The Road Between

OTHER BOOKS BY JAMES T. FARRELL

STUDS LONIGAN

*A trilogy comprising "Young Lonigan," "The Young Manhood of
Studs Lonigan," and "Judgment Day"*

The Danny O'Neill Tetralogy

A WORLD I NEVER MADE

NO STAR IS LOST

FATHER AND SON

MY DAYS OF ANGER

BERNARD CLARE

THE SHORT STORIES OF JAMES T. FARRELL

*Comprising "Calico Shoes and Other Stories," "Guillotine Party and Other
Stories," and "Can All This Grandeur Perish and Other Stories"*

THE LIFE ADVENTUROUS

WHEN BOYHOOD DREAMS COME TRUE

TO WHOM IT MAY CONCERN

$1,000 A WEEK

GAS-HOUSE MCGINTY

ELLEN ROGERS

TOMMY GALLAGHER'S CRUSADE

A NOTE ON LITERARY CRITICISM

THE LEAGUE OF FRIGHTENED PHILISTINES

LITERATURE AND MORALITY

The Road Between

BY

JAMES T. FARRELL

THE VANGUARD PRESS, INC.

New York

MANUFACTURED IN THE UNITED STATES OF AMERICA BY

H. WOLFF, NEW YORK, N. Y.

TO
ESTA AND ROBERT LOEBEL

Ah, love, let us be true
To one another! for the world, which seems
To lie before us like a land of dreams,
So various, so beautiful, so new,
Hath really neither joy, nor love, nor light,
Nor certitude, nor peace, nor help for pain;
And we are here as on a darkling plain
Swept with confused alarms of struggle and flight,
Where ignorant armies clash by night.

MATTHEW ARNOLD (*Dover Beach*)

The Road Between

Chapter One

I

Wasn't it exciting?" Elizabeth asked with childlike spontaneity.

"Yes," Bernard Carr said, wishing he could find excitement and adventure as easily as Elizabeth.

They were sitting at a table near the front window of a large, crowded, noisy cafeteria on Sheridan Square. Outside, it was dark, and the snow was falling. Bernard and Elizabeth had just stolen a few knives, forks, and spoons, and Bernard had slipped them into his overcoat pocket. Taking the silverware had been so easy that he was somewhat ashamed of himself for having been nervous about being caught. For a moment, he had even feared he might be arrested.

"Now we've got all we need, Bernard," she whispered gaily across the table.

Elizabeth looked so girlish and pretty. Her blonde hair was luxurious, and it was combed simply. She had light-blue eyes and the round, eager, shining face of a child. As she smiled at him, she looked more like sixteen than twenty-one.

Bernard was tall, brown-haired, youthful, and looked no different than he had when he'd been in New York in 1927.

Hell, he thought, nothing could happen to him for copping a few knives and forks.

After neither had talked for a while, Bernard said:

"I've got to get going on another novel. I never get time to read anything I want to or to write what I want, running around scrounging book reviews."

"Bernard," Elizabeth said in a serious tone, "maybe I could find a job. I could do something . . . I could be a waitress and

3

maybe work my way up to a hostess in a restaurant. I'm . . .
I'm not unpresentable, am I?"

"You probably wouldn't be able to get a job, honey, and
we'll get along. It's over four months since we eloped, and we
haven't missed a meal yet." He knew he wasn't rational in
opposing her working.

"I'm sure your book will sell, Bernard," Elizabeth said en-
couragingly.

He shrugged his shoulders. In two weeks his first novel would
be published, and he was constantly suppressing his hopes for
it. Last November, when they had come out of Grand Central
Station, they'd both been so happy that they'd skipped hand-in-
hand along Forty-second Street. And all their hopes and worries
since that morning! Now living was a daily grind. No day
passed without worry and anxiety. No day passed but what he
had to fight to hang on to his confidence. Was he a drowning
man grabbing at straws? Back in Chicago, when he'd been
working his way through school and writing his novel, he had
had such a zest for ideas. Some nights they had come tumbling
into his mind so fast he hadn't been able to sleep.

Now, he would drift into daydreaming or else engage in
nostalgic thoughts about Chicago. He was afraid he might be
falling into a rut. Exciting and interesting as New York was to
him, he didn't find the same intellectual stimulation, the same
disinterested curiosity in and enthusiasm for ideas that he had
met at the University.

—All I want is security in this year 1932, he told himself
sarcastically.

"The girls aren't cutting up tonight the way they sometimes
do, are they, Bernard?" Elizabeth said in a quiet, gossipy tone.

He glanced across the restaurant and saw a group of Bohemians. In 1927 he'd wanted to know these people. Now he saw
them as pathetic poseurs. He knew that clowning in a cafeteria
or growing a Christlike beard usually had nothing to do with
a life of art.

"Lesbians quarrel just like other lovers," he said, noticing some mannish-looking girls sitting quietly at a table near the opposite wall. "They must have made up since we saw them last."

"Bernard, we don't quarrel much. We won't be like that, will we?"

"No, we won't." Then, seeing that she was finished, he said, "Well, let's go."

They rose, and Bernard looked anxiously at the manager as he carefully put on his frayed black overcoat.

"Bernard, you forgot the checks," Elizabeth said.

"Oh," he exclaimed, picking them up from the table. He went by the manager casually, paid the checks, and they went outside. They were safe. Again he was abashed for having been so anxious about stealing a few pieces of cafeteria silverware.

"Oh, Bernard, isn't it lovely, like a dream?" Elizabeth exclaimed, looking at the falling snow.

"Yes," he answered quietly.

Elizabeth looked so lovely with snowflakes falling on her face, her black hat, and her raccoon coat. And she had been less afraid than he. Did he underestimate her?

He leaned forward and kissed her.

"Bernard, let's take a little walk."

"All right."

Even though he felt he should work tonight, he didn't want to go back to their dreary room.

II

They crossed Sheridan Square and walked along Fourth Street. The snow glistened in the darkness. It was piled in drifts, packed hard on the streets and sidewalks, gathered in every nook and corner, and outlined every ledge open to the sky.

"New York is transformed by a snowstorm like this," Bernard said.

"Isn't it! I just love the snow, don't you? When I was a little girl, I loved to play in it, but my mother was always worried because she was afraid I'd get my feet wet and get sick."

They walked hand-in-hand, crunching the snow underfoot. He thought of the silence, of the buildings losing their commonplaceness and ugliness in the night, of all the dirt and grime of the street hidden by this wet whiteness. New York had suddenly become another world. He wanted to reach out and absorb what couldn't be absorbed—the colors of the snow, the shadows, the bulky dark outlines of buildings, the dark blue sky. There was a oneness to the surface of the world, a oneness beyond man. It was like a call to him, a dream he could not realize, a calm and peaceful reminder of vain hopes of serenity, a mirror of the impossible appeasements of unappeasable hungers.

"Bernard, we have a good time just being together, don't we?"

"Yes," he muttered, looking across the street.

He noticed several lighted windows and wondered what was going on behind them. Who were the people in these flats? Friends, losing themselves and their worries in laughter and talk? Young writers, like himself, with anxiety in their hearts? He wanted to penetrate through the snow and sky to some core of life, he wanted to reach through these windows to the people behind them, to live with them in their dreams and thoughts, to laugh and love and assimilate sorrow with them.

"Oh, Bernard," Elizabeth exclaimed, "isn't it good that I don't have to go home tonight?"

He didn't understand and stopped.

"Remember, Bernard, how so many times in Chicago I'd have to go home?"

"Oh, yes. I didn't understand you at first," he said, recalling his many fears and worries lest her father find out about their affair. But he didn't want to be resentful tonight.

They came to Washington Square and stopped to gaze at the blanketing snow. Washington Square was the focal point of his past in New York. It was the cemetery of his memories of Eva. But why had he thought of this metaphor?

"Oh, Bernard, I like it so," Elizabeth exclaimed.

"It's almost unworldly," he said softly.

"It looks like something in a fairy story," she said.

The wind whirled the falling flakes, and they saw flying shapes of blue and white. A lone car passed by the Arch; it seemed small, almost fantastic, sliding across this scene. Over on the other side of the Square, the buildings of New York University looked blurred. Everything, even the smallest object or shadow, seemed mysterious and important.

"I feel as if all this were somehow just ours and there were something special in it just for us," she said.

"Yes, I understand."

But at the same time he thought of Eva. The Square brought her to his mind like a ghost. He was sometimes afraid she was a ghost haunting his marriage. He wanted to remember Eva now, and at the same time he wanted to talk with Elizabeth and share the beauty of this scene with her.

"It's so silent—the silence almost talks," he said.

"Yes."

He looked off. He wanted to dream, to dream of all the desires he and all men could never fulfill, of all the loves they could never know, of the eternal lives they could never live.

"Bernard, make me a good snowball," Elizabeth said, interrupting his thought.

He carefully shaped one and handed it to her. She looked at him mischievously.

"I'm going to hit you."

He was touched. She seemed so much like the girl of seventeen he had first known and kissed a few years ago. He was nostalgic for their first days together in Chicago.

"Turn around so I can hit you. I don't want to throw it in your face."

Grinning, he turned around, and she hit his coat.

"There," she exclaimed, clapping her gloved hands.

He frowned playfully and picked up some snow.

"All's fair in love," he warned with simulated sternness.

"Oooh!" she exclaimed. "No . . . no . . . no, please, please don't hurt me," she begged, her gay voice and her smiling face denying her plea.

"I'll give you ten."

As he began to count, she walked away, and after he had reached five, he counted more slowly, and she ran off a few paces. He lightly tossed the snowball at her; it plumped against her back.

"You're mean," she laughed.

He picked up some more snow.

"You're not going to hit me again?"

Silently he made a snowball and flung it at a tree about forty yards off. His throw missed. He threw several snowballs at the same tree, until he struck the trunk squarely. He was satisfied.

"I wish I could just go and roll and roll in the snow," Elizabeth said wistfully as they walked on.

"You'll get wet if you do."

"I wouldn't care."

She moved over to the park railing as though she were going to climb over it.

"Don't be silly," he said a little anxiously.

"Did I scare you?" she asked, turning and laughing when he came over to her. "Kiss me."

She responded passionately to his kiss.

"We're all alone in Washington Square," she said breathlessly.

"It's wet and cold here," he said.

"Take me home," she said.

His feet were wet, and he wanted to get home. He gripped her arm, and they walked on out of the Square. The snow was still blowing in their faces. The wind was growing stronger. His ears burned with the cold. With their heads bent, they hurried along Fifth Avenue. Bernard hoped he wouldn't catch cold because of his wet feet.

"Do you want . . . *tonight* . . . Bernard?" she asked.

"Yes," he answered, telling himself that he meant it.

III

The garbage men outside, handling and slamming cans as though they were committing acts of vengeance, awakened Bernard. Blinking his eyes in the darkness, he became aware of Elizabeth, stirring and whimpering softly in her sleep. And he thought of her as a child he must protect. He wanted to flood her with his affection. He saw the dawn as gray lines around the curtains drawn in front of the small windows high up on the wall. And this was the dawn of the day he had lived for and dreamed of for years. This was the day on which his book was to be published. How inexpressibly lonely he really was. The dawn around the curtain was like the character known to people as Bernard Carr. The rest of him was curtained off. And the world? Should he extend the metaphor and characterize it as a dark and dirty basement room?

He'd wanted to sleep late today. But he still wasn't used to the noises of New York. It was probably the world's noisiest city. He got out of bed carefully, thinking of his morning coffee. His mood was always better after he'd had it. Padding across the room on bare feet, he went behind the screen opposite the bed, fixed the coffee, lit the gas under the pot, and impatiently watched the bluish gas flame.

Would this be a restless, fretful morning? And if it were, wouldn't it prove that he was neither so strong nor so free as he wanted to be? The newspaper reviews would make no lasting difference. Why, then, should he be standing barefooted in this dark and chilly basement room nervously wanting time to pass so he could see them? How much uncurbed irrationality was still in his nature?

If the coffee would only percolate faster! The flame was as high as he could put it.

Suppose his book were really hailed as great? It could become a bestseller.

The publication of The Father *by Bernard Carr is a major literary event. It heralds the birth of a great new American writer.*

Would any critic write such words about his book? He thought for a moment and decided none of the daily book reviewers was likely to. Hampton? He might. He was reviewing it and would probably like it. And Hampton had lined up Bill Barclay to review it, too. Would Barclay like it?

If *The Father* did become a bestseller, everything in his life could be changed. He could give things to Elizabeth. They could travel and live in Paris. But would he ever really see Paris? Would he ever travel? And how would Whelan like it if he became a success? That would be irony! After he'd been fired, after he'd eloped with Whelan's daughter and not been forgiven, then, with one book, to become richer than the undertaker ever could by burying corpses for a whole life-time. The only way he could really thumb his nose at Chicago and the past would be by gaining both money and recognition. His real feelings, his solitary sadness, his hurt and lost sense of boyhood worship, his one-time dreamy love for Elsie Cavanagh, his desire for truth and honesty above happiness and all else—how could they ever understand all this in Chicago? They were afraid of him because he was different.

But what if he did become a success? He was afraid of success. No test he had ever met would be so great. He had been spurred thus far because he was a nobody and had nothing. If he became somebody with money, would he change? Would he become another one of these American writers who was a mere flash in the pan, starting in a blaze of promise and then growing fatuous and selling out?

Tapping his bare foot on the piece of oilcloth under him, he resolved that he would never sell out.

The coffee was ready now. He poured himself a cup, carried it across the room to his worktable in a corner, and switched on the table lamp. He got cigarettes from his trousers, which were in a heap with his other clothes on a large chair. He sat down with a cigarette in his mouth and took his first warming drink of coffee.

The table was cluttered with books, manuscripts, letters, and magazines. His old portable typewriter had been shoved to one side. His eyes fell on a copy of his book. Proudly, he read the title and his name. He winced at the jacket. It was cheap, and he didn't like it. The publishers had used a suggestive cover. But what did this matter? It was his book, his first triumph. It contained a released part of himself. It was his effort to get closer to the very people who would hate it: Whelan, his own father and mother, Elsie Cavanagh. No, she might like it. He opened the book, and as he thumbed through it he choked up. This book wouldn't be liked in Chicago. And it wouldn't be a bestseller, either, except by some fluke. But the notes of his angry defiance would ring for him from beyond the grave. Now it wasn't going to be as hard and as chilling for him to think of his own death as it used to be. Now his life was justified. Whelan could bury his bones. No undertaker of the spirit would be able to bury his book. He was moved almost to tears. He had met with scorn, laughter, contempt in his life. Hardly anyone had believed he could become a writer.

—*I am a writer,* he told himself.

He became tense with a wild elation.

—My battle is won!

He got up and went to the stove for another cup of coffee.

IV

"I made coffee, honey, do you want a cup?" Bernard asked when he saw that Elizabeth was awake.

She yawned, sighed, stretched her arms, and shook her head.

Bernard watched her from the old round table in the center of the room. She curled up. Her rich blonde hair was nicely mussed. Her nose was shiny. Under the covers, her body seemed to him smaller than it had when she'd been asleep and he'd been lying next to her in bed. She smiled at him enigmatically. Her features were regular, except for her nose, which was prominent. He wondered what her smile meant. It seemed to express bewilderment—or was it mere innocence? No trace of experience was written on her face. She was a girl, his girl-wife.

"Sometimes when I wake up, I imagine for a minute that I'm still a little girl."

"But you're a grown-up girl," he answered teasingly, as he turned on the overhead light.

She yawned and stretched again; then she dropped her plump, soft-skinned, pinkish-white arms on the blanket.

"Oh, I used to feel so warm and happy when I woke up when I was a little girl. I'd stay in bed, feeling, oh, Bernard, just like a rabbit in its little burrow in winter. Sometimes I'd imagine I was a Teddy Bear hibernating alone in winter and waiting for my daddy Teddy Bear to come in, kiss me good morning, and chuck me under the chin and play games and tell me nice things." She blushed. "Does that sound silly?"

He shook his head. Affectionate feelings for her slowly rose in his mind. He thought of how as a boy he used to like to lie in bed and dream of Elsie Cavanagh.

"Bernard, come here and kiss me," Elizabeth commanded lovingly.

He went to the bed, bent down, and kissed her cheek.

"Kiss me again," she said as she pursed her lips for him.

He kissed her tenderly. She tightened her arms around him and tried to draw him down onto the bed. Bent over, he responded against his inclination. He was uncomfortable because of his awkward position during their long and passionate kiss. He broke off the kiss, and as he started to sit on the bed, she quickly slid over to make more room for him.

"You are good to me," she said, speaking as though she might be trying to convince herself.

Bernard looked off. His impulses were in conflict. He was disturbed by her sudden welling up of passion. He might not be able to satisfy it. He didn't want to get into bed with her. He didn't know what he wanted to do. . . . A few years ago, there had been times when his desires were stronger than hers.

Now, often they weren't. Maybe he wasn't highly sexed. He became uneasy.

He let his eyes rove about the dreary basement room. This was her first bridal home. But they were past the honeymoon stage. When they'd first begun in 1928, there had been so much fear of detection, fear of her father. But sometimes it had been as wonderful as it had been with Eva. And now? He didn't know how to phrase his thoughts. Sometimes it was naked lust and habit.

Elizabeth squeezed his hand and purred. He stared at the old, dirty carpet that was too dusty and torn to be cleaned. The comfortable but ugly old chair near the bed. His clothes piled on it. The old round table. The dim light overhead. The screen, shielding the little stove from sight, was gray with dust, and its blue latticework pattern was slowly becoming obscured. The rickety straight-backed chairs at the table. The ugly built-in wardrobe. The windows high on the wall, and barred. This was her bridal home, her castle.

"Kiss me, Bernard, honey, and come back to bed and hold me tight."

"All right," he answered grimly.

This was all he was able to give her, he sadly thought. Yes, he could bring ecstasy to her warm young body. But could he bring any real understanding to the mind in that body?

V

"You don't want me to look like an old frump in the morning, do you?" Elizabeth asked.

Bernard pulled his chair in closer to the table and started to eat his eggs. Then, realizing she had spoken to him and that he hadn't answered, he said:

"Of course not."

"When my mother was young, maybe she fixed herself up in the morning. Now I guess she doesn't," Elizabeth went on. "But, of course, it isn't that she isn't neat."

Bernard continued to eat, calm but moody. Elizabeth was

wearing a blue bathrobe. Her hair was combed and her face
made up. She looked as though she were saturated with contentment. He was pleased. He had made her happy. While she'd
dressed, set the table, and made breakfast, he'd lain in bed and
felt sweetly tired. How wonderful it was to have a body! How
wonderful a woman's body was! And he liked his breakfast. He
went on eating with relish.

"Bernard, you didn't tell me how I looked," she said flirtatiously.

He gazed up from the table and said:

"Nice."

She pouted. A moment ago, her face had seemed like that of
a happy woman. Now, she looked like a girl.

He was proud that she had given him her girlhood. But how
much could he give her in return? His book might be the means
of repaying her—if it sold.

"You have lovely hair, Elizabeth."

"Have I, or are you just trying to make me feel good?"

"I mean it," he said, his eyes fixed on its rich texture. It was
pulled straight back and piled high to make her look older, but
it was more beautiful when she didn't do it up this way.

The room shook with the vibrations of traffic passing outside. They heard the front door upstairs slamming.

"Oh, I just feel like singing and dancing," she said impulsively.

She jumped up, put out her arms, and danced around the
table.

He smiled. Then he remembered Eva in her red robe, dancing
around the room, singing, throwing a pillow at him. Soon after,
Sid, her husband, had come in and caught them. He still missed
Eva. But sometimes he wished he had never met her.

"I want to fly in the air. I wish I had wings," Elizabeth half
sang as she danced behind him.

She flung her arms around him, nestled and rubbed her chin
against his cheek, ruffled his hair and kissed him.

"You are my old darling. I'm so proud of you," she said.

She went back to her place and sat down primly.

He heard his own fork clicking against the plate. He observed how dainty her gestures were as she bit into a piece of toast, held it in her hand, and lifted the thick, cracked coffee cup.

"And, Bernard, I just know, oh, I know it—you're going to make oodles and oodles of money."

Bernard frowned. Then he said:

"Oh, I forgot about the mail."

He got up and left the room. Outside, there was a dim hall, an inner wooden door, and a heavy iron door with intricate grating. He quickly went to the mailbox outside the iron door, and the sight of several letters induced a happy anticipation in him. He snatched them out of the box. A Ferris and Winter envelope. His hundred-dollar check. A letter from Bob Whiffle. A manuscript returned from the *American Iskra* in Des Moines, Iowa. Tearing open the letter from Ferris and Winter as he went back inside, he waved the greenish piece of paper before Elsie and said:

"A hundred dollars."

"Oh, Bernard, I'm so happy. I'm so proud of you," she said, hugging him.

She took the check and examined it.

"We'll have to use it carefully. That first hundred and fifty of my advance went fast."

"Oh, we will."

He tore open the letter from the *American Iskra*, a little magazine of the Left.

"Maybe we can move soon and have more room," Elizabeth said cheerfully while Bernard read the letter. "And maybe when your book sells I can get an electric toaster, too. I don't like toasting bread on that awful old little stove here. And I want to fix a little place up nice. I want it bright and sunny, and, with prices the way they are now, it really won't cost much."

"I hope the book sells, but don't count on it too much," he said, looking up from the letter.

She pouted and then looked at him with a long face.

"You can't count on anything in this world," he said quickly and in a consoling manner. Fearing she might break into tears, he added, "Elizabeth, honey—I warned you. We may have hard sledding for a long time."

She pressed her lips together and shook her head slowly.

"Oh, Bernard, Bernard—I know it." She paused, continuing to shake her head. "I know it."

"I'll go out and see if Finch reviewed me—as soon as I have another cup of coffee."

"I hope so," she said.

"And, Bernard, even if your book doesn't make a lot of money, can't I hope and pretend? Don't be a meanie and a kill-joy." She paused, became very earnest, and spoke more slowly. "I feel it, I feel it in me. Bernard, your book is going to sell, sell very well."

"I hope so," he said. He reached across the table, took her hand, and said with resolution and reassurance, "No matter what happens, we're going to get along."

Chapter Two

I

IT WAS a gray day, with a raw, penetrating wind. Bernard was walking along Fifteenth Street toward Seventh Avenue. Weather like this often depressed him, but this morning he wasn't depressed. Back in 1927, he used to tell himself that some day he'd walk the streets of New York with confidence. Here he was, shabbily dressed, his blue suit shiny and unpressed, his shoes unshined. His gray hat looked disreputable. His overcoat was frayed. And yet the day had come when he was walking the streets of New York with confidence. How much better off he was than many who were better-dressed. Everything was possible for him. He was a free artist, with a hundred-dollar check in his pocket. A hundred dollars couldn't go too far. And then what would they do? But he'd been poor and had lived from hand to mouth for so long now that it was pretty late in the day for him to be worrying about money. Without Elizabeth, he'd have no worries. It wasn't Elizabeth, but her father. It was the way she had been raised. She had guts and was a good sport, but still, somehow or other, she always brought money problems back to his mind.

He strode on, noticing that the garbage cans along the sidewalk lay where they had been carelessly flung by the garbage collectors. A wizened superintendent was straightening up some along the rail by one of the buildings. He watched the man's motions for a moment and thought that this was work. And what hopes could a man have with such a job? How lucky he was to have work that he loved—work that gave him a sense of purpose! Even with the depression, wasn't there a future for art? Look at what Jan and other Communists had told him about the respect shown for writers in Russia. Books there sold in editions of hundreds of thousands. Men in the government, like Stalin and Bukharin, read books. And when he was a member of the Russian government, Trotsky had written on literature. Art and literature would survive capitalism.

Bernard passed the superintendent who was arranging the garbage cans. Even though he himself was as poor, or almost as poor, as this man, what a difference there was between them.

He turned the corner onto Seventh Avenue and hurried along to Fourteenth Street.

Bernard bought a copy of *The Star-Digest* at the newsstand and tried to open the paper in the wind. It was almost blown out of his hand. He went down the subway steps, straightened out the newspaper, and opened it to the book page. Finch had ignored *The Father* for a book that sounded like mere academic claptrap.

Disappointed, he went through the turnstile and caught a train immediately. He glanced casually about the car. The few passengers looked dull and spiritless. A neatly dressed young man with spectacles and a briefcase was reading a paper; a fat woman twiddling her thumbs; a man concentrating on a crossword puzzle, patiently trying to write in a word as the car swerved. An angry-looking man with big shoulders glanced at Bernard. Their eyes met. Bernard quickly turned the other way and tried to appear unruffled. He didn't know why the man's stare left him uneasy. He almost never looked people directly in the eye. And if you caught the gaze of others, they usually turned away, uneasy, ashamed, not wanting to meet your gaze either. There was no reason for assuming that these fellow passengers of his would be unfriendly. Yet he'd entered the car with just such a feeling. Wherever he went, except in cases where he knew people, he expected unfriendliness and hostility. Didn't others expect the same? You walked down the street or rode in subways, casually noticed a stranger, and imagined that he was a potential enemy. In cities people were closed in on themselves, closed out from one another. In time, in a big city, people began almost to seem like objects rather than human beings.

Bernard got off at Chambers Street, rushed upstairs and walked toward Broadway. He always had the same uneasy feeling when he came to see Brady. He became apprehensive lest he say something which would cause Brady to break with him and to stop giving him books to review. With Klingal of *The Globe*, or Sherman Scott of *New Freedom*, he felt differently. He lived in the same universe of discourse with them. But Klingal gave him a book only rarely, and he'd already come away empty-handed from Scott's office five times. Without Brady's fatherly interest in him and his career, he and Elizabeth might well have missed many meals here in New York. And yet he couldn't feel comfortable in the old fellow's presence. How could Brady like *The Father*? He hoped Brady wouldn't read it.

Seeing the old *Dispatch* building ahead, a sudden fear crawled up on him. Suppose the *Dispatch* should go bankrupt? Was it solvent? After all, the famous *New York World* had gone under last year. Why should an artist care whether or not a newspaper popular with suburbanites stayed in business or became insolvent? What had that to do with art? But he was worried about it. Dodging in front of a truck as he crossed Broadway, he asked himself what his Communist friends would say of him if they knew that he was concerned about the solvency of the *Dispatch*.

II

Mr. Brady slapped the corrected proof into the box on the side of his desk. This review would go into the paper tomorrow. It would tell another author that he didn't know how to write. And as long as he was literary editor of *The New York Dispatch*, literary standards would be upheld and short shrift made of anyone who wrote a bad book.

Sitting at his large desk, his face crowned with gray hair, he looked stern, businesslike, forbidding. His desk was neat and orderly. On a table beside him were a pile of manuscripts, some newspapers, and a stack of new books with brightly colored jackets. There were shelves on three sides with other books.

In a corner, his secretary, Miss Engels, was typing away. She was dumpy and plain.

"That settles it," he said in a voice of command.

"Yes, Mr. Brady."

"I'm running Kennedy's review of *Dark Horizon* tomorrow. A book club has no right selecting a book like that. A disgrace to American letters. I only wish I'd had the foresight to give it to young Carr, but, then, Kennedy did a good enough job of rapping."

"Yes, Mr. Brady."

Mr. Brady grunted. Young Carr was catching hell in today's review. He was mighty glad that Sims hadn't minced words. He agreed with Sims. Though he hadn't read the book, he'd skimmed through it and read enough to know it was another sample of modern smelfungus writing. *Smelfungus* was his own word, and he was proud of it. He regretted that he hadn't used it in the heading for Sims's review. But, still, what he had written, he thought with gratification, hit the nail squarely.

Young Man With a Cloacal Mind

Young Carr would never know what it had cost him to print Sims's review. For the last three days, he'd been troubled. He wanted to help, and even to guide, young Carr. Now he would lose him. And Carr gave promise of becoming his most brilliant young literary lieutenant.

Mr. Brady leaned back in his swivel chair. The expression of wistful disappointment on his face made him look years older. He remembered the first time young Carr had come to see him several months ago. Old Ned had brought in his name on a slip. He didn't know why the name had attracted him. *Bernard Carr.*

Mr. Brady slowly moved his head from side to side. When he'd skipped through *The Father*, he had almost seen himself as personally betrayed. A young man in whom he had placed such hopes, a young man whom he had wanted to direct and to nurse along, writing such muck. Muck—yes, muck. Smel-fungus muck. It had been raining and dark out that day young Carr had first come in. He'd been looking out his window at the rain falling on City Hall Square and philosophizing about life. Human beings skirting across the Square had seemed so puny and powerless. He was sixty, and not too well. One day, and it wasn't too far off, he would die in harness. The sight of young Carr, shy and idealistic, had been like a ray of light in his dark life. Yes, a ray of light. The boy had been so modest, so sincere, so appealing. He had come to New York with his first novel and a young wife. He had conveyed a sense of quiet courage, of determination. And he, Brady, had given young Carr his chance.

Again Mr. Brady sadly shook his head. Where was his dream now of nursing this young man along, of being the editor who had given him his start? Young Carr, the critic, tearing apart trashy novels, writing with overtones, proving himself a lad of ability, was one person. Young Carr writing that odorous novel was another. What did this boy know of an older man's feelings?

Mr. Brady suddenly sat upright and clenched his teeth. He was a man in harness. He had done right. Young Carr had received only justice in today's book review. Now there was other work to be done.

He picked up a new novel, *Green Fields*, by Bertrand Cecil, and started to thumb through it.

III

Bernard stepped into the forbidding reception room of the *Dispatch*. He wished he hadn't come here today. But he had to live. He looked about at the large, solid table in the center, the leather-backed chairs, the dreary tan walls, the pictures of mustached men of the last century. Lighting a cigarette, he sat down in a corner and waited apprehensively.

"Hello, Carr," Mr. Brady said with unusual curtness, as he marched, heavy-footed, into the room.

"How do you do, Mr. Brady," Bernard responded, standing up.

Mr. Brady stopped in front of Bernard, folded his arms, and looked at him angrily. Bernard grinned meaninglessly and defensively.

"Beastly weather, Carr," Mr. Brady exclaimed with an intensity that deepened Bernard's uneasiness.

"Yes, it's cold, and there's a nasty—"

Mr. Brady interrupted Bernard by asking coldly and cruelly: "Well, did you see our review of your book?"

"No . . . No . . . I didn't," Bernard answered uncertainly.

"I agree with Sims," Mr. Brady declared with an air of finality.

Bernard looked up at Mr. Brady, perplexed. He didn't understand this man, and he never would be able to understand him.

"Just a minute, Carr," Mr. Brady said, turning and marching out of the room.

Bernard waited, embarrassed. This looked like the end of his reviewing for Brady.

He heard stamping feet in the corridor and knew it was Mr. Brady coming back. He asked himself why he hadn't walked out, but now it was too late. Mr. Brady marched into the reception room like a general.

"Here!" Mr. Brady declared briskly, handing Bernard a copy of the *Dispatch*.

Slightly confused, Bernard took the paper. He saw the heading over the review. It wasn't true, he thought. He didn't have a cloacal mind. Determining not to show any perturbation, Bernard read. The printed words seemed cold and insignificant to him. He smirked in self-protection.

This reviewer regards it as a duty to remain always solicitous of the mental health and psychological balance of the book-reading public. He regards this as much a duty as he does the obligation to display a proper concern for the pocketbooks of the public. He believes that it is his duty to warn readers that The Father, *a first novel by a young Chicagoan named Bernard Carr, is unhealthy: but he also wishes to add as his conviction that it will have no deleterious effect on the mature and balanced reader. It will merely bore the mature; it will offend the sense of beauty of the civilized person who loves real literature, has assimilated his Boccaccio, and is not a prude.*

Hovering over Bernard, Mr. Brady almost breathed tobacco fumes into his nostrils. This was all untrue and unfair. Michael MacTavish Sims was trying to hurt him. Yes, it was untrue and unfair. He became pale. His muscles grew taut. He skipped part of the review and read the last sentence, as Mr. Brady emitted a slight, nervous cough and said rapidly and nervously:

"I agree with Sims. It's a good review. I'm glad I published it."

Without talent, young Mr. Carr has given us a distorted picture that is the product of a cloacal mind rather than of an artistic vision.

"Sims doesn't like me, I guess," Bernard remarked.

He looked up at Mr. Brady, but Mr. Brady evaded his gaze.

"One of my principles—" Bernard began, wanting Mr. Brady to know that he didn't demand praise from critics.

"Carr," Mr. Brady interrupted. "Carr, what do you think of Santayana?"

"I admire him, but, as I was saying, one of my principles is—" Bernard started to answer.

"Santayana has a civilized mind, a civilized mind," Mr. Brady said with nervous finality.

Bernard wanted very much to have Mr. Brady know that he didn't want people to praise his work unless they genuinely meant it. But when he tried to explain, Mr. Brady interrupted him once more.

"Santayana has a style. You could well afford to study his style."

"I've read some of his books, and I admire his style, but I can only write my own way."

"You have a fine critical mind. You can become a brilliant critic. You are not a creative artist."

Bernard raised his eyebrows, waited. Discussion with Mr. Brady was pointless.

"I have a book for you. Wait and I'll go fetch it," Mr. Brady declared.

IV

The bum eyed the people passing along Broadway with hatred and contempt. The better-dressed they were, the more he hated them. But at the same time he had to admire people who could be clean and well-dressed and who could work and bathe and shave and get rid of the smells and itch that these human animals had. There were droves of them, these so-called human animals, coming and going, in their pants and their dresses, coming and going here and there and nowhere, filling their bellies as if everything that went down their mouths didn't come out the same as cheap grub came out of his own empty belly. And which of these stinkers and smellers, which one of these odors in pants, would give him a handout?

A young fellow coming out of the *Dispatch* building, with a book under his arm, a book to read, and what could the book do but tell a story, as if all of them, all of the droves and hordes of stinkers and smellers, didn't stink and smell, and smell and stink? He looked like a young, innocent stinker and smeller.

The bum walked up to the tall young man with the book.

The young stinker and smeller was thinking about something, and his eyes were far away.

"Pardon me, lad."

The young fellow took a step in the direction of City Hall Square, away from the *Dispatch* building.

"Pardon me— I haven't eaten in two days, could you give a man a . . ."

The young stinker and smeller dug in his pocket, pulled something out, and, bejesus, the young stinker and smeller was giving him something.

"Thank you, thank you and God bless you," the bum said, taking a dime that the young man was giving him.

"All right, all right, God hasn't any interest in this," the young man said.

He walked on. The bum looked after him. Then he stood waiting to decide which of the walking stinkers and smellers he'd hit next for a handout.

V

Hollow-cheeked, spiritless, and chilled, the ragged man leaned against a railing in City Hall Park and watched the people going by. Did these people ever think of men like himself, these people who wore pressed clothes, clean underwear, and had jobs that gave them three square meals a day? He looked from face to face, and with each face he'd think yes or no, deciding to try or not try for a handout. A young man with a book coming along. Yes. He edged over to him.

"For God's sake, could you help me. I haven't eaten in . . ."

"Sorry."

The young man with the book walked on, abstracted.

The spiritless, ragged man went on, his eyes on the gravel walk. He was in pain from hunger. He'd thought that that lad had a yes face. His empty stomach was making noises. He was weak. Looking at gray stones, and then at this face and that face. Was there any humanity left in this world?

The young fellow with the book was buying a newspaper. He was walking away. One of those with no humanity. The spiritless man looked up and around, hoping to spot another yes face.

VI

Bernard was trying to force himself to concentrate on the first chapter of *Green Fields* as the subway train raced along the express track. He was tempted to give way to a vain im-

pulse. Klingal's review in today's *Globe* stated that Bernard
Carr's book was both powerful and promising. The review was
not only favorable but treated him as an important writer—
an artist. He had been moved, reading it on the subway platform. He wanted to think of the review, of his book, of himself
and of his future. Instead, he was trying to read this novel. He
was always unsure of himself when he started reading a book
for review. He must be sure not to miss anything important.
And he struggled with the book trying to form an honest judgment. But, starting on this novel, he was less tense than usual.
Since he had written a novel that was as highly praised as his
had been by Klingal, couldn't he take his literary judgments
for granted? He knew that despite the book he'd written, the
struggle to think clearly, to write, to be honest, went on in the
same old way. But *Green Fields* wasn't promising. Another
story about the English countryside. The first pages were dull
and written with a merely empty skill. Brady liked to give him
such books. He always rapped them, and Brady seemed to print
his long attacking reviews gleefully. But perhaps Brady had
printed the Sims review of his own book with the same pleasure.
If he found the rest of *Green Fields* as vacuous as the beginning, and wrote a cutting review, would Brentwood Cecil in
London be hurt, as he himself had been hurt by Sims's review?

Bernard decided to read the book at home. He opened up his
copy of *The Globe* and reread Klingal's review. He wasn't so
pleased as he'd been on the first reading. Klingal, writing of
pimply adolescence and sweaty sexuality, really didn't understand his novel. It became painfully clear to him that Klingal,
praising *The Father*, misunderstood it as grossly as had Sims
with his abusive dismissal. He knew he must make it a rule to
ignore all the critics. He must not allow himself to become
either elated or depressed because of what they might write
about him.

VII

Mr. Bertram Ferris sat at his big glass-topped desk, arranging his Sulka tie, reflecting ruefully. He was a youngish man, and he was dressed in such good taste as to be in bad taste.

Somebody, he thought, must have the answer, because there had to be an answer. Five years ago, when he'd gone into the publishing business, it had been so much fun, and he'd believed that it was just the business for him. And he had planned to publish good, distinguished books, naively believing they'd sell well and make money. Now the whole situation was so bitchy that not only wouldn't good books sell, but you couldn't even sell bad ones. It was even hard to sell Veronica Belden's novels. Yes, no matter how you looked at it, everything was bitched up.

The phone rang, and he answered it. Carr was here. Carr was a rather vigorous young man. But the Sims review today had shaken his faith in Carr's book. What a difference there was between now and a few months ago! He'd gambled on this barbarian, thinking he'd have a prestige book, even though he might lose a little money on it, or, at best, only break even.

Again he smiled ruefully. That was 1931. This was 1932. You couldn't cover checks with prestige.

Carr came in, and Mr. Ferris rose, masking a feeling of suspicion with a supercilious smile. He limply shook hands with Carr. They sat down. Mr. Ferris sensed that Carr was ill at ease, and said nothing. Whenever an author seemed uncomfortable in his presence, he felt more confident. He noted that, as usual, Carr was poorly dressed. A strange young man from the wilds of the Middle West. Talented and vigorous, very vigorous, and he scarcely knew how to use a fork.

"I came to ask if I could get the check okayed so I can cash it."

"Of course," Mr. Ferris said graciously. "I'll have Miss Mins, my bookkeeper, phone the bank." He smiled. "Our checks don't bounce . . . yet."

"Well, thank you . . . I was wondering if it would be any trouble if I asked what the advance sale on my book is?"

"Mr. Winter and I were just in conference looking over the figures. I remember them. The advance is seven hundred and forty-four. If it isn't that, it's seven thirty-four. I can get the exact figures for you . . ."

"That's good enough, thank you . . . That means that my advance isn't covered yet."

"Correct. Even a writer can understand that much arithmetic, if I may be permitted a witticism in the presence of one of our serious young authors."

"Because I'm a writer, I don't make a fetish of being dumb. I don't want to belong to the I-Am-Dumb school of American writers," Bernard said.

Mr. Ferris smiled enigmatically and then he studied Carr for a moment.

"Carr," he then said, "I hope you aren't counting on getting rich out of the royalties on *The Father*."

"I never expect to get rich," Bernard said. Then he paused, hunting for words. "I do think I have a right to hope that I can make enough to live on out of my writings. All the time I was working my way through college and keeping up with my studies, I wrote this book. It was hard work. I think I'm entitled to hope for a living from it and my other writings."

Mr. Ferris was impatient with this kind of talk. Young Carr was just too naive for words. Could he believe Carr? After all, he was an author. What hadn't he learned about authors these last few years? Of course, the worst of them were the lady authors. Lord deliver him from them above all others.

"Carr, I want you to know that it isn't going to be my fault if your hopes are dashed."

"I know that. I don't ask for miracles."

"It wouldn't do you any good," Mr. Ferris answered.

He enjoyed seeing Carr confused. He was now completely confident of himself.

"Did you see Michael MacTavish Sims's review of your book? He says you have a dirty mind."

"What do I care what Michael MacTavish Sims thinks?"

"Reviews help to sell books."

"Klingal thinks I'm a good writer and praises my so-called dirty mind."

Mr. Ferris looked impatiently at the clock on his desk. Carr bored him.

"Listen, Carr, old man, I'd like nothing better than to talk with you, but I'm having a perfectly frantic morning, perfectly frantic."

"Oh," Bernard exclaimed awkwardly.

"You'll excuse me?"

"There was just one thing more I wanted to ask . . . I wanted to ask if I could charge a few more copies of my book to my account to send to friends . . ."

"Carr," Mr. Ferris answered, "you're a chump. You've already charged about twenty copies to your account. If these people are friends of yours, tell them to buy your book. . . . Books don't get printed and sold for nothing. I'm sorry. I can't do it."

Bernard said nothing. Mr. Ferris tapped his foot nervously under his desk. He wanted this young author out of his office.

"Well, shall I see your bookkeeper to ask her to okay the check?"

"Oh, yes, yes," Mr. Ferris said quickly; he'd forgotten that. He picked up the receiver of his phone, looked at Carr, and said:

"You must understand, Carr, this is a business."

He asked the operator for Miss Mins.

VIII

Bernard dropped into the big chair with a sigh, opened *Green Fields,* read three sentences without understanding one word, got up, dropped the book on the seat of the chair, walked around the table in the center of the room, gazed dejectedly at his typewriter, turned, strode around the table again, paced back and forth in the basement room, lurched over to the bed, flung himself on it, closed his eyes, opened them, got to his feet, took four steps around the table, took four steps back, and then paced up and down the room counting one, two, three, four, over and over again. He silently cursed Elizabeth.

He sat down at the table, placed his elbows on it, pressed the palms of the hands against his cheeks, and gazed at the wall with an expression of utter despair on his face. He sighed. Noticing the letter from Ilya Ravenov, he read:

Dear Carr:

I can't use your story in American Iskra. *American Iskra subscribes to the Kharkov platform for proletarian literature, which calls on working-class writers to fight against war and fascism. Your story is no-go and doesn't follow the Kharkov directives. It is not proletarian or antiwar. Capitalist imperialism is preparing the workers as cattle for a new imperialist slaughter against the Soviet Union, and your story is no contribution to the fight against war. Carr, it's 1932, too late to write a story about a boy who dreams of being a hero in the last imperialist blood bath of 1914–1918. Your boy character is a rugged individualist.*

Study the Kharkov directives and give us a good rousing antiwar story and American Iskra *will print it.*

Yours,
I. Ravenov

—The goddam fool! Bernard exploded to himself.

To get a letter like this about a simple story that had been based on his boyhood experiences of playing war. But then geting sore at Ravenov wouldn't take his mind off this idiotic jealousy that was torturing him.

Where was Elizabeth? Why hadn't she left a note telling him where she had gone? How long had she been gone before he'd come back home? He'd been back half an hour already, and he'd done nothing but prowl this room like a caged animal.

What an agonizing farce this was! He hadn't wanted to come home. He'd wanted to wander around and dream, and perhaps have something unusual or exciting, something wonderful and extraordinary, happen to him. But instead of staying out, he'd come home, determined to work. And here he was, his will paralyzed, and his mind the prey of all these irrational fears.

She had probably gone for a walk or else to the store for groceries. She enjoyed window-shopping, and might be doing that. But suppose she'd been killed in an accident, run over by a car, and was at this moment lying dead in a hospital or the morgue? Would her death crush him? He'd be free. But the memory of her death might haunt him forever. Would he find another girl? This morning her body had been so warm and soft and moist, and her eyes had been so shining, and afterward she had looked at him with such gratitude. And now, could that body be cold, cold and perhaps mangled? He remembered watching her walk toward him on the campus one day in November, 1928, and he had wondered what thoughts, what feelings were blooming in her, a girl who was his. And he had sadly asked himself if there was anything in the world more lovely than a girl in love. Her face, her eyes, her young body, everything about her had been like music. And now she might be dead. If she died in some accident, her father couldn't blame him. He wasn't responsible. But Whelan would blame him, and might even want to kill him. Should he fight with Whelan about a church burial, about cremation? He believed in cremation. There would be an aura of sad romance in his life if Elizabeth, if his girl-wife, should be killed in an accident on the very day his first book was published.

Hearing footsteps outside, Bernard jumped up. He waited, hoping it was Elizabeth. The footsteps died down. Where was she? What was she doing?

He went impulsively to the table and inserted a sheet of paper in his typewriter. He'd start a story. He ought to do some work on the day his book came out. He had to go on, and he'd hardly written any fiction since he'd come to New York.

There was the story he'd thought of writing over two years ago, *Episode at a Party*. The protagonist would be just an ordinary fellow, who'd have been married five years when the story opened. He and his friends would be going along at a party, having a good time in a dumb way, and suddenly, without warning, the wife would fling herself wildly into the arms of a stranger. The point of the story would be the sense of humiliation the husband felt.

His heart began to pound. He was perspiring under the arms. Suppose Elizabeth had been picked up? Suppose she was with some man this minute and he would never know of it? He knew why he wanted to write *Episode at a Party*. He hoped that if he wrote this story, he would conquer his fear that Elizabeth might humiliate him. For several years now, he had had this suspicion, this lack of trust in her.

He got up, knowing that until she returned and he gained reassurance, he would remain in this torn and irrational mood. He hated and feared his jealousy. He knew it wasn't fair to Elizabeth. And it violated his beliefs and his values. Yet he felt powerless.

Weak, ashamed, humiliated in his own eyes, he put on his hat and coat and went out to prowl Fifteenth Street until Elizabeth returned.

IX

Bernard sat on the bed, emotionally exhausted and longing for deliverance from his jealousy. He'd come inside again because he imagined people might be watching him suspiciously and critically as he'd walked up and down the sidewalk so restlessly. Hearing Elizabeth open the outer iron door, he jumped up. He went over behind the screen to have time in which to compose himself. He heard her come into the room.

"Oh, hello . . . I was just going to make myself some coffee," he said, trying to be casual.

"Hello, honey," she said cheerfully, as she set a small bag of groceries on the table.

"Why didn't you leave a note telling me where you'd gone?" he asked accusingly.

"I just went to the store, that's all. Gosh, I didn't think I needed to leave a note. I didn't even know what time you'd be back. I bought spaghetti for dinner because you forgot to leave me any money."

"When I came back and found no note, I merely wondered where you were," he said mildly.

"You poor dear, you were worried, weren't you?" she said, turning and looking at him proudly.

"No, no, not exactly . . . I just wondered where you were," he said, confused, as his guilt grew upon him.

She smiled at him knowingly. He held out his arms. She came to him. He embraced her, kissing her tenderly.

"Bernard, you are a dear boy," she said as she was nestled in his arms.

"I have a surprise, honey."

"What . . . for me?" she asked, gazing up at him with an open-eyed, childlike expression.

"In a way—"

"Tell me about. . . . Tell me, quick."

"It's about spaghetti."

"You're teasing me."

"We won't eat spaghetti. We'll go out and have a good dinner and celebrate my book. I cashed the check for my advance."

"Just us . . . we'll celebrate."

He released her from his embrace and sat down, dull and listless. She took off her coat and hat and hung them up. Then she put away the groceries and sat down at the table.

"Bernard, let's talk about where we'll go for dinner tonight for our celebration."

Chapter Three

I

How still the house was. You could hear a pin drop. It was Saturday night, and everyone was out. But Mrs. Carr didn't mind being alone. When no one was here, she could think by herself, think of God and Mary, and pray to the Blessed Virgin. Even now, when there was such sadness in her, she was not alone. She was never alone because of Mary in Heaven. There was no sorrow, no ache in the heart of woman that Mary did not understand. For Mary's heart was the heart of a woman and a mother, and it was pure and without sin.

The overhead bedroom light was dim. The room was small, neat, and spotlessly clean. The curtains were worn with washing. The big dresser, set against one wall, was very old. Rocking slowly, with her thin, roughened hands clasped in her lap, she turned her eyes toward the framed picture of the Blessed Virgin on the wall to her right. She was a tall, lean woman whose thinning hair was turning gray. Her face was hard, stern, expressing suffering and dignity. It was beginning to wrinkle. Her eyes were clear and bright, and often seemed to shine. Her lips were thin and tense. Her nose was rather large. She was wearing an old black dress with a gingham apron over it.

Continuing to stare at the picture of Mary, she thought how Mary looked like a nun. Hadn't she often thought that it would have been better for her, and for Patrick, too, if she had gone into the convent? Mary's face, in the black-and-white picture, was so round and so young.

—Mary, my mother, she silently intoned to herself in an appeal.

Mary would understand the feelings of a mother who had lost her son. And she was at fault, grievously, for losing Bernard. Since she had read his book this last week, she had come to know how grievously she was at fault. Could she atone for her sin? Could a mother's silent tears and prayers bring back the prodigal?

For two days now, she had been weeping, weeping with dry, silent tears. This afternoon, when she had stolen over to church, the ache in her had ceased. She had prayed to Mary and to God. She had asked God that not her will but His be done, and that if it only be His will, He take her home to Him like a poor, erring daughter. Yes, in the eyes of God and of His Mother, she was more erring than her son Bernard.

With a great effort, Mrs. Carr held back her tears. She remembered Bernard as a young one. He had been quieter than the others. He had often looked at her with young, accusing eyes. Had he been blaming her, as the boy blamed his father and mother in the book? Had Bernard seen? Bernard well could have seen what happened when Patrick was drunk. Her eyes turned to the bed. The number of years she had slept in that bed with Patrick. The mere sight of it threatened to bring back to her so many terrible memories. In those first days of her marriage, when she was but an innocent girl, her heart had been robbed of love by Patrick in this very same bed. The pain and the shame she had known in that bed. Yes, in drink and in meanness, he had given her a son. And Bernard must know that. She had been accused in her son's book. All these years, he must have carried his accusation against her in his heart.

She was no learned woman. It was many a year since she had read a book. She had read this one because her son had written it. She didn't understand parts of it. But she understood enough. The book had hurt her, filled her with evil feelings. She had longed to be different, to love, and only by prayer had she driven those thoughts from her. Her son's book was evil. But she was more evil.

Mrs. Carr knelt down, gazed at the picture of the Blessed Virgin, and prayed fervently.

II

"Today is no day for me to be showing my face to the world," Patrick Carr declaimed in a voice that rang with self-pity.

He sat in his shirtsleeves at the table in the small, neat kitchen, eating a breakfast of ham and eggs. Patrick Carr was a short, squat man, with a broad face and skin toughened by working outdoors. There were several red blotches from broken veins discoloring his cheeks. His nose was red. His hands were gnarled and looked strong.

Mrs. Carr finished washing some dishes, dried her hands, got herself a cup of coffee, and sat down opposite her husband.

"Woman, are you after not hearing me again?"

"I heard you, Patrick," she said with strain and a quiet dignity in her voice.

"Many a time, I warned you about him. I warned that he would bring no good on this home."

"I prayed for him," she said, stirring her coffee.

"Prayers. Prayers. What good have all your prayers done? What good? Look at my gray hair. Look at me. That a son of mine would bring disgrace on this gray head."

He grimaced as he went on eating.

"Well, I looked at his book," Patrick Carr declared with a mouth full of food. "It's a pack of lies and dirt. He didn't fool me, not one whit. He makes the father a real-estate man because he's ashamed to admit to the world that his own father is a workingman—he, the son-in-law of an undertaker. And the father dying in the end. I tell you—I could die, and he'd have few regrets. Few regrets. Maybe he'd ask his father-in-law to bury me free. Well, when I'm cold and dead, the money for the care of my poor remains will be forthcoming."

Patrick Carr wiped egg off his chin.

"I read the book," she said.

"He thinks little enough of you."

"Maybe our boy should have been a priest," she said.

Patrick Carr leaned back in his chair and spoke dramatically:

"A priest? Well, holy suffering Moses, a priest! With his dirty mind." He leaned forward and grandiloquently began to wave his right index finger at her. "A priest—and there he was with his ears not washed, a milk sopper, looking at the legs of the little girls."

"He read those books he used to get at the library the way you drink."

"And what if I do? It's only human for a man to want a drink with his friends. What other pleasures are there for me in this world? What other pleasures have there ever been?"

Their eyes met, and they both looked off in shame. They were eloquently and sadly silent.

"He wants to make us the shame of the neighborhood. He wants the whole parish to think that he's the son of a drunkard, and that—"

"Patrick," Mrs. Carr interrupted in an intense, hurt voice. "It's us that are at fault, too."

He grunted but did not answer her. Finishing his coffee, he held out his cup for more. She got it for him.

"Ah, I curse the day that he was born!" Patrick Carr said with a bitter whine in his voice.

III

Marie Carr came out of St. Catherine's Church after the ten o'clock Mass. She tried to appear cold and aloof, as if to tell the boys who were standing in front of the church after Mass that she wasn't the kind of girl who was bowled over when she was looked at. She was conscious of her figure. It was soft and svelte, and she was proud of it, and she liked the idea that men and boys would look at her, although, of course, she would never admit that to a soul.

Marie was pretty in an ordinary way. She had dark, bobbed hair, blue eyes, and round, red cheeks. She'd decided to wear her blue suit for Mass, the one which fitted her a little tightly. She always thought more about her figure when she had it on, but now she was kind of ashamed of herself for wearing it to Mass. She was afraid she could easily be bad if she didn't watch her step.

Marie noticed many familiar faces as the parishioners came out slowly. She was behind an old man she had been seeing at church and on the street for years, ever since she was a little girl, but she had never found out who he was. He had not had gray hair then, but now he did. He never talked to anyone, but came to church, knelt and prayed with a solemn face, and then went home, wherever that was. It was funny, the solemn way he prayed. He was different from her father. But her father sometimes was very solemn in church. She then thought her father should have been an actor, and she wondered if he wasn't acting all the time.

Marie wanted to see someone, talk to her friends, and be noticed. Over to the right, by the curb, she saw Timmy Callahan, Kenny Donoghue, and Billy Brennan. She'd gone to school with them. They were too young for her. A girl should go with men older than herself. Oh, how she used to dream and think of Billy Brennan, and now . . . well, she had refused him dates until he'd given up asking. They were looking at her but pretending not to. You could see right through the intentions and tricks of most boys.

"Hello, there. You look like the first rose of spring."

Marie returned Mr. Powderly's compliment with a tolerant smile. He was a fat little man who was getting on toward fifty, and he always gave Marie the heebie-jeebies.

"Excuse me, Mr. Powderly," she said.

Marie walked away from him, wanting to laugh. But even though he gave her the heebie-jeebies, she was thrilled with the thought that a girl like her could have power over men, over boys and men of all ages. She lifted her head just slightly and tried to appear even more aloof and cold and unconcerned and sure of herself. She walked off alone.

Marie daydreamed as she wandered over to Jackson Park.

Finding an empty bench, she sat down, still daydreaming. A young man in a gray suit passed her at a brisk pace, slowed down, turned to give her a quick, shy look, and then hurried on.

She smiled with pride and smoothed out her skirt. Although she was sitting primly, she had her legs crossed, and any man passing could see what nice legs she had. She was proud of her legs. Some girls, like her friend Ellen, were bowlegged. She was certainly glad she wasn't.

She thought that of course she liked to neck and dance a little close, and any girl liked a little kissing and petting from a boy she liked. She remembered how last year, when she hadn't had a petting date for six weeks, she'd gotten pretty nervous and cranky. That was when she started going with George Devin. But just because he could use his father's Lincoln, he needn't think she was going to let him go farther.

She took a pack of cigarettes from her pocketbook and lit one, puffed on it, flung away the burned match. Her mood changed, and she calmly told herself that it was the only thing men wanted. She shook her little head emphatically and with pleasure. Yes, it was true. And when men got what they wanted, well—look at her mother and her father. Did her father pay any respect to her mother? Was her mother happy? Was her mother the kind of woman she would want to be like when she got older?

She had really liked George Devin, up to a point. When he had asked her to go driving with him after dancing and eating, she had said yes. When he'd stopped the car and put his arm around her and kissed her, she had let him, and she hadn't protested when he'd kissed her the passionate way. But when he'd wanted really to get fresh, well, that was different.

Marie pressed her legs together tightly and drew her arms in against her ribs. Oh, she wanted to live and be loved romantically and be kissed. But she couldn't let any boy do that to her unless he were rich and she was sure he'd marry her and take care of her. Oh, she didn't want to end up like her mother, or as an old-maid working girl.

IV

With perspiration on her face, Mrs. Carr basted the roast. Her manner and expression were of calmness and resignation. Her troubled and agitated feelings of last night were quieted. She was doing her duty now, cooking Sunday dinner for her family. It was wrong for her to think of anything but a woman's duty and sacrifice. Strands of graying hair fell down over her forehead, and as she pushed them back she thought that a woman must know her place and keep in it.

V

Marie, after dabbing her face with powder and giving her hair a pat, walked confidently into the parlor. Her father and two brothers looked at her. Jim was the older, but Art was her favorite. Art was twenty-one, slender, dapper and had a pretty-boy face. She noticed Art's eyes on her, and she decided that Art must be as experienced with girls as George Devin. She guessed he tried to do with girls just what George had tried with her. Yes, a girl could really have power over men. This thought left her feeling vaguely guilty.

"You could have come back and helped mother," Jim Carr said. Jim was small, with a thin, angular face.

"I work and pay my board here. I can decide for myself what I should and shouldn't do," she answered haughtily.

"Ah, so she's a grown-up lady now. She's too big to be given a slap on the behind by her father," Patrick Carr said.

"I'd like to see anybody touch me," she challenged.

Marie sat down. Art pulled out a pack of cigarettes.

"Give me one, Art," she said.

He stared at her with surprise. After a moment he said: "Congratulations, Sis."

"I'd be ashamed of myself," Jim Carr said self-righteously.

Patrick Carr watched with interest as Marie lit the cigarette. He wagged his head.

"The girl I marry will never smoke," Jim said firmly, look-ing at the wall.

"I'm your sister, Jim, not your intended," she said with cutting sweetness.

"So now you're an independent lady," Patrick Carr said sarcastically.

"Sis, it's about time you learned to smoke," Art said.

"Oh, I learned before this," she said, raising her eyebrows knowingly.

"Maybe she's going to take after her brother," Patrick Carr commented bitterly.

"At least he had enough sense to get out of this rut," Marie said.

"So, it's a rut she wants to get out of." Patrick looked at his oldest son for support. "Her own flesh and blood live in a rut. She wants to get out of it."

"Father, don't you ever get tired of saying the same things over and over again?" Marie asked.

"Folks, how about cutting out the comedy for today?" Art intervened.

"Ah, when you were a little one with your drawers wet from pee, I told your mother—spare that one and you'll see what happens," Patrick Carr said to his daughter.

The telephone rang, and Marie rushed to answer it.

Patrick Carr nodded as though the phone call were a justifi-cation of him as a father.

"She's a good kid. What the hell do you want to pick on her for?" Art asked.

"You're legally a man now, I see, and so now it's your turn to have your two cents' worth of say. Too bad you aren't like your brother. You could write about it."

"Nix, nix on that. I don't take it," Art told his father.

"Why, George, how nice of you to call," Marie said flirta-tiously over the phone.

"Bejesus, what a family I have. Well, the day will come when they'll have children of their own and they'll know the ache in a father's heart. It's nice you called, George, and, bejesus, come on over and give me a slap on the backside for a thrill."

VI

Mrs. Carr stood behind her chair at the foot of the table, waiting for the family to be seated. The worn linen tablecloth was spotlessly clean, and the silverware was well polished. The family drifted in, Patrick Carr stamping into the room. Art stuck his hands in his pockets and looked off nonchalantly.

"This looks nice, Mother," Jim said, taking his place to the right of his father.

Marie flung a quick look of contempt and superiority at her mother as she took her place at Mrs. Carr's left.

"Mother, don't you want me to carve?" Jim asked, as his mother began carving.

"I've carved the meat in this family all of these years," she answered without looking up.

Patrick Carr rested his elbows on the table, waiting.

Mrs. Carr stopped carving and said:

"We forgot grace."

She bowed her head and folded her hands. Jim piously imitated her. Patrick Carr lowered his head. Marie and Art exchanged bored looks before they bowed their heads. Mrs. Carr finished her silent prayer. Jim prayed for a moment longer than all the others, blessed himself, raised his head, and looked about from face to face with an air of proud self-justification.

Mrs. Carr finished the carving and served everyone.

"What could he do with his hands?" Patrick Carr asked excitedly while they were eating. "Has he hands like these?" he added, raising his own gnarled hands, which were grained with dirt and cement.

Marie looked disdainfully at her father.

"What I want to know is why the loogin, with his brains, didn't have sense enough to forget trying to be a writer and go to an embalming or undertaking school and get himself set with Whelan," Art said.

"Because he's a devil who's too lazy to earn an honest living like any ordinary mortal. He's too good for us. Too good for his family," Patrick Carr said.

"No matter where he may have strayed, he is one of our own. Let us leave him in the hands of God," Mrs. Carr said.

"Woman, for years you've prayed to soften that hard heart of his. And where has it got us?" asked Patrick Carr.

"I saw Kink Mulligan. Kink was sore about the book. I told him I didn't write it," Jim said.

"Again and again, I have said—if he ends up in the looney house, it isn't my doing," Patrick Carr said.

"What would you all say if he became rich?" Marie asked.

Her question startled them. Her father twice started to talk but was too confused. Then he said weakly:

"He wouldn't give us a cent if he made a million dollars."

"People have too much sense to spend money buying a book like that," Jim said.

"If he can make dough writing books like that, I say I'm going to write some books myself," Art said.

"Maybe you're not smart enough," Marie said.

"Whatever his sins be, it is the business of the Lord. Let us not backbite over the holy Sabbath meal," Mrs. Carr said. Her voice was strained with repressed passion.

They all stopped talking and went on eating in silence.

VII

"I see here by the paper that another one of those stock brokers jumped out of a window," Patrick Carr announced gleefully; settled back in the old worn Morris chair, he held the paper before him.

"The guy must have outsmarted himself," Art said coldly.

"We laid off more men. But Mr. Kenman told me I have nothing to worry about," Jim said.

"I should think you wouldn't," Art said.

"I do my job," Jim said proudly.

"Mr. Ellsworth Wimbledon. Landed on his head on La Salle

Street. The papers said that he was despairing because of business. Well, Mr. Wimbledon is no skin off my behind," the old man said, putting the paper down and looking around the room to shake his head with gratification. "Despair about business. What about the money of poor widows and orphans? Despair!"

Art yawned.

"Mr. Kenman would never have to do that. I can tell you—and I know since I keep the books—every penny is accounted for. Everything is on the up-and-up with Mr. Kenman," Jim boasted.

Art stuck a cigarette in the corner of his mouth, let it remain there unlit, and said:

"A lot of big shots ain't as noble as they'd like you to believe."

He lit his cigarette and looked about the parlor with a smirk on his face.

From the bedroom off the hall they heard Marie singing *Cherie*.

Jim Carr started reading the sports section of *The Sunday Clarion*. Soon the papers would be more interesting because of the baseball season. This year he was going to read every box score of every big-league game. But his team wouldn't do much. It looked bad for the White Sox. Lou Fonseca might have a good year, though, and that would make the Sox games more exciting because Lou was one of his favorites.

He leaned back in his chair and imagined he was a star on the White Sox. He'd always wanted to be a ball player, and if he'd had half a chance, he could have been one. But he'd never gotten a break in life—not that he was going to complain, because he was no complainer. And he wouldn't run away from the responsibilities of home as Bernie had. Not that he had any complaint to make against his brother, because he wasn't a complainer, but Bernie wasn't a Carr. He didn't have the Carr feeling.

But what position would he play if he were a star? He could never decide that question. Sometimes he liked to imagine himself a pitcher. But a pitcher didn't get into enough games. He wondered which he would do: break the pitching record of victories held by Cy Young or the record for hitting 300 in consecutive years like Ty Cobb, or the home-run record of Babe Ruth. He guessed he'd rather be a star hitter than a pitcher. He closed his eyes and visualized himself in the White Sox, stepping into the batter's box.

VIII

"I never would have thought it of your brother," baby-faced Ellen said to Marie, as the two of them sat in Ellen's parlor, eating chocolates and talking.

Marie looked around the room at the new furniture. It was so much better than theirs. She didn't like to have people to their house because of the old furniture. But some day she'd find the right man, and then she'd get furniture better than this.

"He seemed so shy, Marie. Except sometimes, when I looked at him and he'd seem to be thinking—he'd be positively frightening.

"Think of it, a book about our own neighborhood. And sometimes I blushed."

Marie smiled tolerantly at Ellen.

"Ellen, aren't we all the same?"

Ellen looked at Marie, startled.

"Marie," she asked self-consciously, "what does it feel like?"

"What do you think I am? A fool? To let some boy get something for nothing out of me?" Marie asked sharply.

"Yes," Ellen said reflectively. "That's what I think. But still, don't you sometimes wonder . . . what it feels like?"

"A girl is a fool to sacrifice herself for a boy," Marie said.

Ellen hesitated for a moment and then agreed.

"Yes," she said.

She reached for another piece of chocolate.

"But, Marie, I feel sorry for you, being the sister of a brother who wrote a book like that. You poor thing, how can you ever live it down?"

"Be careful, Ellen, or I'll write Bernard and tell him about you, and he might put you in a book."

"But, Marie," Ellen said quickly and in a frightened voice, "I'm a virgin. Honest, I am."

Marie laughed.

IX

Standing by the parlor window and looking wistfully down on Maryland Avenue, Mrs. Carr could hear her husband's snores. It was nice and sunny out. People on the street walked slowly, as if they were enjoying the sun. Ah, a day like this was a gift of God.

It was on a Sunday like this, thirty-four years ago, that she'd gone out for a walk with Patrick and he had proposed to her. Her face saddened. She had only been an innocent girl then, more innocent than her daughter Marie. She hadn't been able to look Patrick in the eye, and she'd scarcely been able to talk. Her heart had beat fast. And then, for reasons she'd never know, she'd said yes to Patrick. She could still see her mother standing there in the kitchen when she'd come home and told her.

—Mary, I'm against it.

Mrs. Carr tingled with excitement. Would her son, Bernard, ever understand that she had been young once, and that she had even thought of purity as he must have, as the little boy, Patrick Stanton, did in his book?

She saw an old couple walking along, hand-in-hand. She and Patrick almost never went out together. He hadn't kissed her in at least five years.

—My goodness, what I'm thinking, she told herself.

She turned from the window, embarrassed, even though she was alone.

Patrick Carr's snores could still be heard in the parlor.

Chapter Four

I

SOPHIE ROSSMAN's apartment was in an old building off Union Square. There were about twelve people there when Bernard and Elizabeth arrived. Elizabeth wore a striking dress and looked very pretty. Sophie greeted them with a grin and said in a throaty voice:

"Gee, kids, I'm glad you're here. Paul Drummond, the playwright, just back from the Soviet Union, is coming. He's a swell guy and a swell writer."

"Yes, I've heard of him," Elizabeth said.

Sophie was big and had large bones. Her cheekbones were high, her skin was almost tawny, and her lips were thick. She wore an old pink evening gown. Bernard, on shaking hands with her, noticed the hair under her arms and had an unpleasant impression.

"Comrades, everybody, this is Bernie and Elizabeth," she called.

A thin, swarthy youth named Hymie was entertaining the party with a monologue. He stood near a daybed by one of the walls, talking and gesturing at breakneck speed. His face was expressionless.

"Capitalism is on its knees, see? See, it's down, down on its knees, like Jess Willard when Jack Dempsey gave him K.O. drops. It's floundering; it's punch-drunk, groggy, like a palooka who can't go ten rounds any more. There's Capitalism. It's trying to get up. It's up on one knee."

"Isn't he a funny boy?" Elizabeth whispered to Bernard, who watched the performance with a polite smile on his face.

"Now, I'm History, the referee. I'm counting. One . . .

47

two . . . look at the palooka. It can't see out of one eye. Blood is running out of its nose. It's gasping, it's clutching for air . . . three . . . four . . . five. . . . Its teeth fall out . . . six. . . . It's leaning on two fat arms. . . . Seven . . . groaning. . . . It's groaning. . . . Eight . . . nine. . . . See, it falls on its ugly face! . . . Nine . . . ten . . . "

Amid laughter and applause, Hymie leaped a few feet, stood quiet with his face still expressionless, then raised his arm and barked:

"Ladies and gentlemen, comrades of the working class, the winner and new champion of the world, the Communist Party, U.S.A. That's History. . . ."

"Gee, that would make a grand act at one of our affairs," Sophie said.

"And they say we have no sense of humor," Bernard heard someone say from the other side of the room.

Everyone started talking at once. Sophie led Bernard and Elizabeth to the small kitchen for drinks.

"Gee, I'm glad you came. Isn't Hymie swell?"

Others came in, and Sophie left Elizabeth and Bernard.

"I'm so glad we came. Bernard, let's be gay tonight," Elizabeth exclaimed.

Bernard didn't answer. She slipped away to talk to Florence and Abe. A feeling of his reticence held him by the door near the kitchen. He wanted to talk and make an attractive impression, to have a good time. He remembered Billy Tannehill's party when he'd been in seventh grade. The kids had cracked jokes, but he hadn't been able to think of one. They'd danced, but he couldn't dance. They'd played post office, but he'd been called in only now and then out of pity. Elsie Cavanagh had ignored him during the whole party. Finally he had become so self-conscious that he had pretended to have a headache, and Mrs. Tannehill had given him aspirin, treated him sympathetically, and for the rest of the party she'd kept asking him if he were feeling any better. She was dead now and, come to think of it, she'd been buried by Philip Whelan.

"The leftward swing of the intelligentsia is of decisive political significance," he heard someone say with assurance.

There were several people here to talk to, there were so many ideas to discuss. He was with a friendly crowd, and he needn't fear he wouldn't be liked or that he might make a fool of himself. But he still held back.

Sam Leventhal and Mel Morris came over to him.

"I want to talk with you, Bernie," Sam said ingratiatingly.

"You look as if you're watching everybody and taking mental notes," Mel Morris said genially.

"I was merely sipping a drink and trying to decide which school of proletarian literature and artistic salvation I'd take issue with," Bernard answered dryly, after greeting them with a warm and eager smile.

"I give *schlemiel* capitalism five years," Hymie shouted from the other side of the room.

"Five years?" yelled a young fellow named Jackie. "Five years? Comrade, we're on the Eve. On the Eve."

"Hear them?" Mel asked. "Hell, this is a party. I want to have some fun." He glanced in back of him. "You know, some more pretty girls would advance the Movement . . . Carr, can't you get us half-a-dozen Irish beauties like your wife?"

Mel Morris was young and well built. He had a frank, pleasing face and a disarming grin; he was wearing a loose-fitting gray suit. Sam Leventhal was tall and rather thin, with a mop of wavy, dark hair. He was wearing a neatly pressed dark suit. He spoke in a low, soft voice; his smile was weak but appealing.

"You take Sophie. She's a swell girl. A wonderful comrade," Mel said, making a face and shaking his head from side to side. "But she's not my idea of fireworks. For fireworks give me an Irish rose every time. There's a bloom to unbloom."

"Most Irish girls are just too damned repressed for words," Bernard said.

"But beauty," Mel said. He blew a kiss. "Back home in Indiana, I used to lay one. Boys, even if I say it myself, I'm potent . . ." He grinned warmly. "Real vigorous and virile proletarian potency. But this Irish girl, Nellie Grannon, she licked me. Hell, in the normal course of events, I could manage two babes in the bushes on a good night. But I couldn't handle Nellie."

"If I were young and free like you fellows, I'd take a Jewish beauty every time," Bernard said. He was remembering Eva.

"Comrades," Sam interrupted, "let's not have a split on the national question."

"I got it, Carr. Now we can form a Carr-Morris bloc. Your task is to get me Irish girls. My task is to get you Jewish girls. Then we'll have a Socialist competition."

II

Elizabeth was thinking how wonderful it was to be young. She was so excited, and she wanted to laugh and to flirt, oh, harmlessly, but to flirt just a little. Bernard was over near the kitchen door talking very seriously to Melvin Morris and Samuel Leventhal. She'd already heard so many of those discussions since they'd come to New York, and she didn't always understand them, but she tried to, and it was only polite to act as if she did and as if she were keenly interested. But she didn't want to hear them now because this was a party. Here was Sophie coming over to her. Sophie was a good soul.

"Gee, kid, you look swell. Isn't this a grand party?"

"Yes, it is. What a becoming dress you have on. You look lovely."

"Oh, this—a wealthy sympathizer gave it to me. You should know her, Mrs. Cotterell. I went to see her to get a contribution for *Mass Action*. Gee, she's swell. You ought to meet her. But she's bourgeoise. You should see all the dresses in her closet. She was talking about how she's so rich and about how guilty she feels because she has so much and the workers are starving and unemployed. Mrs. Cotterell is bourgeoise. And so, gee, it was funny," Sophie laughed meaninglessly. "She said she felt bad having so many dresses, and then she showed them to me. So I said, 'Give me one.'"

"That was smart, Sophie," Elizabeth complimented.

"And this is what I got. This, but only twenty-five dollars for the magazine. But, still, that wasn't bad, was it, kid?"

"Most certainly not," Elizabeth said, nodding her head in emphasis. She added disingenuously, "I'd like to meet Mrs. Cotterell."

It might be useful for Bernard and her to know someone that rich.

"Sure, we'll go see her sometime," Sophie said, rushing off to greet some guests who had just arrived.

Sophie was happy and having such a good time. But you'd think that Sophie would at least have shaved the hair from under her arms. She wouldn't think of wearing an evening gown and leaving hair under her arms. Hair on a girl's body was a nuisance, and it wasn't nice. Of course, on her head, that was different. Bernard said he loved her hair, but she almost blushed inside herself thinking of it. She'd bet Sophie never took the hair off her legs. She shaved her own legs once a week. But she was afraid this might make the hair grow faster, and she didn't know which was better, to shave the hair off your legs or to use something.

She looked around with a coquettish gleam in her eyes.

She heard some man she didn't know saying in a loud voice: "Suicide is bourgeois despair. Suicide isn't Marxian. It's individual terror applied to yourself."

III

"I have a scientific plan for the seizure of power in New York. My plan is really scientific proletarian socialism. How are you going to take power if you don't master the science of military tactics?" Jackie told a timid young man.

Jackie was young and pimply-faced. He wore a khaki shirt, open at the collar, and shapeless gray trousers.

The timid-looking young man listened to Jackie, impressed.

Bob Bottomley staggered up to them. He was tall, well built, and good-looking.

"I have a military plan, too," Bob drawled.

"Are you a comrade?" Jackie asked.

"*On the day,* I say, *on the day,* I'll be on your side of the barricades."

"Comrade," the timid-looking young man said in a mild voice, "can you tell me about your military plan?"

"Since we're all comrades, maybe I can," Jackie said. He looked around the room suspiciously. "No, Sophie wouldn't have any renegades or *agents provocateurs* here. Well, comrades, now here is my plan. First, we'll . . . that is, we and the workers . . . we'll envelop Union Square. Then we'll deploy forces. Strong units will go down Fourth Avenue, Broadway, and Fifth Avenue. And then we envelop Madison Square."

"No, no," Bob Bottomley interrupted. "No, you've got to take a town."

"We're going to take New York," Jackie said.

"Padraic Pearse said that the Irish revolution had to be watered with the fresh blood of martyrs. The American Revolution has to be watered with fresh blood," Bob Bottomley went on in his drawling voice.

The timid-looking young man listened with observable awe.

"Did you ever hear of Jackson, Mississippi?" Bob asked.

"It's going to be the capital of the Negro Soviet Republic of Soviet America after we take power," Jackie said.

"You want to take Jackson, Mississippi, first. You lead five hundred hardened workers . . ."

"When the day comes, five hundred million workers will rise all over the world," Jackie said.

"Five hundred comrades. With them, you seize Jackson, Mississippi. First, you take the courthouse and barricade yourselves inside of it. You fight until the last man is killed. The American Revolution will be watered by the blood of five hundred martyrs. The fresh blood of five hundred . . ."

IV

"Carr, I liked your book," Mel Morris said to Bernard. "I felt damned sorry for the son in the book, Paddy Stanton. As I read, I kept thinking . . . poor Paddy, all that he's missing."

Bernard was pleased with Mel's praise.

"I wondered was your book autobiographical."

Bernard shook his head in the negative.

"I'm glad to know that because I thought he was a genuine *schmendrick*. You know what *schmendrick* means?"

Mel paused and then went on.

"But he's got stuff in him. The daydreams he has about the little girl, Audrey. You can make something of him if you write a sequel and show the way out for him. Now that you're here in New York, and know something of the Movement, you ought to do a sequel and show how he finds the Movement, and it points the way out."

"I don't know if he would," Bernard said meditatively.

"Bernie, I said the same thing in my review for *Mass Action,*" Sam Leventhal said.

"And the mother in your book. She's done well—damned good. I like your book a hell of a lot, and that's no crap. I disagreed with Mark Singer. He said you didn't know that when a boy thumbs his nose he's not being a revolutionary," Mel added.

"What the hell does that mean?" Bernard asked sharply, instantly disappointed on learning of Singer's reaction.

"Oh, Mark's a swell writer, the American Gorky, but he's wrong about your book, and I told him so. Mark said that all your characters were petit bourgeois. I told him that obviously you came from that class. Was your old man a real-estate shyster?"

"He's a bricklayer—out of work," Bernard answered.

Mel's eyes popped with surprise, and, turning to Sam, he said: "Carr comes from the proletariat!"

At this moment Bernard heard someone shouting from the other side of the room:

"Our writers will write of the rich, full life of the proletariat."

"That's Bert Anderson talking. He's really talking about you, Carr," Mel said.

"Bernie, that's what I don't understand. You come from the working class, and I don't understand why you didn't write about working-class life," Sam said.

"I wanted to write about values, what some of the values and commandments of the Church mean concretely in actual life. And I wanted to deal with a typical and prosperous family in a neighborhood like the one I grew up in. My own family isn't prosperous or typical. In fact, I think it's a little crazy."

"If your family is poor, how did you go to college?"

"I worked my way through. I even had a three-dollar-a-week job in an undertaking parlor. I hung around to answer the phone in case the other boys were out on an ambulance call. I was fired for incompetence."

They laughed.

"Didn't you get the jitters?"

"No. I watched an autopsy performed on a stiff. A fellow died of a heart attack in his car and they brought him in to our place, and I was put on the coroner's jury and earned a buck. I watched the whole procedure without being seriously bothered."

"I don't know if I could do that," Sam said.

"You can't get at and understand or enjoy life unless you have contempt for it," Bernard said, surprised at his own intensity.

Mel and Sam met his remark with perplexity. Bernard wondered what this remark of his really meant, or even if it had any meaning at all.

"I finally married the undertaker's daughter."

"I'll be goddamned. Is Lizzie an undertaker's daughter? She's such a wonderful, happy girl."

"Mortician or funeral director is the word," Bernard said.

They laughed.

A slender, dark-haired, eager young girl with lovely olive skin sprang into the room.

"Oh, Sophie," she exclaimed breathlessly.

Normally pretty, she was beautiful with the glow in her dark eyes, the radiant smile on her face, and the shy way in which she stopped, became serious, and looked at the floor, embarrassed.

"That's Mildred Feldman. She's a Vassar girl," Sam said.

"Umm, she looks cute and pretty enough to be a colleen," Mel commented.

Bernard stared at her, touched. Her eagerness, her girlishness, her youth, the fine texture of her skin, her slender figure and young breasts, her long hands. . . . He wished he weren't married. Immediately, he became confused and felt badly about his wish.

v

"Oh, Sophie, I left home," Mildred joyfully exclaimed. "I'm so excited."

"Are you, kid?" Sophie said.

"I want to be free. And now, congratulate me. I am free. I'm free," Mildred said, raising her voice.

"But, kid, what are you going to do? How are you going to live?"

"That's not important, Sophie. What do I care how I live so long as I live. I have a little room on West Nineteenth Street. I'm going to be a waitress. I'm going to wait on tables, and every penny I earn will be my own—mine—everything I do will be what I want to do. I'm free. If you only knew how happy I am."

"Well, kid, this is certainly a surprise," Sophie said monotonously.

"But I did the right thing, didn't I, Sophie?" Mildred asked. She went on talking breathlessly. "I want to be on my own. I'm going to live my own life. Oh, Sophie, dear, I just got sick of it, simply sick of it."

"Gosh, kid, you are excited," Sophie said.

"I'm happy, Sophie, happy. Oh, my father and mother gave me every advantage. They raised me to be cultured. Cultured. I've had culture until I could scream. I could have had a wonderful life without having to do anything. Just read books. The latest book-club choice that everybody reads and talks about. Concerts. Dance recitals. Theater tickets. Art exhibits. But what am I going to do with culture? I want to be on my own and meet real people. I don't want my father to buy me a place in the world. I did the right thing, didn't I?"

"Of course you did, kid, only do you think it's going to be easy?" asked Sophie.

"I don't want an easy life. I could have one. I'm good-looking and charming. I have a nice figure, and men like me. And I have clothes, oodles of clothes. This simple suit I'm wearing cost my father eighty dollars. I can marry a cultured man who has money and I can belong to clubs and have dinners and invite writers and actors and artists to my home and have servants and everything I want. I don't want it . . . because . . . because I don't want to be blamed. I don't want to be blamed because my father is rich," Mildred said in a pleading voice.

"We won't blame you, kid," Sophie told her kindly.

VI

"I couldn't come any sooner, kid," Jan Walters said to Sophie.

They sat on the bed in the bedroom off the main room of Sophie's apartment. Jan was a tall, lantern-jawed man in his thirties. He was wearing a khaki shirt. He looked at the closed door of the room. They could hear the noise of loud and excited talk outside.

"Quite a party," he said.

"Oh, it's swell," Sophie said with interest.

They sat in silence for a while, and Jan looked past her at the fire escape. He pulled her to him and planted a long kiss on her lips.

"Gee, we'd better not, Jan. Someone might come in on us."

"I know it, kid," Jan said, releasing her. "Just a kiss. You say Mildred left home?"

"Yes, isn't it wonderful? I'm really winning her over."

"Of course it is. We're on the wave now. This is the wave. That kid coming here when she left home is only one instance of it. Look at those kids out there," Jan pointed at the door. He and Sophie both turned. They heard the gay noise from the party. "Carr, Irish Catholic, with a world of talent. He's come toward us, too, but I wish he'd move faster."

"Oh, Bernie and Elizabeth are swell."

"Damn right, of course they are. I wish I had the stuff on the ball that kid has. He'll come along farther. They've all got to come. Kid, the wave is here."

"And, Jan, I've just collected over three dollars tonight with my *poochka,* and last night I didn't have a chance to tell you . . . I got four subs for *The Fist,* doing door-to-door work, and I made two other contacts."

"Sophie, you do so damned much for the Movement. We haven't a better Jimmie Higgins than you. And you can't have a movement without a lot of Jimmie Higginses."

Sophie listened and watched Jan, wrapt. Her face seemed to soften, to become almost appealingly feminine as she sat on the bed looking at him, noticing the hairs on his chest, which was exposed by his opened shirt. They sat silent. The noise continued.

"Boy," Jan remarked idly, wagging his head as he talked. "The gang's having a good time."

"Gee, isn't it great that they are," she said eagerly.

"Of course, it is . . . Kid, you and I know that you find the real zip, the real joy of life in the Movement." But Jan's face clouded.

"Jan . . . Jan . . . honey, comrade, something's the matter," she said in a low, worried voice.

"I had this long session with Mortimer on the Ninth Floor. He wants to build *Mass Action.*"

"Gosh, aren't we building it?"

"He doesn't like a lot of the stuff we print. Listen, he had so much to say I can't remember it. Sam's poem about the Scottsboro boys has deviations, and it doesn't emphasize the role of the Party enough—"

"But we thought it was a good poem."

"I still do. So do Jake and Mark. Sophie, I caught hell, and what could I do? I tell you, as I walked over here I was in the dumps. But I kept thinking to myself I have no right to be in the dumps. I've been in this game too long. I've gone straight down the line with the Party leadership and done Jimmie Higgins work for it in every struggle with the renegades. And I've worked like a dog on *Mass Action*. Hell, everybody who isn't in the know thinks that Mark does the work because he's listed as editor. I do it, with you, kid. And I catch hell."

"But, Jan, I don't understand," Sophie said, her face appearing almost stupid with lack of comprehension.

"It looks as if I'll be out. . . . I think they're going to put Lloyd Street in to take my place. He quit his job in advertising and has given up doing book translations. He's going to do full-time work for the Party. He wants more action, but if they decide, then he'll be editor of the mag."

Sophie sat pale and speechless for some moments. Her lips quivered.

The noise from the party continued.

"Gosh," she exclaimed.

Jan stared at the closed door with a bitter look.

"Jan, they can't do it. Why, how can *Mass Action* go on without you? Something's wrong."

"I have one ace in the hole. My contacts with Gromov in Moscow. I'm going to try to wangle it for him to bring me over there to work with him. Then, when I come back, my position in the Movement here will be different—a damned sight different."

"Oh, Jan, gee, it'll be swell for us to go and live in the Soviet Union."

Jan didn't respond to her exclamation. She became slowly bewildered.

"But, Jan, won't I go with you?" she asked plaintively.

"Kid, you know what you mean to me. You're more than a sweetheart or a girl. Those are bourgeois terms. You're a comrade. But I'll have to leave you. Annie would raise hell. She blasted my tail off last night about you and me. And I can't swing it. Remember that day last week when we locked the office for an hour . . . Mortimer must have come stool-pigeoning around."

"Jan . . . You know how I feel about you."

"Kid, we Communists just have to have the stiffest upper lips in the world. We're in something bigger than ourselves."

She shook her head, bewildered. He gently poked his fist against her jaw.

"Yes," she exclaimed meaninglessly.

"Jesus, I need a drink. What a day I've had."

They got up and went back to the party. The guests were milling about and talking loudly. The room was thick with cigarette smoke.

"Oh, Paul, gee, I'm glad you came," Sophie exclaimed, seeing Paul Drummond and rushing over to kiss and greet him.

VII

Paul Drummond was a large, gross-looking man with thinning dark hair. He looked about at people coldly and acknowledged successive introductions with weary, bored glances and brief, rude exclamations.

"Gee, I'm so glad you've come. I haven't seen you since you were in the Soviet Union. Paul, you look wonderful," Sophie said to him. "And, Paul, I want you to meet Bernard Carr. He's from Chicago, and he's a swell guy. His novel, *The Father*, just came out, and it gives the Catholics the works."

"I'm glad to meet you," Bernard said genially.

"Hello," Paul Drummond answered dismissingly and without any interest.

"I was looking forward to meeting you," Bernard began.

"It's good to be back, Sophie," Paul said, turning away from Bernard.

Bernard paled. Mel Morris, who was facing Paul Drummond, said:

"I'm Mel Morris, a young comrade from Indiana, and I'm interested in the theater. I want to write plays myself. And I want to tell you I've learned a lot from your plays. I admire them greatly. Some day I'd like to put one of them on."

"Are you a producer?" Paul Drummond asked.

"No, I'm a comrade and just a boy from Indiana. I came here to try to work in building up the Left theater movement."

"I tried that, too. We got nowhere."

"But now it's different. The work done by writers like you and Jake and Mark Singer is bearing fruit. The new generation is going Left. I've read about what has been done in Germany. We can do that here, and more. America is virgin territory." Mel laughed. "I've always liked any kind of ground that's virgin."

Paul Drummond yawned in Mel's face.

"Oh, Paul, we're waiting to hear about your trip. Gee, it must have been wonderful. Gosh . . . how I envy you. . . . Did you see Lenin's tomb?"

"I saw plenty," Paul answered.

"Here's a drink, old man. You're looking in the pink, Paul, and I'm damned glad to see you," Jan said, handing Paul a drink. "We've got to have a long *schmoose* as soon as we can get together."

"Yes, Jan, I've got a lot on my mind," Paul said.

"Here, Paul, sit down and tell us all about the Soviet Union," Sophie said, leading him to a chair.

Paul sat down and looked around with a frown. Meeting Elizabeth's gaze, he smiled, and she returned the smile.

"Well, old man, give us some real dope right out of the feed bag," Jan said, dropping down onto the floor and taking a good swallow of gin.

"I can't give a lecture. When we get together, we'll talk, Jan," Paul said.

"But tell the kids something, Paul," Sophie said.

He gazed coldly around the room, lit a cigarette, and then gave Elizabeth a quick smile.

"They're building Socialism in the Soviet Union, aren't they, Comrade Drummond," Jackie said.

"The workers aren't living on strawberries and cream in Russia," Paul said.

Some of the young people looked at him, distressed, and a few were taken aback.

"Russia," Paul said in the manner of an angry orator, "isn't a utopia. All these articles about pie-in-the-sky in Russia don't make sense. I know what I'm talking about. I've seen Russia. I've just come back from the Soviet Union."

"How were you treated, Paul?" Jan asked.

"I . . . wonderful. Wonderful. But I say you have to be realistic about the Soviet Union. These utopian articles about Russia written by people over here who've never been there . . ."

While Paul paused, Sam Leventhal cut in:

"The yellow capitalist press over here is carrying articles full of lies, lies that there is famine and starvation in the Soviet Union."

"I don't know anything about those articles, but I've seen Russia," Paul said.

"Aren't you for the Soviet Union?" the timid young man asked.

Paul fixed the young man with a fierce glance.

"Do you know my name?" he asked.

"Why," Sophie said, "Paul is one of the founders of *Mass Action*. He's America's leading playwright. Of course, Paul is for the Soviet Union. Aren't you, Paul?"

"All I say is that you have to see Russia realistically. The things I've seen. It's hard. They don't have sanitation like ours . . . some of those toilets—if you can consider them toilets.

And clothes and food! I say it's nothing like the utopian stories about the Soviet Union you read over here."

"That's what the Party leaders in Russia say," Jake suavely said. He was thirty-three, debonair, slender, and handsome. "You can't make an omelet without breaking eggs."

"The eggs are being broken, all right," Paul said.

"If you think of what it cost to build America, or of the Industrial Revolution, of the decades it took, the sufferings of the workers, then you'll understand that the Russian Party tops are expressing a profound historical truth and not a mere platitude when they tell us . . . that you can't make an omelet without breaking a few eggs."

"Yes, Jake, that's true," Sam said to Jake obsequiously.

"I'm writing a proletarian poem on just that. I decided to write it after I heard a lecture of yours, Comrade Jake. I'm calling it *The Socialist Omelet*."

"Oh, Nicky," Sophie said to the anemic young man who had just spoken, "when you finish it, let us have it for the magazine. Gosh, I wish I could see the Soviet Union."

"Drummond," Bernard said, speaking with a strain in his voice, "there's a question I think of sometimes. It's theoretical, but maybe it's important. Isn't there surplus value in Russian economy?"

As Paul turned to stare at Bernard in annoyance, Mel Morris weakly said:

"The workers control Russia, and they can't exploit themselves. If there were surplus value, exploited from the workers in Russia, it wouldn't be Socialist, but it is Socialist."

"No, it's the period of transition to Socialism," said a small, tow-headed lad.

"I told you, you've got to be realistic," Paul said.

"I agree with you, but my question is, what do you say about surplus value in the Soviet Union?"

"The workers are suffering and sacrificing to build, to build, build, and they don't have strawberries and cream, bananas and cream, peaches and cream, or apple pie in the sky," Paul shouted angrily.

The crowd was tense and shocked. Bernard became taut. Looking around, he saw Sophie with her face wreathed in smiles, Jan nodding his head in agreement, and Mel smiling with satisfaction. He saw faces full of belief, joy, hope, and fanaticism.

"Comrade Drummond," a lad named Arnold Gilbert said in a voice that was both cultivated and insolent, "what you say is interesting, what there is of it. But I say, let's be realistic—"

"Hey, Gilbert, let's not have oppositionist speeches," Mel Morris interrupted.

Paul looked bored and angry. Then he watched Elizabeth, who, becoming aware of his gaze, shyly dropped her eyes.

"I'm not making speeches. But I assume that you are all political people, as I am, and I am only making a valid comment," Arnold Gilbert said.

"Well, what the hell's on your mind?" Paul asked sarcastically.

"I gather that it is hard in Russia, a period of crisis. They are sacrificing to build. They have planned economy instead of capitalist anarchy. I go along with you on all of this."

"That's nice of you," Paul said dryly.

Ignoring Paul's sarcasm, Arnold Gilbert continued:

"But Lenin said that without theory there can be no practice. The comrade here, I think his name is Carr, thought he was raising a theoretical question. He was wrong, as I'll point out presently, but first, let me say this—the leadership in Russia is pursuing a theoretically false centrist and right-centrist course, in deviation from a true Leninist line . . ."

"Listen, have you been to Russia?" Paul asked.

"No, I haven't, but I have read all the necessary documents. Now, in the last issue of *Imprecor* . . ."

"Jesus Christ, I've just come back from Russia," Paul shouted loudly in petulant anger.

"When political people lose their heads in theoretical discus-

sion, they only betray theoretical bankruptcy," Arnold Gilbert
continued calmly.

Almost everyone in the room became tense.

"This isn't a meeting, Gilbert," Jan said.

"Oh, let's sing revolutionary songs," Sophie suggested. "Gertrude, you sing that wonderful song for Paul."

"Everybody sing," Gertrude said.

"Come on, Gertie," Mel said. "Majority vote. Everybody demands that you sing."

Mel took her arm and led her to the center of the room.

"There, you're co-opted to sing."

In a nasal voice, but with her eyes closed and her homely face
lit up with fanaticism, Gertrude sang:

> *Oh, 'twas on a bright November morn,*
> *When Lenin threw Kerensky out,*
> *That Yellow Chevalier.*
> *Oh, Lenin is my darling, my darling,*
> *Oh, Lenin is my darling,*
> *My own gay chevalier.*

VIII

"You both don't know what it means to me to get you two
together," Sam said ingratiatingly, as he stood with Jake and
Bernard in a corner. "I've been looking forward to your meeting and listening to you talk for a long time."

Bernard grinned defensively and waited for Jake to talk because he was unsure of himself. He didn't know how much Jake
knew, and he didn't want Jake to catch him up on any inconsistencies.

"Yes, Carr, I'm glad to know you. You're a swell writer. I
read your book last week, and when I finished it, I said, 'This guy
is an artist.' "

Bernard relaxed, smiled modestly, and hoped that Sam had
not been overstating when he'd said that Jake was both the
Belinsky and Plekhanov of America.

"The feelings of the boy in your book, the restraint he feels, his fear of going out and meeting life, his dreams—that's all good stuff, Carr. And the father. He's a dope, a petit-bourgeois dope. He don't know nothin' from nothin'. Your book is the real McCoy. Carr, you're a writer, and you've got a future. That's why I'm damned glad to see you drawing close to us."

"Well, I'm glad to know you think that, and . . . well, thanks," Bernard said shyly, not knowing how to accept praise.

"Don't thank me, thank yourself. I only read the book, but you wrote it."

Bernard couldn't think of just what to say. He started to take things head on by stating his rejection of the theory of dialectical materialism as a statement of scientific method, thinking this might open up any differences between them. But Jake interrupted.

"I was afraid you might not understand the significance of my remark on omelets, Carr."

"I think I did. I've often thought of the cost of American civilization. In a sense, my book deals with some of that cost, psychologically and morally. The promise of American life—"

"Yes, I know that, Carr," Jake interrupted again. "I didn't know how much you know about Bolshevism. Bolshevism is realistic. The leaders of the Party in Russia are realists, men who understand history. I've studied revolutions. Engels said it is an art. It is. It is both an art and a science. The Party leaders in Russia know it. Our own Party leaders know it, too, but, compared with the Russian leaders, all of us in the American Party are small potatoes. Know what I mean?"

"I think I do."

"And that's what Stalin means when he says you can't make an omelet without breaking eggs. My friend Drummond, here, he's an artist. He didn't understand the historical cook-shop or kitchen, if you'll pardon the metaphor. The cook, Stalin, had to be spicy, and Paul hasn't digested the spice. There is the hard side of life in Russia, and there are the model prisons, the crêches, all that stuff. That's good. But the Soviet Union, Carr, stands for something more. Hope. Hope, Carr, and happiness. You know who Saint-Just was?"

"Oh, yes, I've read and studied a little about the French Revolution. I think—"

"I was sure you did. You're an intelligent fellow. Saint-Just, one of the great Jacobins, was a great revolutionist. We Communists are his heirs. He said: *Happiness is a new idea.*"

Bernard's face lit up. The quotation stirred him. He was sorry he had not come upon it himself. He had so much to learn, so much reading to do.

"*Happiness is a new idea,*" Jake repeated.

Sam was watching Jake closely, looking at him and listening with apparent awe. Jake would keep nudging Bernard as he talked, and there were flattering little intonations in his voice. Bernard was disarmed and impressed by Jake. He liked him. But Jake talked so differently, so much more intelligently than he wrote. The few articles of Jake's which Bernard had read had seemed to him abstract, formal, even Jesuitical.

"A poet, a poet of action said that. And, Carr, the Revolution, Socialism, the preliminary step to Communism, is poetry. It means that life, society, is made over into a work of art. You're an artist. You didn't find it easy to write your book, did you? It cost blood and sweat. It was hard, wasn't it?"

"Yes, it isn't easy to write," Bernard said.

"Then think of what it costs when you want to make society, one-sixth of the earth's surface, into a poem, a historical work of art."

Bernard became aware that he was coming under Jake's spell. Others had gathered around and were listening to him. Jackie tried to say something, but Jake and Sam waved him into silence, and Jake went on talking:

"The artist has to be kind of hard. He destroys the gods of the Philistines. The artist of history, the artist of the future of man has to . . ." Jake laughed ironically " . . . break some eggs and leave some eggshells lying on the ground for the garbage man. You can't complain about eggshells on the ground. You can't complain about eggshells that you'll see if you ever go to the Soviet Union, as I hope you will."

"I want to, if I ever can," Bernard said.

"You can," Jake said knowingly. "And then you'll see how they are proving on one-sixth of the earth's surface that happiness is a new idea."

"Jake, you ought to write that," Sam said, spellbound.

"Jake, you're the American Plekhanov," Mel said.

"Now, now, comrades, I'm only a humble cultural worker, only a mere intellectual," Jake said lightly. "Carr, that's what our movement means. Over here we haven't had our 1905 yet, let alone our 1917. But we're growing. Look at the kids here, look at what a good time they're having. Kids who come from ghettos and farms and small towns, just kids. Look at how happy and alive they are. There's one YCLer I know. At nineteen he's been arrested six times in demonstrations. Sam here is a poet. Mel is a playwright. You're a novelist. Five and six years ago when Mark Singer and I talked about a revolutionary cultural movement, we seemed crazy . . . dopes . . . utopians . . . but now it's beginning. All you chaps, and others like you, you have a place with us."

Bernard said nothing. He had listened to Jake without thinking or guarding himself critically. He wanted to agree with Jake, and he remembered August, 1927, when he'd been in the Sacco-Vanzetti demonstration. Could happiness be a new idea?

Over Jake's shoulder he saw Elizabeth talking very spiritedly to Paul Drummond. He became nervously agitated, and all thought went out of his mind. He was glad that Jake continued to talk. He heard the sound of Jake's voice, but the sound registered no meaning for him.

He watched Elizabeth and Paul Drummond across the room.

Jake was speaking about the necessity of hardness. His wife, a round-faced girl, tapped him on the shoulder.

"Jake, it's time to go."

"Honey, can't I stay a few moments to finish what I'm saying?"

"You'll never finish."

Apologetically, Jake left, telling Bernard that he wanted to get together with him soon.

IX

"Let's sit down here," Paul Drummond suggested to Elizabeth, pointing to the daybed on their right.

She heard Mildred Feldman saying:

"But I did do the right thing, didn't I?"

Then Mildred's voice was drowned out in the general hum of conversation.

Elizabeth sat down and demurely straightened her dress and patted her clothes. Paul dropped down beside her. She turned and sweetly and casually said:

"Goodness, I was getting tired, and I didn't know it."

"Parties like this are too big," Paul said.

"But I like parties, don't you?"

"Of course, I do, but when they get this big, and you get damned fools pressing on you, wanting to discuss things with you when they're ignorant and inexperienced, then a party's no fun. I like to be left alone, and some of these kids won't let you alone. Aspiring Tolstoys and aspiring Lenins. What do they know?"

Elizabeth listened with an interested, sympathetic expression on her face.

"Yes, Mr. Drummond, I suppose people do trouble you," she said in a low and understanding tone of voice.

"I shut them up. But let's talk about something else. You know, I like you."

"But you hardly know me, Mr. Drummond."

Paul Drummond smiled at her patronizingly.

"You're not hard to know, are you?"

Elizabeth looked off thoughtfully.

"I wonder."

"You look different from all the other girls here. I've been watching you. In fact, I picked you out among all the girls here."

"That's nice of you. Thank you," Elizabeth said modestly. She thought that Mr. Drummond was somewhat conceited. "I'm glad you did, because I like your plays."

"Are you interested in the theater?"

"Yes, I am."

Paul looked at her carefully.

"Mr. Drummond?" Elizabeth asked girlishly.

"What, Beautiful?"

"Do you think another drink would make me drunk?"

"It would make you charming."

"You don't think it would hurt me?"

"Let me get you one," Paul said, getting up and pushing through the crowd. "You wait here."

Elizabeth sat back and looked around the room calmly and with an expressionless face. When Mr. Drummond had first started looking at her, she had felt kind of fluttery, but now, she didn't. He was getting her a drink, and that was a feather in her cap already. He had picked her out to flirt with instead of any other girl here. And that Mildred Feldman was very attractive and had caused a lot of excitement when she'd first come in. All night she'd been watching boys crowd around Mildred Feldman. But Mr. Drummond had singled her out.

Elizabeth nodded her head in confidence and gratification. Mr. Drummond was the best-known writer at the party, something of a celebrity, and he knew actresses and had even worked in Hollywood. Gosh, he wouldn't like it if he knew she thought he was a feather in her cap.

"Oh, thank you," she said to Paul when he came back with drinks.

She took a glass and looked at it. She didn't really care if she had this drink or not, but she wanted him to bustle for her, and he had. He was kind of nice—not so nice as Bernard, of course, but nice.

"You think it will be all right for me to drink?" she asked, opening her eyes wide.

"Listen, Beautiful, this is 1932. What's going to happen to you if you drink?"

"I guess it won't be bad of me," she said, speaking as though she were reasoning to herself.

She took a drink.

"There's no charm in life unless you're bad. To be bad is only to be natural," Paul said.

She enjoyed the way he fumbled in his pocket, got her a cigarette, lit the match, and put it to her cigarette; and she saw the look in his eyes. He pressed his leg against hers. Elizabeth quickly looked around the room to see if Bernard were watching her. Bernard was in another discussion, talking and listening as though she weren't even in the room.

"Tell me about yourself," Paul said.

He was sitting very close to her. And it was exciting to be a little bit bad like this.

"But you wouldn't be interested in me, because, oh, I'm just an ordinary girl."

"You're charming and pretty," Paul said.

"Oh, thank you," she said demurely.

She took another drink. She felt a little dizzy, and it was such a wonderful feeling. She giggled.

"What did you say?" Paul asked.

Elizabeth turned toward him.

"Do you feel as good as I do?"

"I don't know. I'd do anything I could to make you feel good."

"Do you ever feel like kicking?"

Paul stared at her quizzically. Then he smirked confidently and laid the palm of his right hand on her thigh.

"Why should I want to kick? But I do know what I would like to do."

"I can kick over my head."

"It's hot here. Let's go outside in the hall and you can show me how high you can kick."

Elizabeth gazed swiftly in Bernard's direction. He was looking over at her, and he seemed mad. Well, he hadn't paid much attention to her all night, and he took her for granted. She was attractive, and men liked her, and he had no right to take her for granted, and she wanted him to be a little mad and jealous about her, but not really mad because then she'd be afraid of him. She wanted to kick, to kick her feet higher than her head like a dancer, and she could do it, and maybe if she had gone on at dancing school she could have been a dancer.

Mr. Drummond was caressing her thigh, and his leg was pressed against her, and he was making her, oh, he was making her tingle.

She quickly took another sip from her glass.

"Maybe I shouldn't," she said coyly, her voice a trifle thick.

"Shouldn't what? Why shouldn't you?"

"Kick," she said.

Bernard was talking again. He wasn't even jealous.

"Gosh, it is hot here," she said.

He took her and pulled her up, squeezing her hand. She followed him to the landing outside the apartment.

Elizabeth giggled.

"What's funny, Beautiful?" Paul asked.

"Oh, I was just laughing. Hearing all the noise inside, with everybody just going on, jibber-jabber, jibber-jabber about every subject under the sun . . . listen, jibber-jabber, jibber-jabber . . ."

Elizabeth felt as if she might faint, and Mr. Drummond seemed changed. His face looked kind of handsome. He had her in his arms. He was kissing her, holding her tight, she was losing her breath, and it was like being dizzy.

She was afraid. And yet it had been nice to be kissed.

"Let's go," he said.

"Don't you want to see me kick?" she asked, recovering her poise and looking at him innocently.

Now, it was a feather in her cap, and she was confident of herself, and she wasn't afraid.

"Come on with me and you can kick."

"I can kick over my head. Don't you believe me?"

"Sure, I believe you, but let's get away from here."

"Watch me," she said.

She stood on her toes, rested on the balls of her feet, took a step forward, swung her right foot high, held it a moment while she balanced herself on the toe of her left foot. Paul looked hungrily at her bare thigh as she kicked.

She pulled her foot down, gasped a moment, and then said: "See, I can."

As she stepped backward to kick once more, Bernard appeared, pale and tense. Elizabeth smiled guiltily and said:

"Bernard, I can kick over my head, can't I?"

Bernard glanced at her, turned, glared at Paul, stood between them, clenching and unclenching his fists, struggling to maintain his self-control.

"Let's go home," he said.

"Bernard, let me kick once," she said.

Paul shrugged his shoulders and went back inside.

"I want to go home," Bernard said.

She stared at him and then, becoming meek, she took his hand and said:

"All right, Bernard."

Chapter Five

I

LOOKING over her mother's last letter, Elizabeth was embarrassed. She read the first lines of the second page, written in her mother's large handwriting:

And, Elizabeth, you are still my daughter, my girl. You are far away from me and you are now a married woman, and you have now begun to know of woman's pain and sorrow and shame and sacrifice. I always hoped to help spare you the burden until you were older. But you decided, and you have your husband now. Now you know the Facts of Life. But, my dear girl, you are too young to have children. Do not let your husband give you children yet until you are older.

She was glad she was alone. Mother and Daddy knew that she was not a virgin, of course, but somehow she was ashamed that they did. It was not bad to love someone, and she sometimes felt so good when Bernard loved with her. They liked to call it playing. But Mother's letter made her feel it was bad. Did women get to feel this way when they grew older, like Mother? Did Mother think her Daddy hurt her and made her do things that she was ashamed of? How much did Mother love Daddy?

—Does Bernard love me? she asked herself.

She was sure she knew the answer. When Mr. Drummond had flirted with her, Bernard had become furious. She smiled confidently. He'd been mad at her all the way home from Sophie's party. But he had calmed down, and they had played.

She must be different from her mother. Girls nowadays were different. It wasn't bad. She had told herself it wasn't bad when

73

she'd let Bernard do it the first time. She remembered how she'd been afraid and how she had wanted them just to take their clothes off and hold each other, and how Bernard had been so excited, and how even with him hurting her she had thought it was a woman's power. Bernard always asked her how it felt, and she liked to tell him that was a woman's secret.

Oh, she felt good. Hadn't Mother ever felt as good when she was young? Hadn't she ever sat and thought of Daddy the way she herself was sitting and thinking of Bernard?

She loved her father. He was nice and warm, almost as nice as Bernard. When she was little, he used to bounce her on his knee and kiss her. When her breasts had begun to show, she was sometimes ashamed because Daddy would see them, but still she had sometimes wanted him to see them. Sometimes when Bernard screwed up his face and was snappish and angry, he reminded her of her father.

Elizabeth suddenly got up and went for some paper and a pencil. She had made up her mind to answer Mother's letter. Then she'd get ready to have lunch with Frances Barclay. She thought for a moment, tapping the pencil against her lips, and then wrote the letter without halting once to think of what she was writing.

April 12, 1932

Dearest Mother and Daddy:

I waited to write to you in answer to Mother's letter because New York is so new, and we have so many things to do. But I was so happy to get it, and to know you love me and forgive me. I think of both of you all of the time, and I don't want you to worry about me, because Bernard is good to me, and he does take care of me. A number of important people are beginning to know about Bernard, and they all respect him. Today, while I am writing this letter, he is keeping an appointment with his publisher, Mr. Ferris of Ferris and Winter, to talk about signing a contract for a new book.

Oh, I can't begin to tell you about New York. It's fun to live here and exciting, but of course New York isn't Chicago, and if it wasn't necessary for Bernard to be here, near his literary contacts, we'd both rather live in Chicago. But New York is fun. I have come to know the streets and the stores and I don't get lost when I go shopping. Now, aren't I a smart girl?

There are lots of things and sights I want to see that I haven't seen yet—the Statue of Liberty and Coney Island, and lots more. When Bernard's work permits him to take me around, he does, and we have made some nice friends. We have a full social life, but of course work comes first, and Bernard works hard. He works almost as hard as Daddy does, and really he isn't what some people think a writer is. He believes more in perspiration than inspiration, as the saying goes. Our friends here are of the quiet, serious sort, and I like that, but we have jolly times when we meet them. These first months here have been hectic, and everything has been so new, and Bernard has had to spend a lot of time meeting editors and critics and publishers, but now we are in a comfortable four-room apartment —a sublet from friends—and it is quite easy to keep tidied up. It is new and convenient and large enough for us but not so large as to be a burden. It leaves me lots of time to go out shopping and window-shopping and for reading, and I help Bernard with his work. He says I am a good critic, and he agrees with me now about writing a different kind of book for his second novel.

And, Mother, what is the latest gossip you know? Is Mr. Connerty still quarreling with his oldest married daughter? I so like to get the little tidbits. Please write more of them to me. And, Mother and Daddy, don't worry about me. I'm still your girl, but I'm a big girl now and can take care of myself, and I'm happy and know you want me to be, and, Mother, a little secret. Bernard is really a manageable boy! He wishes to be remembered to you, and love, oh, oodles of it.

From your daughter
Elizabeth

After addressing and sealing the envelope Elizabeth hummed to herself in relief. Her letter was cheerful and would make them feel good. She smiled. Then she looked sadly around the basement room, thinking that her mother and father were all alone now, and they were disappointed in her and thought she was a bad girl, an ungrateful daughter. And if they saw how she was living they would feel, oh, they would feel too terrible for words. When she had first seen Bernard at Daddy's chapel, something had happened to her, and she had known then that Bernard was someone she just had to go to, and she had wanted to the very first moment she'd seen him. She flung herself on the bed and lay with her face on the pillow, sobbing, kicking her feet, and pounding her fists against the bed.

II

"You know," Frances Barclay said to Elizabeth with a touch of aloofness in her voice, "your story is an American romance. A bricklayer's son and an undertaker's daughter eloping and coming here to New York . . . and the bricklayer's son turns out to be an author of unusual talents."

"Do you really think Bernard—" Elizabeth said, sitting across the table from Frances.

"Yes," Frances interrupted. "Yes, I think he is. When Bill and I met him at Arthur Hampton's before we'd read his book, we both had a hunch."

"I'm so glad. Bernard is seeing Mr. Ferris today about a contract."

"By the bye, Bill's review of *The Father* is favorable. But I'm even more enthusiastic about it than he is." Frances paused a moment before adding, "But then, I'm not a critic like Bill."

"Oh, but you've read so much," Elizabeth said.

Frances Barclay raised her brows quizzically but said nothing. She was a plain woman in her thirties, with small crow's-feet around her eyes. But she was dressed smartly, and Elizabeth was quietly watching and studying her. Frances was chic and sophisticated. Elizabeth wanted to impress her, and this lunch was practice, because when Bernard became rich and famous, he would expect his wife to be sophisticated and smart, and she thought she could learn something from Frances.

Inwardly, Elizabeth was gay and excited, even though she was showing it in a way that Frances might call naive. She liked this restaurant. It was jolly, and it was also a speakeasy. She was drinking red wine with her food, and doing it, she believed, just as well as somebody who had been to Paris, like Frances. The place was crowded, and people all around her were talking with spirit, as if they enjoyed what they were saying and considered their own words important. They seemed like distinguished and sophisticated people. Oh, she couldn't wait until the name Mrs. Bernard Carr would mean something and people would turn and look at her when she lunched in places like this.

Elizabeth lit a cigarette with affected casualness. She was sure that if people noticed her, they would think her a real New Yorker.

"Yes, Bill and I know a lot of literary people. Well, your Bernard seemed different to us right from the start. He seemed real. So many literary people aren't real."

"I think so," Elizabeth answered modestly.

How proud she was—proud as a peacock. And she felt sympathy for Frances growing within her. She guessed there was something unhappy in Frances' life. She would like to say something to make her happy, because people all ought to be happy. It was so much fun to be happy.

"You know, I still find it exciting to be in New York. There's such a difference—even in the streets . . . I guess I've outgrown Chicago."

Frances smiled tolerantly and maternally.

"I don't know how to say it. Oh, it's just different. You know, the people in Chicago are nice. They're good people. But they're different, different from people like you, you and Bill, and Arthur and Hildegarde."

"I suppose we're intellectuals," Frances said.

"It's not just that, not only reading books and talking about books. It's everything, the way you live here, and the way you talk about everything. It's being interested and being interesting."

"What I like about you and Bernard is what isn't New York in you both. You're not blasé. Not cynical."

"Oh, I am a little cynical," Elizabeth said quickly.

"Elizabeth, you're a good child," Frances said, again smiling tolerantly, almost as though she were a kindly and understanding mother.

The waiter came with coffee and spumoni. Elizabeth tried to listen to an older man talking to a young girl at the table to her left, but she couldn't quite make out what was being said. She imagined he must be a rich butter-and-egg man, and the thought excited her.

"Simple people are probably happier than the intellectuals," Frances said.

Elizabeth leaned forward, listening.

"Creating something, as Bernard can . . . that's different. But reading books and talking about them and arguing over them . . . there's something artificial about it. I wish Bill could get something else to do," Frances said.

"But Bill is a good critic."

Frances nodded in agreement.

"But what am I saying?" she said, speaking as much to herself as to Elizabeth.

They ate their dessert. Frances felt melancholy. It seemed strange to her that she should be having lunch with this girl from Chicago, that she should have talked almost personally. She had casually mentioned lunch when they'd said goodnight at the Hamptons', and Elizabeth had taken her up on it, and so here they were. The Carr marriage seemed strange to her. All this girl had was her youth, youth and the same kind of ordinary prettiness you'd find in many American girls. Her husband, Bernard Carr, was different. She sensed a torment and chaos in him that might some day break loose in destruction if it weren't harnessed by art. She didn't know why she thought this of him.

What had led such a young man to marry this girl? Yet she did have a kind of youthful charm.

Frances thought that she was now thirty-five and weary, and that once she had been twenty-one and alone and eager in New York. A new generation was now coming to New York searching for what she had once sought.

Reflecting sadly, she was only half-listening to Elizabeth.

"Yes, Bernard is gifted," Elizabeth was saying. "But around a house, goodness, he's all thumbs. He just can't do a thing, poor boy. I'm even afraid to let him help wash the dishes, because I'm sure he'll break them."

"Bill can do anything around the house," Frances said.

"Oh, I wish Bernard could. I wish Bill could help Bernard."

"I wish Bernard could teach Bill how to write," Frances said with irrepressible bitterness.

"But he is a fine critic," Elizabeth quickly remarked again.

Frances was angry with herself for what she had said, and Elizabeth's assurances about Bill sounded hollow.

"You were telling me about Bernard. Go on, tell me more."

"Well, Bernard seemed different, kind of lost and sad. There were other young men working for my father, like Arthur Smith. Father is awfully fond of Arthur, and I think he kind of hoped I might . . . well, yes . . . I might become interested in Arthur Smith and marry him. Arthur now is studying at an embalming school, and he wants to be a mortician himself some day. And Father had only me. Arthur is nice, but Bernard was different. Well, my Daddy fired Bernard."

"Is that why you became interested in him?"

Elizabeth looked blankly at Frances for a moment.

"Come to think of it, I did feel kind of sorry, and I did think that Daddy shouldn't have done it, and, well, I was thinking of this, and I saw him on campus, so I spoke to him. I really did know him, because I had seen him at Daddy's parlor. I saw him again on campus, and he smiled, and I smiled at him, and then, one day I was sitting alone in the Coffee Shop on campus—I used to like to go there because you always met someone there

—and he came in and smiled, and I invited him to sit down with me. He seemed awfully nice, but he was intellectual. I liked him, but, goodness, he said lots of things I didn't understand. And, you know, he seemed a shy boy. And I liked his mouth. He has a strong mouth, don't you think?"

"It's a sensual mouth."

"It's something like my Daddy's mouth."

Frances raised her eyebrows, and this puzzled Elizabeth, but she went on talking.

"So we got to seeing each other, and we fell in love. And after he graduated we eloped—and here we are."

Frances wondered was Bernard Carr still lost? Perhaps, she thought, he had married this girl because she was so young, such a girl. She had never met a young man who seemed more afraid of women, who seemed to dislike them as much as Bernard Carr did. That was the way he impressed her. And, yes, he aroused her curiosity.

Elizabeth smiled foolishly. She lit another cigarette with dainty, girlish gestures, and she began to beam with empty smiles. She sensed that Frances liked her more if she behaved more like a girl than a sophisticated woman, and she was acting on this.

"Well, I have to get back to work at my advertising office. It's been very nice seeing you for lunch, Elizabeth, and I hope you and Bernard will come to see us soon."

"Oh, we'd love to."

Frances paid the bill, and they left the restaurant.

Walking away from Frances and toward Fifth Avenue, Elizabeth thought that Frances Barclay was nice, but sad. Frances had said she wished Bernard could teach Bill how to write. Frances wanted Bill to be a writer, and wished that Bill were like Bernard. That made her real proud. And it showed her there was a difference between New York and Chicago. Because in Chicago people were still . . . well, suspicious of Bernard, and thought he should be something else besides being a writer, but here a writer like Bernard was respected. And here, some women, older than she, too, envied her because she had a husband like Bernard. She sang to herself and thought it would all be so wonderful if Bernard only got a contract and an advance from Mr. Ferris today.

III

Fifth Avenue below Fourteenth Street had become one of her favorite streets. She had come down here just to walk and think and pretend different things. If she walked in a refined way, people would notice her and think she was attractive and well-to-do. Some of the men who looked at her might even think she was a virgin. Sometimes she had such a queer feeling, knowing she was married. Did people look at her and think or know she was not a virgin, and did they try to imagine her in bed with her husband? When she had found out about babies, she used to think of her mother and father together, and now she herself was a wife.

A well-dressed man stared at her. He was older than Bernard, a man of maybe thirty-five, and he wore well-cut clothes. Gosh, she wished Bernard could wear clothes like that man's. The man must have turned around and looked after her. A girl got so she could almost tell which men were or were not going to turn around and look. She had felt this man looking at her from the way he had his head turned just a little in her direction as they passed. If she met some nice man, who wanted to talk and perhaps be given just a little flattery and understanding, and if nothing happened, Bernard couldn't be angry, and there wouldn't be anything bad or wrong in her having tea with some nice, polite older man, would there? She walked on, taking slow, dainty steps.

Her round face became intent. She asked herself who she would imagine herself to be. She'd pretend she was a movie actress. But what would her stage name be? Her mind went blank for a moment. A tall, blond lad smiled invitingly at her, but she didn't see him. The name ought to be unusual and romantic, and . . . kind of mysterious. Perhaps a Russian name would be best. Or should it be Italian?

She couldn't make up her mind and, coming to the drugstore on Eighth Street, she went in and took a seat at the counter.

"Gosh, I wonder what I want," she said.

"I can give you anything you want," the soda-jerker answered insinuatingly; he was a short, bushy-haired lad.

"I wonder if I should have a fudge sundae."

"Why not?" he asked, fingering his checkered bow tie.

"Gosh, I'm trying to make up my mind," Elizabeth said, smiling.

The soda-jerker looked at her wisely and said:

"If you ask me, I always say that the girl who says she hasn't made up her mind has made it up. You have to be careful about the girl who has her mind made up."

"Why?" Elizabeth asked flirtatiously.

"Once they have their minds made up, there's no changing 'em."

The soda-jerker paused, and then he added with meaningful pronunciation, "Their minds."

"Maybe girls just say their minds are made up," she said coyly.

"Is yours?" he asked knowingly.

"Gosh, I wonder what do I want?" she said, slightly lowering her eyes.

"I can give you anything you want," he repeated.

"I wonder if I ought to have a chocolate marshmallow nut sundae?" she asked innocently.

"If it is good for you, you should have it. The nut sundae I can give you ought to be good for you."

"Could I have one, please?"

"With pleasure," he said, bowing slightly.

She sat erect and prim, watching him fix her sundae.

"Here it is. I know all sorts of good things," he said with a wink as he pushed the sundae to her.

"I hope it doesn't make me fat."

"Fat? Why, you're just beautifully slender. You just relax and eat my nut sundae."

"Milk shake, chocolate," a man called impatiently from the other end of the fountain.

Elizabeth watched the soda-jerker fix the milk shake, knowing he was trying to impress her. He was a cute thing. With a guilty feeling about overeating, she began on her chocolate marshmallow nut sundae. She remembered how she had loved these sundaes when she'd been a little girl.

The soda-jerker was busy while she ate. When she finished and was sliding off the stool, he said:

"Come around again and try some more of our *nut* sundaes on a Sunday."

"I will, thank you," she answered sweetly.

"I mean it. I'd like to see you," he said, his tone indicating a proposition.

"Oh, I'll be around again."

"What do you do with yourself at night?"

"Oh, not much."

"That's not right . . . I'd like to see you."

"I'll be here again, oh, for something or other."

"I mean—see you on a date."

"Oh, I couldn't this week."

"Why not?"

"Because . . ." she began.

"You said you didn't do much at night."

"But I have engagements this week."

"Well, when?"

"I'll be here again."

A couple sat down at the fountain, and the man signaled to the soda-jerker.

"Don't forget," he said to Elizabeth before turning to get the order from the couple.

She paid her check and left. Outside, on Eighth Street, she stood for a moment wondering what to do. He was a nice boy. He didn't know she was married, and, of course, she wouldn't have a date with him, but there was no harm in talking to him, and it was flattering to know a lot of boys would like to take you out.

She walked along Eighth Street with no destination in mind. It was such a fine day, and it was so good to be out of the damp, cramped basement room and to walk in the sun and know that spring was here. She stopped at the corner of Eighth and Sixth.

—I am Mrs. Bernard Carr, she told herself. She turned back, walked down to Washington Square, and found an empty bench.

Should she take an Italian or a Russian name for her little dream game? She looked off at the Washington Square monument, and the name Eva came to her mind. But that was the name of that girl Bernard had been in love with. And he used to come and talk with her here in Washington Square. Why, they might even have sat and talked of loving each other on this very bench. An expression of fright came over her face.

She was afraid that Eva had been smarter than she was, and that perhaps Eva had understood Bernard better than she did. She was jealous of that Eva. Eva must have been a nice girl. And if Bernard met her by accident one day, what would happen? Eva was older than Bernard. Older women must like him. Frances Barclay was sweet on him. If she lost Bernard, what would she do? She couldn't even imagine it happening any more than she could think of her Daddy dying.

A frightened look swept across her face.

She got up and walked back along Fifth Avenue. A well-dressed man stepped in front of her near the corner of Eleventh Street. Two cab drivers stood talking. They suddenly rushed to their cabs. The well-dressed man hesitated a moment and then got into the front cab. Elizabeth saw the look of disappointment and then the bitter grimaces on the face of the other driver, as he watched the first cab drive off. She felt sorry for him, poor man. She could tell by his face that he was unhappy about losing the passenger. He must be poor. This depression was bad for people. She wanted it to end somehow. The poor man ought to get some business.

Without thinking, she got into the cab. The driver followed her into the cab.

"Where to, lady?" he asked, smiling genially.

"Oh! . . . oh . . . oh, just take me to Forty-second Street, Forty-second Street and Fifth Avenue."

The cab shot forward, jolting her slightly.

Now the poor man was pleased, and she was glad. Then she frowned seriously. This was a foolish extravagance, and if Bernard knew about it he'd get very angry and bawl her out. But she had only wanted to help the poor taxi driver, and she wasn't doing anything bad, and Bernard sometimes didn't understand her. And maybe he'd get an advance on a new book today. Then they'd have a little money. Since she was going to Forty-second Street, she would window-shop on Fifth Avenue and look at the clothes. She could get some ideas about new clothes and the styles, and Bernard might let her go to Klein's on Fourteenth Street to buy a new spring dress.

Oh, if Bernard only talked the right way to Mr. Ferris and got some money!

Chapter Six

I

"BERT, I never knew how strange the human race was until I became a publisher and had to deal with authors," Terry Winter said.

Bert Ferris, leaning back in his chair, smiled grimly.

"We're all in the same boat now, and it's damned leaky," Winter said, crossing his thick legs and patting his bald head.

"We've got to get a life preserver for ourselves then," Ferris said.

"Bad as these royalty statements are," Winter said, pointing to the papers on his partner's desk, "they've almost sunk us. Our sales this spring are down nineteen per cent from last fall and twenty-seven per cent from a year ago. I don't know where to find new capital to throw into our kitty."

"I wonder if anyone can give me one good reason, Terry, why a man becomes a publisher."

"There are reasons," Terry Winter answered, and his partner looked at him in surprise. "But they are all bad."

The two men grinned dejectedly and were glumly silent for several moments.

"If business gets much worse, not even the Bible will sell."

"I wonder if we can't work some new angle on the Bible," Ferris speculated.

Winter met this with a cold, rejecting glance.

"You really don't cotton to a new angle on the Bible?"

Winter shook his head in the negative. The telephone rang. Ferris picked it up and said hello.

"Tell him I'm in conference and I'll call back," he said importantly. He turned to Winter. "That's Adams."

"We can't give him any more time."

"I know, but if all the booksellers go bankrupt, that's not going to do us any good either."

"Sometimes I think that if I really had any faith in human nature, I'd become a Communist," Winter said.

Ferris was momentarily frightened. Then his face brightened up with an idea.

"I wonder if this would work—a book frightening the pants off everyone with the dangers of Communism. You know, telling them what will happen to them unless . . ."

Ferris looked at the ceiling and thought.

"Unless what?" Winter asked.

"Unless they buy our book," Ferris weakly answered.

"That's your answer."

"Yes, Terry. I guess that's out."

"We need a couple of books that every dame in the country from shopgirl to society matron will want to read, a kind of literary French tickler."

Bert Ferris took a silver cigarette case from his pocket, snapped it open, and leaned forward for his partner to take a cigarette.

Each lit his own.

"If some smart roué would only invent a new vice for the human race so we could publish the first book about it—some kind of sexual miniature golf or flagpole-sitting or dance-marathoning. . . . Bert, do you think we could do anything big with the Marquis de Sade?"

"Let me think about that. Have you talked to Rank about it? It might be up his alley, and since he's our editor we wouldn't have to put out a lot of dough in advances to get the job done."

"He'll be in late this morning," Ferris said, leaning forward and making a note on a pad.

"It seems to me he's late every morning," Winter commented acidly.

"Dan is a priceless asset to me," Ferris said frostily. "He'll be in any minute now. Bernard Carr is due shortly. He's got some idea for a new novel. Dan and I are going to talk with him."

"Another of our contributions to Art," Winter said.

"He has a vigorous talent . . ." Ferris said weakly.

"I still say what I said when that Carr manuscript came in—psychologically, it stinks. But, anyway, see if you can get him to write something for us that'll sell."

"Terry, that's just what Dan and I want to talk to him about."

Winter looked at his partner skeptically.

II

"Carr, all you have to do is to worry about your own book. I have to worry about all the books I publish, and about a hell of a lot more—salaries, printing costs, rent, a hundred and one items. Do you think it's easy to be a publisher? A publisher has a thousand and one worries. The simple fact is that business is just rotten."

"These days, Carr, a writer like you is a luxury," Dan Rank said in an overcultivated voice; he was a slender and elegant young man.

"I want to write what I think I know and feel. I suppose that is a luxury," Bernard said in an outburst.

"Oh, come, come, Carr, let's be practical," Dan Rank said testily.

As Bernard turned toward Rank, Ferris said:

"Carr, publishing is a business."

Bernard sank back in the chair, sighed, and said:

"That's what my father-in-law would say. He's an undertaker."

"He has a better market than we have. A dead person is business for him. A dead book is a loss for us," Rank said.

Bert Ferris smiled at Rank's remark.

"The world is full of honest young writers. I used to know scads of them in Paris who sat all day in the Dôme, drinking and talking about The Great American novel they planned to write. You'll find scads of them here in New York, too, and now, I hear, the exiles are returning. The world is full of them." Rank paused, turned to Mr. Ferris with a knowing glance, and continued:

"Bert, I'd like to say a few things to Carr."

"Go ahead," Ferris said, almost as though this had all been rehearsed.

"Carr," Rank said blandly, "if you could write a different kind of novel, one about New York, perhaps you could get somewhere in this literary business—and possibly we could give some serious consideration to such a project."

"Yes, Carr," Ferris said, leaning forward with his elbows resting on his desk. "We do have an interest in you. After all, we discovered you, didn't we?"

"If you've got your past out of your system, you ought to be able to do a good novel, one with popular appeal and with an adult situation," Rank went on. "A book like that would give you prestige with the literati. You know, neither Bert here nor I doubt that you have the talent."

"And that goes for Winter, also, Carr."

"If you can combine style with something that would have just enough appeal and spice so that the shopgirls and stenographers would want to read the book on the subways, why, then you could give us the kind of novel we could publish."

"A man can write a bestseller and still be a good writer. It's been done," Dan Rank added.

"I'm a writer," Bernard said, hurt, his voice low and throbbing with protest.

Ferris gazed at Bernard, annoyed.

"Carr, for God's sake, don't look so solemn. We aren't trying to rape your artistic conscience," Dan Rank said.

"I'm not solemn," Bernard answered petulantly.

"You could work out our idea for the book," Dan Rank said.

"And will you give me an advance?" Bernard asked.

They gazed at one another knowingly.

"I only wish I could, Carr," Ferris said regretfully.

"How am I going to write this book if I don't have anything to live on?" Bernard asked.

"How do you live now?"

"From hand to mouth on book reviews."

"Isn't that a good apprenticeship for you?" Rank asked.

"I'm to write this book that you've vaguely suggested to me —and I'm to take all the risks," Bernard said.

"But wait a minute, Carr, let's be reasonable. Who takes a risk in publishing a young writer? Didn't we take a risk with your first novel?"

"There's something wrong in the whole damned economy of this business," Bernard said.

"That's what they say in *Mass Action*," Rank commented.

"A publisher, Carr, can't go out in the streets and force people to buy a book, can he?"

"I wouldn't want anybody to do that for me," Bernard said.

"Well, what do you want?"

"There's nothing for me to say," Bernard answered.

"Carr, I think I can honestly say that, as things are, it isn't reasonable to expect us to take a risk, considering that we have money tied up in your first book, money that we'll probably never get back."

"Does this mean, then, that I am free of obligations to you?" Bernard asked tensely.

Again they looked at one another knowingly. Rank raised his eyebrows.

"Do you want it that way?" Bert Ferris asked.

"I need an advance if I am going to write another novel. I'm almost at the end of my rope," Bernard said urgently.

"If you can write the kind of book we've proposed, and if you give us a good first draft of it, then I'll discuss the advance with my partner."

"But you didn't really suggest a book. You suggested my doing something I can't do, something I don't know how to do."

"What was that?" Rank asked insolently.

"Titillate stenographers."

"A man has to prove himself a genius before acting like one," Rank said.

"I want to be released of any obligation to submit my next book to you," Bernard said doggedly.

"Carr, why don't you just think things over first?" Ferris suggested.

"Do you believe it is going to be easy to interest another publisher?" asked Dan Rank.

"No."

"Then why are you so intractable? Do you really take seriously all those sentimentalities about starving in a Greenwich Village garret?"

"My beliefs are irrelevant to the question at hand," Bernard answered.

"What do you mean?" Ferris asked.

"My beliefs don't have a cash value, or cash potentiality, anyway," Bernard declared.

"Oh, come, come," Ferris said. "Come, Carr, don't be so hotheaded."

"I think we're all just wasting our time," Bernard said.

"If that's the way you feel, Carr—" Ferris curtly broke in.

Bernard rose.

"I'm sorry you are so stubborn," Ferris continued, his voice now suave.

Bernard shrugged his shoulders.

"Well, Carr," Ferris said, putting out his soft, pudgy, well-cared-for hand, "I hope you have no hard feelings."

"Why should I have hard feelings?" Carr asked.

Bert Ferris had seemed ill at ease, disturbed. Now his face relaxed in a smile of sympathy and friendliness.

"After all, if I can't make money for you, the question is settled. And apparently I can't," Bernard said.

Bert Ferris's smile washed off his face. He stiffened up but said nothing.

"Well," Bernard said with a nonchalant shrug of his shoulders.

"Good luck, Carr," Rank said as Bernard left.

III

Bernard stood on the corner of Forty-sixth Street and Madison Avenue, dispirited, feeling lost, and staring at the faces of passers-by as though he were trying to find someone. A few minutes ago he had left the office of Ferris and Winter in a mood of proud independence. He couldn't have explained to Ferris and Rank why he wanted to be a true artist. Rank, especially, was too cynical to understand. But he had asserted himself. Now he imagined that Ferris and Rank would merely think he was a conceited fool. He was depressed.

And what could he expect to find in the faces of these strangers? He was staring as though he would find one pair of eyes to look into, one pair of ears into which he could pour words expressing all that was unexpressed in his being. Ever since he had been a boy, it seemed that he had looked at people in this moody way. Yes, one pair of eyes, one pair of lips, one pair of ears, one face, he thought. Only Elsie Cavanagh had had those special eyes, those special lips, those special ears, that special face. The loneliness of his boyhood came back to him. His boyhood need for someone sympathetic asserted itself. And he knew there was not, and could not be, such a person. Yet here he was, gaping at strangers in search of the face he could never find.

He turned and started along Forty-sixth Street toward Fifth Avenue.

One pair of lips to kiss . . . one pair of ears to hear his voice . . . one pair of eyes to look at him with love . . . one vagina. This is what lay behind all those recurrent moods of brooding and melancholy and of Zarathustrian loneliness. He walked more slowly, so absorbed in his own thoughts that he noticed nothing on the street. Here he was, still nursing the feelings of his boyhood.

He automatically turned southward on Fifth Avenue. He

looked vaguely at the legs of passing women. Elizabeth had slender legs. What kind of legs did Elsie Cavanagh have now? Every man must have an Elsie Cavanagh in his life, a little girl, made not of sugar and candy but of innocent dreams. And he hadn't gotten over this astounding fact. He guessed that was why he wanted to be a writer. Yes, his wounded dreams of love had hurt him more than all the lies he had been told. And so here he was, with the emotions of a boy of ten or twelve driving him, driving him with ambition to want to be a great and immortal American writer. And he couldn't tell Ferris or Rank that this was the reason he couldn't concoct the book they wanted. He hadn't clearly known this was the reason when he'd talked to them a little while ago. Now he did.

Wasted days were passing. More days in reading bad books and analyzing them. He was getting nowhere. And he knew now that *The Father* would not be his means of financial escape. All along he had really counted on some miracle.

What was he going to do?

He walked on and stood on the corner of Forty-second Street and Fifth Avenue, looking cater-cornered at the New York Public Library, remembering how he had gone there in 1927 and had written and studied and dreamed of the day when he would have his name on a book. That day, he sadly told himself, had come and gone.

He asked himself—would he be able to write another book? Was he a failure?

He crossed the street dejectedly and, sitting in the sun on the library steps, he took Arthur Hampton's review of *The Father* from his pocket and read it with tears almost welling up in his eyes.

Some years ago, H. L. Mencken called Chicago "the literary capital of America." The raw, smoky industrial city by the blue waters of Lake Michigan, Carl Sandburg's giant, is still producing writers. Grimy, raw, and energetic, there is something about Chicago which is conducive to strong writing. And we have

fresh witness of this fact in Bernard Carr, whose first novel,
The Father, *introduces one of the new generation of Chicago novelists.*

The Father *tells the story of a lace-curtain Irish family, living on the South Side of Chicago. The lace is a little mildewed, but it is the best lace the Stantons can procure to hang in front of the windows of their poor souls. The marriage of Martin Stanton, a real-estate operator who is not above cutting the corners fast, is loveless. They have one son, Patrick. He is a strange fruit of an ordinary and banal home. Half poet and half priest, he feels that his parents bear him no love, and he has no love in his heart for them. He is convinced that he was conceived during a drinking bout of his father, and once, when he was young and his father had been boozing and had beaten him up, his parents inadvertently left their bedroom door open. What young Patrick saw colored his whole boyhood and adolescence.*

This story is rich with the pathos of lovelessness. The father, Martin, is an ordinary homme moyen sensuel. *He dreams of becoming a big-shot in the real-estate business, and he envisions a large, suburban real-estate project in which sales will be limited to Irish Catholics of the better sort. He is here reacting against the ignorance of his own father, who was a greenhorn and a ditch digger. His business dreams are grandiose. He gets along, living well, and for release surrenders periodically to the temptations of the flesh. He now and then finds a girl who might give him what he doesn't get from his wife, he hits the bottle, and he plays poker with the boys. The wife is a colorless, neurasthenic woman, given to nagging and to imaginary ailments. She is constantly at swords' points with her husband, and she adopts a martyred air with her son. He alternates between sympathizing with her and condemning her.*

The love of Patrick's life is the little girl, Audrey, but she is the least successful of the major characters. She is wispy, shadowy, and is seen largely through the daydreams of young Patrick. His piety, his worship of the Blessed Virgin Mary— expressed in moving and poignantly poetic prose—conflicts with his love for this earthly little girl. The boy is tormented with a fear of sin and of death, and he fights to hang on to his purity. His fears and thoughts of death are precocious, and he cannot understand how, in the face of eternity, a man can go on, living and sinning and liking the things of the flesh, as his father does. This sense of death separates him from his own generation, and he has no friends in it. Although he is not a sissy, he is different from the normal boy of his environment. He is intensely lonely, wrapped up in his dreams, and is preparing within himself the seeds of bitterness and revolt.

The end of the book is tragic. The father overplays his hand in the real-estate market, goes bankrupt, and commits suicide, leaving behind him fleeced customers and a wife and son who are penniless. The mother is gray, weary of life, absorbed in her own imaginary diseases. The boy is seething with contradictions and is deeply embedded in the torments of his own adolescence. And over them all hangs the shadow of the coming depression.

This book is powerful and savage. It is one of the most promising first novels that I have read in many a day. It is stamped with the vigor and rawness of Chicago. The loneliness of the boy, Patrick Stanton, is symbolic of the loneliness of the young and budding Chicago artist who rebels against his native city but who is tied to it and loves it perversely. Bernard Carr will be heard from again. He has made a more than auspicious beginning.

IV

Facing Mrs. Lisa Baranov at her desk, Bernard realized that he had never thought old women could be beautiful. She was tall and stately, and had thick, white hair. There was something frail and delicate about her features. And her eyes seemed so alive with beauty.

"I'm glad you came to see me," she said, speaking with an accent.

At a loss for an answer, Bernard grinned.

"But what are you doing here?" she asked ironically.

"Why, I came to ask if I might be given a chance to do some synopses for you. I'm a writer, and I've written reviews for the *Dispatch* and—

"I know, I know," she interrupted. "You're the author of *The Father*, and you want me to give you some work. But why are you here?"

Bernard was visibly perplexed.

"Do you think you'll work your way up to a good job on the Coast?"

"Why, no, no, I need money."

"Do you know you're a talented young man? When I read your book, I lived with your people, and I kept saying to myself . . . 'Why don't they do something, why don't they understand, why don't they do something?' "

"I'm glad to know that."

"The father is a good character. I don't mean that he's good." She smiled. "As a character, he's good. And so is the mother. But the boy . . . boys shouldn't be like the one in your book. Are many American boys like that?"

"No, he's unusual."

"No, no, no," she said, speaking fast and spiritedly. "Don't tell me that—unusual."

"I meant—" Bernard said.

"You mean you didn't mean unusual."

"I didn't mean it in the sense of his being extraordinary or gifted. I meant that he's different from the usual boy."

"You weren't as sympathetic with him as you were with the parents, were you?"

"I tried to be objective."

"Ah!" she exclaimed, tossing her head. "What does that mean, objective?"

Then she leaned forward and looked at him with gentle derision. Bernard smiled. Her personality grew on him as he sat there. He sensed in her a vitality that contradicted her appearance. He had never met an older woman like her. He wanted to go on talking with her.

"Are you writing another book?"

"I want to."

"Then why don't you?" she asked, leaning back in her chair.

He noticed her hands for the first time. They were thin, with long fingers, and the skin was dark—they were an old woman's hands. It was saddening for him to think of this. He thought it must have been sad for her to have grown old.

"Yes, yes," she said, tossing her head to the side in a charming manner as she spoke. "Why don't you write a book, since you want to, and since you are a writer?"

"Well, there's the question of money—"

"Oh, rot, rot, Mr. Carr." She waved her hands dismissingly in front of her. "Was any real writer ever stopped from writing because he was poor? For an artist, what does it matter if he is poor . . . poor in the pocketbook? He can be so rich, so rich. . . ."

Bernard listened thoughtfully. He was sure she had more understanding than almost anyone he'd met since he'd come to New York.

"Do you know where I come from?"

"Where?"

"Yalta. When I was a girl, I used to see Chekhov," she told him, pronouncing the name reverently.

"I like Chekhov."

"And I love Chekhov. How could you help but love him? I was just a girl, and I was full of Zola and Ibsen, but I saw him once. He didn't know me. Oh, I was merely a silly young thing, full of dreams. It meant so much to me. I was so thrilled. Nowadays, in America, young girls are thrilled by some actor like Rudolph Valentino—oh, any number of them. I was thrilled when I saw Chekhov. . . . He was such a gentle man. Oh, what a beautiful writer he was. How true he was. How wise. And how sad."

"My favorite writers are the Russians."

"They are?" she asked, sitting erect.

"Yes, I was just thinking of one of Chekhov's stories—"A

Dreary Story." . . . I was thinking, can you imagine an American writing a story like it, with a title like that?"

"Aren't you an American?"

He grinned sheepishly.

"I liked your book. You could write like the Russians." She laughed, and added, "And then you talk about not being able to write because you're poor."

Bernard broke out into a broad, friendly grin. He was losing his constraint; it seemed to him that he'd known this woman more than just a few minutes.

"I'll write more . . . but today I broke with my publishers."

"Publishers!" she exclaimed disdainfully. "They live well and have good homes, and look at the trash they publish. Mr. Carr, I know what trash they publish, because every trashy, silly novel they issue comes into this office. I have to have six copies of a synopsis of every novel—six copies. That's what you want to do."

"I don't want to. I have to have money."

"Who is your publisher?"

"Ferris and Winter."

"I don't know much about them. What happened?"

"They want me to write a novel that would titillate shop girls. And I asked them, 'Suppose I could, would you give me an advance?' They wouldn't. I asked them to release me of any obligations to them."

"Suppose they had given you an advance, Mr. Carr, would you have quarreled with them?"

"I couldn't write the kind of book they wanted if I tried to."

"Good . . . good. Don't you write trash. Don't do it. Don't spoil and cheapen your talent."

"Mrs. Baranov, Mr. Royce is here to see you," a secretary called from the doorway.

"Tell him to wait."

Mrs. Baranov turned to Bernard.

"Now, you want a book. You know you only get five dollars for this work."

"Well, right now I need money."

She rose and looked on the bookshelves behind her. She picked out a book. As she handed it to him, she said:

"You write another novel, Mr. Carr."

Bernard left her office after getting instructions from her secretary as to the form in which the synopses had to be presented. He no longer was depressed.

v

Two neatly dressed young men sat opposite Bernard in a corner of the large, bright room. Bernard compared his own shabby blue suit with their clothes and asked himself why should he care about clothes? One of the young men was tall. Because of his well-groomed appearance, Bernard guessed that he was an Eastern college man. The other looked merely big and stupid. Bernard stared at them both in a spirit of rivalry. Perhaps they'd get books and he wouldn't. Then he lit a cigarette and wished he hadn't come here. He'd gotten one book and earned five dollars as a result of six visits to this office. He glanced about the office with an assumed air of boredom. He noticed the bright jackets of new books on the long rows of bookshelves. How many of these other authors had had writing experiences like his? Had they known doubts and had they despaired? Had they written fearing they would never be published? Haw they drunk coffee to stay awake and work through lonely nights? He kept watching the two young men out of the corner of his eye. How could such smug-looking chaps know of the agony that made writing worth while?

Hampton was talking with Reva Lublin by her desk at the other end of the room. He was a tall, lean, awkward fellow, and gestured clumsily. Would Hampton put in a good word for him? Hampton went on talking. What was he saying? What would he say to Hampton about the review? On reflection, it didn't seem so good, so understanding, as he'd first thought it.

Still, it accorded him recognition. Hampton was now laughing loudly with Miss Lublin.

He picked up an issue of *Literature* which lay on the stand beside him, and as he thumbed through the pages he noticed the review heading:

The Homespun Fascination of Lydia Griswold

The Father had only received a brief, unsigned notice in *Literature*. And Lydia Griswold, a mere hack, got almost a page. The review was by Virginia Lieb. She had the sensibility of a brick wall, if that. But she could get books to review; he couldn't.

Alvin Swift's Requiem of the Body

The reviewer was Marshall Paxton. He reviewed regularly in *Literature*.

Bernard started reading the review:

When I finished reading this novel, with its beautiful prose and its volcanic emotions, not to mention its penetrating analysis, I wanted to shout and cry aloud from the tops of the skyscrapers—"Genius!" Hardened as I am—thanks to my experiences as a book reviewer and editor—I do not lightly use the word "Genius." When I use it here, I mean it. I was so profoundly moved and stirred by the tides of Alvin Swift's prose, so roused and touched as I grasped his deeply tragic design, a design which induced in me a feeling and an emotion of inexplicable pity and terror, I so felt the wonder, the melancholy, the loneliness, the deep sadness, the profoundness of his tragic account of the simple lives of simple good people that I imagined myself alone in the country, amid the dark mysterious beauties of nature at night, watching the silver glimmers of the moon and the indescribable radiance of a falling star. But this sensitive writer, Alvin Swift, has convinced me that he is no falling star of American letters; he is a rising star. With Alvin Swift, American writing enters a phase of truly tragic themes and noble prose.

Bernard put the copy of *Literature* back on the table and reminded himself that *Literature* was one of the most influential reviewing organs in America.

Hampton was leaving now, walking toward him with a book under his arm. Bernard watched him, envious. Hampton not only got books worth reading from Miss Lublin, but, also, he was paid the highest rates.

"Hello, Arthur," Bernard said, hoping these two chaps would see that he knew Hampton.

Hampton met Bernard with an impassive glance, delayed several seconds before he acknowledged Bernard's greeting with a "hello." Then he stood before Bernard, balancing himself alternately on either foot.

"How are you?" Bernard finally said, embarrassed by the silence and by Hampton's aloofness.

"All right. I'm scrounging reviews."

"So am I."

"Say, old man," Hampton said, "did you see my review of your book?"

"Yes, and I was grateful. I'd like to talk about it. I'm next to see Miss Lublin—but can you wait? She'll turn me down in a hurry. We can have a cup of coffee."

"I have to run."

Hampton shook hands with him perfunctorily and left. Bernard took this as a slight. Miss Lublin was beckoning to him. He walked across the room resentfully, wishing he hadn't come.

Reva Lublin was a plain, dark, chunky girl. Her desk was cluttered with books, manuscripts, and proofs. She was glancing at a manuscript and setting it down. She turned to Bernard, looking both bored and annoyed.

"Well, what are you doing now, Mr. Carr?" she asked in a formal tone.

"Oh, merely planning to write another book," Bernard said casually, as he dropped into the chair beside her desk.

"What can I do for you?"

"I came to see if you had any books," he mumbled.

Miss Lublin turned from him and stared out the window on her left. Turning back with an insincere smile on her face, she said:

"No, I'm afraid I don't have a thing."

Bernard saw a number of new books on the shelves near her desk. If she wanted to, she could give him something. He saw the matter personally. She didn't want to help him. There were no serious standards of merit applied here in reviewing. He knew he could review books competently. Yes, she didn't want to help him. He tried to think of something cutting to say.

"I'm sorry, but there are three persons to review every book that comes out," she said.

His ironical glance disconcerted her. She had given him one book to review because he'd come in with a letter of introduction from somebody, but she couldn't remember who it was now. And she had thumbed through his book and didn't understand it. He was one of the horde of young men—yes, horde—who came to New York to write the Great American Novel, and what could she do about them all? In fact, she didn't like him, but she didn't know why. She was certain he wasn't a reviewer for *Lit*. And he looked at you and talked to you in a mocking manner. She decided to get rid of him. There was too much work to be done for her to sit talking with conceited young men who never should have come to New York.

"I'd like to give you something to do, Mr. Carr, but I can't . . . this week. Our advertising has fallen off badly, and our space has been cut. I'm stocked up with reviews I can't find a place for."

"Well, that's that," he said casually.

"Did you like the review of your book we published? I was sorry we couldn't give you more space, but so many important books have been coming out . . ."

Reva Lublin stopped talking suddenly. She hadn't thought of what she was saying, and she was embarrassed. But he merely shrugged his shoulders.

"Yes, I see that Lydia Griswold has another important book out."

"What's wrong with Lydia Griswold? A great many of our readers find her work diverting."

Bernard didn't answer.

"Try me again next week, Mr. Carr," she said sympathetically.

"Thank you."

"Good luck, Mr. Carr," she said, glad he was going.

Bernard walked off, feeling humiliated. He was angry with himself. Reva Lublin signaled to the stupid-looking young man. She told herself that she was doing the best she could about American writing, and she didn't know why she should let this Mr. Carr get under her skin. He was merely another young man who had written just another novel.

VI

Sherman Scott was a large plump man with blue eyes. Wearing a tweed suit, he sat at his desk in the offices of *New Freedom,* thinking about his career, and about the fact that he had passed thirty-five and could no longer be considered a member of the younger generation.

"Well, Carr," he exclaimed in a nasal drawl, as Bernard entered, "I'll be with you in a minute."

He bent forward and fiddled with some papers on his desk. This was his day to see reviewers and would-be reviewers, and he had lots of other things to do. He spent only two or three days a week at the office, editing the book-review section. And today, when he should be cleaning up his work, he'd fallen into another one of his spells of stock-taking and meditation. He let Bernard sit, and, pretending to be absorbed in letters, he thought that he, a rebel poet and aesthete of yesterday, had become a man sitting at a desk. Of course, *New Freedom* was liberal, and he was a liberal. Yet, only a few short years ago, he had scorned liberals. He was confused these days and not certain what he truly believed. He was writing little. His ambitions of a few years ago were unfulfilled. But how could he quit a job like this, in times like these, and risk living on what he could write and sell?

That was what young Carr here was doing. Carr made him uneasy. He was one of the more persistent and determined, if not talented, members of the younger generation. Carr must feel toward him, at this desk, as he'd felt about editors eight and ten years ago.

Young writers like Carr seemed hard, and tough, and possessed of no literary background. The world had changed under his feet. The literary world had broken under him. What should a man of his generation believe?

And, yes, here he was, a man sitting at a desk.

"Well, Carr . . ." he said, dropping the letters into a box on his desk and filling his pipe.

"I came to see if you had any books for me," Carr said.

"No, Carr, there isn't anything this week."

"Things are going lousy with me. I'm using up all my time living from hand to mouth, and it's hard to write under such circumstances," Bernard said in a spirit of dejection he couldn't conceal.

"Yes, it's tough, Carr," Sherman Scott said sympathetically. The phone rang. Scott answered it.

"Who? . . . Who?" he asked petulantly. "Oh . . . yes . . . Certainly . . . Do you want me to dictate it over the phone? . . . Well, just a minute until I collect my thoughts."

Sherman Scott thought for a minute and then drawled into the mouthpiece:

"Now, I don't want my statement to sound like the usual thing in *The Fist*. Well, old man, here, how is this? Is the girl ready to take it? All right. Now, here it is—quote—Do these visiting Japanese generals know that the American people do not make it a habit to welcome imperialists who shoot down helpless Chinese workers? We would inform these Japanese militarists that, in America, there are many writers, intellectuals, and others who are opposed to the Japanese Imperialists and are telling the American public why they stand for a policy of Hands Off China . . . unquote. That's my statement . . . Yes. . . . All right. . . . Yes. . . . So long, and don't mention it."

Sherman Scott hung up, turned toward Bernard, and said rather sheepishly:

"Some Japanese generals are in New York."

Bernard grinned. He didn't know what to say now, and suspected that Sherman Scott wanted him to leave.

"I'd like to write a series of articles on American culture," Bernard said impulsively.

Sherman Scott sat back in his chair, and his dour silence was criticism. Bernard's self-confidence seemed to evaporate in Scott's presence.

"What do you want to say that hasn't been said?" Sherman Scott finally asked, as he rested his hands in back of his head and reclined comfortably in his swivel chair.

Bernard talked rapidly and with a feeling of desperation.

"I want to analyze the broken promises of American life. The grim contrasts between vision and reality—the split in ideals and actions—these constitute the biggest forged check in history. You know, Saint-Just said that happiness is a new idea. Happiness on the American continent was a new idea. America was a new world on this earth, not a utopia—the city of man, not the city of God. When I read about early American history, read some of the records of the early pioneers, the early settlers, the frontiersmen, I can't help but feel the pathos of all this. They thought they were building something that in a century or so, in our own time, would be a paradise on earth. Your throat chokes when you read of what they thought life would be like in the very day and age in which we live. Up to the Russian Revolution, America, the American Dream, was the greatest promise ever offered to the human race, to man. I

want to write about it, to analyze it, and to use it as a frame
for discussing American culture. Because that split in ideals
and actions, in vision and realization, is seen in our culture.
Our serious literature reveals the costs of American civilization,
and is full of disastrous frustrations, failures, tragedies, and
our popular culture turns the American Dream into a caricature and a juvenile reverie. Happiness has been made threadbare
and banal in our movies and popular stories. Happiness scarcely
exists in serious books. American culture, American literature,
is now a contest between the false and the real. The false talks
speciously of joy; the real, of sorrow. This offers a framework
for trying to understand where we are, where my generation
stands, and where we might go. I want to get at how it is that
capitalism, in a very concrete way, stands behind this, how the
poets, the novelists have expressed this, how and why American
realism has turned out to be the kind of realism it is, how it has
to fight against falsities on all sides, how it bumps its head against
a stone wall of lies."

Sherman Scott's own thoughts pressed on him, and he listened to Bernard indifferently. He had seen and felt a collapse
that this lad, Carr, could only analyze and intellectualize. And
all he'd really ever written were a few poems. He noted Bernard's worn clothes. He himself was comfortable and secure,
and this new generation of writers were paupers. They frightened him. Carr frightened him. He wasn't listening to Bernard.
His own cultural aspirations were now broken idols.

"I don't think that would be for us, Carr. It's a little bit old
hat, but it might be valuable for you to write it in order to
clarify your own thinking," he said, interrupting Bernard.

Bernard shut up, as though he had been guilty of bad manners.

Scott got up and went to a bookshelf by the wall. Bernard
watched him with hopeful eyes. *New Freedom* paid two cents
a word on receipt of the review, and he might get next week's
rent out of this visit. Scott flung the book into a pile of new
books on the floor in a corner. He examined another and threw

it there, too, while Bernard waited, still hopeful. Scott flung eight books on the floor, and Bernard still watched in rising and waning excitement. Turning back to Bernard, Scott finally said:

"We sell those for a reviewers' relief fund. They're no good. No, I'm sorry, Carr. I haven't a thing for you this week. Try me again next week. But I can always give you a loan of ten or fifteen dollars from that fund. Do you want it?"

"No, thanks," Bernard said. "I'm not that badly off," not knowing why he refused the proffered loan.

Bernard picked up the manila envelope he'd gotten from Mrs. Baranov and turned toward the door.

"Well, good luck, old man. Keep your pecker up," Scott said, giving him a friendly pat on the shoulders.

"Thanks, I'll try to," Bernard said.

VII

"Carr, I'm the lost member of the lost generation," Bob Lasker said.

"What's lost about your so-called generation?" Bernard asked. "I don't know what you've lost, but you all found good jobs."

"Come to think of it, we did. But we lost our ambition," Bob said; he was handsome, well-built, olive-skinned. "I'm the best liberal in America. I have no ambition," he said dryly.

They were sitting in the corner of a speakeasy, drinking bootleg whisky. Bernard had met him on the street after leaving Scott's office, and Bob was buying the drinks.

"What exactly do you do at *New Freedom*?" Bernard asked, making conversation.

"You take the Kentucky miners. They're starving, and the company thugs beat them up. So I view that with alarm," Bob said in a dry, cold voice, stumbling over some of his words. "Then, the farmers in Iowa are foreclosed by the banks. So I view that with alarm, too. Then, in Detroit, the unemployed go to an auto plant looking for work. And fire hoses are turned on them in zero weather. So . . ."

Bernard laughed, but with bitter feelings of his own powerlessness.

"Liberalism is an inspiring occupation," Bob told him. "Every week we have an editorial luncheon at *New Freedom*. We have guests who give us the lowdown on everything in highbrow language. Last week, an English economist gave us the lowdown about Russia, and do you know what they are doing over there, Carr?"

"What?"

"They are conducting a fascinating experiment in planned economy. Yes, it's fascinating. The Englishman said so. Carr, I was inspired. Liberalism is an inspiring profession."

Bob signaled for more drinks. The waiter brought the drinks, Bob paid, and they took sips.

"My job is to be a factotum. I'm an important man on *New Freedom*."

Bernard smiled weakly. He was thinking that Lasker had a regular job and didn't get any writing done, and that Sherman Scott wrote little. A job like theirs wasn't what he wanted. Yet they had security. Should he envy them?

"Not a day passes without its little inspiration. As a matter of fact, I contribute inspiration myself. Do you read the editorial paragraphs of *New Freedom*?"

"Not often."

"It's a pity. Some of them contain my best thoughts. Whenever I am pricelessly brilliant, I attribute my profundities to Shrewd Observer. That's me, Carr—the Shrewd Observer."

They had more drinks and sat in silence. Bob knew he should get back to work. Sherman Scott had left a whole batch of proofs on his desk to be corrected. But he wanted to sit here and crack jokes which had long since grown stale.

Bernard was grateful for the drinks. But this was wearisome. He liked Bob but felt he had nothing in common with him. Bob's blandness and humor were, in essence, mere weakness. People who joked like Bob were really escaping. Their humor wasn't healthy. Why did he bother to sit here like this?

"Are you a Communist, Carr?"

"Sometimes yes, sometimes no."

"They aren't like liberals. They're hard. The liberals are gentlemen."

Bob gave funny imitations of all of the editors of *New Freedom*. Bernard laughed. They had another drink. Then Bernard glumly asked:

"Did you ever have to live on book reviewing?"

"I couldn't do it," Bob said.

"It's tough. Your time is wasted, and you have a hell of a time preserving the continuity of your own thoughts."

"Don't think too much, Carr. It only gets you into trouble. If you think a lot, you might become like an editor of *New Freedom*. Every day I warn myself of this danger. But to date I've bravely resisted. But now, Carr, I have to return to the slavery of inspiration," Bob said.

They parted in front of the speakeasy. Bernard started home. He didn't want to go home. He didn't want to go anywhere. He walked on, clutching the manila envelope. He felt almost as if he were in a dream. He wondered if he were drunk. He could almost feel a moody state of depression growing within him. Ferris, Lublin, Sherman Scott. . . . He was getting nowhere fast in New York. He was disintegrating. Bob Lasker. Bob was a nice fellow, but dissatisfied. This weak and empty bitterness. Meaningless barroom chatter. Yes, a wasted day.

He'd paid for his education with his youth. And was it all for this?

—You don't love her!

A voice within him spoke these words accusingly. He knew they were true. He couldn't silence the voice. He walked fast, wanting only to move, to eliminate all thoughts from his mind. He had a headache and felt sickish. He was a failure, and he feared he was always going to be a failure. He wanted to give up.

—You don't love her.

The voice spoke to him again. He shook his head in vehement denial. He was stricken with a nameless terror. He started running. Then he walked as fast as he could, anxious to get home as quickly as possible. The voice repeated the accusation to him with monotonous insistency.

VIII

Elizabeth greeted Bernard with a hopeful smile.

"I just got home. I was window-shopping," she said.

Bernard dropped into the big chair. He didn't know what to say, and he didn't want to talk. He was neither drunk nor sober, and his emotions seemed limp. He hadn't kissed her. He knew he ought to get up and do it, but he didn't move.

"Bernard?" Elizabeth exclaimed in worry and surprise.

He didn't answer. He and she would never know each other. She seemed like a stranger. If he told her the truth, he would hurt her, hurt her terribly. He ought to tell her the truth, and he couldn't.

"Bernard, what happened? Tell me the news."

"Well, I wasted the day. I didn't get any books from Scott or Lublin, and I have no publisher. It's been a rotten day."

"Did you fight with them?" she asked in alarm.

"Not exactly. I merely drew the correct conclusion. I told them that inasmuch as I couldn't make any money for them, that was that, and I wanted to be free of any obligations to submit my next book to them."

"But, Bernard, why did you say that? Couldn't you have soft-soaped them?"

"How?" he asked with irritation.

"Bernard, you know, you don't always use tact," Elizabeth said, accusing him in a soft, sweet tone.

He didn't want to describe the interview. He seemed to have forgotten what had been said, and he wasn't sure he could give a lucid and full account of it.

"Briefly," he said, "they wanted me to try to write a novel to titillate shopgirls. They wouldn't give an advance until they saw the manuscript. Now I'm going to write to Ferris and ask him to give me my release in writing."

"Don't, Bernard, don't cut off your nose to spite your face."

"I'm going to write the letter," he said coldly.

"Bernard, I think I know about some things. I do. Bernard, if you do things like that, you'll get a bad reputation."

"What the hell do I care about a bad reputation!"

"Bernard, if I ask you not to, will you not write the letter, for me, for my sake?" she said, going to him, sitting on his lap and embracing him.

She kissed him passionately, and he felt rising disgust. He determined to control his own desires. But he found himself feeling pity for her. He embraced her firmly, and tenderly returned her kiss.

"Elizabeth," he said calmly.

"Bernard, don't talk to me now. Don't! Don't! Make love to me. Please, please make love to me," she begged, breathing fast.

He kissed her again, but only in pity.

"Oh, I love you," she said, looking at him with eyes so bright that they seemed almost to be burning.

She caressed him with restless hands, and he became submissive. He wanted only to forget, forget for at least a little while.

IX

Lying in bed, Bernard looked at Elizabeth's breasts and then watched her put her robe on. He thought about her body. At times, her breasts didn't seem to be quite the same young breasts he had looked at the first time he'd seen her naked. Sometimes, with shadows on her skin, her abdomen looked creased. Yes, her breasts were getting larger. His mother's breasts hung. He always thought of his mother's breasts as milkless. He couldn't remember suckling. Even now, the idea that he had suckled at his mother's breast was revolting. There was nothing inherently ugly in suckling. How touching was

De Maupassant's story. But he couldn't remember the title of it. The word *Idyll* was in the title. When he was twelve, he'd seen his mother's hanging breasts, and he'd been hurt with shame for her, for himself, and for all men and women. He didn't feel that way now. He was relaxed. His thoughts after leaving Bob Lasker must have been merely the effect of drink. He was sober now, and at peace with himself. His mood was one of mellow disappointment.

All his problems seemed so far away. The outside world of agitation and hurry and economic insecurity—he couldn't feel its pressure now. The disappointments he'd met with today weren't so important, either. If death could only come, when it had to, in this mood of relaxation and calm resignation. He was sad, and yet so pleasingly sad.

He dozed off blissfully, and when Elizabeth woke him up, the table was set and a plate of scrambled eggs was waiting for him. She handed him his old bathrobe. He got out of bed, put it on, and sat down with her to eat.

They ate quietly. He was really hungry. His thoughts were listless. Today he'd just had to get things out of his system. Yawning, he looked up from his food and picked up his coffee cup. Elizabeth reached over and took it from him, got him more coffee, and meekly put the cup in front of him.

She sat down and watched him closely.

"Darling Bernard, I want you to patch things up with Mr. Ferris because . . . because I don't want you to act like a foolish boy."

When they had first gone together, he had liked her to call him a boy. Now it was boring, boring and irrelevant. A sense of the pathos of their relationship drove all other feelings out of his mind.

"What do you want me to do? Be a damned fool? I couldn't go back to him again, and, anyway, it would be useless to try to."

"But, Bernard, why couldn't you?" she asked, speaking slowly and intently. "Couldn't you think of a book which he would like and which would sell and make some money for us, and then you could write the books you wanted to write—and it wouldn't matter?"

"Elizabeth," he said, trying to speak casually and calmly, "I told you, long ago in Chicago, that you'd have to do without things with me."

"I do go without," she said in a voice of petulant protest. "And do I complain?"

He gazed at the faded wallpaper behind her. How useless it was to talk, to explain! She was a girl and wanted the joys of a girl. Why shouldn't she want them? But he could give her so damned little. In sex she had been happy. And now, what did that happiness mean? What did cement together people in love? What were human emotions all about? He felt as though he could cry, cry in despair.

"But, Bernard, do we have to, do we have to always go on not having anything, living in this dump?" She burst into tears and screamed hysterically. "I'm sick of it! I'm sick of it! I'm sick of it!"

She sobbed like a child having a tantrum. He wanted to soothe her. But what could he do? Wasn't he sacrificing, too? It wasn't easy for him. And if he conceded to her now, he'd be taking a step on the road of compromise. No, he couldn't concede.

She put her head on the table and continued to sob. He stroked her hair. He took her in his arms and kissed her tenderly and soothingly until her tears dried. He felt utterly helpless.

"Bernard," she said, gazing up at him with tears streaming down her face, "you're mean."

He didn't answer.

Her eyes were red from crying, and she didn't seem so pretty to him now. And this red-eyed blonde girl was really his wife.

"You're cold and hard, and you're mean. I hate you! I hate you! I'm sorry I married you," she screamed.

"Elizabeth, why don't you stop crying?" he asked.

"You don't care. I know you don't care that I'm not happy."

"What am I doing to make you unhappy?"

"I don't even have a new dress for spring."

"As soon as I get some money, I'll buy you one."

He let his tongue play on the cavities in his mouth and thought of mentioning his decayed teeth.

"Duffy has a job reviewing books for that new magazine, *This Age*. You couldn't get a job like that," she said, almost melodramatic in her effort to be scornful.

"I didn't even know about it until I heard that Duffy had got the job."

"Others get jobs. You don't. You don't try."

"Elizabeth, what's eating you?"

"What do you want me to do, sit here in this dump while you go out and fight with publishers? You're just mean and selfish."

"Do you think I'm having a picnic?"

"If my father knew how we lived, what do you think he'd say?"

"He ought to say that he has a better business than I have," Bernard said, immediately regretting his remark.

"My mother at least has enough to eat, and I did, too, when I was home. You're always hinting about my family. What about your own family?"

"What do I care about your family or mine?"

"Well, I care. I care about my family, and, Bernard Carr, you are mean, just mean to say nasty things about my father."

"I don't know what I said that's nasty about your old man."

"He's not my old man. He's my father," she said, getting up and stamping her foot on the floor.

"Oh, Elizabeth, what the hell are we shouting at? Let's stop being imbecilic," he said.

She sat down and cried. Then she whimpered. He thought of the meaninglessness, the misery, the frustration, the stupidity of the life in his own family in Chicago. And her family! There were differences in his attitude to the Carrs and to the Whelans. If he hated both, he hated them differently. How strange it was that he and Elizabeth Whelan Carr should be here, quarreling so stupidly in this basement room on Fifteenth Street in New York City. He, the son of a drunken Chicago bricklayer, and she, the daughter of a smug Chicago undertaker! They had escaped from Chicago. They'd violated the pattern of their environment, their social background. But they were quarreling according to that pattern.

"Elizabeth, let's stop quarreling," he said quietly.

She went to him, kissed him, and said penitently:

"I'm sorry, Bernard. I love you. I do love you, and I'm sorry."

He blamed her for their stupid quarrel. He hadn't been able to stop it until she'd had a tantrum. But he knew that such quarrels were episodic. No, he wasn't sure. But they were ghastly. He gazed fixedly at the wall, fearing his thoughts were like some poison which could seep through his mind.

"Forgive me, Bernard," she begged with trusting, wide-open eyes.

"Of course I do," he answered grudgingly.

Yes! Yes! He meant it insofar as he could mean anything. The voice in him today had said the opposite. He wanted to mean yes. But in the deepest layers of his nature, in the core of his being, there was a no. And there was a feeling of lonely separation from people, all people, as well as from Elizabeth. Sex, love, marriage, kisses, rapport in conversation—nothing could ever consume this loneliness. Had Eva? No, even she hadn't.

"It was merely a foolish spat," he said.

She nestled in his lap. He stroked her head.

"I feel almost like a comfortable kitten, just the way I did in bed when I was a little girl."

He caressed her hair, but thought how there was something inconsolable about personal life. He had to live for more than personal life. He had to achieve, achieve and fight. But then, didn't he want to do this so others might find joy and comfort? The achievers and the comforted—this seemed like a possible division of people. He had to achieve, and to comfort and protect Elizabeth. Could he do both?

"And I am so proud of you. I know you are going to be a good writer, Bernard."

Eva had said he was going to be a genius. Not that he was. Elizabeth said good.

Chapter Seven

I

"DON'T let the boss see you readin' that book," Smith told
Stallings in a friendly manner as they sat looking bored
in the back room of the Whelan undertaking establishment.

Smith was a bushy-haired, stocky lad of twenty-five, and
Stallings was a small, thin, bespectacled, intellectual-looking
youth.

They had coffee cups before them on the old table in the
center of the small room. There was a stove in one corner, on
which there were some cans and articles of food, and a cupboard
in another. The chairs were nondescript. The sink near the
stove was old and cracked. The windows were barred and
looked out on a vacant lot and the side of a three-story apartment building.

"Mr. Whelan doesn't read books, too, does he?" asked Stallings.

"He reads *Casket and Sunnyside*," Smith said.

"What's that?" asked Stallings.

"An undertaker's magazine."

"It has a cheerful name."

"It's a good magazine."

"What's all this about the boss getting sore if I read a book
like this?" Stallings asked.

"The guy who wrote it is his son-in-law. He came here to
work like you, and copped off the boss's daughter."

"I like his book," Stallings said.

"If the boss hears that, you'll sure find yourself out on your
ear. He seems to like you. You aren't like Carr. You don't talk

so much. God, he talked! He and Clarke were at it about religion, hammer and tongs, all the time. But the boss's daughter Elizabeth was the sweetest and most innocent girl. I couldn't understand why she did it. He wasn't the type for her. The boss has never really gotten over it. He doesn't say much about it, but he feels it. Yes, he feels it. It's a big disappointment to him."

Smith seemed to be thinking of something.

"He had plans for her," he remarked wistfully.

"Who?"

"His daughter. She was a wonderful girl. I don't think Carr loves her. I think he married her to inherit the business. The boss has no other children."

"Good evening, gentlemen," Clarke said; he was tall, thin, and tight-lipped.

"Look what Stallings is reading," Smith said.

Clarke reached across the table and picked up the copy of *The Father*.

"Filth," he said with quivering lips, as he slammed the book on the table.

"Why do you say it's filth?" asked Stallings.

"Because filth is filth," answered Clarke.

"Well, what's the pow-wow about?" asked Mr. Whelan, suddenly appearing in the doorway.

He was a big, ruddy-faced, dignified man with sandy hair, shot with gray. He wore a neat, conservative, brown suit.

"I was just telling Stallings that that book is filthy," Clarke said self-righteously.

Mr. Whelan came forward, picked up the book, and then put it down on the table again without a change in his expression.

"You, Stallings, I don't think I'm going to need you. You can move. I have too many fellows around here, and there's been too much discussion since you came here. Every time I hire anybody from the University we get long debates," Mr. Whelan said in a cold and very restrained voice.

"What did I do?" Stallings asked.

"Nothing, except what I said. This is a mortuary establishment, not a debating society or a branch of that Bug Club over there in Washington Park."

"All right, if that's the way you look at it," Stallings said.

"Of course it's all right. Whatever I say around here is all right."

Stallings left the room to go to the small cubbyhole where he slept.

"Any calls?" Mr. Whelan asked.

"No, sir."

"What do they think the world is over there, with all their talk of philosophy and what the hell else they don't talk about? And literature, what they call literature. I'll call up a Catholic college and get some decent Catholic lad to sleep here nights and answer my telephone. Maybe I'll find a lad I can break in the way I helped you, Smith."

"Yes, sir."

"And I want you to pick up a stillborn at the Jackson Park Hospital. Here's the name, Smith." Mr. Whelan handed Smith a slip of paper. "Bring it in and leave it here in the morgue. We'll take care of it tomorrow. It's only an accommodation, and there's nothing in it. But we have to do it."

"Only an accommodation," Clarke said, parrotlike.

"Oh, Mr. Whelan, those new thank-you cards came. I put them on your desk. A good job. Dignified," Smith said.

"I'll look at them."

"I hear Donovan's in trouble," Smith said, getting up from the table.

"He ought to be. His father was a fine old man, old Jim Donovan. He built up a solid business, but then Tom Donovan comes along with a lot of fancy notions. When he went away to college, he was taken in by a fraternity, and he got a swelled head and a lot of fancy notions. That new chapel he built must have cost several hundred thousands. Well, now he better go to embalming school and learn something. He's in deep. He's never going to be able to pay for that chapel. Why, he paid more for the brick on the outside of it than my entire service cost me, and I have a good service and never stinted on the cost of it, or the upkeep, either. Young Donovan is running around now like a chicken with his head cut off." Mr. Whelan smiled cruelly. "He's nosing up to some Protestant ministers, looking for afternoon cases."

"Like everything else, you have to be a businessman in this business, or in any other," Smith said.

"That's what I believe," Clarke said, looking at Mr. Whelan for approval.

Mr. Whelan took a cigar out of his breast pocket and casually lit it.

"Yes," he wagged his head. "Yes, boys, you've got to keep your feet on the ground in this business."

"They're better on the ground than under the ground," Smith said, and they all laughed.

"That's a good one. Smith, you do have a sense of humor," Clarke said.

"Say, Smith, what about that new Zero Fluid?" Mr. Whelan asked.

"Oh, yes, Mr. Whelan. I inquired about it. It's good. They told me about a case where they used it. The relatives were away and couldn't get back for the funeral. They had to put the case in a vault, and he was buried nine whole months later. They made a few injections, of course, while they had him stored in the vault, but the case looked just the same as he did when they prepared him. Lifelike."

"Say, that's pretty good," Clarke said, looking at Whelan.

"When I get started, that's what I'm going to use, Zero Fluid," Smith said.

"Those Zero people keep on their toes," Mr. Whelan said.

"I saw Mr. Connerty on the street. He's going to be a case soon," Clarke said.

They all looked at Clarke in disapproving silence.

"He looked pretty feeble," Clarke added nervously.

Mr. Whelan shook his head slowly, sadly, knowingly.

"Yes, old Mr. Connerty is failing. He's failing. But, Smith, you'd better run over and pick up that stillborn now. I'll be here until you come back, and then I have to go."

"Yes, sir," Smith said.

Mr. Whelan turned and went to his office. He passed Stallings's cubbyhole and noticed that the lad was packing. He was sorry he'd lost his head, but he couldn't bear the sight of the boy, once he associated him with that scamp, Carr. And, come to think of it, Stallings had talked radically about religion and politics. Carr used to argue with Clarke about religion. At first, he'd been amused and had taken to Carr. If he had never hired Carr four years ago when the University Employment Bureau had sent him on, his whole life would be different.

He stopped and half turned to go and talk with Stallings. This boy wasn't Carr. He was really a quiet and serious type. But then, he'd done it, and he couldn't go back on what he'd done in front of the other boys.

II

Stallings heard Mr. Whelan in his office. He was glad to have been fired, especially for reading a good book. An undertaking parlor was no place to live. All last week he'd gone to bed with the creeps because corpses were in the place. And, watching Smith embalm an old lady, he'd almost vomited. The smell of the corpse alone had been too much for him. Smith had told him you get used to it.

"Once anybody dies, they're just dead meat, that's all," Smith had said.

Stallings wondered how Bernard Carr had stood it here. Carr had probably had this same room, and had packed just as he was doing right now. Carr's book was perceptive, even if it didn't point the way out. He guessed Carr must have been as revolted as he was, working here in the odor of death.

"Stallings," Mr. Whelan said, suddenly standing in the doorway.

"Yes, sir," Stallings said, masking his resentment.

Why had he called this capitalist *sir*?

"If you haven't any place to go now, you can stay here tonight. I don't want to have you just left out on the street."

"That's all right, thank you."

"I have nothing personal against you. I think it will be better if I have another type of lad here."

"That's all right," Stallings said.

"Well, when you're ready to leave, come to my office and I'll pay you. If you need a recommendation from me, I'll gladly give it."

"Thank you."

Mr. Whelan returned to his office, and Stallings went on packing. He silently called Whelan a hypocrite, and he was glad to think Carr had gotten revenge on him. He was like Carr, and one day would be a writer, too, though he wouldn't write fiction. Carr had once published a review in *Mass Action*. After he worked his way through school, he'd go to New York, and they'd meet, and he'd tell Carr of how he was fired by Whelan.

Everything was now clear to him. He could thank Whelan. For he had been wavering. Only yesterday, he'd disagreed with Andy Morgan, the leading Communist student on the campus. Andy had said no bourgeois was any good. Look at the way Whelan had treated him. Yes, he was going to throw his lot in with the Communists.

He went on packing.

III

"I was passing by, so I thought I'd stop in," Mr. Whelan said to Mr. Connerty.

Mr. Connerty's palsied hands shook almost continuously. He sat forward in the comfortable chair of the comfortable parlor.

"Philip, I knew you were coming," he said in an aged and weak voice.

"You're looking good. Yes, you bear up very well, Mr. Connerty, with your years."

"The life is hardly in me," the old man said weakly.

"There's more life in you than there is in many a man, Mr. Connerty."

"Eighty-six," Mr. Connerty said.

Mr. Connerty's wrinkled face became dreamy and vague. Whelan sat immobile, controlled, reserved.

"Do you still take your daily walk, Mr. Connerty?" he asked, his voice formal.

"Every day," he bragged. "Every day. . . . You are well, Philip?"

"Yes. Yes, thank God, I'm very well, and so is Mrs. Whelan."

"And the little girl? Didn't you have a little girl?"

"Yes, she is well," Mr. Whelan said, his lips tightening.

"I was telling you about how I want my funeral run," the old man said.

Mr. Whelan raised his eyebrows a trifle.

"I want to be waked three days. Three days," Mr. Connerty said petulantly.

"Of course, God willing, Mr. Connerty, that will be a long way off in the future."

"Three days."

Mr. Whelan waited, a solemn expression on his ruddy face.

"I don't want one relative to carry me to my grave, my last resting place. Not one. Not one of them is to be a pallbearer."

"Of course, Mr. Connerty."

"I want the finest casket that money can buy, the finest casket," Mr. Connerty interrupted.

"There are some fine and durable caskets, ones that are not too expensive. There's one all-metal casket called the Nobel that has a fine record for endurance."

"What's all-metal?" asked the old man, his eyes opening wide, his hands still shaking.

"It will endure longer."

"That's what I want," the old man said.

"As I say, Mr. Connerty, the Lord willing, that is a long time off. But you can rely on me to carry out your wishes to perfection."

"That I do. Philip, you are a man of your word. Now, Philip, when you wake me, wake me three days."

"Yes," Mr. Whelan said solemnly.

They sat, and Mr. Whelan continued to look at the old man with false solemnity.

"Three days."

Suddenly the old man was asleep in his chair, breathing with slight noises.

IV

Philip Whelan rubbed his hands over his rough, graying whiskers and stared blankly into the bathroom mirror. He felt rotten this morning. He could hardly feel worse with a hangover. He usually enjoyed shaving, but this morning he dreaded it. He was sorry for himself. A lot of fellows he knew complained about having to shave. Danny McCall used to say that it was more botheration and nuisance for a man to have to shave than for a woman to have the monthlies. Danny was gone these last five years. Funny that he should be thinking of Danny McCall now. Danny's son was doing well in the McCall place over on Halsted. A decent, regular lad, and he gave good, honest service. He was proud of his embalming jobs, and he did good ones, too. Danny died the night Elizabeth graduated from high school. That had been a happy night in his life.

He saw himself as a stranger in the mirror. A paralyzing and agonizing feeling of guilt came over him. He was afraid. That dream he'd had last night. Sometimes dreams bothered him more than anything else. After a man had handled and seen as many corpses as he had, there was almost nothing that ought to give him the heebie-jeebies. And it wasn't because he didn't have feelings or didn't feel sorry for other people, either. He did. He was human. The public just didn't know how human an undertaker was. An undertaker had to face life and go on as if he didn't see and touch and handle death more than anyone else did. And he did go on. He didn't want to. He didn't want to shave and dress and go to his business today.

That dream that Elizabeth was dead . . . it didn't mean anything. He wasn't a superstitious old woman.

He began to lather his face, enjoying the feel of the soft brush and the warm soap.

He had had this dream before. She had lain dead, wearing her high-school graduation dress and holding her diploma against her heart in cold, stiff hands. It had been dim all around the coffin, and he had been looking at her corpse, thinking that she was dead, really dead and embalmed with Zero Fluid, and there was nothing he could do about it. The diploma, which he had paid for, had had something to do with her death. And then Danny McCall had closed down the coffin lid. He'd waked up in a sweat, and he'd hardly slept again until dawn.

Hell, it was only a dream. But whenever he had this dream, he had a rough time of it with himself.

He began shaving carefully and slowly, putting the straight razor to his face. He flipped the soap off the razor and into the bowl with a neat, enjoyable snap of his wrist. He never could understand how some fellows could prefer a safety to a straight razor. There was no comparison. What he liked about shaving was taking your time, the warm water, the idea that you would get the bristles off your face, sting it with a lotion, and then see yourself in the mirror clean-shaven and ruddy.

God, he didn't wish or want his only daughter dead. How could a man want to have such a dream?

With one side of his face clean, he wiped his razor dry and sharpened it on the strop, which was attached to the wall near the mirror. When his daughter had been a tot, she used to ask if she could watch him shave, and he always said no because she was a girl. She had been such a pretty tot. And she had run off in secret, marrying a scamp, betraying him, betraying his faith in her.

He went on shaving.

V

Ruth Whelan was a plump, fading, little woman of fifty. She was nervous this morning because at breakfast Philip had been so downcast, and when she had asked him if anything was the matter, he had been snappish. She was afraid he would never get over the blow of Elizabeth's elopement. And Mrs. Whelan knew he secretly blamed her. It wasn't her fault. This morning, Philip had acted as if one of those spells of his were coming on. Ever since Elizabeth had run away, she had been fearing one. Nobody knew what she had to go through.

Fanny, the maid, was cleaning in the parlor. The laundry had been taken care of, and she was ready to go out shopping. If people saw her on Seventy-first Street, they would never know she was putting on a brave front. Oh, nobody, nobody could know.

The telephone had just rung, and she had almost jumped. How relieved she had been when it was a wrong number. Sometimes she wanted to tear the telephone right out of the wall and never hear it again. It had rung at breakfast, and Philip had changed when he'd heard it. Something came over his face. She had waited at the table while he answered, wanting to know who it was. This time, was it somebody she knew? Was it that old Mr. Connerty who kept wanting Philip to see him so that they could talk about how Mr. Connerty was going to be laid out and buried?

How would she be laid out? How would she look in her casket? Would Philip embalm her, dress her, lay her out himself? Last week, she had been talking to that nice young Mr. Smith, and she had thought that when she went, he might take off all her clothes in the morgue, let the blood out of her, and shoot that terrible fluid into her, and handle her naked, dead body, see it, touch it, work on it, and she had been so ashamed and so afraid . . . oh, the thought had made her almost sick.

She was dressed in a simple, blue suit. The skirt was a little short, because she had always had shapely ankles and legs and she was still proud of them. Her hat, with the thin, meshy, black veil, lay on the dresser. She liked veils, because she thought they made her look more interesting and younger.

Instead of putting on her hat and going out, she sat down and sighed. This morning, the call had come from a family named Hannon. She didn't know them. The mother had died. Philip had said they were well-to-do, and she hoped that this case would bring him out of the spell. A year ago, he had come home drunk, and she had put him to bed and looked at him lying on that very bed at her right, and for a minute she had thought him dead.

"Fanny," she called, putting on her hat. "I'm going now. Is there anything we need that you didn't tell me about?"

"Not as I can think of, Mrs. Whelan."

"Well, I'm going."

She walked down the street. Whenever she went out shopping, she always hoped she would meet someone and that something interesting, something she didn't know what, would happen.

Mrs. Whelan walked along the quiet, sunny streets of homes and apartment buildings, taking short, even, slightly dainty steps, and now and then swinging her large black pocketbook. Once or twice her lips quivered slightly. She was thinking that it was spring, and of how sad the spring sunshine could sometimes be, and she thought that they must be having weather like this in New York, and that Elizabeth and Bernard would be taking many walks. She imagined they must be very happy. Oh, she had been a girl, and she had once been happy. And she remembered how on the day of her first wedding anniversary she had waited all day for Philip to come home and take her out. She had been so full of hopes and had put on a new dress. She had wanted to look so pretty for him.

And he had come home and said he had a case. She had told him that his father could go and take care of it.

—Don't be silly. This is business.

She remembered him telling her that, talking to her as if she were just a girl who didn't understand. She'd flung herself on the bed and cried, and somehow she'd known that she could no longer expect to be happy.

She came to Seventy-first Street and, crossing the tracks to the South Side of the street, she thought that, yes, it was because of Philip, not her, that Elizabeth had run away. Philip had expected his daughter to be an undertaker's wife, just as his mother and his wife had been. Walking on Seventy-first Street, she was certain this was why her daughter had run away. And, seeing other women out shopping, she thought of how her life was so different from theirs. When they heard the telephone ring in their homes, they didn't jump the way she did.

VI

"An Englishman was asked the question 'What is a corespondent in a divorce case?'" said Ole Hanson, the hardware merchant. "Now, I'm not good at imitating the blimey way an Englishman talks, so you boys just imagine the English saying it. He said, 'A corespondent in a divorce case is a gal who hangs her fur on another woman's peg.'"

There were four men having lunch in the small restaurant on Seventy-first Street; they laughed at the joke.

"'Another woman's peg.' I'll remember that," chuckled Arthur Billings, a middle-aged salesman.

Mr. Whelan forced out a second laugh. He was thinking about himself. Here he was, vigorous and still feeling in the prime of life. Sometimes it was hard on him. He wondered about Hanson and Martin, who owned the radio store. Billings was younger than they and a salesman. A salesman could take chances that he dare not take. Not many people ever even stopped to think of the discretion, as well as the hard work and the sense of responsibility, demanded of a man like him.

No one had any more jokes to tell, and they talked about the depression. Hanson complained about business.

"The papers," Billings said, "tell us the worst is over."

"I was saying to my missus last night, prosperity might be just around the corner all right, but which corner?" Martin said.

"Conditions are different from what the papers say they are.

But, then, it's better that the papers don't tell everybody how bad things are. If everybody knew how bad business is, you couldn't tell what would happen. Why, the jiggs in the Black Belt could go wild. I hear that the Communists are trying to inflame them against us."

Hanson reminded them of the story of a girl that had recently been in the newspapers. She came from a good family in Minnesota, and was a college graduate. She was discovered living with a Negro Communist, brought into court, tested for her sanity, and declared sane.

"Some of the people in this world are rotten—just rotten," Mr. Whelan declared venomously.

He had read about this in the newspapers, and he wondered what was happening in the colleges. What ideas had Elizabeth had put into her young mind? She'd done something almost as bad as what that Minnesota girl had done. Mightn't it all have turned out different if Elizabeth had gone to a convent?

After they all expressed their indignation concerning the story, they again talked about business.

"I still figure it this way—after the elections, things will pick up," Billings announced.

"Too many people try to live beyond their means," Mr. Whelan said bitterly. "I see it in my business. They could have a modest, dignified, and economical funeral, but they put on the dog. The same way, there are people living in this neighborhood who can hardly pay their rent, but will they live within their means and in a neighborhood that's in accordance with their income?"

Mr. Whelan didn't understand his own anger and became self-conscious. He shouldn't get so angry. For the rest of the lunch, he was silent, and then he walked over to the Prairie Bank and Trust Company on Stony Island, near Seventy-first Street. He thought about what kind of funeral he could sell in the Dolan case, which he'd just gotten this morning. The Dolans were well-fixed.

The fat, little, gray-haired bank guard greeted him. He

nodded. Mr. Cavanagh waved to him from his desk behind the railing up front. He waved back. He always had a feeling of quiet and personal assurance when he walked into this bank. But then, the fruits of many years of Whelan's service were deposited here. He endorsed his checks and filled out a deposit slip at the stand. Three hundred and fifty dollars from the Collins family. A twenty-five-dollar money order on account from Joe Peters for Mrs. Peters's funeral. There was an honest man, hardworking, steady, and he had kept his word about trying to pay. If there were more workmen like Joe Peters in this country, the country would be better off.

He stood in line behind a little old woman who wore a black shawl. She wasn't long for this world. Who was she? And might he know anyone in her family? Mr. Whelan watched the way she clutched her bank book and then the five-dollar bill she received from the teller. She went off hugging an old black pocketbook. She was a poor woman, and it touched his heart to see her. He had laid many such old Irish women away to their last rest.

Mr. Krug, the young man behind the window, greeted Mr. Whelan obsequiously and commented on the weather in a respectful manner. He got his deposit book out, made his deposit, bade Mr. Krug good-by, and walked out of the bank.

People often said things like:

—There goes Phil Whelan, the undertaker.

He liked to be recognized. He liked it best just to be thought of as Phil Whelan.

He started back to his establishment, crossing Stony Island Avenue at Seventy-first Street. He felt very secure. His fat cigar, his fresh-looking, eighty-dollar blue suit, his polished black shoes that had cost eight-fifty, his starched white shirt with medium-high collar, his restrained two-fifty blue tie, his brown Stetson, all these helped to give him a feeling of solidity.

Going on to Seventy-first Street and Cornell Avenue, his gait was slow and even. He thought of how good a community this was on the Southeast side of Chicago, and that it would go on this way after the depression. Depressions could come and go, but it was people, solid people, who made a community good or bad. And he had given solid service to the people of this community. He saw the sign in front of his establishment in a mood of gratification. That sign meant that the name of Whelan was important and worthy on the Southeast side of Chicago.

He owned that big front lot across the street, too, and some day it would realize a pretty penny. Some day after this depression there would be buildings, stores, and apartment buildings along here, all the way from Stony Island to South Shore. Yes, this was a fine community.

Suddenly a question squirmed in his mind.

—What for?

He was angry. Rage blotted out his satisfaction. That dream he'd had. Burying his own daughter. If he'd dreamed of the son-in-law. How gladly he would bury the scamp! What would happen to his business after he was gone? What about his will? He'd been stalling with himself about this question. God, suppose something should happen and the business went to that scamp, Carr? He had to make up his mind. He went into his establishment feeling impotent rage and a sadness. But he couldn't stop to think of his own troubles now. He had to meet the Dolan family to discuss the interment of their mother.

VII

Philip Whelan sat under a lamp in the corner of the parlor and stared at the dedication page of *The Father*.

To My Wife
Elizabeth

What was that joke young Billings had told at lunch today? A young bride serves her husband raw carrots and lettuce for breakfast on the first morning after her marriage, and the groom wants to know why.

—I want to see if you eat like a rabbit, too.

He'd laughed for the sake of politeness, but he'd thought of
Elizabeth in a robe serving that scamp breakfast after they'd
slept together. How could a girl like Elizabeth have done it?
He couldn't understand it. God, she always seemed so sweet
and innocent. He grew taut with the dammed-up energy of his
resentment and sorrow. Then he sagged a little, and his face
relaxed. He glanced around the parlor. This furniture. Good,
well-polished, comfortable furniture. It must have cost about
a thousand dollars to furnish this parlor. He didn't remember
exactly what he had paid for all these things. The big, comfortable sofa, the fine chairs. The baby grand piano was closed. No one
ever played it. When Elizabeth had been a little girl in grammar school, and she'd just started music lessons, he used to
imagine how, when she'd become a beautiful young lady, she'd
play for him, and how he would sit back, close his eyes, and
listen. He had looked forward to such scenes, dreaming of the
contentment they would bring him, believing they would become beautiful memories. And there was the unused piano,
without a speck of dust on it. Its closed top covered his hopes.

The mask of solemnity with which he faced customers was
gone. His expression was relaxed. He looked tired and hurt, and
there were grotesque suggestions of youth in his face. He
leaned forward, pressed his lips together, and rested his chin
in cupped hands.

The apartment was quiet. Ruth was asleep. He ought to be
turning in. He was pleased with the way he had handled the
Dolan funeral. The biggest case he'd had in months. He'd clear
over three hundred on it. Mr. Dolan had complimented him,
too, saying that the old lady looked twenty years younger in
the casket.

Had Elizabeth been sheltered too much, or not enough? Why
hadn't he trained her to work for him? Ruth had never liked
his profession. Too bad about her. Now, when it was too late,
one could see the fruits of Ruth's doing. He fixed his eyes on the
piano and thought that, yes, in a sense, Elizabeth was dead in
his life. If she came back to them, he'd treat her very kindly,

but he could never be the same to her. She hadn't told him a thing. She hadn't told her mother. Hadn't she trusted or loved him all these years? She had betrayed her father's love and trust for a Cheapandbum writer.

He yawned and started wearily out of the parlor. The telephone rang. With a quickening of energies, he answered it. It was a case. He took down the necessary information and hung up. As he started to get ready to leave, his wife called anxiously to him from her bed.

"Is it anyone we know, Philip?"

"No, dear. Some poor girl. You go back to sleep now and get your rest, dear."

VIII

The room was cluttered and dirty. Mr. Whelan sat down at the dining-room table as Smith and his new man, Curley, carried the girl's body out in a box. He heard the sound of a mother weeping in the kitchen. The girl's brother, a lad of seventeen, stamped noisily in and out of the room. Mr. Whelan remained poised and calm; he was proudly conscious of his self-control. Without having to think about it, he knew that he could come into any situation of death and sorrow and be controlled, even masterful.

The father was a man in his late forties, or perhaps his early fifties. He was gray and haggard. There were circles under his eyes. He sat down at the opposite side of the table, looking dully past Mr. Whelan. These people were poor, and this was not going to be a profitable case. There was no room here for salesmanship—unless there was an insurance policy. The weeping in the kitchen grew louder, and the father jumped up and went out to the mother.

Mr. Whelan calmly waited. A young girl. Dr. Dunley had told him about it briefly on the phone. The poor girl had tried to perform an abortion on herself. A tightening of the lips betrayed to no one the emotion behind Mr. Whelan's impassive face. He had lost a daughter, too, even though she was alive. In his heart, he had buried his own daughter.

The lad stamped into the room and fumbled among a pile of papers and clothes on the top of an old bureau in the corner.

"You can't find anything in this goddamn place," he shouted.

Mr. Whelan ignored him.

He stamped into the front of the house. There was a murmur of voices and quiet weeping coming from the kitchen.

The father came back slowly.

"I'm very sorry that you must witness this, Mr. Whelan," the man said in shame.

"Mr. Coyle, this is your loss. Mrs. Coyle's loss. Your son's loss. Who am I to tell you how to express your grief? I am here only to serve you. Part of my service is to soften the blow, to give dignity to grief."

The shaken father looked at Mr. Whelan with trust and gratitude.

"Now, first of all, I have to ask you some questions—you understand, I need to put this information down."

"Yes, I know. I understand. I know."

"What is the girl's name?" Mr. Whelan asked with authority.

"Madeline," Mr. Coyle answered, his voice changing so that he spoke with an effort to be persuasive and impressive.

"The full name, please?"

"Madeline Elizabeth Coyle."

Mr. Whelan wrote. His lips tightened again. Madeline Elizabeth. Elizabeth. This poor fellow.

"Age?" he asked in his cold, official voice.

"Twenty years."

He wrote it down.

The son was stamping about in the parlor now. The mother still wept in the kitchen.

"Her birthday?"

"Who cares when she was born?" the son screamed.

Mr. Whelan ignored this. His face did not change. He waited for Mr. Coyle's answer, fountain pen in hand.

IX

Three straight funerals. The Crane funeral had only been a hundred dollars, and, on top of it, he'd had to see that old quack Dr. Cain and be insulted getting the death certificate. And he'd lost forty dollars, to boot, burying that poor Coyle girl. Thanks to the Coyle's parish priest, the story had been kept out of the papers. All this loose talk of people about his profession, and this attitude of doctors like that fossil, Cain—what would they say now, knowing this story? Could that poor fellow, Coyle, have handled the arrangements and details? These cost time and money. The public didn't know about such things. It was good that the profession had hired this new crackerjack press agent to tell the true story of funeral direction.

He was very tired. But he wasn't going to get drunk, the way he'd done a year ago after a rush of business. He'd merely sit here and have a few drinks and think. After all, a man really had no one to talk to, and sometimes he had to talk to himself. And you needed a few drinks so you could talk to yourself.

He sat in a corner of a clean, small speakeasy on Clark Street. There were prosperous-looking men at other tables. The patrons were quiet, and the waiters in white coats moved about quietly serving them. There was no bar.

Mr. Whelan looked at the glass of whisky in front of him. Coming here, you could be sure you weren't getting dangerous rotgut. He'd buried more than one fellow who'd died of rotgut since the Volstead Act was passed.

He drank, enjoying the feel of the whisky as it went down. He wished that he had someone to talk to. He looked at his watch and thought he'd better call up and see if there were any calls. He went to a booth in a corner, phoned, and got Smith. Smith told him they'd just been called to pick up a man named Burton on South Shore Drive, and that it looked like a big case.

"He's a millionaire. I'll drive out, and we'll go together to get the body. Phone and tell them I'm on the way over," he instructed Smith.

After talking a moment longer, he hung up, got his hat, and left the speakeasy. What luck that he'd thought to telephone Smith. This was the best kind of case to get. There was more pleasure in your work burying the better class of people, and you could give the service you were capable of giving. You could show some showmanship, and, after all, there was an element of showmanship in his profession. But he felt foggy. He went into a small, dirty restaurant, sat at the counter, and gulped down two cups of black coffee. Then he got into his car and drove out South, hoping his head would be clear by the time he got to the Burton home. He had a splitting headache.

x

The maid, Fanny, was thin and homely. She silently served their dinner in the clean and characterless dining room. Mrs. Whelan had just told him about her bridge club. He had listened without interest. Then he said:

"You've got to hand it to Father Delaney; he's a smart priest. He's suave—the kind of a priest I like to do business with."

"I don't know him," Mrs. Whelan said.

"I had to take this young fellow to see him. His mother wanted to be buried in sacred ground. She was like all unbelievers. When their time comes, they change." His voice became cruel, and he knew that unexpectedly he was talking about his son-in-law, and that his wife understood this. "I can't be one of those dogmatic fellows who lays down the laws of God and man. I'm in business. If I didn't tell him how to straighten things out and how to talk to Father Delaney, somebody else would."

"So what did you do, Philip?"

Beaming with self-gratification, he answered:

"I told this young lad what to say. He and I went to Father Delaney and he said, 'Father, you know my mother?' He told the name. Well, Father Delaney will stretch a point now and then in a human way, and so he said to the lad, 'Of course, of course, son. She was a good friend of mine, may God have mercy on her soul. I'll pray for her.' And he turns to look me in the eye, and he says, 'Phil, this lad's mother, may God have mercy on her soul, was a fine woman.' So, to make a long story short, the burial was arranged."

Mrs. Whelan thought how sometimes Philip had not been as willing to stretch a point with her.

"But, Philip," she said, "if the woman didn't live up to the faith?"

"He's a nice decent boy. And she was his mother and lived a quiet, decent life. What sin could she have on her soul?"

"It doesn't sound right to me."

"It was good enough for Father Delaney," Mr. Whelan said sharply.

She didn't say any more but told herself it must be all right. All these years, in fair weather and in foul, hadn't she gone to church and lived up to the faith? If women who didn't live up to it were rewarded like those who did—was that fair? And when Elizabeth had run off, Philip had talked of how she had deserted the Church. Yes, he was harder on his own than on outsiders.

He ate slowly, hoping he wouldn't have any more cases for a little while. He had conducted the Burton funeral today. He knew that Ruth was criticizing him by her silence, and by what she had just said. Elizabeth's elopement hadn't affected her the way it had him. Sometimes he suspected that she was even pleased.

"Philip, you look tired. Are you feeling all right?" Mrs. Whelan asked.

"Any man would be tired after what I've been through. But there's nothing the matter with me," he answered with a vague note of irritation in his voice.

He resented her sympathy and he tightened up with fear. After all, men could work at a fast clip and suddenly have a coronary or a stroke. But his heart was good; yes, he had a strong, stout ticker in him. Still, you never could be sure. But Ruth knew there was nothing he could do but go on. When his own

father had been fifty, he'd been ready to take over. If they'd
had a son! Still, was it fair to blame her because of those mis-
carriages after Elizabeth was born? She'd nearly lost Elizabeth,
too.

"Ruth, my dear, I'm not cross. I'm tired, but there's nothing
wrong with me," he told her, noticing how distressed she looked.

"I understand," she said with emotion.

"Especially with this depression, I have to keep on my toes.
Every day I have more competition. I'm being undersold by
these fellows who buy Cheapandbum caskets from those fly-
by-nights. I could buy 'em myself. I have no love for the casket
outfit, but I'm like them—I have a long reputation to maintain.
And people can't always pay their bills. I've got about six thousand dollars outstanding. With all this recent business I would
have lost money if it weren't for the Dolan and Burton cases,"
he explained, talking about business in order to drown the feelings that were threatening to break forth into words.

"Philip," she suddenly and nervously asked, "are you in
trouble—are you worried about money?"

"You know I'm not. But I have to hustle. Something else is
happening. The foreigners are starting to muscle in on us, just
like they've come into politics. Of course, out here, it's
not such a problem. It's tough on fellows like George Loomey
down near Saint Ignatius. But they're coming in. There are
more of 'em in our profession than we need. Foreigners, politicians, young fellows from college with no training or experience
but just their old man's money to blow—some of these fellows
who go in for show and fancy stuff—well, that's competition."

She agreed, but asked herself if she dared suggest that he sell
out. She didn't make the suggestion. She was afraid of him. But
if he went on this way he might have an attack. And if he died,
what would she do? Would Elizabeth and Bernard come back
and learn to run his business? They could stay here, and she and
Elizabeth could run the house, and in time Elizabeth would be
having children and would need her.

She shouldn't have thoughts like these. Why, it was almost

like wishing your husband dead. She didn't wish him dead. At her age, you couldn't help but think of who would die first and when the Call would come ringing.

He looked so tired.

"Ruth, I'm fagged out. I feel like taking in an early movie."

"All right, Philip, let's."

She smiled tenderly. She thought that he was all she had in the world. And, yes, he was a good man.

XI

Looking at the sky, with his hands in his pockets, Philip Whelan stood in front of his building at Seventy-first and Cornell Avenue. A mood of awe and fear came over him. He thought of his son-in-law. How could he, how could anyone, say there was no God. He sighed with weariness. He walked off and stood on the sidewalk, looking at the lighted sign.

W
H
E
L
A
N

It was always so gratifying to look at that sign.

His chapel was the only building on the block. With nothing on either side of it, it stood out, stood alone. He gazed at the sign in a continuing mood of satisfaction.

A car stopped at the curb. An old woman and a young man got out, and Mr. Whelan watched to see if he knew them. But he didn't. It was clear they were coming to the Callahan wake, and he smiled and stiffly said:

"Good evening."

"Good evening," the old lady responded; the young man mumbled inarticulately. He watched them go into the chapel. Several people came out and stood talking for a moment on the sidewalk. He looked at them, but saw no one he knew. He almost never forgot a face or a name. A man in his business shouldn't forget names or faces.

He looked up at the sky again. He shook his head, thinking how beautiful it was. Yes, life was really strange. A man who had seen as many dead bodies as he had, who had handled death, who had seen as many grief-stricken people as he, could well know that life was, indeed, strange and mysterious.

Inside, Mrs. Marion Callahan was laid out, and overhead was this blue sky with so many stars out tonight.

He became moody, but decided there were some thoughts a man ought best forget. He had overheard many of the mourners speak of how beautiful and young she looked, how lifelike. This was another case well-handled. The Callahan family would remember their mother as looking young and beautiful and lifelike. And Phil Whelan had done that. He had given them a last, beautiful memory of their mother. He walked back into the funeral parlor. He had to see the Callahan boy about the pallbearers for tomorrow, and he knew now that he'd have to arrange for another limousine for the funeral.

Chapter Eight

I

"BERNARD, I'm worried."

Guessing what she meant, Bernard looked apprehensively across the table at Elizabeth.

"How long?" he asked anxiously, leaning forward over the plate with the remains of his scrambled eggs.

"Gosh, it must be over three weeks since I should have had the curse," she said.

"But . . ." he said, his shoulders sagging. He didn't finish his remark.

"It's not just my fault," she said sadly and in obvious bewilderment.

He looked upset.

"Bernard, don't be angry with me," Elizabeth said.

He smiled tenderly and then said very slowly:

"I'm not, Elizabeth."

"Maybe, maybe I'm just late."

He nodded.

"Well, there's no use in worrying," he said with growing agitation.

He heard vague sounds, footsteps outside, footsteps on the floor above. A telephone rang upstairs. He listened to these sounds as though they were significant.

"I can take something," she suggested.

"We have time. There's no need to worry yet," he told her with a forced smile.

"It's not two months yet, Bernard. Something can happen."

Two years ago, her abortion. How he had worried then. Now they were married and her old man couldn't say anything. But what had Whelan to do with the problem? This was something he must face. He'd faced it before when she'd been pregnant. He had seen her through then. Now he had to face it and be responsible.

He'd have to get a job. How could he write? His career could be ruined.

"Bernard, please don't worry. I'll do something. I'll do something. Something will happen."

"It won't do us any good to worry. Worry is merely a waste of emotion."

They were both trapped. He glanced idly around their sordid basement room. Yes, trapped, and in a dump like this.

"Bernard, are you angry with me, or disappointed in me?"

"No."

"Kiss me."

He pulled her head down, kissed her forehead.

"We'll manage, Elizabeth," he said, trying to be reassuring.

II

The sky was overcast. It was raining. The demonstrators turned the corner of Union Square onto Sixteenth Street, file after file, carrying their drenched banners and cards with painted slogans. Bernard, watching from the corner, saw Elizabeth, trim and girlish in her yellow slicker. Sam Leventhal was beside her. He had decided to go home and not parade but work. But, seeing her, hearing a band playing *The Internationale*, he impulsively joined the marchers; he heard spectators on the sidewalk cheering his action.

"I didn't expect you, Bernard," Elizabeth said, smiling with joy as she took his arm.

"I changed my mind about working."

"I'm so glad," she said, squeezing his arm.

"I'm glad you're with us. It was swell of you, Bernie, to join us. I knew you would," Sam said.

"Say, Carr, what are you doing here?" Jackie called from behind Bernard.

"What do you think?" Bernard asked nervously in reply, but without looking back.

"How do you feel?" he asked Elizabeth, bending down toward her.

"Fine," she answered.

As they marched, she let go of his arm and swung her arms at her sides. Yes, she was so pretty, so young in her slicker and with a tan beret protecting her lovely hair. He was proud of her. But his face clouded with gloom. Was she feeling well? Nothing had happened. She was marching in the parade, hoping the long walk would make her come around. Not precisely a revolutionary reason for being in a May Day parade, he reasoned. But, then, this reason could be compatible with revolutionary reasons, couldn't it? And he was marching, sacrificing time that he badly needed for work. He had intended to see her march by at Union Square and then go home and work. But here he was.

Jackie barked out:

We build proletarian culture!

Others took up the cry. All around him, young people were marching and shouting:

We build proletarian culture!

The shouting died down, and they marched on, southward. A narrow squalid street. Bernard didn't know its name. Men and women hanging out of windows, some looking with friendliness, some dull-eyed. The rain came pelting down.

He turned, bent toward Elizabeth again, and asked:

"How do you feel?"

She smiled at him wanly.

"Come on, let's make a noise and show the bourgeoisie," Jackie suddenly boomed out.

"There are no bourgeois around here," Bernard said, turning toward Jackie.

He couldn't really hope too much. And yet, if there was hope, must it not come this way? He had burned his bridges. And, yet, maybe the feet of these marchers were the footsteps of the future, and his footsteps were mingled with theirs, with the thousands of footsteps of the future.

He took Elizabeth's arm and walked on.

III

We write books for the working class!

"You're not shouting," a girl snarled behind him.

He didn't answer, but he felt uneasy. He just couldn't bring himself to shout. He guessed that he wasn't a shouter.

"You, why don't you shout?" the girl screamed at him.

He turned and glared at her, feeling nervous and unsure of himself.

"Yes, I was talking to you," she said aggressively.

How ugly her voice sounded! How thin and homely she was!

"What did you say?" he asked contemptuously.

We write books for the working class!
We write books for the working class!
We write books for the working class!

He grinned self-consciously, turned, and walked on with a sullen expression on his face.

Was he weak? Damn it, he knew that he wouldn't be railroaded and bullied into shouting by this comrade.

"Are you afraid?" the homely girl screamed at him.

"I don't like her," Elizabeth whispered to him.

"You do the shouting," he said.

"What are you marching for?" she asked.

"He's all right. I know him, he's a good writer," Sam said to the girl in a mollifying tone.

"Then why doesn't he raise his voice for the workers?" she asked.

"Who the hell do you think you are, Krupskaya?" asked Bernard, turning around again.

"Are you a bourgeois?"

"Do you write books?" he asked.

"I'm not an intellectual," she answered shrilly and with almost inexpressible contempt.

"Then why do you shout that you write books?" he asked.

"Comrades, we're all comrades," a little fellow said in a piping voice.

"Let's make some noise," Jackie yelled.

They trudged on.

The rain had stopped. Above the narrow street with the dirty old red and gray brick tenements, the sky was dark and low, dark clouds floated heedlessly by. A fat woman stared down lackadaisically from a fire escape. The homely girl shouted up at her:

"Comrades, join our ranks."

"Where did she get that voice?" Bernard asked under his breath.

In the rear somewhere behind them a band was playing *The Internationale* as though it were a funeral dirge.

They marched on, spiritedly, shouting in unison and with contagious enthusiasm:

We fight for the working class!
We fight for the working class!
We fight for the working class!

IV

"Well, at last it's stopped raining," Sam said, edging beside Bernard.

"We don't necessarily advance the cause of Socialism by getting wet," Bernard said.

Bernard looked up, noticing a gray-haired old woman staring at them. What, if anything, did this parade mean for her?

"It's a good parade," Sam said.

"Yes. It's good, with so many marching in the rain. But don't be deceived."

"What do you mean?" asked Sam.

"A parade like this isn't power. Faith isn't power. It's power that counts. Did you see the cops with clubs all along the way?"

"We'll take power when the conditions are ripe," Sam said.

Marching along, Bernard became moody and thoughtful. What of Moscow today? Crowds marching in triumph to *The Internationale*. The days of the French Revolution, when crowds marched to the *Marseillaise* or sang the *Carmagnole*. Yes, some day, perhaps, out of these buildings grained with dirt there would come swarms, and they might march in triumph.

"How do you feel?" Bernard asked Elizabeth in a low voice.

"Oh, all right," she said.

"Are you tired?" he asked.

"No . . . no, not particularly. But it is a long parade," she said.

"We can drop out if you're really tired," he said.

She had walked and walked for several days, and she was still walking, and there was no sign of her coming around.

"Let's step out," he said.

"No, no, Bernard, I want to march. I had cramps a little while ago. I think I did. I think maybe something might happen."

He took her arm. Step by step they trudged forward. It was becoming wearisome with the halts, the slow movement forward, the standing and waiting. How much longer would it be? And he hoped. . . . He looked at Elizabeth. She seemed tired, even grim. There was a smudge of dirt on her nose.

—-Yes, she's brave.

v

Entering crowded Chatham Square, they straightened ranks, and everybody marched with more spirit. Mark Singer was ahead of Bernard and Elizabeth, and the cultural group in which they marched sang:

Give me that good old Communist spirit,
Give me that good old Communist spirit,
Give me that good old Communist spirit.
If it's good enough for Comrade Singer, then it's good enough
    for me.

Elizabeth swayed her shoulders, and with a bright, happy glow in her eyes she lost herself in this revival singing. Bernard didn't sing. He felt alone. He didn't know why he should find revival singing so distasteful, but he did. It wasn't what he thought should happen in a May Day parade.

Then they sang *The Internationale* again. His mood changed. He sang with the others, but in a low voice. Elizabeth hummed because she didn't know the words. They marched through a double line of spectators, and the air reverberated with cheers which echoed in his own mind. The cheers persisted, rose, drowned out both the words and the tune of the song. He marched erectly, deeply moved. He felt himself one with many, and he remembered the August night of 1927 in Union Square when Sacco and Vanzetti were murdered. He was afraid he might cry. He was now one with many, linked in the bonds of solidarity. He was glad he'd marched today.

With raised, clenched fists, they passed the reviewing stands, singing *The Internationale*. Eldridge and other party leaders were on the crowded stand, and on either side there were wet American and red flags. A loud speaker barked. Tears welled in Bernard's eyes. He suddenly thought that there was pathos, sorrow, death, joy, and hope in this parade, and that it was all symbolized in the song, *The Internationale*, which was being sung today in many lands and in many languages. He marched on past the stand, with Elizabeth clinging to his arm, his head high.

VI

"Fakers," a little man with a mustache shouted.

Bernard looked up at a group on a balcony, apparently editors of the Yiddish Social-Democratic paper, *The Jewish Daily Examiner*.

"Betrayers of the workers!"

"Social-fascist dogs."

The screaming increased in volume, grew into a mad beast-like roar. Bernard glanced around, amused, thinking of how much bitterness these left-wing squabbles created.

"Dirty dogs!" a fat woman screamed in hatred.

Bernard was frightened. Yes, this was like the roar of beasts.

"Ach, I spit on the pigs," a man on his left said.

Bernard turned, looked from face to face. Yelling men and women with their features contorted in mob hatred. A screaming round-faced woman whose hair fell down on her cheeks and forehead; a girl of sixteen shouting hysterically, an old man with a drooping gray mustache and quivering lips trying to shout with his cracked voice; hard and work-worn faces, faces lined and seamed as though with dirt; used, rubbed, weather-beaten skin; waving fists and arms. A constant roar, and accusations, insults, screams of anger, mad denunciation, becoming part of this churning, roaring sound of hatred.

"Agents of the capitalists," screamed a shrill-voiced woman.

Again the roar, and somebody yelling:

"The Communist Party."

"We are not fakers," a young girl yelled beside him, her spittle hitting his ear.

He shuddered, clenched his lips, stood tense, and gripped Elizabeth more tightly.

The spirit of the parade, all of its hope and faith, was now turned into this fierce collective hatred of the Jewish Social Democrats standing on the balcony.

"Down with the Social-Democratic dogs!" a man yelled, and this became a mob roar.

A beautiful girl beside him screamed this cry, her soft, sensitive face becoming ugly, stretched out of all proportion. Then he saw the bewildered face of a fat policeman with a defensive smirk on his face.

The roaring continued, while from behind him came the strains of *The Internationale* and the cheers of the crowd by the reviewing stand. He was dazed by the noises. Then he struggled with a rising wave of disgust. Did one have to accept hatred to become a Revolutionist? How could a writer hate like this? But this was no time to think about these questions. He was very disturbed.

"Down with the labor fakers!"

"Down with the traitors of the working class!"

"Death to the Social-Fascist dogs, betrayers of the working class."

He began edging Elizabeth out of the crowd.

Chapter Nine

I

THE basement room was quiet. Bernard listened to Elizabeth's soft, even breathing. He was too restless to sleep. He wanted to think. Working alone at night, while millions slept, his mood had been one of consoling loneliness. He'd revised and rewritten his story, *Someday*. It had already been rejected about twenty-four times. Would it still be rejected?

Millions of people were asleep now in Chicago, too. His mother. His sister, Marie. Was old man Whelan out on a case? Smith at the undertaking parlor? Would Smith have made a better husband for Elizabeth than he?

—You'll never get anywhere doing what you're doing.

And

—What'll it ever get you?

How many times had he been asked these two questions— and by how many persons? Those who belonged to his Chicago past would never understand him. Could they ever understand enough of life to become tolerant? Understanding life probably meant knowing that there was nowhere to go. It didn't matter if he never got anywhere or if he never got anything. Other than his integrity, he had nothing to lose. He wanted only to learn, and he had learned enough to see that the discovery of knowledge was the beginning of the discovery of the unimportance of man in the world.

He looked over at Elizabeth. There was an almost heartbreaking pathos about her as she slept. Had he finally married her because she, she and marriage both, helped him to feel more important in his own eyes? He really couldn't be sure that he knew the reasons why he had married her. Her youth and innocence had appealed to him strongly. Wasn't she the Elsie Cavanagh he had happened to marry? Somewhere he had read that thrilling phrase of Robespierre's, "the dread of unimportance." In Chicago he had known that dread. And hadn't he often felt most unimportant because of girls? Elsie Cavanagh had never treated him as if he were important. Was it because of this that he had yearned and hungered for that one pair of eyes, that one pair of lips, that one girl? And didn't this all help to explain why he wanted to write? Not only girls, not only Elsie Cavanagh, but the Church and his family, almost everything in his boyhood had made him feel unimportant.

And his mother? Wasn't she a good Catholic because she knew that nobody was really important? Growing more uneasy, he suspected that he was more like his mother than he cared to admit, even to himself. She'd unconsciously taught him this sense of the unimportance of people. And the boy in his book, Patrick Stanton, felt this same unimportance in people. Patrick Stanton was like his own mother. She cultivated holiness so that she might be important in Heaven. He wrote so he might be important to posterity. Was his heaven any the less illusory than hers?

Elsie Cavanagh. What was she like now? She was supposed to be engaged to Marty O'Hara. He was under indictment for embezzlement and might go to jail. In grammar school, Marty O'Hara had been stuck-up and arrogant. He'd had a feeling of rivalry toward him. His father had been a greenhorn, and had built up a chain of banks, and now the banks were closed, and father and son were indicted. He laughed to himself bitterly.

But how could a skinny little sixth-grade girl hurt a boy so that he'd carry this hurt for years? It wasn't a hurt any more. He'd written out that hurt. He'd written it out by describing a boy's adoration for his girl character, Audrey. But nothing he had written touched those lines by Francis Thompson:

> *Go, and too late thou shalt confess*
> *I looked thee into loveliness!*

These two lines explained the story of Elsie Cavanagh in his life. Through her he had read the world into loveliness, and all because of a "dread of unimportance."

He became so agitated he paced about the room. To understand—this was the greatest adventure in the world. And yet it was the saddest and the loneliest. Did it mean destroying all the loveliness one had read into the world?

He looked at the neatly typed and marked copy of his story, *Someday*. A man in his forties going back to Mass in the church of his boyhood, wanting to see his childhood sweetheart as a woman, wanting to regain some shred of the lost loveliness that was only illusion. That was *Someday*.

He looked again at Elizabeth asleep.

Elizabeth . . . Eva . . . Elsie, and his fictional girl, Audrey. When he and Eva had broken up in 1927, he had written in his diary:

Between the fires of the beginning and the frozen dead atoms of the end, I loved you, Eva.

Was he ready to write his novel about Eva? He started undressing for bed.

II

Bernard was reading a novel for review, and Elizabeth was reading another that Mrs. Lisa Baranov had given him for a long synopsis.

Mildred Feldman, Sophie, and Sam Leventhal dropped in on them for a visit. Bernard's eyes lit up at the sight of Mildred. She was wearing an old black dress with a rip in the sleeve, but she looked beautiful nonetheless.

"Oh, isn't this wonderful?" Mildred exclaimed, glancing about the room.

"As soon as we can, we're going to move," Elizabeth said.

"It must be wonderful to be a poor revolutionary writer and live like this, just like the workers do. Why, it's almost the same as sharing the life of the workers."

Bernard kept looking wistfully at Mildred. She was so young, so lovely, and so free.

"I can't tell you how happy I am now because I'm on your side," Mildred said. "My room isn't as big as this. It's so small that there's hardly space to move in it. And there are bedbugs, too, but I don't care. I'm so happy living in poverty."

"Poverty is debasing," Bernard said.

"Oh, I never think that way. I see all those poor people on the East Side, and I tell myself, 'Now, I'm like them, I'm like one of them,' " Mildred said with a ring of sincerity and a purity in her voice. "I'm ready to starve and die with them."

"Gee, kid," Sophie said, facing Mildred, "you have the makings of a real Communist in you."

"Oh, I'm not good enough for that yet," Mildred answered.

"None of us are, if you take us merely as we are, Mildred," Sam explained. Mildred listened attentively. "What makes the difference between us and the bourgeois is the Party. The Party makes better people out of us."

"A movement or an organization can't be any better than the people in it," Bernard declared.

Sam looked uncertainly at Bernard, as though he wished Bernard hadn't said this.

"I know many Catholics who'd say that the Church makes them better than they are. In fact, the Church says that without it nobody would be any goddamn good at all."

"But, Bernie, we're not a religion. We're the only revolutionary party in the world fighting for the workers," Sophie said.

"How does the Party make you better?" Bernard asked.

"Bernie, gee, I thought you knew that," Sophie said, staring at him obtusely.

"What would there be for me without the Party?" Sam asked.

"I can't answer that question," Bernard responded.

Sam smiled ingratiatingly and said:

"What I mean is, there wouldn't be any place·for me. The capitalist magazines don't want my kind of poetry."

"They don't want my work, either," Bernard said.

"That's why you belong with us. It's just as Jan and Jake say: if a young writer wants an audience, he's got to come with us. In a couple of years millions will be on our side."

"Oh, I can't wait for that day. Just think of it, to be one of millions, to be like millions and millions, to think that you yourself don't count, but that only millions count," Mildred said, her face almost ecstatic.

"You can help, too, kid. Gosh, you could go back to school and organize for us, and let your father give you an allowance and give us what you don't need," Sophie told Mildred.

"But, Sophie, I can't. I left home. I'm never going to see my father and mother again."

Bernard noticed Elizabeth open her mouth to speak, but she said nothing. She turned away with inexpressible fear on her face. He wanted to go over to her and comfort her, but he didn't move.

"Gee, Mildred," Sophie said. "When you took me to your house that time, I thought your mother and father were nice . . . nice for people who are bourgeois."

"They are. They're very nice. They were too nice to me, too good. They raised me to be too special. Oh . . . if I could only describe how I feel, working on my feet as a waitress. The girls are all so human. They aren't like me, talking about Ernest Hemingway and Gertrude Stein and concerts. They're real."

"I don't think it hurts anyone to get an education," Bernard said.

"I had to quit college in my second year," Sam said. "But I don't regret it. I learned more in the Party than I ever could learn at Columbia."

"I adore hearing the waitresses talk. I was always bored listening to the girls at school or to the people who came to our house. All those poor girls want something better. One of them, her name is Annie, she's wonderful, she says she could be a great actress if she only had a chance. She tells me everything. She told me about a dream she had. She dreamed she was in a woods, and rich people were sitting at tables, and she had to keep running to them as fast as she could with plates and plates of food. And no matter how much she brought, she had to bring more. And the next night I had the same kind of a dream, only it was the poor and the workers I was serving, and I was happy. I was doing something. I was sorry when I woke up."

"That dream is symbolic. Even the dreams of the proletariat are different from those of the bourgeoisie," Sam said.

"Gee, Mildred, you're wonderful," Sophie exclaimed.

"Who would like a cup of tea?" Elizabeth asked in a quiet and rather formal voice.

III

Elizabeth looked wan and ill. There were circles under her eyes. Her feet ached, and her ankles seemed swollen. Her whole body, all of her, was tired. She hesitated for a moment in front of the Forty-second Street library, tempted to take a bus. Then she moved on frantically, forcing herself to walk fast.

She could tell, from the way Bernard kept asking her if anything had happened, that he didn't want her to have the baby. She didn't know if she herself wanted it or not. She had drunk almost a whole bottle of medicine. If she couldn't bring on the curse, it would be simply terrible for her and Bernard. Her back began to pain. This might be a good sign, a beginning. A little while ago, when she was passing St. Patrick's, she thought that she'd had a cramp, but it had only been another false alarm. She was afraid, and she wasn't absolutely certain of what she was afraid. The feelings she had were just awful. They couldn't be worse even if she knew she was going to die any minute.

She drove herself on along Fifth Avenue. People were looking at her as if something were wrong with her. Oh, she was so tired, too tired to think of anything. She wanted this to happen, and, after it did, to go to bed and sleep for a long time.

In Chicago, that time she'd drunk the whole bottle and had come around, she had slept wonderfully. She wanted to sleep the same way now.

By an effort, she forced herself on at a fast pace. When she got home, she undressed quickly and took a hot bath in the bathroom on the first floor, letting the water get as hot as she could stand it and staying in the tub until she almost fainted. Weak and perspiring, with a mad look in her eyes, she went downstairs to their basement room, took a big dose of castor oil, and pitched into the bed. She fell asleep almost immediately, and her drawn face relaxed.

IV

"Did anything happen?" Bernard asked eagerly as he got home and saw Elizabeth lying in bed looking worn out. He had just made another futile round of literary offices.

"No," she said in a choked voice.

"What's the matter, Elizabeth? Are you sick?"

"I'm just tired," she said in a weary voice. "I walked and walked, for blocks. And I took a hot bath and castor oil," she added in a faraway voice.

"Elizabeth, what's the matter?" he asked excitedly, seeing her face in pain.

"I . . . I got cramps," she said in agony as he went to her.

"I'll go get a doctor."

"No. . . . No. . . . Just help me out of bed."

He helped her out, got her robe, and assisted in putting it on. He guided her to the door.

"Don't come with me," she pleaded.

"Maybe I'd better. . . ."

"No . . . please, Bernard."

She walked slowly to the bathroom. Relieved that she didn't want him to go and stay with her, Bernard was torn and agitated. He couldn't sit still and he struggled to be calm. Maybe he ought to get a doctor. If she aborted and had a hemorrhage, it would be a mess. He had to make the right decision. But he'd done nothing illegal. It would be easy to get a doctor. She wouldn't die. What was happening to her upstairs?

He was in a panic.

He casually noticed a small medicine bottle on the table. After he examined it and discovered it was practically empty, he let out a violent curse. He started to the door but turned and wearily sank into the big chair. Elizabeth's action awed him. He knew that he was at least partly responsible for it, for he must have conveyed some feeling of alarm to her. Her courage was foolhardy, an act of desperation. Were they going to have a mess? This was ugly, ugly. But having a baby now before he was artistically sure of himself. . . . Was Elizabeth in pain? In danger? He jumped to go to her, but she fell into his arms at the door.

"Oh, I had terrible cramps," she said in a weakened, frightened voice. "Hold me."

"Tell me how you are," he asked, holding her.

"I feel better . . . but nothing happened."

He looked over her shoulder with a defeated and guilty expression on his face.

"Elizabeth, you were terribly foolish," he said, speaking softly. "You mustn't do things like that again."

"Don't scold me."

He led her to the bed and tried to comfort her.

"We can have the child. We'll get along."

"Bernard, I can have another abortion."

"No," he said decisively.

"I'm not afraid, Bernard. I'm not."

"I am," he told her.

"But, Bernard, if nothing happens?"

"We'll be parents, that's all."

She was watching him attentively. Tears welled in her eyes. "You don't want me to have a child . . . you don't want it."

He couldn't answer her. It was true, he didn't want a child.

"I hate you!"

"Elizabeth. . . ."

"It's not my fault," she sobbed.

He took her hand. She looked at him blankly. Slowly, her face changed. Her eyes began to shine through her tears.

"And you'll love my baby . . . our baby?"

His answer was a tender smile.

He sat by her, still holding her hand, and with the expression of an attentive child she watched him.

v

Mr. Capper, of the Personnel Department of the Nation Oil Company of New York, was proud of his ability to show a poker face. He looked on life as a poker game in which you had to have a good poker face in order to win. He guessed that Mr. Carr was an unusual young man. He was a college man. Mr. Capper didn't know if he could place him, but he might if Mr. Carr clicked.

Mr. Capper was deliberately silent for several moments. Not a muscle moved in his youthful face.

"How did you happen to come here looking for a job, Mr. Carr?"

"If I have to get a job, there's no use going to a little peanut stand and asking the owner to let me sell his peanuts. You're a big company. I thought you'd have something."

"Did you make Phi Beta Kappa in three years or four?"

"Four. I had to work my way through school, and I wrote a novel at the same time."

"Most young men write novels, or else dream of writing one. I suppose the manuscript is pretty dusty now."

"It was published."

"What's the name of it?"

"*The Father.*"

Mr. Capper jotted down the title on a pad.

"I'll read it."

"I hope you'll like it."

"What experience have you had?"

"I've worked in a book store, a cigar store, an undertaking parlor, a branch want-ad office of *The Chicago Clarion*. I've waited on tables in a fraternity house and worked at jobs on the University of Chicago campus. I tutored summer-school students. And I've written a lot of book reviews, mostly for the *Dispatch*."

"What brings you to an oil company for a job?"

"I have a wife. We're going to have a baby. I need a job. I've invested my youth in a so-called education."

"The market's glutted with education, isn't it, Mr. Carr?"

"A chap I know in Chicago took his diploma to a grocery store and wanted to exchange it for food."

"What happened?"

"He got publicity in the newspapers but nothing to eat," Bernard said.

Mr. Capper didn't laugh. He was trying to estimate Bernard. Educated, cynical young men were good bets. Babbitry, Boy Scoutism, Service, and the American Dream had had their day. Cynical, educated men would win the poker game in these times. If he helped employ them, and held them to him, they'd be useful. This job of his was only a stepping stone. He wondered if this chap would be useful.

"Tell me some more about yourself, Mr. Carr."

"I'm twenty-six years old. I need a job. I don't think I'm dumb."

"You're rather blunt and cynical, aren't you?"

"I'm merely trying to talk straight. I've always done whatever I said I'd do. If I say I'll do my best, I'll do it."

"Did you think there might be some kind of writing you could do for us?"

"No, not particularly."

"What did you think you might do when you came here?"

"I don't know. There must be hundreds of things that have to be done in a corporation like this. Anything. I had selling experience with Monahan's *Blue Book*. Maybe I could sell."

"I'm afraid there isn't anything, Mr. Carr."

"That settles another question," Bernard remarked casually.

"Do you know any languages?"

"French badly—I could work it up for reading, if necessary."

"Mathematics?"

"A little. I know a little of everything, including mathematical logic."

"Do you want merely a temporary job here?"

"I don't understand what you mean."

"I mean temporary—to tide you over?"

"I'm open to conviction."

"What does that mean?"

"If you give me a job and I can get somewhere, I wouldn't consider it temporary."

Mr. Capper made some notes.

"I'll keep you in mind and file your name and address, Mr. Carr. That's all I can do."

"Thank you."

Mr. Capper rose and shook hands with Bernard.

In the crowded anteroom a number of men were waiting to be interviewed. As Bernard passed through it, he was followed by glances of curiosity, hostility, despair.

VI

Bernard sat in the sun on a bench in City Hall Park, with a novel and two newspapers beside him, trying to make up his mind what he'd do after lunch. He'd had no luck looking for a job this morning, but Mr. Brady had given him a book and also promised to print a long, critical letter on Plekhanov on next Saturday's book page. He'd get twenty-five dollars for the letter and twelve-fifty or more for the review. If Elizabeth weren't pregnant, he could manage to support them both.

These last months suddenly seemed to him to have been not quite real. He had been floundering badly. What kind of impression must he have made on others? Did they know how unsure he'd been? Did they know that in a half-conscious way he'd been fighting a battle within himself? Now, the time of floundering was over. The odds of the world were against him, and he'd have to summon all his will and energy to overcome those odds. To lack confidence and will was to practice sentimental self-indulgence.

A lunch-hour crowd came and went in the park. On benches all around him he saw stolid, unemployed men. He looked about with bright, clear, confident eyes. Several men, who looked like Tammany politicians, strolled by. They seemed to be unworried and at peace with themselves. A big, red-faced man reminded him of Whelan, particularly because of the way he walked. How describe it? A measured tread? A dignified walk? A sureness of foot? A man walking through life who thinks he knows the road from beginning to end?

He suddenly wished he could listen to some music or go to the museum. He wanted to hear or to see something that would represent all that was wordless in him. Some unarticulated emotions of men could never be put into words. The hunger for the ideal. There is no ideal. The ideal was merely a vast, unreachable, and unreal sky in the head of man. Today, the real sky was clear and blue, and the clouds seemed like soft white and white-gray gauzelike stuff. And there were other skies. Heavy skies, low skies, sunset skies, the skies of Walt Whitman's "mad, naked summer night." And there were skies inside of him. A sky and the skies. The sky was a sidereal universe, a world of stars and planets, of heat and cold and dizzy speeds, a catastrophic chaos, unfixed and unfixable, raging and whirling. The whirling sky.

VII

"We're in the hands of a receiver, Carr. I've got to lay off two more clerks," Mark Alberts said, fingering his mustache.

He pointed around at the large bookstore, with its rows and tables of books.

"There's hardly anybody in here. Look at the clerks standing around. And we're one of the biggest retail book outfits in America, Carr. Well, that's the picture."

"I see."

"Take a book like yours. We can't sell it. I read it. I liked it. It's a good book and I ordered five copies. We sold one. Why, we're not even selling many bestsellers."

"You don't know of anything I might get in the book business, do you?"

"Hell, no, I wish I did," Mark Alberts said gloomily.

"Well, thanks just the same."

"Drop in any time you're around. I'll be glad to see you," Mark Alberts said, shaking hands with Bernard.

VIII

Guy Watkins had a dedicated look in his eyes. He sat between Bernard and Jan Walters at a table in the cafeteria at Fourteenth Street and Sixth Avenue, fingering a half-drunk glass of milk. He was thin and wiry, and didn't look to be a man of forty-four. He wore an old suit and a khaki shirt without a tie.

Guy liked the cut of Bernard and, listening to him talk, thought a good new generation of radicals was coming into existence, and with modest pride he could say that he had helped to form them. His observations in New York and all over the country on this last tour offered only one more confirmation, proving the scientific truth of his views and prognostications. The depression, the inevitable decay of capitalism, had produced its storm birds of the Revolution. He would no longer be a lonely voice. But for years now he had never for one minute doubted. Before the Russian Revolution, during the War for Democracy when he had almost been lynched, he had held to the faith. But how often had he not been tempted to doubt? How often had he not thought that he would die before that great dawn of Socialism?

Bernard felt relieved to be with these people after another futile job-hunt.

"This has been another wasted day for me," Bernard said.

"For a revolutionist every day is like a piece of cloth with twenty-four squares in it. You have to cut that cloth up perfectly. Every square should be cut evenly and right on the line. Not one thread must be lost. And then the squares must be harmoniously arranged."

"You want to listen to this, kid," Jan told Bernard. "We are the only people in America who have no time to waste. Isn't it so, Guy?"

"Look at the men sitting here, idle," Guy said, taking in the cafeteria with a gesture. "It's the same all over America. Workers, unemployed, sitting on park benches and curbstones, and in coffee pots and cafeterias. And the idle factories. American capitalism has now gone into its inevitable decline. Neither miracles nor sunspots can change that fact. Even if it hadn't, what would happen? These same men would go to ball games and yell like fools because somebody named Babe Ruth hits a little white ball four hundred feet instead of two hundred feet. Capitalism can't produce men, only bellies for bread, eyes for circuses, and backs and heads for wage labor. Only the rebel can be a human being under capitalism. Only he can plan and think."

Bernard saw in Guy Watkins a vital force, a will, a drive, and a self-restraint that he had achieved in himself only rarely. He asked himself how much real conjunction there was between his aims and those of Guy Watkins. As they went on talking, Guy Watkins's words acquired an added personal authority. Jan spoke as one who belonged to the Party, Ferris as a publisher, and Scott Sherman as an editor. He could speak only for himself. So did Guy Watkins. But Watkins's experiences included trials by fire. He had opposed a war during wartime and had spoken to hostile audiences. And he had studied the economic mechanisms of capitalism and imperialism. He was part of the history of American radicalism and was linked with the time of Debs. Bernard wanted to learn from him, to impress him, but at the same time he didn't want to be afraid of Watkins.

"I'm going to write about the psychological effects of capitalism. Most of my material is collected and filed," Guy Watkins said. "But that book won't be ready until 1939."

"You have your own five-year plan, Guy," Jan said.

"Socialism doesn't mean only planned economy. It means the planned life," Guy Watkins answered with a proud seriousness. "You can only change the world by work."

"Guy, even though you aren't a Party member, you're a real Communist," Jan said.

Bernard was thoughtful. He was strangely attracted to, and at the same time frightened by, this man.

"Everything done by the Russian leaders is justified by all that is implied in the Five-Year Plan," Guy Watkins said.

"And it's succeeding," Jan quickly added.

Guy clenched his fist, and his face tightened. He talked with such tensity that his voice seemed like a hammer driving each word, like a nail, neatly and unfailingly into place.

"The energies of a whole nation are concentrated and planned on one goal. In the Soviet Union, they are remaking human nature as well as the social world of man. Under capitalism, man conquered nature. Under Socialism man will conquer human nature."

Jan looked over at Bernard with fatuous self-justification.

"Here, demoralization, idleness, waste, vice. Look at what we could do! Look at what we might accomplish and build!"

Guy's clenched fist came down firmly but softly on the tile-topped table.

"Anything we do to end this capitalist hell is worth the cost."

"And we're the only ones who can do it," Jan said.

To Guy, Bernard and Jan had become mere listening vehicles and instruments of communication. He wanted to imbue them with his own fierce conviction. He was ecstatically keen. To him, history was like a clear page, with every letter legible. Only the storm birds were needed to fly far and wide to give vision and ambition to others. He talked with passionate fervor, as though he were making a soap-box speech. For Bernard, the cafeteria became transformed. He felt his own power growing within.

"No power on earth can stop the march to Socialism," Guy proclaimed.

"And the new wave is here," Jan said. The casualness of his voice struck Bernard as being in marked contrast to the ardor of Guy Watkins's certainty.

"Every day, something happens. Capitalists lose hope, jump out of windows, and leave residues of undying hatred in the hearts of the workers," Guy went on.

"And every day the Soviet Union grows more powerful," Jan said.

Bernard thought how his own days were passing. They were all silent. Guy Watkins finished his glass of milk.

"Well, Bernie, what do you think?" Jan asked.

"Of what?" Bernard asked.

"Of Socialism?"

Bernard smiled in answer.

They got up to leave.

Bernard walked on home, carrying a book and a large manila envelope. Suddenly he realized with some shock that Guy Watkins had told him nothing that he hadn't already known. Yet the man had spoken as though everything he said were being uttered for the first time.

Fourteenth Street looked dirty and dismal. The sidewalk was gray and dusty. It was noisy. Although there were quite a few people on the street, Bernard felt separated from them. Last May Day, and in Union Square when Sacco and Vanzetti were murdered, he hadn't felt separated. In the French Revolution, one wouldn't have had the feeling of separation. Jan always talked of a new wave. These people didn't look like part of a wave. If the wave did come, how would he act? He knew there was something of the same spirit in him that he sensed in Guy Watkins. If he had the courage, this spirit would be tempered. And then?

He walked on, a shabby young man with an indifferent look

in his eyes. His pants were baggy, his shoes unshined, the seat of
his old blue suit shiny. Tonight he would sit down and work.
He told himself that the day would come when his words would
help to cut all the apathy, all the indifference, of life. Yes, he
was convinced. He had a mission no less than Guy Watkins.
He would write yet—write words that would be tender and
soft, words that would explode like bombs and cut like a blade.

But then he asked himself, after all, do I have the heart of a
Jacobin? His question disquieted him.

Chapter Ten

I

Mrs. Carr did her housework in much the same way as she
breathed. She had done it for so many years that she
scarcely needed to think of what she was doing. Her days passed
so uniformly that the differences between yesterday, today, and
tomorrow were almost negligible. The weekdays were marked
off in her life by what she did. On Friday, she cooked fish or
eggs. On Tuesday, she did the washing. On Monday and Thursday, she scrubbed floors. She neither resented nor enjoyed her
housework. Long ago, she had adopted the practice of offering
up to Mary, along with her morning prayers, all the tasks
which she performed, and she did her housework as a duty, a
penance, and a prayer. Her motions were slow and wearied, but
these weary motions had become a habit. She did not fuss in her
kitchen. She did one thing after another at the same pace, with
the same thoroughness. While she worked, she thought only
intermittently. Thoughts and memories would come and go in
her mind as though there were pauses and spaces between them.

It happened to be today, rather than yesterday or tomorrow.
She had cooked breakfast for her three grown children, and
they had gone to work. Patrick was still in bed. Since he was
out of work, and seemed almost to have given up the idea of
finding anything, he slept late. She kept a low flame going under
the old coffeepot so his coffee would be warm.

This morning there were fewer pauses and spaces between
her thoughts and memories than usual. It was a fine, sunny day,
and it was May. She tried to pay a little visit to church every
day in May, and she was always pleased when the weather was
good. Beautiful days in May seemed like a special sign of the

167

glory of Mary. This afternoon she would put on her best black dress and run across to St. Catherine's Church.

She methodically stacked the dishes in the dishpan. There was an almost lifeless expression on her face. Her hands were large and bony, and the skin on them was dried; they bore the marks of years of housework. Her tall figure moved noiselessly between the table and the sink.

When Bernard had been a boy of ten or eleven, he had been devoted to Mary, and never before nor after had she been as close to him. She had been most hurt and saddened by the parts of his book that told of how the boy placed himself under the guidance of the Blessed Virgin. Thinking of this again, sadness passed like a quick shadow across her face. Clocklike, she washed the breakfast dishes. She used her hands and arms as though they were heavy. There was no grace in her motions. They were not awkward, merely tired and slow. But, occupied with the first of her endless domestic duties, there was an awesome dignity in her straight, tall figure, and in her eyes—eyes which seemed to look inward and to see things that others did not see.

Patrick Carr stamped out to the kitchen. She hustled to give him a cup of coffee. He yawned and blinked; his unshaven, weather-beaten, red-blotched face was coarse with sleepiness. His iron-gray hair was uncombed, and the two top buttons of his faded blue work-shirt were open. His sleeves were carelessly rolled up, exposing hairy arms. He finished buttoning his fly as he gave his wife a squinting glance. He let out a meaningless grunt as he sat down.

His morning depression and grouchiness were accompanied by a throbbing headache. A moment ago he had wanted to remind himself of something about these headaches, but he couldn't remember what it was. He gulped down his coffee and sat back waiting to be served. In a moment Mrs. Carr set bacon and eggs before him and poured him a second cup of coffee.

Mrs. Carr went on with her housework. He kept glancing at her, wanting to say something friendly. He could think of nothing to say. The pain in his head seemed to drive his thoughts

away. As he ate, the pain began to subside. There was no need
for him to worry. No one could go through life without a pain
or an ache now and then.

"If I didn't get up this morning with another headache, I'd
be out looking to see if I could find anything to do," he said.

"It's a good thing the children are working, but then I can
always go back in service if the worse comes to the worst," she
answered in a matter-of-fact tone and without turning away
from the sink where she was drying dishes.

"I'll find something to do, headache or no headache," he
said, his voice full of self-pity.

His eyes became melancholy. By God, not a word of sympathy about his headaches, but only about how she could go back
to work if she had to. He wanted to believe that there was love
in her heart, but there wasn't. If there had been, he'd be a different man than the man he was.

With the dishes finished and placed in order on the pantry
shelves, Mrs. Carr poured herself a cup of coffee and sat down.
She and her husband didn't look at each other. The silence between them became like a weight on Patrick Carr. He decided
that it was impossible even to pass the time of day with this
woman. And yet he had lived with her all these years. This
morning, he had wanted to talk with her, wanted to let her
know that, after all was said and done, he was a man with
feelings. He sighed heavily, wearily, and gazed past her at the
spring day.

Mrs. Carr was having this cup of coffee because she somehow
sensed that Patrick wanted to say something. There was sorrow
in her heart for him, seeing him the way he was, sighing and
not working, moving about the house in the morning, complaining of his headaches, and keeping something on his mind.
She wanted to tell him that she had sorrow for him in her heart,
but she couldn't. The words wouldn't come. It had been years
now since she'd been able to speak of anything that was on her
heart.

"Woman," he said, holding out his cup for more coffee.

She took the cup from him and went to the coffeepot on the stove.

Brooding over his coffee, and needing to talk, he said:

"Well, it well might be that his nibs is living off the fat of the land."

"You and I are old enough to be thinking of our own souls and of what we'll be answering to when our time comes."

"Woman," he proclaimed in a manner approaching the oratorical, "to err is human." He paused dramatically. "And I erred."

"I have no recriminations to make."

"And well she mightn't," Patrick Carr said, looking at the kitchen stove, as though it were a sympathetic audience.

"If it be the will of God to punish me for my sins or the sins of others, I will not question His will," she said with a strange intensity in her voice.

"The will of God—in the name of God, woman—God is too busy to be thinking about the human frailties of a man who's worked as hard as I all my life, in season and out of season."

He got to his feet slowly, cupped his hands behind his back, lowered his head, thoughtfully contemplated the worn oilcloth on the kitchen floor, and walked slowly past his wife.

"I tell you, woman, it's comforting to a man's vanity to know that God is always willing this and that for him," he yelled as he left the kitchen.

He tramped into the parlor and sat in his old rocker. He rocked, letting his arms hang awkwardly over the sides of the chair. Ah, as far back as he could remember, that woman of his had been the same, sour and dour and thinking of duty and of God in Heaven, and she didn't even seem to sit down over a toilet seat without it seeming to be her duty. And for years and years now, he'd watched her going about with a face like mortal sin.

He became drowsy.

If he only had the doing of his life over again. When he'd first known Mary, she'd been shy and pretty. He grew drowsier.

Yes, shy and pretty. How proud he'd been to win her, fool that he was. Shy and pretty. . . . His thoughts grew vague. He closed his eyes and slumped in the chair. His head dropped, and he fell asleep with his mouth open.

II

Patrick Carr walked eastward along Sixty-third Street, enjoying his hazy thoughts. It would be good to be young. And if he were, wouldn't he see to it that he was a free man without caring a come-as-you-please for any soul, man, woman, or child? To have spent his life living with the likes of Mary Carr. With her, it was sin and damnation if you sneezed. It was hell-fire and brimstone if you blew your nose. It was verging on a mortal sin, if not a sin against the Holy Ghost, if you took a leak in obedience to the call of nature. And so here he was, a man of fifty-four!

He saw a nurse wheeling a crippled little old man. He glanced off guiltily for fear of meeting the invalid's eyes. God in Heaven, it was better to be dead than to be in a state like that. If he had the misfortune to have a stroke, God Almighty, what would happen to him? His woman would care for him without complaint and with the most sour-faced look of martyrdom known to man. He'd rather be dead than have such a fate befall him. He was better off dead than alive. Then she could pray for his soul to her heart's content. And his educated son could write a book about him and get rich. His reflections roused him to self-pity. None of these people passing him on the sidewalk could even imagine that they were seeing a man whose story would, if ever told, wring tears from the hardest of hearts.

He was planning to go over and sit in the sun in Jackson Park, but when he came to Sixty-third and Stony Island, he turned south and walked on to a dingy speakeasy below Sixty-fourth Street. He found Mr. Garrity sitting alone at a corner table and joined him. A scar-faced husky served him with a glass of beer. He drank.

"It's a fine day, Mr. Garrity."

"Yes, so 'tis. 'Tis always easier to bear the vicissitudes of life on a fine day," Mr. Garrity said.

Mr. Garrity was a small, neatly dressed man with a red face. His wing collar gave him an eccentric appearance. His thin, angular face was mournful. He sat in rigid dignity. He looked at Patrick Carr without appearing to see him. He nodded his head meaninglessly, as though he were agreeing with something that Patrick had said, although both men were now sitting in silence.

"Well . . ." Patrick Carr said, lifting his glass.

Mr. Garrity raised his brows in response, and Patrick Carr drank.

"What's that you were saying, Mr. Carr?" Mr. Garrity asked.

"It was the she-devils who gave us Prohibition. They'll be the ruin of the country before they're through," Patrick Carr said bitterly.

He was thinking that a place like this wasn't like a good saloon in the old days. It wasn't friendly. If you tried to pass the time of day or be sociable with one of these young hoodlums, it was enough to get your face bitten off or a bullet in your back. And these hoodlums were making money selling this rotten twenty-five-cent beer while many a decent, honest bartender was walking the streets out of work, with his job stolen from him, thanks to the blue-nosed she-devils.

"Women," Mr. Garrity exclaimed.

He took a sip of beer. He was thinking of what he wanted people to say and think of him when he departed from this life. He wanted them to say that he bore his vicissitudes well. Then he said with wistfulness:

"Oh, don't tell me about women."

Patrick Carr agreed with a vigorous shake of the head.

"It's long since I learned to let what women say go in one ear and out the other," Mr. Garrity said.

Patrick Carr felt close to Mr. Garrity and, at the same time, superior. He knew that Mr. Garrity was henpecked, and, with all that he might think of his own woman, she couldn't hold a candle to Garrity's she-devil.

Mr. Garrity, continuing to think wistfully on the vicissitudes of life, remarked:

"It's always the same . . . every man for himself, and devil take the hindmost."

"There's no lie in that," Patrick Carr affirmed.

They sat in silence, each thinking his own thoughts and nursing their beers to make them last a long time, because they couldn't afford to drink them too fast.

III

Marie sat down at the supper table, all smiles. She felt fine after having taken a quick bath. She'd thrown on her bathrobe over her underthings.

"Sis, I know you got something on tonight," Art said, raising his eyebrows as he gazed across the table at her.

"You ought to, because I told you I had a date," she answered lightly.

"You going out stepping, Sis?" Jim asked her.

Mrs. Carr finished serving and sat down to her own supper. She looked at the empty chair left for Patrick. They all ate. She had made hamburger and fried potatoes and a salad of lettuce and tomatoes. Particularly since Patrick wasn't working, she had to be careful to make ends meet and to save what little she could, but she managed to do it and to have enough food on the table every night. Eating in silence herself, she watched her three children and listened to them. They were good children. If you raised good, decent children, you fulfilled your responsibility to God as a parent. But the one child who should be here, wasn't. Bernard was as different from his two brothers as night from day. If he didn't help to save souls, he'd lead them to damnation. To save his soul, she'd gladly sacrifice her own. Yes, willingly, she'd spend eternity in Hell if she could save her strange son.

"If Pa comes home drunk and makes any fuss or trouble while George is calling for me, I'm going to give him a piece of my mind," Marie declared.

"His cronies will pour him home about midnight, if I don't miss my guess," Art said.

Jim listened in silent displeasure. He wished his father didn't drink, but, after all, his father was his father, and he wouldn't speak against him. If his father were only like Gerry's father, sitting home at night with her mother, looking so kind and wise, never quarreling. He wondered when he would tell them about Gerry. He'd been planning to all week. Tonight, with his father out like this, wouldn't be a good night.

"Where does he get the money to drink?" Marie asked suspiciously, turning to her mother.

"I never give him more than twenty-five or thirty cents. I can't give him the money you children earn if it's going to take food off the table."

"I gave him a dollar this morning," Jim said defensively and with a guilty look on his face.

Art's glance told Jim he was a sap.

"He must have found a sucker," Art said.

"He is your father," Mrs. Carr said to Art in a reprimanding tone.

"Oh, Mother," Marie exclaimed, becoming suddenly resentful of her father. "I don't know anyone, anyone whose father acts like he does."

She shook her head emphatically and looked angrily from one to the other as though to challenge disagreement. Art watched her with amused admiration. Jim busied himself with his food. Mrs. Carr said sadly:

"It isn't for us to judge."

Mrs. Carr watched her daughter. When she had been young, a girl wouldn't have dared talk of her father as Marie did, no matter what the father said or did. Patrick wasn't a good father, and it had always been hard on all of her children because of him. And she so often wanted to be a better mother, but she couldn't talk to her children, tell them things a mother ought to. She had never been able to talk to them, even when they were little. What did they really think? The thoughts of the boy in Bernard's book had troubled her. Whenever she remembered it, she would feel that there was something she ought to do, but she didn't know what.

"You might be better off thinking more of your soul and less of your life," Mrs. Carr said, speaking out of a sense of duty. But she wanted to talk to her daughter, tell her of what had happened when she was young.

"The way I think is that we had a better chance than Dad did," Jim said dully.

No one was interested in him. They went on eating. Marie was happy, satisfied with herself. Her date tonight, her anger against her father, both helped her feel so good. She knew that her own life was going to be different, that she was going to be happier than her parents had been, and she just couldn't feel anything but happy tonight.

IV

Art Carr stood on the southeast corner of Sixty-third Street and Cottage Grove, looking as though he owned the corner. He couldn't think of anything exciting to do tonight. He didn't want to spend anything because he was saving to buy a second-hand jalopy, and he only had thirty-five bucks put by. He could kick his tail around the block for having lost eight bucks playing stud-poker last Sunday. He'd wanted to add a little to his kitty, and so eight bucks went down the drain. When he did get his car, life would be plenty of fun, more exciting than it was now. Then it would be easier to pick up babes, and you could have cheap dates.

"Say, you're Bernie Carr's brother, aren't you?"

The chunky young fellow who had come up to Art and spoken to him seemed familiar, but Art couldn't remember his name.

"I'm Pinky Cullen. I went to school with Bernie."

"Yes, I heard of you."

"I used to think Bernie was a nice guy. But I'd be ashamed of him now if he was my brother. He did a mean thing writing a book like that."

Art nonchalantly lit a cigarette.

"And to think he would do what he did to make money," Pinky went on.

"Listen, Pinky, I don't know you, but I heard Bernie mention your name. I'm not the guy who wrote his book."

"I know," Pinky said, suddenly becoming apologetic. "It's only this . . . seein' you, I remembered who you were—and, you have to admit, don't you?—it was a bad thing to do . . . writing a book like that?"

"It didn't phase me—one way or the other. In fact, I didn't read it."

"Writing a book like that—why, it's like spitting on your mother's dead body!" Pinky said intensely. "And, well, seeing you here on the corner, I had to get this off my chest."

"Oh, that's okay, Pinky—it's always best to get a load off your mind," Art said.

"Well, glad to have seen you, Art," Pinky said curtly, holding out his hand.

"Yeh," Art said, shaking hands with him.

Pinky passed along Sixty-third Street. Art glanced after him, puzzled. Why should Bernie's book have bothered the guy? But then, it wasn't his lookout. Bernie's book just didn't interest him too much. But it did give him an idea about Bernie he'd never had before. Bernie took life too hard. As he remembered Bernie from their kid days, Bernie wasn't exactly like Patrick Stanton in the book, but, damn it, he'd kept thinking that there was something there that Bernie was writing about himself, and that he'd taken life awful damn hard. You would end up a sucker if you took it all too hard and too seriously. Or would Bernie? How would Bernie end up? Come to think of it, Bernie had always seemed to have something on his chest. He had a lot of ambition, and maybe he might become some

kind of a big shot, at that. That would be funny, having a
brother a big shot.

But, more important, when and how would his own ship
come in? He'd gone along for some time now, thinking that
some day, somehow, his ship would come in. But he hadn't
always believed it. Still, sometimes it was consoling to pretend
to believe. And maybe it would. You never could tell. But how
in hell could it? He didn't look for any advancement where he
was. A thirty-five-bucks-a-week payroll clerk at the Austin
Steel Fixtures Company didn't become president of the corporation. Still, he was doing pretty good to be working, and it was
a break to be working for a big company instead of a little one.

He sauntered on, thinking he might get some pickup in Jackson Park.

V

"I haven't laughed so much as I did tonight in one whale
of a long time," Jim Carr said.

"I laughed until my sides almost split," Gerry Murray said.

"I sure got a kick out of that movie tonight. I sure did laugh,"
Jim said.

They were eating waffles in the Circle Restaurant on Clark
Street. It was large and only half-filled. The walls were plastered with prose and verse poems about Idaho baked potatoes
and other foods.

Gerry Murray was tall and thin, with a surly expression on
her bony face. She had high cheekbones, and small, suspicious-
looking dark eyes. Her face opened up in a smile. She enjoyed
her dates with Jim. He was her first steady. Being engaged, she
didn't feel out of the swim, as she used to when she'd go out to
a movie or somewhere with a girl friend. She didn't feel lonely
any more, and she didn't go around being so sensitive, because
now she didn't have to fear she'd become an old maid. How
she used to be hurt if she heard jokes about old maids! Now,
she told jokes like those herself.

"Gee, Gerry, you're a swell kid," Jim said with emotion, as they gazed across the table into each other's eyes.

"Oh, Jim," she exclaimed with gratitude.

It was more wonderful than she could ever find words to describe to know that she had found someone who had asked her to marry him, someone who had said he wanted to live his whole life with her.

"I knew it, too, when I first saw you, Gerry. And then when we got to talking, I knew it twice. Remember? We talked about the White Sox. Well, I found out you liked baseball, and that you were a White Sox fan. And the same way, you like the pictures I like, and we laugh at the same pictures and the same things in the picture."

"I know we'll be happy, Jim," Gerry said.

"The way I see it, Gerry, I earned the right to it, too. Until the day we're married, Gerry, my mother gets my pay check every two weeks. And I haven't missed one day's work in four and a half years. And that day I was out, four and a half years ago, I was so sick with a cold I had a fever over a hundred and I got up to go, and if it wasn't for the way my mother insisted on my not going, and my almost fainting in the bathroom, I would have gone to work."

Gerry beamed at him.

"I sometimes think of you, Jim, almost, almost as if you were my brother."

"And I think that we are, in a way, like a brother and sister, as well as engaged."

Jim thought how he could talk to Gerry in a way he couldn't with anyone else, not even his own mother. Gerry understood his slant on life. That was what was so fine about knowing her. He had always wanted to think that the family was together. He liked that word, together. It meant a lot to him. But then Bernie had walked out, and the family wasn't together, and the rest of them just weren't together the way he wanted them to be. But he and Gerry were, and they always would be. And no matter what happened or what was on his mind to make him worry, he forgot it when he was with Gerry. Like the other night, when he had put his head on her lap and closed his eyes, and she had run her fingers through his hair, it had been like being in Heaven. With Gerry, everything he thought of was important.

"Well, kidlums, no spika da English?" he asked after he had finished the plate of waffles.

She smiled tolerantly across the table.

"That's it," Jim said, as though he were addressing a third person, "she's a dandy girl, a dandy girl, but she no spika da English."

"Sometimes, Jim, you're so funny."

He laughed loudly and coarsely.

"I was wishing, Jim—wishing we didn't have to wait."

His face clamped up. There was his mother. Could he get married with things as they were at home?

Gerry watched him carefully. She couldn't be absolutely sure until they were at the altar. And, oh, she so much wanted to see that day, wanted to prepare for it, with showers for herself, and to talk about it, and count the days, with the fuss of getting her wardrobe together, and making her bridal dress and the fittings, and the thinking about it all, and all the fuss and feeling of importance it gave you. She just knew she wouldn't be able to sleep the night before her wedding.

"I got the dirty end of the stick in my family," Jim said with bitterness.

"It isn't fair to you. It isn't fair to you or me, Jim. The oldest should be the first to be allowed to get married."

"Bernie is my brother, and I'll not say a word against him," Jim said, still bitterly. "I know he's smart—but I'm not proud of him."

"I blushed when I read his book."

"I can say it to you, but I wouldn't say it to anyone else— I'm ashamed of that book. When I see the name of Carr on it . . . I feel like hanging my head. That's the honest-to-God truth, Gerry."

"How can he be so . . . so different from you, and still be your brother?"

"I've thought about it and tried to puzzle out what makes Bernie tick. I can't make it out."

"My girl friend—you met Catherine, Jim—she was shocked. It made her mother's hair stand on end."

"No matter what the others do—I'll never disgrace the name of Carr, and when you take my name, I know you won't, Gerry kid."

She smiled at him meekly.

"We'll do our duty, no matter what anybody does."

"Yes, we will," she said with restraint.

"You're swell, Gerry, honest," he said.

He looked at her tenderly.

"Jim, we can wait a little while," she told him.

Gerry was so fine and pure, he thought. Sometimes, when he thought of their getting married, he didn't want to face it, didn't want the time to come when he would take her purity away from her. Had his father felt this way about Mother before they were married?

"We'll go on saving, Jim, and you know how I feel. . . . You know I'll wait."

He looked at her like a grateful boy. She knew she needn't worry now, with that look on his face. But, oh, she had a right to happiness. She had a right. She would wait a little until they saved enough, but, once they did, then she would have her happiness. She hated that brother of his, Bernard.

"Gosh, it's late," she said suddenly.

"Tomorrow's another workday," Jim said, getting up from the table.

VI

Art let out a big yawn, and the girl beside him sighed softly.

They sat on the bench and didn't hear a sound. Art sniffed, enjoying the smell of the lake in the air. He heard the wind quietly scratching the leaves in the trees. This was his favorite

spot in Jackson Park. In fact, you had to remind yourself that
it was Jackson Park and so close to home. It could even be some
spot not in the United States, not in this world. He didn't go
for moonlight and roses and romance. That kind of falderal
wasn't his style. Still, he did like it here. It was a little better
here than any place else in the park, and safer. The trees were
like guards, standing in the darkness. They were black against
the sky, and they seemed alive as you looked at them.

He let out another yawn. He didn't know what to say to
this tramp beside him. He wanted to get rid of her, but he
wasn't sure as to what was the best way of doing it. He felt a
little bit like a dog, and wanted to go home and take a bath,
and he'd have to get a prophylactic at a drugstore, because you
couldn't trust a tramp like this. Why, he'd hardly had to work
on her. She was a rabbit all right. Still, he'd been pretty damned
potent. Maybe if he gave her a half a buck or so, it might be
the best way to get rid of her. He stretched his legs and looked
up at the black, waving leaves overhead. A damned pretty sight.
How might he feel if he had a babe he was in love with, sitting
here and looking at them? Only what did it mean to be in love?
Would it be any different than it had been with this poor tramp?
Could he get more excited than he'd been, no matter who the
babe was? Could any babe get more excited than she'd been?

"I'm gonna sleep good tonight," the girl said in a husky,
coarse voice.

"What'd you say, babe?" he asked, although he'd heard her.

"I said I was going to sleep good. How do you sleep?"

"Like a rock. The minute I hit the hay, I'm off, sawing
wood."

"That's why I like love. It makes me sleep better. Put your
arms around me."

"Babe, I don't like to admit it, but my oats just ain't right
now."

She giggled. Then she said in an earnest voice:

"I just want to feel I'm cuddling. If you cuddle, you feel near
somebody. Then you don't feel nervous or afraid."

Art was bored, and yet he listened. This babe made him leery, but at the same time he felt kind of sorry for her. She was just a poor tramp. She was husky, all right, and not bad-looking, although he hadn't lamped her clearly in good light.

"It's getting late," he said casually.

"Sit here a minute," she said in a pleading voice.

"All right. But I work for my living."

"I lost my job, and since then, has my old lady been a sourpuss! Even if I was workin', she wouldn't want me to have any fun. She's a worse sourpuss than my father. You'd think neither of them ever was young."

"What kind of work did you do?"

"Me? My last job was a waitress. But I didn't like it none. My feet got tired."

"You don't like being on your feet, huh?"

"Standing on your feet . . . but, say, did you mean that . . . dirty?"

"No, I was kidding. And, after all, babe . . ."

He got up. She stood up and walked beside him, smoothing her hair. He was weary, and his eyelids felt heavy. What kind of a tramp was this babe? And to have her walking at his side meekly, like a trained dog, was annoying. He'd have to shake her.

"Say, isn't it a grand evening?" she remarked, as they walked on along a path.

"Yeh."

"I like it like this at night, soft. It's a kind of a soft night, isn't it?"

Art was only half-listening. He felt dirty. You felt so much better chasing it than afterward.

"Have you got something I can remember you by?"

"What?"

"Anything. A match cover, anything for a keepsake. When I like anybody, I like a keepsake, and then, some night, if I can't sleep and get nervous, I look at my keepsakes, and it makes me feel better."

He handed her a book of matches. They crossed the drive-
way and walked on silently to the park exit at Sixty-third
Street and Stony Island. They stood, not looking at each other.
She seemed so meek and so guilty. He didn't feel right, either.

"You need carfare home or anything?"

"Oh, no."

"Aren't you going to give me your phone number?"

"I haven't any."

"How am I going to see you again?"

"I can buzz you."

"I'm in the same boat. . . . Let's see. . . . How about
meeting me right here . . . at eight o'clock, next Friday
night?"

"I can't . . . not Friday."

"What is it? A steady?"

"No. I just can't say."

"Monday."

"All right."

They stood, still not looking at each other. Then she quickly
and suddenly kissed him and hurried across the street. He
watched her, relieved and yet saddened. There was something
sad about the poor tramp. Hell, she was nice-looking, and built,
really built. He couldn't get it.

He crossed the street and went into a drugstore.

VII

Hearing the handsome saxophone player sing softly was like
being petted and caressed. Oh, if she could only marry someone
like the saxophone player, who could support her in decent style
and hold her in his arms and sing to her, his voice going straight
through her. She'd close her eyes, let her head go back, and let
his lips meet hers, and that would be the beginning of a wonderful life.

"You're suddenly quiet," Charles Ralston said to her as they
were dancing at the Bamboo Inn.

"Oh, don't you like this music, Charles? And he's a divine singer."

"I heard better."

"No matter how good anybody is, there's probably something better."

"You and I look pretty good for my money."

He was a conceited boy. Still, he was a good dancer, and good-looking, and he was fun. She liked his light, curly hair. He was tall and might even be taken by other people here for a college football player. She liked being out with a good-looking boy. Girls looked at you then, sometimes green-eyed with envy.

When the dance ended, she and Charles went to their table. The Bamboo Inn looked tawdry and run-down. There was only a small crowd, and the Chinese waiters stood around looking bored.

"Yes, as I was saying, this depression doesn't cause me any worry, because I'm not a sap. I get enough to have a good time." He became mysterious. "I can't tell you about them, but I've got connections."

A fatuous grin came over his weak but pretty face. Across the table from him, she seemed even prettier. She must go for him, he decided, because of the way she was listening. And then she wasn't pulling away from him on the dance floor.

"You're luscious and gay," he said.

"Oh, Charles, you're just flattering me," she said, enjoying the compliment even though she knew it was an exaggeration. If someone like that saxophone player would only tell her things like this. She tried to imagine that Charles was the saxophone player.

"And what else am I?" she asked.

"What are you?" he asked insinuatingly and with a smirk. Marie felt his knees touching hers under the table.

"Just a working girl," she said.

"You'll go far. If I didn't think so, I wouldn't have dated you."

"Charles, you frighten me. I can't possibly live up to your ideas about me."

"Listen, Marie, let's not kid ourselves. We're okay."

"Are we?"

"Aren't we?"

"I'd like to think we are."

"Well, there's the noise again," he said, as the orchestra began tuning up.

They danced. Marie liked dancing with him better than talking. The orchestra played soft, slow music, and Charles led her slowly around the floor. Moving, feeling him so close to her, feeling her skin tingle and almost losing her breath, she closed her eyes and believed she was something wonderful and alive, and that the music was only for her—that it was talking to her and for her alone. And it meant everything in life that she wanted and didn't have. It meant all there was to know in life that she hadn't found out. Her heart was beating very fast. She was no longer just Marie Carr but the girl she wanted to be, the happy, beautiful person she knew she could become. Her face became softer, prettier, more girlish. She looked over Charles's shoulder, and the other couples were like figures in a dream. And she was twirling in a dream that would never end.

The music stopped. Charles applauded politely.

"Oh!" she exclaimed breathlessly.

"You're some stuff, Marie."

His remark broke the spell.

"Charles, I'm too tired to dance any more."

"Oh, one more."

They left the floor. What had happened? One minute she was in a wonderful world, as if the songs she heard were true. The next, here she was, seeing Bamboo Inn as a dull place, looking around and seeing people like herself wanting to have a good time and looking bored. And Charles was bragging, but she had closed her ears. He was trying to make her think he was tied up with gangsters. As if she cared. Oh, what had happened? She was sad and angry. Was this all she could get out of life?

"What's the matter, Marie?" Charles asked her, leaning across the table, his voice quivering with alarm.

"Nothing's the matter."

"You changed so."

"I'm just tired. I want to go home, Charles."

They left and turned off Sixty-third Street. Neither talked. He was disappointed and kept wondering what had happened, what he had said or done.

"I liked the dancing, Charles. I just got tired. After all, I have to get up at seven-thirty in the morning."

"It's only twelve-thirty."

He took her arm. She walked along, indifferent. She wanted to get home and go to bed. It hurt you to dream, because you woke up sad, as she was now.

When they came to her door, she said nothing as Charles walked into the outer hallway with her. She sensed that something would happen, but she didn't care. She allowed him to kiss her, and she kissed him back. They heard footsteps outside and sprang apart. Marie waited, rigid with fear that it would be one of her brothers or her father. A man passed by. She thought of her independent mood at supper, and of how she had been so frightened just now.

"Charles, good night and thank you for a wonderful time," she said with determination.

He slunk away. She went upstairs quietly, and when she got to her room she sobbed. But she didn't really know why she was crying.

VIII

Patrick Carr opened the front door, plunged through the opening, slammed the door, staggered into the parlor, awkwardly switched on the light, and shouted:

"I am Home, Home Sweet Home, Home," he shouted.

He sang *When You and I Were Young, Maggie.*

"You stop that," Marie yelled, rushing into the parlor in a bathrobe.

"Some day, my lassie," Patrick Carr said, taking off his coat and sitting down. "Some day, my young lassie." He untied one heavy shoe and plumped it down on the floor. "Some day, my young lassie, you won't be as young as you are now." He took off the other shoe and dropped it on the floor with a thud.

He stood in his stocking feet in the center of the parlor. His face was streaked with dirt. Art came into the room in a rage. He whiffed the odor from the stocking feet and made a face of disgust. The father folded his arms and looked with proud defiance from one to the other of his children.

"It's after two o'clock—what the hell's the idea?" Art asked.

"For you I have a riddle," Patrick Carr said, waving his finger at Art. "What is there that a son knows that his father didn't know before him?"

Jim quietly entered the room in his pajamas.

"You have no right to do this. I have to get up and go to work in the morning," Marie said.

"When you were an infant in arms, wetting every diaper put on you, many's the night I lay awake listening to you bawl and howl," Patrick Carr told his daughter. Then he announced theatrically: "I have a piece to speak."

"Father, why not go to bed?" Jim asked.

"What in the name of God and the Blessed Virgin is going on here?" Mrs. Carr asked, coming into the room, her hair matted.

"A conclave of the clan of Carr," Patrick Carr declared ironically. He sat down in his big old chair and made a face at his wife. "I'm now in the bosom of my family . . . the bosom . . ." He made another face. ". . . of a refrigerator."

"Father, the neighbors . . ." Jim began.

"Now, if my educated son was here, he could write a book."

"For crying out loud," Marie shouted at him.

The old man raised his thick brows, pulled off a sock, lifted his trouser leg, and, showing a dirty, bony ankle, he asked his daughter:

"Isn't this as pretty as the ankle on your own limbs?" He

waved an arm in the direction of his daughter and said with
melodramatic, thundering accents: "Take care, you, take care
lest those limbs of yours don't become the limbs of Satan."

"Father, you're disgusting," Marie said, but she was blushing.

"In the name of God, Patrick, go to bed," Mrs. Carr said.

"It's a cold bed I'd be going to, too," he said.

"Listen to me," Art said, stepping forward and tying his
pajamas, which had become loose. "I don't care what you do, so
long as you cut out this crap and let us sleep. See?"

Marie looked gratefully toward Art as he walked out of the
room. She followed him. She felt so very sad.

Patrick Carr spotted *The Father* in the small bookshelf in
the corner.

"The sins of the father," he sneered.

He got the book and held it up for his wife and Jim to see.

He began ripping pages out of the book. Mrs. Carr suddenly
snatched it from his hand. He gazed at her, stunned. Then he
sat in his chair and mumbled.

"Father, you better go to bed," Jim said.

The old man got up and staggered out of the room.

"Go to bed, James," his mother said gently.

Jim kissed his mother and went back to bed.

She sat looking sadly at the book with the torn pages. Then
she got up, turned out the light, and went back to bed. She lay
beside her husband, who reeked of alcohol, snored, and moaned.
She prayed for everyone in her family until she fell asleep.

IX

"Why, Mother, what happened to you?" Marie asked, as she
came into the kitchen.

"I slipped and fell," Mrs. Carr said.

"Mother, he beat you. Where is he? He's a drunken old bum."

"No matter what a parent does, the Commandment of the
Lord says for a child to honor her father," Mrs. Carr said, wearily sitting down at the other end of the kitchen table.

"What honor is he worth? I don't know why my brothers

just don't beat him up, yes, beat him up. He's just a stinking disgrace."

Mrs. Carr's face seemed to melt. She looked softly and tenderly at her daughter.

"Yes, he beat me. He beat me up," she said slowly.

Mrs. Carr turned a sad, beaten, swollen, and discolored face toward her daughter, and looked at her as though to say she wanted to be a loving mother. A few wisps of gray hair fell over her forehead.

Yes, Marie thought, Mother loved her. But she herself was bad. She had been so depressed all day. She was bad. She knelt, put her head in her mother's lap, and sobbed. Mrs. Carr stroked her daughter's hair.

"Always be good, my daughter."

Marie got up, wiped her eyes, and then kissed her mother.

"People looked at me in the street," Mrs. Carr said. After a pause, she continued, "I held my head high. The opinions of this world are not important. Marie, you are a girl. When you're my age, you might know this the way I know it."

"Mother, I'm sorry," Marie said, deeply moved, not fully knowing what she was sorry for.

She remembered how, after she had gotten over the fright of the curse the first time she had it, she'd thought that if she hadn't been born, maybe her mother's life would be easier. She'd imagined that somehow she and her brothers had done something to Mother, and that in some way they had caused her mother to sin.

"I'm going to write Bernard," Marie said, suddenly wishing Bernard were there and could explain something to her, because there was something she wanted to know very, very much. She was surprised that she was thinking of Bernard in this way.

Jim came home. Marie told him what had happened. With his hat still on, he turned helplessly toward the wall and exclaimed:

"I'm ashamed. I couldn't face the world if it knew that my father . . . my father . . ."

Marie asked herself why she thought of Jim as being like her father. Jim didn't drink, and when he got married he'd never beat his wife. But when she was little he'd wanted to see her and finger her. But maybe all brothers, all men, were like that. Perhaps she hated men. Oh, she knew now that she wanted to get out of this house. She wished she had never been born a Carr. She looked at her mother guiltily and took back her wish.

Mrs. Carr began to prepare supper.

Art came in, smiling cheerfully, and when they told him, he said:

"If I'd been here, I'd have clipped him. Where is he?"

"Don't you hear him snoring?" asked Marie.

"I'll take care of him," Art said curtly, turning to leave the kitchen.

"Arthur!" his mother said in a commanding voice. "Don't you lay a hand on your father."

Art dropped into a chair meekly.

"Mother, let me help you fix dinner," Marie said.

"Goddamn it!" Jim said angrily.

"I feel the same way," Art snapped.

"For my sake, forgive your father," Mrs. Carr said, turning from the stove.

X

Jim, Art, and Marie sat in the parlor.

"What in hell kind of a family are we?" Marie asked.

"Just a happy family," Art said sarcastically.

"I don't know what to say," Jim said.

"Don't say it then," Art said.

"I'd never let any man get away with that on me," Marie said, walking about the room nervously.

"You'll always be able to take care of yourself, kid," Art said.

Art rubbed his chin and sank back in his chair and seemed to be thinking. Marie looked worried. Jim wished his father hadn't done this awful thing. What would Gerry think? Would she break off the engagement? If Bernie had done his duty, he could be married now, and he wouldn't be in this fix. He was the one who was put behind the eight ball. And think of it. Last night he had kissed Gerry good night and come home seeing the world through rose-colored glasses, thinking he was going to tell everyone and fix it up for Gerry to meet the family. Now, how could he? How could he marry and leave home? Art and Marie couldn't carry the load, and he couldn't bring Gerry to live here. He had nothing against his father, only he wished his father were a man like Mr. Murray. He could take Mother to live with Gerry and him, and they could be very happy. Gerry would go for his mother. But where would his father go? And how long would it go on like this? Yes, Bernie should have stayed home and shouldered some of the burden.

"Let's stop acting like it was a wake," Art said.

Patrick Carr entered the parlor, quickly filling the room with the odor of his feet and of alcohol. His face was dirty and purplish. He blinked and rubbed his eyes, sat down in his chair, and said:

"I never saw my children look so solemn."

He wiggled his big toe through a hole in his sock.

"Like the rest of the world, I suppose they condemn their old father," he went on. "They're supporting themselves now, grown men and women. And, mind you, one of them is a genius, a genius."

The father farted.

"Father, you're vulgar. I despise you!" Marie shouted.

"Well, here I am. Tell me I'm no good. Tell me what you think of me. Tell me I'm an old drunken sonofabitch," Patrick Carr said with a surly whine in his voice. "Maybe you'd all like me to go to sleep and never wake up," he complained.

"Who said that?" Art asked.

"Maybe I should be condemned. But there's two sides to every story," Patrick Carr said melodramatically.

Art was afraid of what he might do. And this man who looked like a West Madison Street drunken bum was his father. Yes, there sat his father. Look at him, weak and gray-haired, feeling sorry for himself, nothing but a goddamn mess. And he had once feared him!

"Listen," Art said angrily. "If you ever hit my mother again, I'm going to bust your drunken face."

Jim and Marie were shocked.

"Bejesus, he's man enough to lick his father," Patrick Carr said, rising in comic majesty.

"Sit down before I knock you down!"

"Art!" Marie shouted.

"Don't do it, Art," Jim cried frantically.

Mrs. Carr appeared.

"God will never forgive a boy who hits his father, Arthur," she said.

They all looked at her. Art's lips trembled.

"If your writing brother was here now, he'd write the Carr Declaration of Independence from your father for the whole shebang of you," Patrick Carr said weakly.

He staggered out of the room like a beaten man.

XI

He couldn't face her. He sat on the bed in his dirty pajamas, his head lowered, his gray hair standing up like bristles, and he rubbed his hands across his stiff hard whiskers. Then he looked with sad watery blue eyes at the picture of the Bleeding, Sacred Heart of Jesus on the Wall. He hadn't wanted to hit her. The drink had taken hold of him. He would let the children know that he didn't even know that he'd struck their mother. But she'd wanted to be struck. How did he know she wanted to be struck? He didn't know. He had had this thought, standing drunkenly in the kitchen, seeing her standing there, not saying anything, looking at him, and it seemed to him that she had wanted him to hit her. By God, he was right, too!

He dropped back on the rumpled bed with a sigh and felt his aching forehead. He groaned, closed his eyes, and turned his face down into the pillow as he rolled over onto his belly. Yesterday he had felt like a king, like a king afraid of neither man nor woman nor beast. He'd felt like a king when he'd hit her. Oh, he'd gone wild with anger. The drink had taken hold of him.

He slept for about a half hour and woke up with a splitting headache and a terrible fright. He'd been dreaming that he was dying. He looked with bloodshot eyes at the yellow ceiling and asked God for mercy and forgiveness. Slowly getting out of bed, he found his slippers on the floor, put them on, and padded out to the kitchen.

"Do you want your breakfast?" she asked him, as though nothing had happened yesterday.

Seeing her bruised, discolored face, he was overcome with remorse.

"Just a cup of black coffee."

She brought him coffee.

"Woman, I'm sorry. Something came over me with the drink."

She almost broke, and he knew it.

"I humbly ask your pardon and forgiveness," he said melodramatically.

"It's not for me but for God to forgive, Patrick."

He lifted the cup of coffee, drank, made another face, set the cup down, and rested his elbows on the table. Through the kitchen door he blearily saw the back porch, old, dark gray, splintery, and swept clean. Beyond the porch railing, a piece of grass, the backyard fence, the green of a yard across the alley, the back porches and the old grayed brick of the three-story building on the other side of the alley, and a patch of the blue spring sky. He remembered the time when he'd been young and had thought of the day when he and Mary would be old and happy and respected, with their family grown, owning their own home. And here he was, an old man now, and thinking that he wouldn't be living long. He knew he wasn't a well man. Slowly he finished his coffee and staggered back to his room, pitched into bed, and lay there, trembling at the thought of his own death. A cold sweat broke out all over him.

"Mary," he called in fear.

She hurried into the room.

"I'm sick. I'm cold. Put a blanket over me."

She got a blanket and carefully covered him.

"Take care of me, Mary," he whined.

"I will."

"Forgive me, Mary," he pleaded.

"I do, Patrick," she said softly, laying her hand on his sweating, aching head.

Chapter Eleven

I

ELIZABETH was waiting for Bernard to come home and hoping this would be the time he'd have good news. She'd just finished reading a rental-library love story. By reading it, she was able to help Bernard. And the book had helped make the time pass for her. It had carried her thoughts away from this basement. She knew that she was imagining and that she couldn't be the girl in the book, because you knew a dream was only a dream and not real life. But she hadn't wanted the book to end, because the descriptions of hotels, and parties, and yachts, and gambling, with the women wearing evening gowns and the men dancing attention on them, had thrilled her. But she had finished the book, and she wasn't a rich society girl dancing in a whirl at Palm Beach.

Bernard came in, moody and depressed. He checked himself as he was about to ask her if anything had happened, kissed her perfunctorily, and sat down at the table. She asked him what was new and proudly told him that she'd finished the book from Lisa Baranov.

"I might get a job at twenty-two bucks a week with a new company that's opening up a chain of low-priced food places. It's called the New Era Food Stations, Incorporated."

"Oh, you poor thing," she said.

"There are men who'd murder for such a job in these days," he answered dully.

"But can't you make more just freelancing and doing book reviews, especially now since I can help you by reading the books Mrs. Baranov gives you for movie synopses?"

"Brady's the only one who'll give me a decent chance to review. I can get a book a week most weeks from him, and that will give me twelve-fifty to fifteen a week. Possibly I can get a book a week from Mrs. Baranov, and that's five more a week. But we'll be better off if I can land this job and do some reviews on the side."

"But what about your own book, Bernard?"

"I'll write it. Don't worry. Honey, we've been living here on false hopes. You just don't come to New York and get rich overnight. It might be years before I can make a decent living writing. I can't indulge in pipe dreams or bang my head against stone walls."

"Bernard, if Mildred Feldman can get a job, I can."

"Elizabeth, you won't be able to work long."

"Oh, but I don't show. It isn't quite three months yet."

"I'll take this job if I can get it."

He sat at the table, dispirited.

"Do you want me to tell you about the book so you can do the synopsis now?"

"Let me skim through it first," he said, picking it up and opening it.

He looked at it for a moment and slapped it down on the table with a sigh.

"I don't know why such tripe must be published."

"But, Bernard, some people forget their troubles for a little while when they read a book like this. It doesn't do any real harm, does it?"

Bernard looked up again. He wondered if there really were any conclusive and convincing answer to her question.

II

Bernard, Bill Barclay, and Arthur Hampton were talking together by the bookshelves in a corner of the Barclay living room, while their three wives sat across the room on the sofa. The furniture was good and had been selected carefully and with taste. Bill Barclay was a tall man of about thirty-five, with a lined and weak but kindly face. There was an expression of sad accusation in his eyes, and he spoke in a slow, dull manner.

"Now that my position as a book reviewer and critic is secure, the next step in my career is to publish an article. I can place one in *The Elite*, and I've found a subject. I'm going to do an article on Christian Science."

Art Hampton said it was a good idea.

"I didn't know you were interested in Christian Science," Bernard said.

"I'm not particularly interested in it," Bill declared.

"Then why bother to write about it?"

"I just explained that."

"I'd tackle it, Bill. It's time now for you to do an article," Art said.

"Why do the article if you aren't really interested in the subject?"

"Oh, I didn't make myself clear. I have the interest that any civilized man has in a subject like Christian Science. I'll read up on it, consider both sides, and then I'll do the essay."

"You're merely picking a subject out of a grab bag."

"*The Elite* has never published an essay on Christian Science."

"Do you believe in it?" Bernard asked. "Or do you think it's false and dangerous?" Bernard asked.

"Oh, like any other religion, it's an organization of nonsense," Bill answered.

"Does it pose any particular problem for you?"

"I'd have to read more about it before I could answer that question."

"Mary Baker Eddy was one of the classic paranoiacs in history. She was serious. Her serious delusions deserve serious annihilation."

"You take everything awfully hard, Bernie, don't you?" Art said paternally.

"What about book reviews? Don't you take what you get?" Bill asked.

"Yes, but if the book's no good, I attack it."

Art Hampton grinned at him genially.

"That's something else I wanted to talk about with you, Art."

Bernard understood now that Bill was seeking Art's opinion, not his, and that what Bill really wanted was assurance. Was it that Bill didn't value his mind, or that Bill was afraid that he wouldn't get from Bernard the assurance for which he was looking?

"Don't you think, Art, that in reviewing a book for *Lit.*, you have to be guided by relative considerations? Let me give you an example of what I mean. Now, when I was reviewing Duffy's *Defeated Laughter*—"

"Sherman Scott's white-haired boy," Art interrupted.

"It should have been titled, *Cry, Clown, Cry,*" Bernard said curtly.

"He's a rival of yours," Bill said. "But, as I was saying," he continued before Bernard could talk, "I had definite criticisms I wanted to make, but if you compare the book with most of the novels praised in *Lit.*, it's good, sincere, and promising. That's one of the reasons I praised it more than I would have if I'd judged the book according to ideal standards."

"That's a nursemaid's theory of book reviewing," Bernard snorted.

"But what would you say if Art and I imposed the harshest standards on your own work?"

"I've never asked anyone to like or coddle my writing," Bernard answered.

"Bernard," Frances said, coming over and interrupting the conversation, "whenever I've seen you socially, you've always gathered the men together in a corner for serious talk. Don't you like women?"

Bernard was too flustered to answer.

She led the men across the room. They sat down, but no one spoke for several moments.

Bill sadly watched Bernard. He liked him, yet Bernard's sharpness had hurt him. After all, he had praised Carr's book and given him a push. He feared for Carr's own sake. An intolerant spirit and art were incompatible.

"You boys act like husbands in Kokomo, Indiana," Frances said.

"We were discussing a writer named Duffy. Henry James would have written like him, except for the fact that Henry James at least knew how to write," Bernard said.

"What's your favorite novel?" Frances asked.

"*The Red and the Black,*" Bernard said without thinking about the question.

"Why? Do you compare yourself with Julian Sorel?" Frances asked.

"Julian was probably smarter and more sensitive than I. But he should have fought to the last ditch."

"Except that he was worn down. His speech to the jurors," Frances said thoughtfully. "Do you remember it, how he says that he, a poor peasant boy, can expect no mercy or justice from these rich people? And the way he speaks of Napoleon. 'How can we poor wretches get anywhere now that the great Napoleon is gone?' It goes something like that."

"Yes, I liked it. But Julian somewhere says or thinks—he'll wear the uniform of his generation . . . That was his mistake. I won't wear the uniform of my generation."

Frances Barclay didn't like what she thought she saw in Bernard's eyes.

Elizabeth listened as though she understood every word. She was proud to think that her Bernard seemed to be making a good impression. She formed her lips at him in a kiss.

"Fran, don't you think we ought to have the sandwiches and coffee now?" Bill suggested.

"Oh, let me help you fix them," Elizabeth said.

III

The office of *Mass Action* looked like a barn. The dirty, yellow walls were plastered with slogans, posters, pictures, and covers of past issues of the magazine.

When Bernard entered, Elizabeth, along with several other
girls, was bent over a long table by the wall, wrapping and sealing copies of the latest issue. A group were seated in Jan's office
to the left of the entrance. Sophie rushed up to Bernard with a
wide grin on her face and told him that Elizabeth was doing
swell work helping to get out the new issue, and that the new
issue was swell. She handed him a copy. Under the blocked
letters on the cover there was a bold drawing of parading
workers; they had powerful hands and arms, foreshortened
torsos, and broad, Slavic faces with prognathous jaws. The
workers in the lead of the group carried aloft the slogans:
DEFEND THE SOVIET UNION and DOWN WITH WAR. Bernard
thought the cover was ugly; none of the figures in the parade
was individualized.

Sophie called Elizabeth and left Bernard. Looking up, Elizabeth smiled and came over to him. Her face was smudged, and
her hands were dirty. The three other girls stared sullenly at
Elizabeth. They were all homely.

Bernard kissed her on the forehead:

"I got the job with New Era, honey."

She made a long face.

"We'll have minimum security now, dear. . . . Did my
story *Someday* come back in the mail?"

"No mail came . . . and oh, Bernard, I've been working
hard." She lowered her voice. "These girls were just so in-
efficient, but I got them working together. But, gosh, I must
look a mess."

Sophie rejoined them and said enthusiastically:

"Oh, Bernard, you should have seen the way your wife organ-
ized those kids. Say, she'd be a swell organizer. There's a writers'
meeting in Jan's office. Go on in. Jan's going to the Soviet
Union."

"Wonderful. Some day . . ."

"But first I want you to meet the kids," Sophie interrupted.
She introduced him as Bernard to the girls, Rachel, Mildred,

and Susan. The girls mumbled acknowledgments and went on working.

"Bernard, will you wait till I finish here? It won't be long."

As he turned to go into Jan's office, David Bergman, a tall, fat, gross young fellow, asked:

"Is this Carr another *schmendrick*?"

"I met him—a *nebbich*," a squat, bushy-browed fellow said.

"He's just *luftmensch*," a little fellow added, expressing his contemptuous attitude toward Bernard by gesturing with his hands and shoulders and making comic faces.

Some of them laughed.

Bernard joined them nonchalantly, looked them all over, shook hands casually with Jan, and congratulated him on the news about his getting to Russia. Some of the others frowned. Bernard was introduced all around, sat down, and lit a cigarette.

"We've just finished a meeting and were *schmoosing*," Jan said. "In August, Lloyd Street is going to take over."

Bernard looked at Street. He was medium-sized, light-haired, and chubby. He met Bernard's glance impassively.

"I hope the literary section will be developed," Bernard said.

"We've got to write for the workers and poor farmers. We'll have a firm orientation," Street said, speaking with sincerity and emotion.

David Bergman sat back in his chair, folded his arms ostentatiously, smirked, and said smugly:

"It's about time we clarified the whole question of the orientation of *Mass Action* . . . the face of *Mass Action* to the workers, not to the intellectuals."

"Street and I talked with Mortimer on the Ninth Floor. He agrees with us, doesn't he, Lloyd?" David Bergman went on.

"Right along, I worked for that slant," Jan said nervously and defensively.

No one spoke for a moment. Bernard sensed suspicion among them and decided to think a moment before he said anything.

David Bergman leaned back in his chair, folded his arms again, and asked:

"Why can't one of our writers do a story or a novel about an American *apparatchik*?"

Bernard felt definitely out of place. He didn't even know what an *apparatchik* was, and he didn't want to ask any questions for fear of showing his ignorance.

"Mortimer has been saying that our writers ought to use our leaders as literary heroes," David Bergman went on. "I'd say that for anyone—that is, of course, anyone who is conscious—there is no other life in these times, no other life but the life of an *apparatchik*."

Street seemed to be very concerned. He kept staring at the floor.

"It's the poetry of action," he said suddenly, as though he were speaking to convince himself of something.

Dave Bergman then went on to elaborate on why it was necessary to produce a great proletarian novel about a Party functionary. Bernard tried to listen, but his thoughts wandered against his will. Idly glancing around, he noticed the picture of Lenin hanging behind Jan's desk. Lenin's eyes seemed sharp and piercing, and his face was strong. Offices like this must have been very familiar to Lenin. The problems of money, of volunteer help, of getting out publications under difficulties—all of this must have been part of his own daily experience in years of exile. If anyone had gone to one of the little offices where Lenin had edited a revolutionary paper, would he have known that history was being made there?

But these boys weren't Lenins.

"This whole civilization is doomed," Street said, waving his arms. "This culture is doomed with it. Action or doom is the issue today, and culture must be action."

"Writing is a form of action," Bernard said.

"What do you mean, writing is action?" Street asked Bernard aggressively.

"It expresses ideas, emotions. It fixes ideals and aims, doesn't it?"

"We've outgrown that," proclaimed the little fellow. "Art is a weapon. It has to go off like a gun."

"Can you throw a book at the class enemy on the barricades?" a thin, mild-looking young fellow asked.

"Just a minute," Street said to the others, and then, turning to Bernard, he almost commanded: "Go ahead."

"Writing can affect people's lives. It can move them. It can be remembered and can live for decades and centuries. You have to think before you act, and you have to feel, too. Even talk like this is a form of action. Even our dreams are a form of action," Bernard said.

"What are you writing now, Carr?" Street asked.

"A love story."

Dave Bergman sat back smugly in his chair, his big head cocked.

"I say that it's about time writers stopped deluding themselves, deluding themselves with the idea that they're superior beings, above the battle," Dave Bergman said with finality.

"If you got to write," a little fellow said, "write about the coal mines, the way workers work, their great proletarian heart."

"And the dirt farmers," added Lloyd.

"And the hunger marchers, the unemployed with their bellies pinched."

"What do you say, Carr?" Street asked.

"What should I say?" asked Bernard.

"Are you with us?"

"I'm not against you politically, but as a writer I'll go my own way."

"In ten years, writers like you will be forgotten," Street told him.

"I'm not afraid of oblivion," Bernard said quietly. He got up and added, "I have to go home now and work."

IV

"You can see how Jan Walters deviates and makes concessions when you listen to Carr talk," the bushy-browed fellow said.

"A scribbler. He's not one of us," Dave Bergman said contemptuously.

They were sitting in a cafeteria.

"If he's a real writer, it's going to be tough for him in this doomed system. He wants to be free—when freedom is an illusion," Street declared, holding his coffee cup before him. "If he is a sensitive writer, he'll have to come to us or else his dreams will be crushed mercilessly. My college dreams of being a free artist would have been mangled if I hadn't found the Party."

"Lloyd, you and I can do a little modest boasting. We broke with the bourgeois world before the depression. History didn't have to knock us on the head with a club and steal our wallets in order for us to see the logic of events. Now, fellow travelers from the intelligentsia are going to come a dime a dozen. It's good. They'll have their use, but they can never be trusted," Dave Bergman said.

"Before the Wall Street crash, I was an unconscious revolutionary," Katz said.

Bergman looked sharply at him and thought:

—You sonofabitch, you're still unconscious.

Bergman rose and went to the counter and came back with a second piece of pie.

"Bergman, you couldn't pose for a picture of a lean and hungry worker with a pinched belly."

"Comrades," Dave said, holding out a finger, grinning fatuously, cocking his head to one side, "comrades, Communism stands for guess what? Communism stands for the full life, the good life, the rich life, the life of strenuous joy. Comrades, when we make a Soviet America there'll be more and more chickens in every pot and more chickens in every bed. Comrades, there will be more food, more fun, more diddling, and more of the bourgeoisie in the graveyards. Comrades, long live Communist diddling."

Some of them laughed.

"Say, I was thinking . . ." Dave Bergman cut in, "I was thinking—what dopes Americans are. You know, outside of ourselves and a few intelligent capitalists, a few intelligent people in the summits of the bourgeoisie, there isn't anybody in America who knows the score." He rapped the table sharply. "Politically speaking, most Americans don't know their ass from a hole in the ground."

"I was talking to Jackson. He's worrying about the German situation. I told him, the men in the Kremlin, our leadership and our comrades in the Kremlin, they're smart. They won't miss the German chance," Lloyd said.

"When we win Germany, Europe is ours," Dave boasted. "Think of it, comrades, a *bloc* of the Soviet Union and Germany. Why, before the American bourgeoisie wakes up, Europe will be ours, and then it will be too late for them."

A dream lit up their faces. Their eyes shone.

"The one thing never to do is to doubt. The intellectuals doubt. We—we must act," Street said insistently.

They talked on, but Lloyd Street didn't listen. He was thinking about Carr. Was Carr really confident and convinced about art, or was he a poseur? He remembered his own days at college, six or seven years ago, when he had talked about poetry all night in bull sessions, and had walked alone by the Hudson River on misty nights, looking at the water and at the Jersey shore, reciting poems, thinking of his future. And one day he had given it all up. Did this fellow Carr dream as he had?

The memories of his abandoned dreams abashed him. He wanted to apologize to himself for them. He had been young, naive, confused, adolescent. He had imagined that you could find certainty in art. Now he knew better.

He looked around the cafeteria and then he stared at the others, comrades of his . . . comrades . . . and yet he didn't really know them and they didn't really know him. He felt no warmth for them. They, like himself, were but instruments, instruments of the terrible and glorious purpose of the Revolution and the future. He knew that he had chosen the right course. He was right and sane in the terrible future awaiting mankind. Carr was wrong, all of the Carrs of America and of the world were wrong. He looked at his comrades with bright, fanatic eyes. They were discussing petit-bourgeois skepticism.

"In a time like this," he said intensely, "only cowards will doubt. Skepticism is moral cowardice."

v

After they came out of the movie on Fourteenth Street and had a soda, they all strolled slowly over to Fifth Avenue and then on down to Washington Square.

Bernard and Abe walked together, and Elizabeth and Florence tagged behind. Abe Ratunsky was big, dour, and silent. He had a moon face and soft eyes. He seemed to be more interested in his cigar than in Bernard. Bernard couldn't think of anything to say to Abe and relapsed into his own thoughts. Their two wives were chattering away behind them, and now and then they would laugh. Bernard liked Florence's clear laugh. She was a dumpy, clean-looking girl with fine texture to her tawny skin, a frank, round face, large dark eyes, and thick lips with faintly noticeable traces of down on the upper lip. They'd all met at Sophie's and had quickly become friendly. Bernard didn't know exactly why. He liked them, but he closed up in their presence. He believed they were in love and very happy. They seemed happier than Elizabeth and he.

He thought how most lives were directionless. Abe and Florence led directionless lives. Yet, how much worse to have direction. One couldn't relax easily. He wasn't relaxed. He had paid for relaxing at the movies tonight with self-condemnation. A double feature full of false emotions. Wasn't there something weak in you when you needed daydreams and reveries full of false emotions? Art should rouse true emotions in you. He should have said this at *Mass Action* this afternoon.

Florence and Elizabeth were following along slowly, noticing the clothes on the women they saw.

"Even with times as they are, I'd have a baby at the drop of a hat if Abe wanted one," Florence said. "Abe says he doesn't want to be responsible for bringing a human being into this lousy world."

"I got caught, but, Florence . . . you know, I'm sometimes glad. Do you believe me? I am."

"Of course, I believe you."

"I think Bernard will be a good father, too . . . don t you, Florence?"

"Certainly. . . . And Abe would be a wonderful father. He's really too sensitive. He keeps talking about the imperialist war and says we'll all be killed in it."

"Florence, do you really think there's going to be a war?"

"Don't you?"

"I just can't imagine people being so foolish. Why should they want a war? I don't want a war, do you?"

"No," Florence said bitterly and with fear in her voice. "But there's no way out for the capitalists but war. Oh, God, Elizabeth," Florence became emotional. "God, they're building, they're building in the Soviet Union, and that's what the capitalists will destroy. It will be like ripping babies out of a womb. It'll be ripping the future right out of the womb of humanity."

They sat on a bench near the arch in Washington Square, the wives at one end, and Bernard and Abe at the other.

Bernard stretched out his legs and thought how strange it was that he should be writing a book about himself and Eva. Florence and Eva came from the same background. Could there be anything of Eva in Florence? No, they were different.

"Abe," Florence called. "Let's stay out late and not go to work tomorrow."

"Why?" he asked, a trifle annoyed at having had his thoughts interrupted.

"I want to feel free."

"Oh, let's stay up all night," Elizabeth said eagerly.

Bernard shared this desire. Next week, a real grind would begin at the hamburger stand. To be able to stay up all night and sit, talk, dream, do nothing, would give him a feeling of freedom.

"All right," Abe said reluctantly.

Elizabeth clapped her hands and said:

"It'll be fun."

"Hey," Florence called out to Abe in a husky voice, "why don't you come up and see me sometime?"

"You don't look like Mae West to me," Abe said.

"She's a *shicksa*," Florence said.

Florence started singing, *I'll Be Glad When You're Dead, You Rascal, You,* and Abe joined in. Then he sang it alone.

"Don't you love that song?" Florence asked Elizabeth.

"You better. If you don't like Louis Armstrong, and if you don't think that Mae West is *zoftic*, you're no friend of mine," Abe said.

"Bernard, you're so quiet tonight," Florence said.

"I liked the song," he said.

"Oh, let's sing some more," Elizabeth said.

Abe, Florence, and Elizabeth sang. Bernard listened moodily.

"Sing *I'll Be Glad When You're Dead* again," he said.

Florence and Abe sang it with enthusiasm. To Bernard it was singularly disturbing.

"I like its frankness. It's our favorite song, isn't it, Abe?"

"It's about the only thing we agree on—that's why we're so happily married."

"Elizabeth, he is really nice, even if he is so sour," Florence said.

The girls teased Abe about being nice. Abe was annoyed. Then they all were quiet. Bernard wondered what Eva might be doing at this moment. Did she ever think of him? Had she read *The Father*? She'd broken with him in order to save him the kind of struggle he was now facing. How would she feel if she knew? He sat up, startled as he asked himself if she had really lacked confidence in his ability to struggle through if he were saddled. Somehow he believed this was true. He gazed off at the trees.

"Abe and I can't decide about using our savings for a trip to Russia," Florence said.

"We might be on the breadlines when we come back," he said.

"We could probably get work in the Soviet Union. I'd work in Russia. It would mean something there."

"They wouldn't welcome a salesman," Abe remarked with bitterness.

"Abe, you know your father was a poor immigrant when he came here. And the Party might help us, even if we are only fellow-travelers."

"Why don't you go to Russia?" Elizabeth asked. "Bernard and I are going to travel some day . . . aren't we, Bernard?"

"Yes," he said.

Travel was one more of the sacrifices he'd have to make. How would he ever get to Europe, to Paris, to Moscow? He'd stopped dreaming of travel.

"It isn't merely the idea of traveling that appeals to me. It's going where there's hope," Florence said.

"I had hopes I'd be a big shot when I went to college six years ago. Hopes!" Abe said.

"To have hopes, and to do something," Florence went on.

"But, Florence, you're getting along nicely, aren't you?" Elizabeth asked.

"But what's that? I'm a secretary for a capitalist. What am I doing? You're doing something. You're having a child. How wonderful that can be. You can bring him up decently, to be a revolutionist—that's doing something. Oh, I know the Party may be stupid sometimes, but it's made a beginning. A number of the people in the Party have children—even Party leaders. They can be trained to be fighters from the beginning instead of being raised as petit bourgeois the way we were. Elizabeth, you and Bernard, you can train your child. Why, that's wonderful. Just think, you may be walking around with the American Lenin inside of you."

"I was looking at the stars—isn't it a wonderful night?" Elizabeth said in sudden joy.

VI

"When I see Elizabeth, it makes me think of when I was a girl. She's such a girl, Abe, dear," Florence said, clasping Abe's hand, as they walked along Fourteenth Street toward Union Square.

"Yes."

"At first I thought it was a strange marriage, but now I think they're in love. It's nice to see people in love, darling."

"Yes."

"Oh, you're just a moody boy again, Abe darling."

"I'm sleepy."

"There were times tonight when I wanted to cry. Abe, dear, I wish we could have a child."

"So do I. But to bring a child into a world like this. . . ."

"Yes. If only we had Socialism, it would be easy. Abe, dear, think how wonderful it will be some day for women to have free and healthy children in a free world with a planned economy."

"The Soviet Union can't be quite as idyllic as some of the comrades say," Abe said with a yawn.

"I know it can't. I know it, darling. But they're making something. And over here we're making nothing. That's why I wanted to cry. These two kids, having a child. It's brave. In a way, it's wonderful, and yet it's so sad."

"He has a chance to write," Abe said.

Florence just squeezed his hand.

"I know why I like to see them. Because we're happy, and when you are happy yourself, you are happy if you see other people happy."

"Yes, except that if you wrote that in a composition in college you'd flunk," he said.

"You devil, I love you," she said, looking at him with bright, shining eyes. "Abe, I want to start trying. You've got to say yes, for me, for the world."

He looked at her uneasily. She dug her nails into his hands.

"I don't want to live merely for myself."

"All right," he said.

She smiled and cuddled against him.

"Tonight," she said softly, "you're really going to come up and see me?"

"Hm!"

"And you won't think of Mae West, either."

She looked up at him with burning but tender eyes.

VII

Bernard and Elizabeth strolled slowly toward Seventh Avenue. Fourteenth Street was deserted. Across the street a man was sleeping in a doorway.

"Do you think Florence and Abe are happy?" Elizabeth asked.

"Don't you?"

"Do you think they're as happy as we are?"

"How do you measure happiness?" he asked.

There was a gray vaporishness in the air. The moon was out, clear and bright. New York was so still. Its millions were asleep. All these lives. Yes, directionless lives. How many of these strangers could he ever touch, understand, describe? New York was still strange to him. And at this moment it was like something new. He wanted to feel the night more intensely. He squeezed Elizabeth's arm. He was making a fresh start now. But he was full of yearnings, and he knew that it was too late for him to yearn.

"Do you remember nights like this in Chicago—the time we went over on the rocks by the lake? It was in August, 1928," Bernard said.

"You kissed me . . . and I was afraid."

"Elizabeth, sing *I'll Take You Home Again, Kathleen*."

She sang in a low, soft voice. He listened, holding her arm, looking ahead at the wide deserted street, and at the sky and the moon, and he thought of his mother.

"Sing it again."

She did. His mother was a poor faded woman. Eva must be

fading a little now. And Elizabeth would fade one day. All life would fade.

I'll take you to your home again . . .

He had no real home in this world, and he never would have one. He wasn't sure that he even wished for a home in the world. It was best, perhaps, to be a child of restless change, and to find your own direction.

"There," she said, finishing the song. "It's a sad song, Bernard. And you are a sad person, aren't you?"

"No, not particularly."

"Yes, I think you are."

Possibly he was. Yet the sadness he felt now was sweet.

"Tell me, Bernard, about Eva," Elizabeth asked disingenuously as they turned the corner at Seventh Avenue.

"What's there to tell?" he answered, making an effort to be casual.

"Oh," Elizabeth said, "just tell me."

"But I told you," he said with a note of irritation in his voice. "I had an affair with her. It broke up. I don't know what happened to her."

"But you never really told me much about her," Elizabeth persisted.

"There's nothing much to say. After all, you went out on dates, didn't you, before I met you?" He sounded stupid to himself.

"But I merely went out with them," she grinned.

They said no more until they got home. Then, as they were undressing, she teased:

"My darling boy, Bernard, he doesn't want to talk about Eva."

"That's not so."

She looked at him meekly and asked:

"Why are you writing a book about her?"

"I have to write about something, don't I?"

He glanced aside in order to escape her prying eyes.

"Was she lovely, Bernard?"

"You have no reason to be jealous."

"But, Bernard, did I say anything about jealousy?"

"No, but you seemed to convey the idea that you're jealous."

"I am jealous in a way. I'm jealous of any girl who ever knew you."

"Isn't that irrational?"

"I'm afraid you still really love her, Bernard," Elizabeth said.

"A lot of good it would do me."

"There, there," she quickly accused. "There, I knew it."

"What did I say?" he asked.

"You didn't deny it," she added.

"I didn't deny what?"

"That you love Eva. She knew you before I did."

Bernard faced her with mixed sympathy and resentment.

"Tell me, tell me," she said with a frantic tone, "tell me you love me more than Eva."

"Yes," he answered, smothering his resentment but aware that his sympathy for Elizabeth had suddenly vanished.

They finished undressing. Elizabeth went to bed, and Bernard sat at his desk.

VIII

"I slept so well," Elizabeth said joyfully.

"So did I."

"And your breakfast is all ready."

He nodded drowsily.

"But you don't even say anything," she said.

"But I am grateful," he said without enthusiasm. "I'm not quite awake."

She looked so young and alive, but yet she somehow seemed to be made up especially for him. She'd combed her hair neatly, and her face was washed and powdered and rouged. Momentarily he entertained the queer suspicion that she was many different Elizabeths, a series of different faces and personalities. And he thought of the strange and triumphant dream he'd been having when he woke up.

"Tell me how I look."

"Nice."

"Nice? Do I just look—nice?"

"You know what I meant—you're pretty," he said, frowning, unable to bring himself to use the word beautiful.

He'd vaguely dreamed of war, and of Tolstoy, and that he had been doggedly moving up a small hill, flinging statues of himself at people who were grinning stupidly. He'd picked up and thrown one statue of himself that looked like Napoleon and it had broken into numberless pieces. What wish did this express? The wish to be free? The will to be a conqueror? No, it must mean the wish merely to be himself.

He got out of bed, flung on his bathrobe, yawned, rubbed his hand over his whiskers, lit a cigarette, and sat down at the table.

"My, Bernard, you're silent this morning."

"I was thinking," he answered, looking away instead of at her across the table.

That dream. Had it meant that he didn't love her, that in throwing statues of himself he had been trying to destroy his past? Hadn't one of the persons on the hill looked like her father?

He thought of how he'd have to spend the day in making the rounds of editorial offices.

"Bernard," Elizabeth said softly. "Bernard, remember the first time. . . ." She paused and blushed. ". . . the first time we woke up in bed together?"

He nodded his head. A sense of sadness and loss came with memories. He recalled his anxiety when he'd signed a false name on the hotel register, and his feeling of bravery, of adventurousness and mystery. She had been only seventeen. There'd been danger, danger and liability before the law if they'd been caught.

"You said such dear, sweet things when we woke up. And remember," she went on, leaning forward, "remember, we had breakfast in bed. It tasted so good."

She had worn transparent, black lacy pajamas, and he'd wondered if her father knew that she had such pajamas. He'd wanted to be one with her, to lose all sense of himself in union with her. And now, was that all past? He let his eyes rove about their dreary basement room. In terms of her father's world, he had brought her to this state of degradation.

"And you still do love me?" she asked.

"Yes."

"And you're not—not disappointed in the sight of me when we wake up?"

"Of course not."

"You are a sweetie."

He looked around their basement room again.

"Maybe it will be nice to have a child," Elizabeth said, as though talking to herself. "I want it to be a boy."

"So do I," he said, thinking he ought to say something.

"And I want it to look like you."

"Couldn't you want him better-looking?"

"Bernard, maybe you won't like when I begin to show," she said, agitated.

"Honey, honestly, I will," he exclaimed. He went to her, kissed her, pressed her head against his stomach, and caressed her hair.

"I don't want it to be a girl," she went on in a way that touched him. "But if it *is* a baby girl, I hope it will be beautiful when it grows up, much prettier than me."

"Yes," he muttered.

"I like to look nice—for you, and for myself, too. But I know I'm not beautiful, beautiful the way I'd want my baby to be beautiful if it's a girl. Because I'm not just me any more. I'm part of you. I'm you now."

She was striving to say something more, but she didn't seem to be able to find the right words. Her face was intense, expressive, her eyes glowing, and her lips were tight. She looked like a woman who was inwardly tense rather than a girl.

"I have you growing inside of me, Bernard."

He didn't know what to say. Was the mystery of woman to be explained by possessiveness? Did women see men as mere instruments to be possessed and used? He'd often thought of his mother as witchlike and ghoulish. And he'd frequently dreamed of a tall, thin, deathlike figure, and he knew that this figure represented his mother.

"But you don't want it?"

He feared she would cry.

"Why do you say that?" he asked, his voice strained.

"I can tell. I can tell. The way you sighed."

"That doesn't mean anything. I often sigh."

"Bernard, you must—you have to—tell me, honestly tell me —you really don't hate me because, because I . . . ?"

"Honey, we'll see this through, and we're going to come out on top," he said with quiet determination.

"Bernard, I know you'll be good to me."

Chapter Twelve

I

WONDER and absorption were written on Bernard's face. He wore a black jazz-bow tie, a white apron trimmed with black, and a white cap. He stood behind the counter in the small New Era stand on Fourteenth Street between Second and First Avenues, staring at the endless succession of people on the sidewalk outside. He was crystallizing an impression of New York. Here in New York you were flung up against humanity even more than in Chicago. You were never free of it. It was pressed against you. Without necessarily thinking about it, you were aware of humanity day and night, of millions walking by you, living lives parallel to your own, working and loving and suffering. The noises and roar, the rumbling traffic, the endless human and mechanical sounds of the city were but part of this one general, nervous beat of humanity upon your senses. Even asleep, you weren't free of it, with the sounds of footsteps outside and the noise of passing automobiles. And Fourteenth Street was like a walking museum of humanity. Old and young, men and women of almost all races went by. He saw so many of them for fractions of a second. The entire East Side seemed to pour past his stand. The immigrant women with their shawls, gray-haired old women bent with work, women worn out with maternity and housework, the old men, the bearded old Jews, the immigrant workmen, the slick-looking East Side lads in their cheap, flashy clothes, the noisy kids, the young girls with thin legs and the ones with thick legs, the girls and women in cheap print dresses, the girls on the arms of the lads, the married couples, the mothers with babies, the mothers screaming at their restless children, the big, maternal women from Ireland

217

and Poland and Russia and Bohemia and Lithuania, from unknown and scarcely pronounceable corners of Europe, all these
types, and others, too, passed by. Street vendors with their carts
and boxes of useless trifles and shoddy goods, housewives with
their bundles, students with books, all coming and going.

There was such a sad poetry in all this life, in the clothes
he saw, in the bags and bundles and books and papers people
carried; and the endless movements of hands and limbs were full
of suggested meanings. And there was a babel of sounds, the
snatches of Yiddish, of broken English, of gutter English which
he could hear now and then in the general echo of noises.

The stand was narrow, with a long counter, and with a store-
room in the rear. He had work to do, dishes to wash, forms to
fill out for orders and supplies. He attended to all this in a dull,
dreamy fashion. He looked at the rat traps under the counter.
Yesterday, he'd caught two. He found it distasteful to bait the
traps, take out the dead rats, and drop them in the garbage
can in the rear. The nickel hamburgers were small and placed in
small, doughy biscuits, and he guessed that one would have to
eat between four and five at a nickel each in order to get as
much as you did in a ten- or fifteen-cent hamburger almost
anywhere else in New York. One sandwich was just enough to
whet the appetite for a second, and he was sure this was something consciously planned by New Era. It worked like a charm.

At times the counter would be full, with people excitedly
calling their orders to him, and he'd get confused, especially
when he had to fry eggs sunny-side-up or make egg sandwiches.
Often he dropped thin little cakes of hamburgers on the grill
with nervous feelings. He was unsure of himself frying hamburgers, he was afraid he wouldn't fry them just right. And
he was undecided about the coffee he made in the glass
coffeepots. He worried about how much coffee to use in each
pot, and how long to let it percolate. He met his customers with
uneasy feelings, never knowing whom he'd offend. He knew he
wasn't an efficient employee.

But he did know he had changed since 1927, when he'd

worked as a clerk in a cigar store on Broadway. He didn't snap at the customers, nor treat them rudely; he wasn't surly, as he had been in those days. He tried to be efficient, even though he wasn't very successful at it. His mind kept wandering and he would forget to take off the hamburgers quickly enough when customers wanted them rare. In the last two days, he'd eaten six that he'd fried too well and explained the shortage by saying the customers had run out on him. He often spilled coffee on the counter, left soap in the glasses, and was conscious of his awkwardness in nearly everything he did. He had planned to try to write or read on duty, but it was hard because of the interruptions and the noise on the street. He wished the weather would change. If there were even an all-day rain, he'd have only a few customers, and his time would be his own.

Alternately he felt dull and interested. He looked eagerly at the faces of many of his customers, hoping to learn something for future use in his writing, to catch some phrase, some expression of joy or sorrow, of hope or despair, some secret of someone's life. And then the inner strain and tension of observation would grow to the point where he'd close up and serve his customers mechanically, forgetting what they looked like, facing and serving them like a semiautomaton. He kept watching the clock, noting the minutes, counting the time until he could close shop, and this alternately induced a restlessness and apathetic dullness in him.

He resented this job, the hours of real work of which he was robbed. And yet his resentment was not truly deep. The passing contacts with persons who came in, the endless parade on the sidewalks, the release from the tension of writing brought him a full and simple kind of pleasure. Since he had to work, he could excuse himself from writing, from carrying on his own inward struggle. Standing behind the counter, he became immersed in the details of the job and in the people around him, and he lost his sense of difference from others. The people could look at him as they passed and might think he was one of them.

They could understand the work he did, and if they knew he was doing this to support his young and pregnant bride, they would even think he was honorable, that he was doing what they did, and that he faced the same problems they faced. There were moments of ease and relaxation that he had rarely known for years. He told himself, half in jest, that he was beginning to understand the old conundrum about being either Socrates or a contented cow. Sometimes he would stare at the people on the street and think of himself as merely another human cow contentedly chewing the cud of his anonymity.

The workday of nine hours seemed long, but then, when twelve o'clock came, the day seemed to have been short, and he would close up the stand with mixed emotions of eagerness and regret. His job became a little haven. By his fifth day it began to seem to him as though he had been working for New Era for a long time. He looked out as it was growing dark and reminded himself he had been working only five days. Tomorrow was Thursday. He would be paid, and he'd be off all day Friday and not have to come back to work until Saturday afternoon. Fourteenth Street was as crowded as usual. A radio blared jazz music from the window of a store down the street. Auto horns honked. He had the illusion that he heard some far-off human cry of excitement, as though people were shouting somewhere in the distance. He looked at two squat girls with coarse faces and thick legs and wondered who would ever want to marry them and sleep with them. He was sorry for these girls. They passed out of sight. A stupid-looking man of about thirty-five came in. He wore a leather jacket and a dirty khaki shirt, opened at the throat, and his hair was cropped close.

"Hello, Scissors Bill."

"Hello, Leather Jacket."

"Here's where you and I are exploited again. One of your measly hamburgers."

"That helps pay my salary," Bernard said, as he turned, pulled up a hamburger, and dropped it on the grill.

"They only pay you twenty-two dollars a week?"

"That's a good salary these days," Bernard said, standing over the hamburger, waiting for it to turn brown and sizzle.

"Scissors Bill, don't you know you're a wage slave?"

"My employers here are really nice fellows," Bernard said, serving his customer.

Two other customers came in, and Bernard was busy waiting on them. Leather Jacket finished his hamburger, and as he left he looked at Bernard with contempt and said:

"After the Revolution, Scissors Bill, we won't have any use for guys like you."

"Who's he?" one of the customers asked.

"A Fourteenth-Street character," Bernard said.

"Where I come from, they lock up guys like that," the customer commented.

Bernard washed some dishes and waited for more customers. This morning he'd been down to see Brady and had gotten another book to review. He wouldn't be able to get much work done on his novel on Friday, for Brady had told him to try to deliver the review Saturday morning. If he did a review a week for Brady, they'd run over thirty a week, and he could easily save five dollars a week at a minimum. And then, suppose *Someday* were bought? How had other writers felt when they'd had to take jobs which prevented them from writing—Dreiser, Knut Hamsun? One had to be a writer to understand what this meant.

A customer came in and broke the flow of his thoughts. Serving him, Bernard's mind seemed dull. Then he went to the back end of the counter, took a small notebook out of his pocket, wanting to write, but nothing came to his mind. The time was passing slowly. It was almost dark outside now. He had to make more coffee. Then he ought to sweep the floor.

Two more customers came in.

II

Elizabeth, Sophie, and Florence were eating ice cream and chatting. Sophie was glad they had dropped in to see her be-

cause she hadn't known what to do with herself. She had no
Party assignments tonight, and Jan had a meeting. She grinned
and listened while Elizabeth and Florence talked about Bernard
and Abe in an affectionate, possessive, and criticizing way.

Sophie was vaguely unhappy. Florence had Abe. Elizabeth
had Bernard. Elizabeth was only twenty-one. Florence was
twenty-five. And she was already twenty-nine. She was secretly
afraid that her thoughts were bourgeois, and that if Jan knew
about them he'd criticize her. She ought to be as hard as some of
the comrades. Was it harder to be hard if you were a woman?
Elizabeth and Florence both seemed to be happier than she. But
wasn't she a Daughter of the Revolution? Some day, wouldn't
all that she did be remembered? Wasn't what she was doing
more important than what Elizabeth and Florence were doing?
But still she was vaguely unhappy, and she wanted to tell them
how she felt. She would tell them, but she was afraid to. They
weren't Party members, and they wouldn't understand her.
And if they knew she had these unhappy feelings, they might
not come closer to the Party. She couldn't tell them. A Party
member couldn't face the world with tears or a broken heart.
A Party member must set an example of Communist joy to the
whole world.

Elizabeth smiled with reserve and primly faced them.
Florence liked Elizabeth's assurance. And Elizabeth was
almost beautiful, especially because of her hair. She and Elizabeth were so different racially and socially. She had come to
admire Elizabeth very much since they'd first met, and she admired her especially for having thrown security to the winds
and eloping with Bernard. With nostalgia and regret, she remembered how happy she had been when she and Abe had first
gone together. Then every second of her life had been full and
rich. Even sorrow had been interesting and important. And
ugliness had seemed beautiful. She and Abe were both children
of the ghetto, and together they had known such wonderful
feelings and aspirations. She remembered how on a warm Sunday afternoon they had sat in Central Park and Abe had read

her some of T. S. Eliot's poetry. She had been so moved by that line about April, April the cruellest month. But that particular April had been the most glorious month of her life. Now her marriage didn't seem to be so romantic as Elizabeth's. For though she treasured her deep and quiet feelings with Abe, she nevertheless admired and even envied Elizabeth! She had never really known a girl like Elizabeth before. It was such a surprise to find out that she and Elizabeth had so much in common and could like each other. And she knew that Elizabeth was a girl like herself and was willing to sacrifice. Oh, if she'd only become pregnant. She was going to try to persuade Bernard and Elizabeth to move to Brooklyn. Last night she'd gone to sleep imagining herself and Elizabeth taking their babies out together. Elizabeth was on her side. And wasn't Elizabeth's romantic elopement and the life she was now living merely a symptom of revolt?

"Gosh, I was dumb. Kids, I was just a dumb stenographer working for a cloak-and-suit man," Sophie was saying. "I lost my job in 1929, and that's when I came to the Movement. It wasn't interesting working for a cloak-and-suit man, typing business letters, and you never met anybody important."

"Sometimes I feel my job is so stupid," Florence complained.

"Gee, kid, I thought you had a good job. Aren't you a private secretary?" Sophie asked.

"But it's stupid. Stupid. What do I care what my boss buys and sells? And what good am I doing for the world? I'm not doing anything important. Look at Abe. One week last December he made fifteen dollars. That's the most he made in any one week in nine months. Abe has brains. But who wants to pay him for his brains?" Florence asked.

"And Bernard is working at the hamburger stand," Elizabeth said.

"Elizabeth, Bernie will have to get in touch with our food workers. Maybe he could help us to organize a New Era cell. He's a food worker now," Sophie said.

"But Bernard needs all his spare time for his novel. I hardly talk to him. He gets home after twelve and works almost every free minute he has," Elizabeth told them.

As they went on talking, Florence thought about herself. Had a college education contributed to her own happiness, or to Abe's? So many times she imagined that perhaps she and Abe were unhappy because they were educated. They were separated from their own world, their own people. Education had not really given them a sense of belonging as Americans. It seemed as if they had no place to go in America, except to the Revolution. But the Revolution was not for writers and intellectuals and petit bourgeois. She wasn't doing anything for the Revolution except giving Sophie a small contribution for the Party or the magazine once in a while.

Sophie was trying to get Elizabeth to join the Party.

"Gee, kid," Sophie was saying, "we could use you. You're Nordic and so pretty, and you could do some organizing. Why, the way you put the kids to work last week in the office. . . . I didn't know you had it in you."

"Do you think so?"

Florence thought that if the Party were bigger, there'd be a place for Abe. But there didn't seem to be any sense in his joining now because he just wasn't the type who could do the kind of work that was needed.

"But, Sophie, I don't know anything about politics."

"We'll teach you. The Party knows. It's scientific. And we could use you."

"Didn't Elizabeth tell you, Sophie?" Florence interrupted.

"What?"

Elizabeth became embarrassed.

"Is it still a secret?" Florence looked inquiringly at Elizabeth.

"I'm dying to know what this is, kids," Sophie said.

"I'm going to have a baby," Elizabeth said shyly.

After a few moments of silence, Sophie said:

"Say, that is news. Swell, kid." And then she added, "Are you afraid?"

"Should I be?" Elizabeth asked.

"Isn't she a sweet kid?" Sophie asked, turning to Florence.

Florence agreed. Elizabeth was proud. She was younger than either of them, and yet she felt more grown up. And she sensed that Sophie was really unhappy, and it might be that Sophie wanted what she had, to be married as she was and to be pregnant. She sat beaming with satisfaction. She felt important, and not just because she was Bernard's wife, but in her own right.

They went on talking in an idle manner.

III

Joseph Leonard had stopped by to see Bernard at the hamburger stand and had waited for him to close up. He seemed soft and spoiled, and there was usually a pouting expression on his face. He wore a fine, double-breasted suit and could well have been taken for a young businessman.

They walked a bit and then sat for a while in Madison Square. A homeless man was sleeping on a bench near them. Joseph wasn't completely at ease with Bernard, because he wasn't sure of his judgment that Bernard was a gifted writer. Today he had wondered seriously about Carr's talent. But, then, his original impressions were always the best, and these had been favorable to Bernard. He had just finished his own novel, *The Sun Returns at Morning,* and he believed its style to be superior to that of *The Father.* He was certain he had revealed a power of imagery of which Bernard was incapable. Carr's book had impressed him because of its unusual psychological insight, an insight which was surprising to him, for when he'd talked with Carr, Carr hadn't seemed to show a corresponding insight in conversation, even though he was pleasant and congenial and honest. But tonight Joseph was very tolerant of Bernard. He himself had surpassed Carr. When his novel was published, he would be known as the most promising writer on the American literary horizon. And Carr wrote reviews and might do one of his books.

"Don't you resent having to work at a lousy job?" Joseph asked.

"I'm beginning to think that hatred, bitterness, and resentment are luxuries I can't afford. They waste emotions," Bernard answered.

"You said you were writing a new book?"

"Yes."

"I hope the Union Square boys aren't influencing you," Joseph said.

"They won't," Bernard answered with finality.

"I wonder what you'll think of my book," Joseph went on.

"I'm looking forward to reading it. Maybe I'll like it. I have the feeling or impression that you're a writer," Bernard said.

"You might review it."

"I don't know if I can or not. Who did you say was publishing it?"

"The name doesn't mean anything. It's a fellow named Mannix who runs a small bookstore. He's interested in new writers. He liked your book."

"I don't know if I can review it, but I'll ask around. Of course, if I don't like it, I'll say so."

"I think you'll like it. It's good. It can't have much of a sale. A good book can't sell."

"Sometimes one can."

"If you want to be a successful writer in America, you have to be able to become a whirling dervish, or else to trade in Mongoloid adolescence, cheap hard-boiledness, or some such shoddy goods. This is neither the place nor the time for writing."

"Maybe there's never the place or time for writing," Bernard said. "You know, Joe, when I go about New York and see so many poor bums, I think that perhaps the literary artist in America is just a spiritual bum."

"What makes you say that?" Joe asked quickly and aggressively.

"How many people care if you or I write what's called a good book?"

"Maybe you're right."

"You know, Joe, there must be hundreds of chaps in America like us, dreaming of being writers, seeing it as the be-all and end-all of their lives. Out of these hundreds, a handful, one, two, three, five, or six will break through. What'll happen to the rest?"

"A lot of them are goddamned fools."

"Most of them are going to fail," Bernard said.

"Do you care?"

"I suppose not—no more than they care about me. The point I was coming to is that there's a kind of terrible cruelty about writing. There's room for all kinds of doctors and lawyers and teachers, but there's very little room for real writers. The artist who designed the Flatiron Building over there had a place. We haven't. This country can go to hell as it is, without us. That's what I mean when I say that sometimes the artist is a kind of spiritual bum."

"Well, why do you worry about it?" Joseph asked.

"There's nothing else in this world that I want to be. If I fail, it will mean I'm a mistake. That'll put me in the category of most people—they're mistakes."

Joseph laughed. He agreed with Bernard, but he was inwardly nervous. Would he be one of that handful from his own generation? Would his name be drowned out, and would the names of some hacks be where his belonged?

"Do you think this novel you're writing will sell?" he asked.

"I don't even know when it'll be finished. And it's likely to be considered bitter. After all, this is the land of Horatio Alger."

"Horatio's been having a little trouble since 1929, hasn't he?"

Bernard laughed with pleasure.

"At seventy, Horatio is where he was at seven. He began shining shoes at that age in front of a bank. He was such a fine shoe shiner and he shined with such pluck that he became president of the bank. The bank has been turned into a speak-easy, and there is Horatio, age seventy, shining the shoes of

the gangsters as they come out of the speak that used to be his
bank. That's the story of Horatio Alger, 1932, isn't it, Joe?"

"That just about sums it up. It doesn't make much difference
to us, does it?"

"Who can be the American hero now?" Bernard went on.
"The banker and businessman, the politician, the priest, have
had their day. The gangster, maybe."

"It won't be the artist," Joseph nervously said.

"Maybe writing is merely a grim joke," Bernard said. "In
terms of the world, we're fighting a losing battle."

"I had a chance to be almost anything I wanted. My old man
is disappointed in me."

"What does he do?"

"His bank's still open."

A ragged man passed them, carrying a stack of newspapers
under his arm and mumbling to himself.

"I'm not going to lose," Joseph asserted.

Bernard wanted to say that he felt that his battle was already
won, but that nobody knew it. He didn't, because it would seem
like bragging. Instead, he asked:

"Do you know Rimbaud?"

"No."

"In his *Seasons in Hell* there are four lines that I like. Translated, they'd run something like this—*The wolf cries out under
the trees—and spits out the beautiful feathers of the fowls he
has gorged on. . . . Like him, I consume myself.*"

"That's good. He was a poet."

"The wolf is the poet, the artist—only I don't intend to consume myself. So there we are—we'll have to be wolves, howling
under the skyscrapers. Maybe whoever wins will shoot us."

"So what?"

"Howl loud enough so that our howls are remembered after
we get shot. Shortly before I came here, one day in the Loop
I met a chap I'd gone to high school with. He's pious and is
studying to be a priest. We argued about the Church, and he
asked me if I was crazy enough to think I could lick the Church

and outlive it. I told him I knew I couldn't do that. . . . But
I also told him that I'd try to write a book that would live as
long as the Church, if not longer."

Listening to Bernard, Joseph had become increasingly agitated. He knew that he was afraid of the future. He wished he
had Bernard's confidence.

"What'll you do if you grow old and fail?" Joseph asked.

"This might be an age when people don't grow old."

"But if you do?"

"It'll be tough on me, I guess."

They both got up, yawning.

"It's late. I hope Elizabeth's asleep and isn't worried about
me," Bernard said.

They walked out of the park. Under the lamplight, Joseph
noticed Bernard's clothes. He himself always dressed well. He
wondered—would this shabby Irish lad of his own age go farther than he? Would they both get nowhere? He envied Bernard his poverty and thought that it had given Bernard so
much more experience than he had gotten.

"Bernie, if I mention something, I hope it won't hurt your
feelings," he said in a solicitous, tactful way as they started to
cross from Madison Square.

"My feelings don't hurt easily," Bernard said.

Joseph took his arm and continued:

"You know, I have some good suits, and I was wondering if
you'd let me give you a couple."

"I'd be grateful. That's the way I got the one I'm wearing,"
Bernard said.

IV

As Bernard pulled a green envelope out of the mail box, he
realized he'd unconsciously believed he would have good news
about this story. He tightened up. Knowing what this meant,
he tore open the letter, looked at the one-hundred-dollar check,
read the note of acceptance, and hurried inside.

"Something's happened," he shouted.

Elizabeth became apprehensive.

"I sold *Someday* to the *American Mercury* for a hundred dollars."

She hugged him with joy.

"Oh, my darling, I knew something good was going to happen."

She danced around the room.

"I'm so proud of you, Bernard."

"We haven't had this much money at one time since I signed the contract for *The Father*," he said, quietly excited.

"Oh, I wish you were off today so we could celebrate."

"I'll take the day off," he said. "You can call up and say I'm sick, dead, or even buried."

"Bernard, couldn't we go out and dance tonight to celebrate?"

"Let's."

"You are a dear, you really are."

"If we're careful, we can live on this while I make an effort to finish my novel, or at least get enough done so that I can try to get an advance from some publisher. I'm going to be sick for a couple of weeks or a month. We've got to take a chance."

"But—can you get it done that soon?"

"I've got to."

She was thoughtful for a moment.

"It's too early to call New Era. You call them later this morning—and say my father died and I had to rush to Chicago."

She looked at him, disturbed.

"What's the matter?"

"I don't know," she said in a quavering voice.

"Don't you think it's a plausible excuse?"

"Oh, I couldn't say that," she said, fearing to tempt fate.

"It doesn't mean anything. I just know that I have to take this chance. I'm going to go at my novel until we're broke and then try to get an advance."

"I know you can do it, Bernard."

He went to his disorderly worktable in the corner and dug out the manuscript of his new novel. Could he go on now at breakneck speed? You weren't supposed to write books like this. Joe Leonard would probably disapprove of his writing at the speed he planned to. He bent over the manuscript. This was his only chance, his last one. And possibly his career hung on what he would be able to do while this money lasted. He had to succeed, to prove himself, or else he might sink back into the ranks of beaten mediocrity. He'd try to write this novel not merely because of economic need but also as a form of warfare, conducted in defense of his freedom.

"Elizabeth, tonight we'll celebrate my decision as well as the sale of *Someday*."

"We haven't danced since we came to New York," she said.

He didn't fully believe in his decision or in his ability to carry it out. He turned back to his typewriter and slowly put a sheet of paper in it, trying to find confidence and assurance in the fact that he had carried out decisions to get an education and to write *The Father*.

"Bernard, you have such will," Elizabeth said.

He was flattered. He wanted to be thought of as having *will*, wanted people to think of *the will of Bernard Carr*.

But did he have the right to take this chance? The New Era wouldn't hold his place open for so many weeks. If he failed, they'd be broke and so much nearer the birth of the child. Wasn't he selfish? Had he a right to risk Elizabeth and their unborn child to his ambition? But wasn't he risking the very justification of his own life also? He began to doubt his decision, but he knew the decision had been made. He must plunge in and go ahead.

His mind went blank. He faced the empty white paper in his battered old portable typewriter. And he thought that, yes, writing was lonely and cruel, more cruel than he had even realized last night when he'd talked with Joe Leonard. How lonely it was to be by yourself, cut off from the world that was all about you, shut up with yourself, forced to drag feelings out of yourself and to put them into words which were so much paler than those feelings. And how cruel to be shut up in the loneliness of writing and to know that you could fail, that, no matter how you drove yourself, you might not be able to come through with the right words and conceptions.

He idly typed out his own name. Then the name of Elizabeth, and then, of Elsie Cavanagh. He looked past the typewriter at the sooty wallpaper. He pushed down the lock on the typewriter and typed:

E V A

v

"Let's not play games," Bernard said, sitting on the bed in an awkward position; he was fatigued after having worked intensively for most of the day.

"Bernard, just do it for me, please."

Elizabeth looked trim in her pink girdle. As she bent down and fastened her garters, she resembled a model in an advertisement.

"You grudge this to me. Is it a lot for me to ask?"

"I'll do it."

"And don't sulk. After all, can't we pretend? We don't play and pretend any more."

"I'll go in a little while."

"No, please—go now."

He wished he were able to throw himself into the spirit of her childish play. He was touched. And he enjoyed being washed and clean, shaved, dressed up, and having his hair cut.

"Aren't you going to kiss me good-by?" she asked in disappointment as he turned to leave.

"But I'm a ghost," he teased. "I don't exist. I'm your fellow, and I'm not here. I'm not on my way to call for you yet. I'm a lug who has a big date tonight with his girl."

"You aren't a lug," she said in playful indignation. She started rubbing cold cream on her face as he left.

The spring twilight was invading the streets of New York. There had been a shower, and the sidewalks were drying. New

York appeared fresh to him after the rain. Some children were playing in the gutter. Two boys and a little girl watched a match float toward a sewer. He had done that once, imagining that matches were battleships. Dirty matches in rain water could never become dream boats.

It was as though he hadn't been on the streets in a long, long time. He was excited. There was a common life of people coming and going, and of playing children. He could sense what lost and hidden drama and poetry there was on this street, on any street of New York. He must seem like another commonplace young man. Was anybody commonplace, if you knew him, and knew why he suffered? Everybody wanted something, just as much as he wanted to write. If they couldn't get what they wanted, they had to pretend that dirty matches in a pool were dream boats. All frustrated people became like children. But what did it mean not to be frustrated? Was it worth while to be grown up, rational, civilized?

How poor are they who have no patience.

This line ran through his mind like a motif of self-justification. He couldn't remember where he'd read it.

He turned the corner onto Seventh Avenue and proceeded toward Fourteenth Street. It was noisy.

How poor are they who have no patience.

Yes, he must have patience. This book was but part of a whole lifework. What he was struggling to do was to create, to build, to produce a lifework.

He walked on.

VI

After Bernard went out, Elizabeth sat down on the bed and looked gravely into a hand mirror. She wasn't pretty with the cold cream on her face. Her hair was let down her back. She felt it and knew that it was very fine. But her face! She was glad Bernard wasn't here. He didn't know that it wasn't merely because she was playing games that she'd insisted on his going out. Living in this one room, she couldn't dress and fix up alone. Even when you were married, you liked privacy. You didn't always like Bernard to see you putting on your girdle and making up. If he always saw her this way, how could he think she was beautiful, or know her real self?

She set down the mirror, held her legs out before her, looked at them with studious pleasure, and nodded her head thoughtfully. She did wish her ankles were just a wee bit thinner. She puckered up her lips and thoughtfully decided she had a good figure. It wouldn't be—soon. Bernard said that she didn't show yet. But she was afraid she did a little. Her breasts were a little swollen, just a little bigger. Maybe they made her look, well . . . a little matronly. But she was starting to stick out and she wasn't going to be able to wear her girdle much longer.

But she'd promised herself that for tonight she wouldn't worry about anything. And here she was beginning to worry. She got up, flung a bath towel around her shoulders, and sat down at the small dressing table behind the bed. The mirror was small, and the light here was so bad. Oh, when would she have a bright, clean bedroom, with a big mirror and a good dressing table?

Bernard never thought of such things. She hadn't either when she'd run away with him. She had never understood what it meant to be poor. Here she was, young and poor and married, and she had nothing, no furniture, no sheets or dishes or silver. Everything you needed cost money. When they had come here so happy and having so many dreams and hopes, she'd never expected their life to turn out the way it had. Bernard thought that they'd managed well because they were able to eat every day. But that wasn't happiness, just not starving. Bernard didn't understand all the things a girl needed. He wanted her to be attractive, but it just never dawned on him how hard it was to look your best all of the time when you didn't have the money you needed. And the time she spent going to the five-and-ten-cent stores, looking around to get what she needed cheap. At home she'd merely had to ask for the money or go to the drugstore and charge her purchases. And with the baby coming, and all that it would cost, how was she going to be able to keep herself attractive? There wouldn't be any money for the things she needed, and if she didn't want to nurse her baby, it would cost more money to buy milk, and if she did nurse the baby, her breasts might get big and ugly. Oh, she did hope that somehow everything would turn out right for them.

After she had combed her hair and done it up to make herself look sophisticated, she put mascara on her eyelashes and eyebrows, rouged her cheeks and lips, and then put on powder. Looking contentedly at herself in the mirror, she sadly remembered the excitement of her first dates back in high school. She wanted to feel the same way now. But she was playing a foolish game of pretending that she was a virgin and that Bernard was a romantic boy. Daddy and Mother used to ask her about the boys who took her out, and the next day they'd want to know if she'd had a good time. Those dates had made her feel so important. Now she had to play this game of pretending, to make herself feel important. She wasn't a girl any more.

The doorbell rang. Elizabeth was surprised. She didn't move until the bell rang again. In her underwear and girdle, and with the bath towel around her shoulders, she ran out and opened the door. She squealed at the sight of Bernard.

"Goodness, I'm not ready. Don't look at me," she exclaimed excitedly and then she scampered back into the room.

Bernard entered, dropped into the large chair, and sighed.

"Bernard, pretend you're in my parlor," she said.

He nodded his head with a weary look on his face. He felt like a fool.

"You sit down, please, and Miss Elizabeth will be ready soon," she said formally. Her voice then changed as she said hurriedly, "That was the maid talking."

He shook his head, bored.

She went to the dresser and slid her black silk dress carefully over her head.

"Oh, I'm so sorry I had to keep you waiting," Elizabeth said in a stereotyped voice as she came forward with her hand held out.

An illusion took control of him. For a strange moment he thought of himself as a boy in Chicago, taking out a girl who was young and unknown to him.

"Oh, Bernard, I was stupid. I just wanted to pretend. I'll be ready in a jiffy, and we'll go out and dance and have a good time."

He nodded with a feeling of uneasiness. He knew they wouldn't.

VII

Bernard and Elizabeth sat at a table flanking the dance floor in the center of the Kit Kat. It was about eleven-thirty, and the place was noisy and smoky. The walls were painted a glaring blue, and colored balloons hung from the ceiling; the four-piece orchestra sat on a dais at one end of the dance floor. Chinese waiters moved about between the tables, serving. Here and there men drank from flasks with surreptitious gestures.

"Bernard, are you glad we came?" she asked.

"Yes . . . yes—I needed relaxation," he answered.

She let her eyes roam about the place. Most of the people seemed gay and happy. Why couldn't she and Bernard be gayer? They had been gay at places like this in Chicago. Bernard was very quiet.

The orchestra began to play, and Elizabeth beamed with pleasure.

"Oh, Bernard, dance with me."

They danced, but the floor was too crowded. Bernard perspired. His feet became weary. He was glad when the dance ended. Then he and Elizabeth sat at their table like a married couple.

"That gray-haired man across from us—isn't he the life of the party," she commented.

"He looks like a high-blood-pressure case. He looks too full of beefsteak and booze."

"He's enjoying himself."

Bernard glanced across the floor at a noisy, elderly man who was with a common, overdressed red-haired girl.

"The red-haired girl he's with looks like a hooker who's taking him for whatever the traffic will bear," Bernard said.

It was now too noisy for them to talk. They sat. He was getting a headache, and he thought that he'd come here to celebrate just five years too late.

People all around him were exploding their energy in conversation, laughter, and dancing. He'd once done this. Tonight he couldn't. The feelings, the desires, and emotions these people were shooting off like firecrackers were the counterpart of the feelings, desires, and emotions he was channeling in his book. So often, when he'd been working, studying, writing, he'd thought of himself as sacrificing pleasure, sacrificing the chance to dance and play. Tonight he'd come out to dance and play but he wasn't interested.

The elderly man roared with pleasure. The red-haired hooker with him pasted a smile on her face. A long-haired Bohemian looked at a short-haired girl with an air of supercilious boredom, and the short-haired girl responded with her own look of supercilious boredom. A cadaverous, tight-lipped young man, whom Bernard had watched dancing clumsily, smiled weakly at his partner, a skinny, dull girl. They touched hands across the table. A group of middle-aged people rocked with laughter as one of their party flashed a pocket flask.

Then the orchestra played, and Bernard and Elizabeth watched the dancers. The elderly man flailed the air with his hands, smirked, pulled his partner to him, and shimmied with her. The faces of many of the dancers became like masks.

"Finish this dance with me—please, Bernard."

He rose, took her in his arms, and a couple smashed into him.

"Bernard, don't hold me so loose."

She felt the pressure of his arm and the palm of his hand tightening against her, and it made her feel warmer and more secure. She pressed herself more firmly against him and looked

up at him mischievously. He forced himself to smile, and she
thought, oh, she wanted to make him happy if she could, and
he must be a really unhappy person. She nestled her head against
his shoulder. Her hair was touching his cheek, and they were
dancing so smoothly, the music seemed to become part of her,
and she could feel him holding her tightly, and she believed
that, no, nothing that wasn't good could ever, ever happen
to her.

"Bernard, you are a sweetie pie," she told him as the dance
ended, but he knew that if she didn't smile, she'd cry.

A sleek, black-haired man called for attention from the dais
and announced that George Benson Giddings, a well-known
Village poet, would give a recitation. There was lackadaisical
applause. George Benson Giddings stepped into a green spot-
light on the dance floor. His weak face looked dissipated and
satanic in the strange light. He recited a poem, entitled *Moonbeams*. His voice throbbed as he paraded commonplace meta-
phors about love and moonbeams. His final, sighing line proclaimed that silver moonbeams are not real. He recited other
poems. The face and the voice were strangely familiar to
Bernard.

When the recitation ended, and the lights were turned on,
Bernard remembered the poet. In 1927, in Washington Square,
he had seen Giddings drunk. Giddings had talked about Stephen
Foster and he'd also denounced capitalism and the Puritans.
Three months ago, Bernard had seen him selling dirty postcards
near the New York Public Library on Forty-second Street. And
here the poor fellow was again.

The orchestra played fast, wild jazz, and the dancers became
frenzied. After the dance, the talk became loud, nervous. It
rose to a roar that sounded inhuman. He saw fragments of
people, heads, arms, profiles, hands, parts of torsos, and as the
noise beat upon him, he told himself that these people were all
escaping from something. And then, he speculated—wasn't this
their manner of running away from death? He gazed about at
all these noisy strangers in a mood of pity and awe. He saw them

as trying to make their flesh as alive as possible because one day it would be dead. And he saw himself tied to them because his flesh was as mortal and as corruptible as theirs. His head throbbed.

Elizabeth smiled at him strangely. She was afraid. She wanted the music to start so she could dance again, with Bernard holding her tightly.

The music started again.

"Bernard . . . please, let's dance again."

Her agitated voice distressed him. He rose to dance with her. The tune was *It's Three O'Clock in the Morning*. He waltzed her, and she said:

"Bernard, this is one of our songs."

"Yes."

He pulled her to him in a protective gesture and held her closely until the dance ended.

Chapter Thirteen

I

Bᴇʀɴᴀʀᴅ ran his hand through his wet hair. Sweat was
rolling down his face and was breaking out all over him.
His shirt was drenched. He bent forward and finished typing
another page. He leaned back in his chair. He didn't want to go
on working. He took the paper out of the machine, laid it on
the stack on the floor at his right, put a clean sheet into the
typewriter, stared at the ceiling thoughtlessly, and sat tense,
ready to write. But he didn't write.

Elizabeth was in the bathroom, cooling off. She had been
meek, utterly meek all day after having had a tantrum last
night when they'd come home from their celebration at the
Kit Kat Club. Walking home, she'd been quiet, and she'd said
that she'd had a good time. Then, suddenly, on Fourteenth
Street, she'd said she thought something was happening. And
how they had rushed home! But it had been a false alarm. And
then she'd cried and called him names, and he'd thought for a
while that she was mad. Now she was so meek.

It was distressing to think about that unpleasant scene. And
how far could, or should, he go in blaming himself? These
scenes interfered with his work. Elizabeth could have her tan-
trums and seemed to get over them. But it was only after she'd
gotten over one and had asked his forgiveness that he felt their
effect. Only then would he brood over them. But now he had
to work. That was all there was to it.

He took off his shirt and sat before the typewriter, bare to
the waist. Sweat rolled down his chest. He was uncomfortable
under his arms; the hair seemed matted. He was uncomfortable all over.

And now, his character Lou, based on Eva's husband, Sid—what would he be saying, sitting at home at night?

Noises on the street outside. Vibrations and rattling as another heavy truck passed by. A child screaming.

If he could work on all day in this heat, that would prove his desire to work, to sacrifice, to give himself completely and in dedication to his writing, wouldn't it? It would show his ability to stick to it. He looked up with despair on his face. He thought—no one would care if he did or didn't prove this. No one would care too much if he failed. Sacrifice, dedication, didn't necessarily make a good book. And the world cared nothing about what it cost a writer to produce a book. There wasn't even any necessary conjunction between the bread-and-butter problems of the world and these silent, personally terrible problems of a writer, was there?

It was as though the writer were outside this world, a total stranger in it. At this instant, in this hot basement room, he was outside the world, all alone, all alone and utterly unimportant in the eyes of the world. And yet he felt such power within himself. Last night, the people at the Kit Kat had had their moments. These were his moments. And he wouldn't trade them for anyone else's moments.

But all this, too, was merely further distraction. He tried to visualize the room in which his characters sat, but it was very vague in his mind. Clean, with modernistic furniture, nondescript pictures on the walls, and a random assortment of books on the shelves. The husband was sitting totally unaware of his own insensitivity, oozing contentment as he digested his meal. His unhappy wife, beautiful and shy, was nervous. She had a headache. She sat, silent, ominously silent. Her silence was forced upon her because her instincts, her need for love, were blocked, frustrated. Her silence was the most polite way she knew of accepting the bad bargain she'd made with this man. And the man would say with utter lack of awareness:

"That was a fine meal. Yes, a fine meal."

Bernard lit a cigarette. Sweat stung his eyes, and he blinked.

He closed his eyes. He wiped them with a crumpled dirty hand-kerchief. He went to the sink and gulped down a glass of water. Vague thoughts were running through his mind. He didn't know what they were. If he went on working, perhaps they'd crystallize.

He sat down, looking at his typewriter, absorbed. His trousers stuck to the hot seat of the wooden chair.

His husband and wife continued to sit, neither knowing the thoughts of the other. She would suddenly fear she might even be going crazy. Her feelings, her nature, are smothered, and her husband assumes that she is as contented as he.

And all this must be objectively presented, the balance between them equal, with no devices falsely to create sympathy for one or for the other. He despaired of describing this scene. But he plunged into work, striving to suggest the unspoken pathos that would hang like a veil between the two. He wrote a page but impulsively snatched it from the typewriter and tore it up. He shook his head as though he were shaking confusion out of his own mind.

Eva sitting in her living room, wistfully dreaming. Elizabeth sitting here. Eva dreaming, hoping—feeling what? She had never had her Prince Charming. He himself had been the closest approach to a Prince Charming she would ever know. And she sat in her living room, a girl on the other side of the American Dream. Sid would look up from reading the comics, or, no, he'd be working a crossword puzzle to improve his mind. He'd glance around at the furniture and at his quiet, beautiful wife, gloating in a commonplace pride of possession. His entire ego would seem to be expressed in this pride of possession. He would sit there, looking up from his unfinished crossword puzzle, gazing at what he owned—furniture and a beautiful, unhappy wife. And vague dreams of love would shyly form in her mind. Shyly afraid of her dreams, she'd merely sit. And her headache would be a small godsend for her, excusing her in her own eyes from having to talk to him, excusing her when they went to bed.

Bernard wrote on, thinking first with the husband and then with the wife. Finishing eight pages, he sat back in his chair, unable to go on. His own sadness, his own problems had mingled with those he was trying to describe. He looked at the small stack of manuscript on the floor. These pages represented progress. And he thought how this would evolve into a tragic book, and that sadness was the binding link between people, that it was central in the condition of man.

His own mother, his father. They had often sat together in one room, saying nothing. Could his mother in her silences have ever had dreams and yearnings like Eva's, dreams and yearnings which should be common to all women? Had her very womanly nature become so chilled that it was frozen completely? The thought of his mother evoked a sudden awe in him. She seemed to reveal to him all the sadness, all the misery, all the tragedy in people's lives. For the real destiny of the race was a composite of these small and awe-inspiring individual destinies.

Would this ever change?

His mother sitting in a rocker. Her black dress, her wispy gray hair, her wrinkled grayish skin. She was so repressed that her face was becoming almost stony, stony in its firmness and rigidity. What heart was behind that face? But this was not his problem. Eva's heart was his problem, and she was different from his mother, warm and unhappy with her great unfulfilled capacity for love. Yet Eva and his mother had both had husbands unsuited to them. He looked up at the ceiling and asked himself if it weren't true that in the same way these two women had also been unsuited for their husbands?

—Can I blame my father?

Intellectually he didn't blame him. He merely hated him, that was all. His hatred was irrational. God, what had it been like when they had slept together, when his mother had lost her virginity? Had his mother ever lost herself in sexual ecstasy, and had this frightened his father? Was there any parallel between his own feelings after sex and his old man's? Had his mother lain down naked, her face unchanging, fixed in a hard and stony expression of suffering, her very face an accusation of the sacrifice she was making?

He fingered the pages he had written and decided that here he would introduce Eva's decision to have a child. She'd hope that a child would save their marriage and save her life. And then she would look at Sid with anguish in her heart.

He wrote rapidly now, with energy, heedless of the heat.

II

"Gosh, there's nothing to do in this heat," Elizabeth said as they ate a salad.

Bernard nodded perfunctorily. He wiped the perspiration from his face and sighed. In this heat Elizabeth seemed plain to him; she couldn't keep any powder on, and, with her nose shiny, her face seemed ordinary.

"You poor boy. I hate to see you working so in the heat."

"I don't mind it," he said casually, but he wondered how long he could sustain himself at the pace he'd set today.

"When you're this way, you're away from me." Her voice became agitated. "I can tell you are, I can tell by the look on your face. I don't know you when you're like this. You're not *you* any more, *you, my Bernard,* a part of me. You're someone else."

"I have a right to work, haven't I?" he replied in a slightly whining voice.

"But I'm a little jealous of your work," she said with both sadness and coyness in her voice and manner.

"When you write a book you've got to give yourself to it, completely. If you don't, how can you mean what you write? How can you respect the book yourself?"

"I know, Bernard . . . but can't I still be . . . still be a little jealous?"

Trying to conciliate her with a smile, he reached across the table and squeezed her hand. But he was troubled, because he was so fearful this book might hurt her. He wanted to abandon it and write something else, but he knew he wouldn't, that he couldn't. He would know no rest, no relaxation, no calm until he had finished this draft. Resolute, he assured himself that now the book was started, nothing must be allowed to stand in the way of his finishing it.

"You still seem so far away," Elizabeth said wistfully

—How can I explain to her? he asked himself.

"Elizabeth, when I write, the things I try to say become more real to me than anything else. I can't help it."

She shook her head as though she understood him.

"Yes, Bernard, I know. It's only that I feel lonely when you are this way," she said.

He wanted to tell her that he was lonely, too, intensely lonely. Locked out of the world and trying to touch it with his heart and his mind. And he only touched it with words. No real human contacts seemed to promise to bridge this gap of loneliness as did the imaginary sense of contact gained in writing. Was he more lonely than she? Was there a common loneliness in all human relationships, and did this exist regardless of how much men and women loved one another? His face clouded, his eyes still far away, and he didn't even see her frightened expression. He must try to suggest this fundamental loneliness and make the book more than a mere literal example of a bourgeois marriage. It must be that, and more. And this scene in his own life, was it not a variation of scenes he would describe, a variation of scenes his mother and father had experienced?

"I'll get this book written," he said, talking to himself as much as to her.

"I know you will, Bernard," she said earnestly.

He shook his head with a sad kind of determination.

"If it weren't hard to write, there'd be little use in writing."

"I know, I know, Bernard. I saw you writing in this heat, working so hard, concentrating. I was proud of you. I thought to myself, I told myself—'That's my Bernard.'"

Her expression of possessive affection sounded a warning as much as it pleased him. He wanted to be his own Bernard, not her Bernard, not anybody's Bernard.

"Elizabeth, make me some coffee," he said. He added,
"Please."

"In this heat?"

"I have to keep awake," he said, feeling groggy.

"But, Bernard, if you drink so much coffee and go on this
way, you will hurt yourself. Your heart."

"I don't care," he said resolutely.

Immediately, his heart pounded. He told himself that he
didn't care, and then he thought that while he did care and
while he did worry, he had to disregard his worry. If comple-
tion of this book meant sacrificing his health, his life, then he
had to make the sacrifice. Suddenly he sat rigid. Into his mind
there came the dreamlike image of himself as a corpse lying in
a coffin.

"If you really want the coffee, Bernard, I'll make it," she
called from the small stove.

"Yes, I do."

III

Elizabeth pulled the sheet over herself and looked up at Bernard with affectionate eyes as he put on his underwear and
went slowly back to his typewriter.

Bernard was displeased with himself. He'd just made love
with Elizabeth, his wife, as though it were merely a duty. But
then, what difference did it make? What difference did anything make now, except his book? He must live in his work;
all else in life was secondary. After all, real marital relationships were different from the banalities of popular songs and
sentimental love poems. But, then, this was no reason for dis-
illusionment. Yet he knew he was still hurt and angry because he'd learned that these lies and illusions were, after all,
merely lies and illusions. He was angry because there was no
Arcadia, no Eldorado, no Atlantis, no heaven on this earth or
anywhere else. The ideal was not real. And that was the sense
of his writing. And his Eva would want a child because there
was no ideal for her either. He stared at his typewriter, wondering if Elizabeth felt as cheated as he did. Was that why she had

had a tantrum last night? He seemed too listless now to work. He might take a walk. He didn't move.

After sexual experience, one could experience a range and variety of emotions, and he was trying to put this, too, in his novel. He realized now that he couldn't have written it at the time he'd known Eva, and why he had needed to wait so long before he could handle this story. He had had to live more. And yet, from the standpoint of the world of romance, he had done so little living. These recurrent feelings that he'd been cheated by life seemed to him to express an anger at not having gotten the things he told himself and others he didn't want. Elsie Cavanagh? Did he want her? No! Shouldn't he feel gay, joyous, over his having been able to liberate himself from lies? It was out of disillusionments, sufferings, frustrations, wasn't it, that one gained insights? And didn't that suggest that the artist's destiny was an unhappy one? Didn't that signify that the artist must bear the burden of other people's pain, even of their unknown, their semi-conscious, pain?

"Bernard, do you know what I'd like?" Elizabeth said coyly.

"What?"

"Candy."

"I'll go get some."

"But you're tired."

"No, I haven't been out today."

"No, don't bother, it's late."

"It's only a quarter after nine. I'll get it."

"You're a darling to go out to get me candy."

"What kind do you want?"

"Oh, any kind. Just get me a surprise."

IV

Bill Barber went to his office every day in a mood of keen anticipation. He liked his work as an editor for Tolan and Rand, and he wanted to make the most of his opportunities. At twenty-nine, he had landed an important position in the publishing business, and he frankly admitted to himself that he was ambitious. Publishing needed new blood, and he was absolutely confident that an energetic young editor like himself could go far. He knew that he had clearly taken the measure of many of the leading figures in the trade, and he regarded himself as their equal or even their superior. Tolan and Rand had been put on a solid financial basis. Its reputation was good, and its lists had been among the best. Barber was certain that he would play a major part in building up T & R as the outstanding American publisher. He believed, too, that there would be a new renaissance in American literature, that many new writers would come forward, especially with the depression, and he was constantly on the lookout for those new writers. Every morning he went to the office hoping this might be the day when he would make a great discovery. He liked writers, and was aware that his future depended on them, and especially on his discovering new ones. The idea of being the editor who would discover a new Dreiser, a new Lewis, a new Sherwood Anderson appealed to him strongly. He himself had wanted to write, but he'd given up in college. Business appealed to him as much as it repelled him. Publishing was an ideal solution for him. The compromises that had to be made, the deceits involved in the business could be compensated for by helping to publish, by fathering, good books. He wanted nothing so much as to find a young writer of talent, or, even better, if possible, a genius.

He was more eager than usual as he waited for Bernard Carr to show up for an appointment. Arthur Hampton had phoned him and asked him to see Carr, and he respected Hampton's judgment. In fact, during his telephone conversation with Hampton, he'd impulsively asked if Carr were a genius. Hampton had said no, he wasn't, but that he had great promise.

Barber had attended to his morning dictation, including three letters to young writers in which he'd used business conditions as an excuse for rejecting their manuscripts. He felt very sorry for unsuccessful writers, but, leaning back in his chair and linking his hands behind his head, he checked his pity. After all, he decided, no one put a gun to a young fellow's

head and told him that he must be a writer. It was easier to
reject a manuscript now than it had been for him three years
ago when he'd first come to work here. And the depression
helped him to let them off easy. He grinned. About the only
good the depression had done the book business was that it had
offered a new and easy excuse in letters of rejection.

He wondered about Carr and wished he'd finished his book.
He only hoped Carr filled the bill. Depression or no depression, he'd push through any really promising young writer.
The depression would end. For his money the Democratic candidate, Roosevelt, stacked up as the man who was going to save
capitalism in America, and he knew that the best investment
T & R could make was in any young writer who really had the
goods to deliver. Costs were down, and it was easy to get writers
and books. He wasn't one of the prophets of doom. Why, goddamn it, he had faith in this country, and in the future of
American literature. Well, he certainly hoped Carr would be
the goods.

His phone rang. It was to announce Carr, and Barber told the
girl to send him right in. He waited, eager and hopeful.

"I'm glad to meet you, Mr. Carr," Barber said genially, as he
rose and extended his hand.

Bernard and Barber tried to size up each other as they shook
hands firmly.

Bernard noticed that Barber's desk was orderly, and that he
was young and well-dressed. He had a pleasant manner, a pleasant face, and seemed to Bernard a contemporary.

And Barber liked Bernard's looks.

"I come from the North Side of Chicago," Barber said, making conversation.

"I come from the South Side."

"Yes, I know. What do you think of Chicago?"

"I'd offer no objections if it seceded from the United States,"
Bernard said.

"New York is more sophisticated, isn't it?" Barber replied,
smiling.

"Yes," Bernard said, but immediately he knew that he couldn't truly call himself sophisticated.

"Of course," he began, talking slowly and haltingly, "I don't like the part of Chicago I came from. I'm glad I got out of it."

"You went to the University, didn't you?"

"Yes, I did. It's a truly formidable citadel of knowledge."

"But you did get an education there, didn't you?"

"I got about six different kinds of education."

"What did you take? English, I suppose."

"I majored in social science."

Barber and Bernard lit cigarettes.

"Well, what's on your mind, Carr."

"I'm writing a book."

"Sitting where I am, Carr, it sometimes seems as though everyone in the United States were writing a book. How much have you done?"

"I've got about seventy pages of this draft done, despite the heat," Bernard said, smiling modestly.

"Thank God, it's a little cooler this morning. What about your book—is it good?"

"It's what I want to write, and it'll be the best I can do, especially under my circumstances."

"Will you consider me too personal if I ask you about your circumstances?"

"I'm married, and we're going to have a baby. I had a job making twenty-two a week at a hamburger stand, and I picked up some money doing reviews, especially for the *Dispatch*."

"I like your reviews, except one you did of a book of ours— *Holiday Season*."

"I didn't like the book."

"I thought it was clever."

"I don't always appreciate clever people," Bernard said.

"Why? You're not afraid of them—are you?"

"They get too smart for their own good."

Barber raised his brows and scrutinized Bernard a moment.

"Now, about the book you're writing . . ."

"I quit my job at the hamburger stand—that is, I invited being fired by not going to work because I sold a story to *The American Mercury*. I decided to get a draft of my book done, or as much as possible done, so I could try to get an advance."

"Do you want an advance on what you've done?"

"I'd take it."

"Can you go on and do more under your circumstances?"

"I can go on for at least a month on what money I've got, perhaps longer."

"It might be fairer to you if I could read more than what you've already done."

"I'd agree, but I was talking to Art Hampton and . . ."

"Yes, he spoke very well of you. And he said you were uncompromising."

"I didn't decide to become a writer in order to write like . . . oh, Lydia Griswold."

"Who?"

"Lydia Griswold . . . I was taking a name out of the air. Her books are praised regularly in *Literature*. What I mean is—it isn't my intention to become a hack—even a glorified hack."

Barber looked questioningly at Bernard, but he was impressed.

"How is your book going? I'm just reading it."

"Not too well."

"Who's your publisher?"

"Ferris and Winter."

"Aren't you under option to them?"

"I broke with them, and I hear rumors now that they may be bankrupt anyway."

"Are they?"

"You'd know more than I would."

"I haven't heard that," Barber said with finality. "But what happened?"

"Ferris and his man Friday, Friday Rank . . . do you know him?"

"I've met him."

After Bernard described his last interview with Ferris and Rank, Barber asked:

"Do you want to send me what you have?"

"I could." Bernard thought a moment. "I'd rather get more done and bring you more, or maybe the whole draft in a few weeks."

"Is that a bargain?"

"Yes."

"I'll count on it and read it as soon as you bring it in."

Bernard lit a cigarette and remarked dryly:

"Of course, it isn't my ambition to bankrupt every publisher who publishes me."

"Here's the situation, Carr. It takes time to launch a good new writer these days. But I pride myself that we are a little different from Ferris and Winter, not that they weren't all right. They're nice fellows. We're bigger, and we want to develop a good list of new writers." Barber smiled quietly and added: "I don't think we're going bankrupt either. At the same time, I have to be realistic and practical in this business. I can't give you an advance merely on a gamble. But if my associates and I like your manuscript, we can give you as good an advance as any publisher in New York, and we can handle a writer like you . . . that is, like what I assume you to be."

"I'll have a better chunk of it to show you in a few weeks. Can I have a quick decision?"

"Definitely. I'll expect to hear from you."

"You will," Bernard said, rising to shake hands and leave.

v

As Elizabeth sat making over an old dress, her robe opened, exposing her left breast. It was slightly swollen, and Bernard was touched by the sight of it. Bernard, wearing his pajamas because of the heat, looked at her possessively. Then he calmly turned back to his typewriter. She uttered a meaningless exclamation. He swung around from the table and apprehensively asked:

"What is it, honey?"

"Oh, nothing. I was thinking to myself."

"About what?"

"Gosh, I don't know, just thinking."

He turned back to work.

He'd skipped part of his novel in order to work out a scene late in the book which had just occurred to him. He was trying to describe Eva nursing her baby. Reflective, he leaned forward, struggling to bring to mind what he wanted to and what he ought to write. He had some vague distaste for the subject. He wasn't sure why he felt this way. Then he realized that he had practically never thought of girls as mothers. Mothers were a different species of women from girls. They were older and unattractive, like his own mother. You rarely thought of them as attractive. Yes, in his mind motherhood had always been unattractive. Pregnant women had always seemed ugly to him. He stared at the ceiling, vacant-eyed, wondering wasn't there something wrong with him for seeing motherhood in this light? Shouldn't he look at it more humanly? It was an indignity which nature forced on girls. He'd always assumed that pregnancy and motherhood were ugly.

And yet, for girls, for women, there must be a deep and intense joy, a profound gratification, in having a child. For some, it was worth the risk of seeing girlhood and beauty end, it was worth the risk of life itself. His character, Eva, would feel an intense gratification, a fulfillment which no man could ever know. She would lament because motherhood signified the end of girlhood, but at the same time she would be joyful, deeply joyful. And for the husband—Sid—the child would mean a continuation of ego. Just as he wanted to speak from beyond the grave with his work, so Sid would want the child to be his voice from beyond the grave.

Eva would sit nursing. The infant would greedily suckle. There would be a beautiful and calm expression on Eva's face. She'd sit alone in her beauty, with no one to see her. He felt close to Eva, and he was guilty about his attitude toward pregnancy and motherhood. He liked to look at breasts and touch them, but he didn't like contact with them. Why? The unremembered shames of childhood, infancy? There could be no shame in the infant. All the warmth of life would be centered for it in its mother's red nipple. This feeling about suckling came later. How describe the first days of an infant? It was blindly and helplessly plunged from the womb, cannonaded into the world in a bath of blood, powerless, with no words, no control.

Bernard closed his eyes. It was as though he saw darkness with an inward eye. He felt that there were lost memories behind this darkness in his mind. And in the infant in his story—what?

Next year, Elizabeth would be nursing his own son. And her son would live in a wordless world and fasten its little mouth on her red nipples. He had such a sudden rush of thoughts that he typed at breakneck speed, scarcely able to keep pace with them.

Elizabeth hummed as she continued to sew. Pausing to mop his face, Bernard recognized the tune of *O Chi Churnia . . . Dark Eyes*. Eva had had dark eyes. Elizabeth's eyes were blue. Dark eyes. The promise and symbol of love and passion, and of all that neither love nor passion nor life itself could ever give him. This song was forever associated in his mind with both Eva and Elizabeth. Two loves. Eva's name had just come to mind before Elizabeth's. Did this mean merely temporal priority? How infinitely sad this song was to him.

Eva's face, her darkish skin, her dark eyes, her wild dark hair, her smile. She had given him the first real smile of love in his whole life.

How beautiful she had been. How understanding and how tender. She had loved him.

Would he be able to make her a beautiful symbol of the trapped girlhood and womanhood in America?

Eva had been so shy and reticent. Eva. His first real excitement in the flesh of a woman. The memory was probably rooted structurally in his brain. This really was a more poetic idea than the usual conceptions of romantic love. For Eva to be a special nervous structure in his brain, a special synapse.

And in this book, breasts, the red nipples of Eva, must become forever fixed in the baby's life. And as she sat with it at her breast, her dark eyes would light up with sorrow as well as joy.

Elizabeth put her dress down on the bed and yawned in boredom.

"Bernard, you do look tired. Haven't you worked hard enough for today?" she said, as he got up and took a few nervous steps about the room.

"I'm all right. And it's only eight-fifteen. I'll get a lot more work done tonight."

"I was thinking," she said, pausing and then continuing, "I was thinking maybe we could take just a little walk. Bernard, you ought to get a little exercise."

"I'm going too well now to stop."

"Just a teenie walk. A little air will really be good for your health, Bernard."

"There's no air in New York. Hell, the air itself is sweat."

"It ought to be cooler at night."

"It's never going to be cool again," he said. "When I feel like work and am working as well as I am now, the only thing for me to do is to go on. I can't waste a minute."

"Yes, Bernard. But you have to take care of yourself."

"Honey," he said, a hard, firm quality in his voice, "I believe in blowing myself, putting everything I have into a book."

She looked at him, alarmed, and he immediately smiled.

"You change so. One minute I'm afraid of you and the next minute you smile so sweetly, like a boy."

He said nothing.

"Darling," she said with feeling. "I know. I know. I just thought a walk would be good for us, for your health. And I wanted to put on this new dress," she said, pointing to the dress she had just laid on the bed.

"Let's take a walk," he said unexpectedly.

She kissed him gratefully. Feeling empty, he waited while she dressed. They went out and strolled toward Fifth Avenue. They walked on past the darkened high school on the opposite side of the street. Fifteenth Street was deserted. New York seemed silent for a moment.

"You might say something about my dress. Does it hang right?"

"Yes, it does."

"But," she teased, "you didn't look at it."

"Yes, I did. I looked at it before we left."

"Do you mean it, Bernard? Or are you just telling me that to make me feel good?"

"Of course, I mean it."

"Men! You see so little and notice so little. We do so much to make ourselves look pretty for you and you just tell us that we look *nice* and that's all. You don't pay any attention to us after . . ."

"Yes, we do—I mean I do." He became earnest. "But, honey, when I have my work on my mind, I have to block out other things."

"Yes, darling, I know. I just like to be told sweet things. I like . . . I like a little flattery."

They walked on to Fifth Avenue in silence. He began to feel the heat. All things were now sweating. They turned southward.

Fourteenth Street. Below Fourteenth Street, Fifth Avenue was different. It wasn't depressing. They might run into someone they knew. Something might happen.

"It's nice to get out and see people. I get such a cooped-up feeling in that basement," she said lazily.

"Uh huh!" he exclaimed.

"When we can afford it, this is the part of New York I'd like to live in," Elizabeth said dreamily.

He was going to remark that they couldn't hope to be able to live on lower Fifth Avenue, but he said nothing. People who lived here could eat without worrying about it. And yet some of them must be worrying now. They didn't know what would happen to them, and to their America. America was theirs, and it was Mr. Whelan's. It wasn't his. He was merely a poor American writer, he thought with sentimental irony.

"Let's get a soda," he said, as they approached Eighth Street.

VI

"Last night, Bernard, I dreamed your book was finished and that it was a masterpiece," Elizabeth said shyly.

"That doesn't prove anything," he remarked curtly.

Bernard frowned with displeasure. He had not succeeded in his efforts to reason Elizabeth out of her superstitions. He didn't want to try now, because he didn't know how to phrase his arguments so they would really convince and change her. So often, the effort to change anyone's mind seemed to be hopeless. And a familiar and yet strangely disturbing apprehension came over him. If dreams did forecast the future, there would be a psychic world, and then all he had thought, all of his rationalism, would turn out to have been an error. And he'd really staked his whole mental life on his rationalist views. Suppose Elizabeth were right? But, no, he could make no concessions to her superstitions.

"Bernard, sometimes I think dreams are . . . are prophetic."

He didn't want to discuss or argue this question. It would take time that he ought to spend in writing. And he didn't know how to explain rationalism convincingly to her. Again he frowned with displeasure.

"It doesn't do any harm to think that, especially if the dreams are happy ones and mean we will get things and be happy."

"We'll never grow up if we think that our wishes will come true merely because we wish them to. . . ."

"I'd like to think that dreams do mean something. Don't try to make me not think that."

"I can't prevent you from believing whatever you want to."

Suddenly there was a loud peal of thunder. She shuddered. Her face became pale.

"Bernard," she screamed.

He jumped.

"Hold me, quick," she pleaded frantically, plunging into his arms and nestling against him.

There was another loud crash. She trembled in his arms

"It's only thunder," he said, trying to be reassuring.

"Hold me! Tight!"

He held her more firmly. She looked up at him, wide-eyed, like a terrified child.

"You're strong," she said.

Another peal of thunder, but less loud.

"Nothing is going to happen to you," he said softly.

She shook her head, looked at him flirtatiously and said:

"Bernard, don't laugh at me. I can't help it . . . you know I've always been afraid of thunder."

"I'm not," he said, masking his displeasure.

They heard the rain on the sidewalk outside. They went and looked out from the doorway and saw it coming down in splashing silver drops. Bernard tingled at the sight.

"It's quite beautiful," he said, after looking at the rain for some moments.

"Yes."

Arm-in-arm, they went back inside.

"It's going to be much cooler working now," he said, going over to his typewriter.

"Yes. I wonder what I'll do today."

As he worked, he was aware of her moving restlessly about the room. He couldn't stop working now and amuse her, tell her what to do, could he? He heard her flop down on the bed and sigh.

He thought of suggesting that she read what he'd already written. Especially since he was writing about a girl, she might be able to help him. But he was hesitant about her reading this manuscript. He went on writing. He heard the rain outside.

He became so absorbed in his work that time and place lost all meaning for him.

Elizabeth fell asleep.

VII

"Aren't you going to ask me to read what you'-: written?" Elizabeth asked with an enigmatic grin on her face, as Bernard paced around the table, trying to think his way through a scene.

"Oh, yes, I was just going to suggest it," he answered absent-mindedly.

"Maybe I might have one or two little suggestions to make, because, Bernard, after all, you are writing about a girl, and a wife . . ."

Again she smiled enigmatically. He handed her his manuscript.

He went back to his table and stared uneasily at the typewriter. Would this book hurt her because of Eva? He fell into a desolate mood. He wished he were writing some other book. Yesterday he'd been so painfully conscious of Eva. He'd remembered her so vividly. He'd wanted her so much that he'd almost lost his objectivity.

He went on working with grim determination.

VIII

Bernard rubbed his itchy whiskers. He hadn't shaved for three days. He hadn't dressed for two. His legs ached. His back ached. He felt cramped and sluggish as he sat at the table and stared past Elizabeth.

"Bernard, I like your book—so far."

He smiled but couldn't relax. He'd been writing with conviction. The greatest power in the world was the power to move people by artistic expression. If he could but attain that, others might have the political power and even the wealth of this world. And this book might move people, move them deeply. He knew now that he was really fulfilling himself.

"Bernard, you are developing as a writer—growing. It makes me so happy."

"Do you think the girl's emotions are true?" he asked eagerly. She shook her head and said sadly:

"I was hurt when I read some of these pages."

"But why?" he asked, struggling to conceal his agitated emotions.

"I don't know. I couldn't help it. She wants the second baby. She doesn't try not to have it. I was hurt."

"But they have money to take care of the baby. This book isn't about us, you and me, Elizabeth."

She looked off at the wall.

"I think she must be a nice girl—Eva."

"It isn't precisely Eva."

"Oh, yes, it is. Don't fool me, Bernard. It is. It is a nice picture of her. I liked her, even if I am jealous."

He stood looking past her, tense.

"I think I understand," she said with resignation and as though she were speaking to herself.

"If I can finish this now and get an advance," he said, his words sounding hollow in his own ears.

"I think lots of readers will like your book, Bernard."

"I wonder," he said, moved.

He wanted his book to be liked.

"Is there anything you'd criticize?" he asked stiffly.

"I don't know," Elizabeth said, talking with a sudden affected seriousness. "Of course, there is the style. There are rough parts. And you repeat some words."

"I meant to."

"But is that good style, Bernard?"

"It isn't good textbook style, but what do I care? Do you think that the thoughts, the feelings, I give the girl are true?"

"She doesn't love her husband."

"No, of course not. That's central in the novel."

"And she doesn't know what to do."

He puffed on a cigarette and waited eagerly for Elizabeth to say more. Yes, one of the pleasures of writing came with talking about your work, hearing others talk of it. And he realized that his emotions were deeply and personally involved in this book.

"Bernard," Elizabeth said, worried, "I sometimes have headaches and feel nervous and worried, and I even think maybe I am unhappy."

He could talk straight now, couldn't he, really talk with her, bring out whatever feelings they had. But he said quickly:

"But, honey, you're a different character."

She picked a caramel out of the bag on the table and smiled at him. At this moment, eating candy, smiling at him, she didn't seem unhappy or troubled.

"I'm going to get on with the book," he said.

She sat, relaxed, smiling, with the caramel in her mouth.

"How soon will you finish?"

"I'm over half through with this draft."

A feeling of unhappiness came over him. The Eva of this book would die.

They sat for a few minutes, and then he went to the typewriter and thought again of the end of his book. After Eva died, he'd describe the boy, squawling, crying, wetting its diapers. A new life. A baby, without words, without real consciousness. Anticipating the future with a squawl. And the baby would be the child of her lover. The end of his story—death and a crying baby, a little bastard baby.

He looked at Elizabeth. God! If she died, and if he were left with their child! If life imitated art in his own experience.

IX

Bernard had changed his whole conception of the end of the book, and he described the girl dying from an abortion instead of from childbirth. Her lover walked the streets of New York in the sun, a stranger, hurt and bewildered, staring at other strangers and thinking they knew nothing of his sorrow and his guilt. He fought back tears. He wandered aimlessly. He was free and alone and hurt, and he thought he would always carry a scar and a bitterness in him. He walked the streets, his life one of the millions of lives reflected, concealed, revealed obliquely on the crowded sidewalks of New York. Love had given his hero a feeling of dignity and importance. It had rescued him from anonymity. And now love was dead. The hero walked about, bitterly quoting Shakespeare:

Men have died from time to time, and worms have eaten them,
But not for love.

Bernard's throat choked up. The final scene which he had just written took hold of him. This novel had to move people. It would! He looked at the pile of manuscript. Finished! He had done what he had said he would do.

Elizabeth was sleeping. He heard footsteps on the sidewalk outside. He was alone. He picked up and read the last page, his eyes filling. He put the sheet on top of the others, sat back in his chair, lit a cigarette, and looked at the wall. He wanted to sleep, and he wanted to walk. He wanted to get drunk. He wanted to do something.

He went over to Elizabeth, bent down, and kissed her.

"Darling," he whispered softly.

She opened her sleepy eyes.

"I finished my book," he whispered.

She blinked.

"Oh!"

She shook her head. Her face broke into a smile.

"Bernard, I'm so happy," she said, flinging her arms around him and kissing him.

He was uncomfortable as she hugged and kissed him.

"Maybe I shouldn't have waked you. But I wanted to tell you. I had to tell someone."

"Someone?"

"Aren't you someone?" he covered up.

"Oh, Bernard, darling, I'm so happy."

"There it is," he said, pointing to the stack of manuscript on the table.

Neither of them spoke for several moments. Then he said: "Well, I'll go to bed now."

"How do you feel, Bernard?" she asked sleepily.

"I don't know."

"You come to bed and put your head on my shoulder, and I'll pat you to sleep."

Now he wanted to be by himself. He wanted to think, to be alone.

"Don't look so sad, darling."

"I'm not sad. I'm merely tired."

He turned out the light. He climbed into bed. He kissed her. He lay on his back, staring into the darkness. She kissed him and patted his hair. He didn't want to be kissed or touched. He feigned sleep and lay near the wall, his eyes open, staring at the darkness. That last scene. Eva dead. The lover walking the sunny sidewalks of New York. He lay, agitated and unhappy, unable to sleep.

Chapter Fourteen

I

BARBER sat in the comfortable modernistic chair, put the
manuscript down on the small table beside him, took up the
glass on the table, drank, and then became thoughtful. He
looked at Martha, who was curled up on the couch and reading.
She was demure and dark.

"This fellow, Carr, is a writer," he said.

"What?" she asked, bored, as she looked up from her book.

"Carr. You don't know him. He's a strange chap from
Chicago."

"Bill, don't let your enthusiasm carry you away again," she
said.

"Oh, I like this book. I haven't any doubts about that. I'm
just wondering . . ." he said.

She turned back to her book. He watched her. He didn't
enjoy admitting it to himself, but Carr's book was hitting
home. Sometimes he became concerned because of the silences
between Martha and himself, and because of his own fits of restlessness. Would the day come when he'd no longer love Martha?
When she wouldn't love him?

"Of course, attitudes have changed. We're no longer in the
Victorian Age," he said, taking another sip.

"What's that, darling?" she asked, looking up.

"I was asking myself if this book might be a little too hot to
handle."

"Do books always have to deal with sex?" she asked.

"This one is art. It's true. It swept me away, and it almost
tears your heart out. I want to recommend it, and I want to
help this fellow. He's broke, and his wife is having a baby.
He's a bright Irishman."

"You know, Bill, you can't take too many risks. After all, it isn't going to be good for you if you sponsor a book that will cause a censorship case involving a lot of trouble and expense."

"But I know I must recommend it . . . in fact, I feel that I'll have to go to bat for it. It's the real goods. I'd like you to read it, darling."

"Tell me about it," she said, shaking her head, sitting up, and smoothing out her dress.

He gazed at her legs appreciatively.

"It's a love story about an unhappy marriage and a lover. It's simple and direct, but it has impact, terrific impact. I'd rather you read it than have me describe it."

"Bill, I'll read it before you decide," she said.

His lips became momentarily tense.

"Yes, I'd like to know what you think."

She sat back, yawned. He took another sip of his drink.

"Bill, it's such a nice night. Let's take a walk."

"All right," he said, rising, and going to the closet off the living room for his jacket.

Carr's book had left him in a vaguely troubled mood.

II

Bernard wanted to keep on an even keel while he was waiting to hear of Barber's decision. He remembered how, on that day in 1930 when Elizabeth had had her abortion, he had had the same kind of desire and determination. He was resisting his inclinations to become hopeful and confident, to dream that now the worst was over for them. But he was confident. He expected Barber to accept the book and give him an advance. In the same way, he had been sure that *Someday* would be sold, even though it had been rejected so often.

They sat contentedly on the grass in Central Park, looking down a small hill at a bend in the lake. Behind them was a path. Now and then they heard someone going by. The water looked dark and stagnant. Sandwiches and cakes were spread out before them on a gay paper tablecloth that Elizabeth had bought in a Woolworth store. All morning, while she'd prepared for this little picnic, he had been touched, even though she had fussed more than was necessary. He'd eaten all he wanted, but he was idly finishing a bottle of stuffed olives.

"Remember our picnic lunches in Jackson Park, Bernard?"

"Yes."

"I remember how you always loved stuffed olives then."

"I'm eating them."

"Are you tired?"

"No, I'm just full and stupid. I couldn't write now if I had to."

"In Chicago, you used to tell me about the things you planned to write. You knew then, didn't you, Bernard, that you'd really become a writer . . . I knew it, too. I think most everybody who knew you knew it. There's something about you, Bernard, that . . . well, that makes people notice you. I noticed you the first time I saw you in my father's parlor."

"Maybe I'll write a sequel to *The Father* now. I could write that or else do a book about my own family."

"You're not going to start working on another book right away?"

"Not immediately, but soon, with the grace of Barber and his associates. But I do think he'll take my book. And I'm going to apply for a Loewenthal Fellowship. It'll be a little too late to have a baby on the Loewenthal, but we might be able to buy milk and shoes for one on it."

"You deserve a Fellowship."

"I've got to have a project. I'd like to get one for a study of Irish literature, but I'll have a better chance trying for one in creative writing."

"Now you're the way you used to be, Bernard."

"What's that?"

"Oh, full of plans, not frowning so much or screwing up your forehead, and . . . oh . . . being grouchy and moody."

"Was I hard to take, finishing the book?"

"You were worried, worried for me, for us, and for our baby, weren't you, Bernard?"

"Yes, I suppose I was." He took another olive. "But just let a hole open up in the line, I'll always go through it."

He was somewhat surprised at his own extraordinary confidence. But with all his passing anxieties, and even self-pity, in his low moods, he hadn't failed once in anything important since he'd gone back to Chicago in 1927. He remembered how he'd written Eva a letter in December, '27, telling her that although it looked as if he'd failed, he hadn't. And he'd told her that he would chain his spirit of rebellion. Now it was the end of June, 1932, and he had done what he'd told Eva he'd do. She had been a stepping stone in his life. Would she like his book?

"I wonder how much advance you'll get, Bernard."

"Two weeks ago I thought I was writing a book that would never be published. Now I think the chances are with me. In the meantime, we have thirty-three dollars between us and the streets. But we aren't the slaves of fear."

"Bernard, put your head in my lap."

He stretched out with his head in her lap. She ran her fingers through his hair. He closed his eyes.

"Bernard . . . what are we going to name our baby?"

"Vladimir Ilyich," he said in a calm and dreamy mood.

"That's a horrible name."

"It's Lenin's name. Lenin did something in this world. And he didn't lose."

"But do we have to call him Vladimir? And what was the second name?"

"Ilyich."

"Ilyich? Vladimir Ilyich Carr? That sounds awful."

"We can break his Irish past with a name."

"Bernard is such a nice name," she said thoughtfully.

"It's bad enough that the poor kid will have me for its old

man. I don't think I ought to burden our child with my name
—make him a junior."

"Don't say that, Bernard. I know you are going to be a wonderful father."

"There's a screwball on Fourteenth Street who calls himself
Comrade Leather Jacket because he says that names are counter-
revolutionary and bourgeois. He wears a leather jacket even in
the heat."

"Why is he so silly?"

"Because the Russian Cheka wears leather jackets. He probably goes around killing people in his mind the way men often
walk along and undress the women they pass on the street."

"Do you do that?"

"And in Russia some people are giving their kids names like
Dialectical Materialism, Dialectical Materialism Sverdlov . . .
Dialectical Materialism Carr. . . . How does that sound?"

"Bernard, do you want our baby?"

"Of course."

"Do you—honestly? Are you really not angry—not afraid it
will be a burden, too much of a burden on you?"

"It doesn't do any good to avoid responsibility."

She went on stroking his hair, but she looked wistfully off at
the trees. His answer wasn't the one she wanted to hear.

Bernard hadn't realized how tired he was. He couldn't keep
his eyes open and fell peacefully asleep. Elizabeth gazed down
at his sleeping face. It looked worn and yet boyish. She gently
stroked his hair. Yes, she told herself, she did love her Bernard.

III

Sitting in the softly lit, small speakeasy having lunch with
Arthur Hampton, Bill Barber was pleased with himself. Taking
people out to lunch was one of his duties, but often it became
the most pleasant part of a busy day. Good conversation, good
food, and good liquor were among the best of the social rewards
he could reap because of his position in the New York literary

world. He liked and respected Arthur Hampton and was enjoying his lunch.

"I wanted to talk to you about this chap Bernard Carr," Barber said.

Arthur grinned and waited for Bill to go on.

"Do you think he's got it?"

Art Hampton hesitated and thoughtfully gazed upward for a moment before answering:

"Yes, he probably has. Did you read his book?"

"You mean *The Father*? It's damn promising. And I've just read the manuscript of his new novel."

"How is it? He's worked fast to finish a book so soon after his first one."

"I can't make up my mind about it. It's got something. I know that. But I'd like to have an honest, objective report on it. Art, would you have time to do me a favor and read it and give me a report on it?"

"Why, yes. I'd be glad to."

"I'd be grateful. I'd rather not tell you about my own impressions of it so you'll read it without any prejudice. I haven't made up my own mind as yet."

Martha hadn't been impressed by Carr's novel. But he wouldn't tell Hampton this. What kind of editor would he be if he didn't have the capacity to make his own judgments, to say yes or no on his own? Even though Martha insisted that it was merely an ordinary book, and that, after all, many people fall in love and go to bed together, still he was strongly inclined to say yes on the Carr manuscript. It had haunted and troubled him now for the last two days. When he'd lain in bed that night after finishing it, its effect on him had been particularly strong, in fact, almost shattering. Damn it, it was a poignant love story. That first feeling of love, that first love of a woman's body, was never to be recaptured. And once it was gone, perhaps the best thing in life was gone. All the changes from those first ecstatic feelings, on through to tragedy, were either stated or implied in the book.

"Yes, I'll be glad to read the manuscript. I'm busy as the devil at the moment, but I can squeeze it in." Hampton said, as he pondered how much he could charge·Barber.

"And you'll write a report? Especially if you like it and recommend publication, your report will be helpful to me."

"My usual fee, you know," Hampton said with hope, "is twenty-five dollars."

Barber thought for a moment. He got manuscripts read for ten and fifteen dollars. Still, Hampton was rapidly gaining a fine critical reputation and in the future could be a useful man to him in many ways.

"That's all right. It'll be worth it because I know your report will be perceptive. Can you do it quickly? I don't want to keep Carr waiting any longer than I have to. You know about his circumstances."

"Yes, I do."

"Carr has lots of drive and guts."

"Yes, he has, and I think he's got self-confidence. When I read that first novel of his, Barb, I could see he was a new writer who bore watching. I'll be glad to give you the report in a couple of days."

"That'll be fine. I rather like this guy Carr, and I don't want to keep him on tenterhooks," Barber said.

He felt a little sorry and guilty already about Bernard, because he'd let two days go by while he'd postponed making up his mind. He'd been lucky in catching Hampton at home this morning and finding him free for lunch, and he was banking on this report. Martha considered Hampton a good critic. At breakfast this morning, they'd talked about the manuscript again for a few moments. He'd told her he was convinced that somebody was going to publish the book anyway, and that he didn't want to let a promising writer go to any rivals, and she'd answered that such a consideration was one thing, but that he seemed to talk about the book as though it were literature.

"One of the questions I'd like you to answer in your report

is this, Art—do you think Carr is a good long-term investment for us? You know, I'm looking for new writers with staying power."

"Judging from his first book, and from the way he's got another done when he's in such a tough spot, I'd be inclined to think he has, Barb. But I'll be in a better position to answer after I've read this second book," Hampton said confidently.

"You know, Art," Barber said, "one of the secrets of how to keep going in the book business is to have a good back list. Right now, we have a pretty fair one . . ."

"Yes, I think you do."

"I'm thinking of the back list we'll have in ten or fifteen years. Of course, I'd like to get bestsellers, but I also want to see that we maintain a policy of publishing distinguished and solid books season after season. Damn it, I know the way this country is bollixed up, but I'm not fooling myself. I don't think prosperity is just around the corner. I'm not Hoover . . . knock on wood on that one."

They laughed, and Barber rapped lightly on the table.

"But I don't think we've come to the end of everything in the world."

"Neither do I," Art said.

They were both quiet for a moment and let their eyes wander about the speakeasy. Both were thinking, each in his own language, of the air of sophistication and culture of the place. And they asked themselves—would this all end? Would the basis for the life they lived be knocked out from under them? Were they living on quicksand?

Barber had a moment of gloom and apprehension. All that he was working for, all his ambitions, could be torn from under him.

They finished lunch and left, Hampton going back to Barber's office to pick up Bernard's manuscript.

IV

Bernard and Elizabeth listened to the ticking of the clock in their basement room. Every time he'd started to say something in the last fifteen minutes, he'd checked himself. He was too listless to make conversation. Elizabeth glanced over at him as he slouched down in the old chair. A gleam of interest lit up her face. He expected her to say something. Then the interest started to fade. They looked at each other as if they were strangers. There were footsteps on the sidewalk outside. Someone was walking briskly somewhere. Elizabeth inclined her head toward the front wall. The footsteps died down, and the ticking clock dominated the room. Bernard slumped down further in the chair.

"Bernard, maybe you'll hear from Mr. Barber in the morning."

He mumbled agreement. He heard the clock again. He was waiting, stupidly waiting.

"Barber promised to let me know about the book as soon as he could. It's only eight days. He and Tolan and Rand have other things to do besides deciding about my book. To them, we're merely one item of business."

"I'm sure the book is going to be accepted. . . . Bernard, I am, because, oh, they'll just see it's a good book."

"That's not the point. The point is, will it sell?"

"Don't you think it will, Bernard?"

He shrugged his shoulders because he didn't want to explain his contradictory thoughts and feelings.

"You worked so hard on it, Bernard."

"Who cares? I've worked hard for over four years now. If I'd stayed here in 1927 and gone on working for Monahan's, without even working very hard I might have become a successful and useful citizen by now. Who knows?"

"But, Bernard, I'm glad you didn't, because then . . . I never would have known you."

"You might have married a more worthy citizen—an embalmer who does respectable work, a salesman, who knows?"

"Bernard, please don't be bitter."

He let out a hurt laugh. "The fate of a book isn't very important."

"But it is, Bernard, it is."

Disregarding her pathetic efforts to give him the reassurance he didn't want, his voice became cruel.

"Almost nobody cares. Who cares if a literary tradition is carried on? Who cares if this country ever has a literature or not? A decent, self-respecting writer finds no silver linings. And now, what the hell is left in this country but the delusion that there's still a silver lining? You can't walk four or five blocks in New York without someone begging from you. Thousands are sleeping in Hoovervilles. And in the movies, the lovers live happily ever after. Nobody cares. What I write is up to me. What happens to what I write is out of my control."

"Bernard . . . don't you think people can be happy?"

He wished he could tell her he believed people could be happy. But he realized he had known for a long time—he almost always had known—that happiness was an illusion. She leaned forward, watching him, waiting for him to speak.

"We're not allowed to be by this society," he told her, but as he spoke, he secretly questioned the validity of his own words and knew that, at best, he was uttering an incomplete truth. "I don't mind giving everything I have to writing. But worrying about getting the book published, worrying about its sales, about what the book reviewers say is different."

"Maybe they'll all like it and it will sell thousands of copies. Bernard, that's possible."

He lit a cigarette and sat thinking. His emotions seemed spent. He didn't want to think or feel. He didn't want to go on struggling and struggling. He might have to go on this way for his entire life. He might win recognition only from posterity. Bernard sat up in a state of sudden shock. Posterity at this moment consisted of trapped embryos like the growing, trapped organism inside of Elizabeth. Did he want others to bear all the burdens and sacrifices to create the posterity which might accept him?

"Bernard, what's the matter?" Elizabeth asked, agitated because of the strange, shocked expression on his face.

"Nothing—I was thinking."

"Bernard, tell me, what's the matter?" she insisted.

"I was thinking about what I ought to do—maybe I'd better go out and get another job."

"Bernard, it's not my fault."

"Who said it was?" he asked sharply.

"But . . . but you say things that make me afraid you blame me."

"I do not. Can't we talk about our problems rationally without . . ."

He didn't finish his sentence. He wasn't sure what he was really trying to say.

"I sometimes feel, Bernard, that you talk as if you blamed me about your writing. I want you to write. I was glad, glad when you quit your job and wrote your book. I was, Bernard."

"I know it. I didn't mean you, honey. It's this system, this society—the conditions we have to face that I'm blaming."

She didn't quite believe him, but she smiled, wishing she could. She resented him, telling herself he didn't understand her and thought more of his work than he did of her. She could be sad and cry now if she let herself go, but she wouldn't. And she thought of her father and wondered how she could get help from him. But she wouldn't mention this to Bernard.

v

Art Hampton sat in a reclining position, absorbed in Bernard Carr's manuscript. Reading rapidly, he kept putting page after page on the small table beside him with mechanical regularity. Hildegarde watched him with glowering eyes. An opened book lay in her lap. All day she had felt oppressed. Something dangerous and catastrophic had loomed over her, but it had not struck.

Before she had given up painting, she had tried to paint it, to make it a symbol of tortured striving for beauty. How wrong she had been! What did he know of the tortures of the soul? There he was, working away at a hack job. And she had wanted him to be a great artist.

As Arthur read, he was vaguely conscious of Hildegarde's eyes on him, and of her mood. They saddened him, and the anguish of Carr's love story only deepened this sadness. All that he knew and wanted to forget about life threatened to burst forth within him.

"Is Bernard's book any good?" Hildegarde asked.

He looked up and yawned. He seemed utterly calm and controlled.

"It's a real advance over his first book."

"Then they'll murder it."

"No, Hildegarde, I have a hunch it will sell. Of course, a great many may be bought for the wrong reasons. But I have a hunch it will do well."

"It almost breaks my heart to see a man with your talents and education wasting your time reading manuscripts of writers who aren't fit to shine your shoes."

"I'm just about ready to do a book of criticism. I think I'll wangle Barber into a contract."

"Then you'll be attacked. You'll be so envied."

"All most of these babies in New York can do is to envy."

Hildegarde's resentful mood had disappeared. She regretted the thoughts she had just had about her husband, and she saw him, as she saw herself, a victim of the world.

She picked up her volume of Emily Dickinson and read, slowly and quietly, reciting the words to herself. The hatred vanished from her eyes. She was like Emily Dickinson. Even though she had been a wife and a mother now for so long, she believed there was something indefinably virginal in her nature and her sensibility, something too rare for the world ever to understand. Like Emily Dickinson, she was one who knocked at every door and didn't know when the dawn would come, and she, she also, had tasted a liquor never brewed. She read:

> *I could not die with you,*
> *For one must wait*
> *To shut the other's gaze down,—*
> *You could not.*

Hildegarde looked over at Arthur with these lines running through her mind. Again she saw that expression of intense absorption on his face. Was he finding some expression of his own feelings in Bernard Carr's book, just as she found expression in Emily Dickinson? And did he ever wonder which of them would shut down the other's eyes? She read some more, said good night to Arthur, went to look at their sleeping seven-year-old son, and then she went to bed and lay in the darkness, thinking of Emily Dickinson and telling herself she wanted to be a debauchee of dew but that she didn't know how.

Arthur went on reading Bernard's book. Hildegarde remained fixed in his mind. The girl Bernard pictured seemed like all women. Her dreams and emotions, her desire for love revealed something deep in the nature of all women. Could men satisfy that nature? He paused and asked himself—was he inadequate?

He thought of Carr. Yes, Carr was an artist. And art was the only justification in life. Was he himself an artist? He gazed about his living room. His eyes were fixed on his books. Then he rose and stood gazing at one of Hildegrade's pictures. Her tree leaves were so dreamlike and delicate, and yet they were twisted and painted as though their very frailty made them symbols of unhappy dreams. He noticed that Hildegrade had left a volume of Emily Dickinson opened on the chair. He picked up the book and read four lines she had marked:

> *To shut the other's gaze down,—*

Carr's book was leading on to death. Death was so bound up with feelings of love. Had Hildegarde sat reading and thinking of death while he was reading of these feelings in Carr's novel?

He finished reading the manuscript. He sat in awe, thinking of Bernard's description of the heroine dying, and in order to hold off the feelings that were threatening to overcome him he began searching through the pages of the manuscript for stylistic flaws.

VI

July 6, 1932

Dear Carr:

I've talked over Unshapely Things *with my associates here, and Mr. Rand as well as an outside reader share my enthusiasm. We are ready to offer you a contract and to advance you three hundred and fifty dollars, half on the signing of the contract and half on the delivery of the final revised version of your novel, provided you can make some revisions which will give us assurance we will be safe from attack by Wright, the so-called vice crusader. These are minor matters, and I am sure we can agree about them without damaging the sincerity or the artistic merit of your book.*

Will you give me a ring so that we can arrange to discuss this, and perhaps have lunch?

You have done a swell job, and I am convinced that in publishing Unshapely Things, *we'll be publishing a book that is a permanent contribution to American letters.*

Cordially,
Barb
[(William Barber)

VII

Barber was happy and confident working at his desk. After reading Hampton's report, he was convinced that, in Carr, he had a discovery.

He could promote and sell Carr's novel honestly, with a feeling of personal integrity. If Carr only turned out to be agreeable about changing some of the sections which went too far, everything was set.

With his morning dictation finished, he was reading a manuscript, when a sentence in it caught his attention.

"*And since these findings of bourgeois anthropologists are in flagrant contradiction with Marxism and Marxian dialectics, they are therefore wrong.*"

God, wasn't that fanaticism? How could a man think this way? Oxman, the author, was brilliant but erratic.

His phone rang. The switchboard operator announced Bernard Carr. He put the Oxman manuscript aside.

Bernard seemed shy to Barber, and Barber noticed he was wearing a good suit and that his shoes were shined. The last time Carr had been in, he'd been dressed poorly.

"Well, I'm glad to see you, Carr. How are you?" Barber said cordially, shaking his hand and smiling.

"Oh, all right, thanks," Bernard said.

They exchanged a few remarks.

"I agree to what you say about my book in your letter. I think it can be toned down," Bernard then said.

"Swell. Swell. I thought you would."

"Yes, but I don't think there's much to do. What I mean is I don't think there's a big job here."

"When do you want to start on the revision?"

"Right away. But I can wait a couple of days if you want to give me some notes."

Barber thought for a moment. He was getting to like Carr a lot, and he was really surprised that Carr was more reasonable than he'd expected him to be.

"You take the manuscript, and we'll see how it shapes up after you've revised it. How's that?"

"I think I can do it."

"When do you think you can get the manuscript back?" Barber asked.

"I can't say—but I want to get it done soon. I'd like to have it published this fall."

Barber again hesitated a moment before speaking.

"Could we plan on September first for the delivery?"

Bernard nodded.

"Now, for the contract. You don't have an agent, I take it?"

"No—but I'd like to get as much of an advance as I can."

"I know, Carr—but there's a limit here. Most young novelists in your boots would probably get two-fifty these days. We're giving you three-fifty."

"Could I have two-fifty now and a hundred when I deliver the final manuscript?"

"If you want it that way. Now, for the rest, suppose I have one of our regular contracts drawn up?"

Bernard nodded.

Barber picked up the phone. He felt important, and he was really keen on this book now.

"Miss Coyne, Mr. Barber. I spoke to you about the Carr, Bernard Carr, contract. . . . Will you please draw it up with the date of delivery for September first? Can you get that ready—I'd like to have it signed when I come back from lunch. . . . Thank you, Miss Coyne."

Barber turned to Bernard, wondering if his voice had been casual enough.

"Well, it's done, and we can have it closed after lunch. And, Carr, I've got a hell of a lot of confidence in you, a hell of a lot."

"I'm very glad," Bernard said with feeling.

"Carr, you don't know how good this makes me feel," Barber said with sincerity. "Say, let's go out and celebrate and have lunch. I know where we can get a good drink and a fine meal."

VIII

"After the way I worked and worried, haven't I a right to celebrate?" Bernard asked in a defiant voice.

"But, Bernard, I was waiting on pins and needles for the news. I didn't know what happened or what might have happened to you."

Bleary-eyed, he leaned drunkenly on the table and looked at Elizabeth.

"I can always take care of myself."

"I was worried and nervous, Bernard—that's all."

He knew he should have come home to tell her the good news. But after having lunch with Barber, he'd just wanted to see someone, someone to tell the news to, and he'd stopped up at *Mass Action* and had some drinks with Jan and Sam Leventhal. Jan had been happy because he was going to the Soviet Union, and Sam because a fifteen-line verse of his had been translated into Russian and published in the Soviet Union. They'd only talked and had drinks in a speakeasy.

"I feel bad—that you wouldn't come home to tell me the news—first."

"But you knew when I left."

She looked at him, disappointed.

"Jesus Christ!" he exclaimed in sudden anxiety.

"Bernard," she asked, almost jumping. "Bernard, what's the matter?"

Her hands trembled and her lips quivered. She became pale.

"The manuscript. And I haven't a carbon."

Her mouth popped open. An agonized look swept onto her face. Bernard's hands sank to his side, and his shoulders sagged. He faced her, looking crushed, helpless, guilty.

"Did you lose it, Bernard?"

"I don't know. I don't know where it is. I can't remember," he said in a weak, spiritless voice.

"Oh, Bernard," she exclaimed, her voice throbbing.

He dropped into the big ugly chair and sank his head against his chest.

"Did you lose it?" she added urgently.

"I don't know," he answered without looking up.

"Think back, Bernard. Where did you last have it?"

He shook his head from side to side and stared at the rips in the rug. He was sober now, and his head throbbed.

"Tell me, Bernard," she asked in a persistent but almost hysterical tone of voice.

What a damned fool he was! And he had no one to blame but himself. Now he was beaten. Beaten. How could he write it over again? And he had Tolan and Rand's money in his pocket. What would Barber think of him? Would this queer him with Barber? Then he looked up at Elizabeth. Her face was pale, and her lips were quivering. She clasped her hands tightly before her.

"I didn't have it when I got to *Mass Action*. I'm sure of that."

"Where were you before you went to see Jan and Sam?"

"There was the speakeasy for lunch. And Barber's office. I walked from Barber's office to *M.A.*"

"Did you take it with you from Mr. Barber's?"

"I don't know. I don't think I did," he said, his face blank.

"Maybe Mr. Barber has it," she said.

"Let me think."

"Bernard, what are we going to do now?" she said, struggling with herself not to cry.

He drew his elbows in against his ribs, and his whole body became taut.

"I couldn't have dropped it on the street. I knew what I was doing. I wasn't that drunk." His face lit up. "I remember. I didn't take it. I forgot to ask for it. No, Barber said he wanted to go over it tonight, and that he'd send it to me tomorrow by messenger."

He sagged.

"Oh, Bernard—I had such a scare!" she said in tears.

"I did, too. But now I'm sure. I'm absolutely certain."

She smiled and sobbed at the same time. He rose, and she went to him, clung to him, laid her head against his chest.

Chapter Fifteen

I

THE group sat on the roof of the building off Union Square where Sophie lived, looking down on the anti-war demonstration. The Square kept filling up, and the crowd was a mass of human beings, differentiated only by the color of their clothes and by slight movements. Surrounding the Square and lined up along the walks were policemen, their blue uniforms giving the impression of a pattern around and within the crowd. A band played *The Internationale*. Cheers were heard. The group kept watching, and after some slogans were shouted, growls came from the demonstrators.

"It's a thrilling sight," Florence remarked. She was wearing a white linen dress, and her arms, neck, and face seemed even more tawny than usual.

"Three years ago we couldn't have filled the Square with anti-war demonstrators," Sam Leventhal said.

"This demonstration is bigger than the one I was in the night Sacco and Vanzetti were murdered," Bernard said.

"The progress we've made heartens me," Sam said.

"It's the nuts to me," Mel Morris said enthusiastically. "This is the first big demonstration I've ever seen in Union Square. It's the biggest one I've ever seen. Back in Indiana, when I was first coming over to the Movement, I used to have daydreams about demonstrations in Union Square the same way that lots of lads dream about girls."

"Aren't you thrilled?" Florence asked him.

"I know I oughtn't to admit it in front of sophisticated New Yorkers, but I am. It's a beautiful sight, a wonderful sight. Just think of it, there are thousands, thousands of comrades right down there. What do you think of it, Bernie?"

"It's interesting, Mel," Bernard answered, leaning forward in a camp chair, his eyes riveted on the crowd.

"Will there be any excitement?" Elizabeth asked.

"Isn't this exciting enough? If those people, and if the masses they represent, can't stop the attack on the Soviet Union, then we'll all be in the imperialist war," Abe said with emotion.

"Gee, that's swell, Abe," Sophie said, looking at him with admiration.

The crowd below was continuing to grow. Watching it, Bernard found the spectacle both monotonous and fascinating. There were eddies of motion within the crowd. Men and women hurried and scurried across the streets into the Square. Groups came out of the subway station east of the Square and became lost in the crowd. Policemen moved about, and he saw one of them gesturing. The spectacle was a kind of mass pantomime. Distance and height seemed to endow it with a quality of unreality, and Bernard kept forgetting the political significance of the demonstration and saw it as something not quite real and human, something alternately dull and exciting.

"Some day they'll have to tear down all the buildings around here to make room for the millions who'll demonstrate," Mel said.

"I'm writing a poem about that. I've called it *A Vision of Union Square*," Sam said.

"We'll live to see it happen, Sam," Mel said.

"Maybe," Bernard commented.

"Oh, I wish Jan could be here. He thought he'd be leaving in September, and suddenly it was all arranged for him to go. I'll write and tell him about it. He can tell our comrades in Russia—I mean, the Soviet Union—about it."

"By the time they hear of this demonstration in Moscow, it will number millions instead of about fifteen thousand," Bernard said.

"Bernie, you're really cynical, aren't you?" Mel asked, but good naturedly.

"Oh, Bernard isn't cynical," Elizabeth said.

"Mel, I was just thinking—when I sit down and write, I can't think of choosing sides. For instance, if I'm describing a capitalist—suppose I'm putting my father-in-law in a book. I have no use for him. I hate everything he stands for. Should I, then, just write a caricature of him, dipped in hatred?"

"How can you do a friendly picture of him if he's a capitalist?"

"But if I don't show how it all appears to him, what am I doing but sounding off? I have to show him as he seems to himself, and as a fellow human being who one day will die, just as I will. You know, the richest boy in my class was a banker's son named Marty O'Hara."

"I'll bet he was a pk?"

"Yes—but I envied him. He was dressed better than I, and copped off the girl I adored—Elsie Cavanagh. She's engaged to marry him. And the future looked as if it would be all roses and gravy to him. That's why I envied him. He didn't have to worry. The same way, I envied kids in high school who were sure of going to college, who might inherit their old man's business. This guy—Marty O'Hara—his old man came over here, a greenhorn. He built up a chain of banks and they went bust— and the old man and Marty are going on trial in Chicago this month for criminal embezzlement. That's the guy I envied. But if I write about him, I want to do it fairly and objectively."

"He'll get off in the capitalist courts."

"No, you can't take sides so simply," Bernard said.

"Bernie, I really think you're confused," Mel said.

"That's Eldridge," Sam interrupted, as they heard a speaker talking through a microphone.

A roar went up from the crowd. Then they heard a magnified nasal voice screech in a flat and unconvincing tone of voice.

"Only our Party can stop the War being plotted by Hoover and Wall Street along with the Japanese imperialists. Only our Party can fill Union Square, yes, fill our American Red Square with a revolutionary demonstration against imperialist war and for the defense of the Soviet Union, the fatherland of the workers of the whole world. The yellow Socialists . . ."

A growl rose from Union Square.

"Hoover isn't plotting a war. He's probably praying to God to work a miracle that will keep him in the White House," Bernard said.

"Don't you read *The Fist*? It's proved that there's a war plot," Sam said.

"Oh, that reminds me," Bernard said. "I read an editorial in *The Fist* which said that Trotsky was a social fascist, and a political sonofabitch with other faults, because he said that Japan wasn't going to attack Siberia this year."

"That proves that objectively he's an agent of counter-revolution," Mel said.

"It doesn't look to me as if there's going to be a war right now. I read the papers sometimes. I don't think Hoover's plotting a war. Hell, his Secretary of State, what the hell's his name? . . ."

Bernard paused and looked around. No one seemed to know the name of the Secretary of State. Then he remembered.

"Oh, yes, Stimson. Hoover didn't put his ideas through. Maybe Trotsky is right."

"Bernie, our Party knows what's going on. If the Party says that there's a war plot, there's a war plot," Mel said with great assurance and mystery. "The Party knows what's going on in every country in the world."

There was another roar from the crowd. They all watched again. The heads, the shirts, the colored dresses, the straw hats, the figures and parts of human figures that were visible, all formed a kind of senseless kaleidoscopic pattern which changed continuously in little details. And the speaker went on, his magnified nasal voice recurrently swamped by traffic noises. An airplane roared overhead, and they looked up.

"I'll bet that plane was sent over here to intimidate the workers," Sam said.

"Bernie, you don't think there's going to be an imperialist war?" Mel asked.

"Of course, I do."

"What's wrong with *The Fist,* then—it's exposing the war plans of Wall Street."

"I don't think it's coming immediately, that's all. But maybe my generation will still be a war generation."

"What are you going to do about it?"

Bernard looked up at Mel before he asked:

"What can I do?"

Abe was visibly distressed.

"We've got to stop the war," Sophie said.

"I just can't imagine a war," Elizabeth said.

"If the capitalists attack the Soviet Union, I don't know what I'd do. I'd just feel like jumping out the window," Florence said.

"We know what to do—Lenin told us. Turn imperialist war into civil war—turn the guns around," Mel said glibly.

At this moment there was a chanting mass roar from Union Square:

> *Down with Imperialist War!*
> *Down with Imperialist War!*
> *Down with Imperialist War!*

II

Elizabeth sat in their new attic room, thinking how much happier she was here than she'd been in that dirty old basement on West Fifteenth Street. This room was large and sunny and quiet, and the rent was only seven dollars a week. There was a kitchen on the floor that they could use, and this, along with the big space outside their door, gave her the feeling that they were living in more than one room. Bernard liked this place, too, except that he'd been worried about her climbing three flights of stairs, but she'd wanted the place so much that he'd given in, like the dear that he was, and now she had a home she could live in until they could afford a real apartment. She knew that things like this didn't mean as much to a husband as to a wife, but she thought Bernard was happier, too. He was working hard on the revision of his book, and he talked more and was very hopeful about its sales.

She was going to write her parents at last to tell them the news. She'd put off doing this, and Bernard had been after her. He'd written his own folks and to friends, and maybe if she didn't write, her father and mother would find out from someone else. That would make them feel bad. She wanted them to know and to be glad, but every time she'd started to write, she just hadn't done it. Her parents knew she was a married woman, and she herself didn't understand why she didn't want to tell them the news.

Her face saddened. Maybe she hadn't been a good daughter. Sometimes when she was alone like this, and she thought of them, it was hard for her to keep from crying. Bernard couldn't understand this. She didn't like the way he talked about his own mother and father. He told everybody that his father was a drunkard and his mother was superstitious. He didn't seem to miss them. Much as she loved Bernard, she missed her mother and father. It made her sad when she thought of them alone together and growing old, or of Mother alone at night when Daddy had to go out on a case. They had always been good to her. She wanted to see them, and sometimes she was afraid she'd never see them again. If she died having Bernard's baby, they'd be alone together, and she'd be dead without having seen them again.

She wiped away a tear.

It was August already, but it seemed such a long time from August to December. She was afraid so often, not knowing what would happen to her. Bernard was sweet and dear, and she knew he loved her, but sometimes he was forgetful, and even if he wasn't forgetful he was a man, and he wouldn't know how she felt. And pains and morning sickness, and sometimes just crying because she wanted to cry, and her dreams which frightened her, and, yes, this funny feeling she had that she was going to die. She had nobody to talk to. She had talked to Hildegarde Hampton, but she couldn't ask the questions she wanted to, just as there were so many questions you couldn't ask people in New York because they were so sophisticated and knew so much more than you knew and might laugh or think you were funny if you told them about your thoughts and daydreams.

She told herself:

—I want my mother.

Filled with an inexpressible longing, she wrote:

Dearest Mother and Daddy:

I have so many things to say, and I was lonesome and thinking of both of you and thinking maybe you'll think I am a bad girl for not writing to you. Specially because I have such news. Mother, I am going to become a mother myself. Bernard is so happy, and I am happy, and I am feeling very well. I didn't write sooner to tell you because, Mother, I didn't know, and then, Bernard was writing his book and I was helping him and reading it for him, and there was the question of the contract, and he talks over everything with me, and he's revising his book, and he has been so busy. We have moved, and you'll see I have a new address on the envelope. It is a nice place. We are only here temporarily because we are going to settle in an apartment, and we have not made up our minds. One day we think we would like to live in Manhattan, and then we think perhaps we would be better off in Brooklyn, and then we think about Long Island. We are taking our time, and in the fall or after the newcomer arrives in December, we will decide. This new place is comfortable. I have fixed it up cheerfully, and made curtains myself, and I am proud of them, and it is quiet and sunny and easy for Bernard to work in. And, Mother, I have learned to knit, and I am knitting things, because I am going to have everything ready early, and Bernard is going with me—he is so good to me, really he is—to buy things in a store, and, Mother, you write me and give me advice.

I was thinking since you and Daddy like to go away on Labor Day, you might make a trip to New York. You have never seen New York, and I could see you both, and we could talk and talk, and if you saw me you wouldn't worry, because I am happy, even though I do miss you both very much. Bernard has to be in New York because of publishers and editors, but I miss Chicago.

Please write me, Mother. And tell me about yourself and Daddy. And here's a great big kiss for my Daddy, and a big kiss to you, Mother. And, Mother and Daddy, don't be worried or disappointed, for I am happy and well, and maybe you will both come here for your Labor Day trip.

Your loving daughter,
Elizabeth

III

"Maybe we were wrong about that boy. He will turn out to be a decent kind of a lad, after all," Mrs. Whelan said, while her husband sat holding Elizabeth's letter, leaning forward and gazing moodily down at the dark carpet on the parlor floor.

Whelan looked at the expensive parlor rug and struggled with himself so as not to give away his emotions. Of late, he and his wife had not talked much about Elizabeth. And having avoided discussion of their daughter, they had not had much to say to each other except commonplaces that meant nothing. He had tried to sink himself in his work. He had gone out for new business, attending meetings of the Order of Christopher, trying to make contacts with Protestant ministers and with rabbis in order to get afternoon cases, and making every possible new contact. He had more than kept his head above water, but he had refused to ask himself why he was doing this. He had acted as though he would go on burying people forever, as though there were no other end in life than that of burying others. Now, threatened by a rebellious flood of his own feelings, struggling to maintain an unforgiving attitude which really caused him suffering and sadness, he was surprised by the question which entered his thoughts. Had he been working this way with the hope of leaving it all to a grandson who would carry on?

"She waited a long time to let us know," he said coldly.

"But now she'll understand more, Philip . . . she's no longer a girl now."

This touched the old wound. He had gone on for years, thinking of Elizabeth as a girl, his girl, his daughter. Before she could even walk, he had looked at her with awe and embarrassment, and he had thought how some day she would grow up and belong to some man. His loss had hurt doubly because it was to this Carr. At times he had imagined her coming home meek and asking forgiveness, and he'd thought of himself forgiving and trying to forget. And he had fancied Carr dying. No one knew better than he how easily people could die, how they were snatched away by accidents and unexpected illnesses in the prime of life. At times, and in moments of his greatest bitterness, he'd told himself that all he would ever do for his scamp of a son-in-law was to give him a free burial. And he'd even leave any gold in the scamp's teeth.

So often he had silently felt disdain for so many people he'd seen lose their control in the face of death. Now, he must manage his own feelings. Elizabeth wasn't dead. She was only dead as his little girl.

"She hasn't asked us for anything, Philip. Ber—he must be supporting her."

Mrs. Whelan sensed her husband's mood and feelings. Her own emotions were mixed. She had complained more than Philip after Elizabeth's elopement, yet she had felt it less. At times she'd even been glad.

Elizabeth, she often told herself, had run away from Philip's business. If it was hard to be an undertaker's wife, it must be hard to be an undertaker's daughter. And she wanted to go to New York to see Elizabeth, to see how she lived, and to talk to her as woman to woman. She believed that Bernard must have turned Elizabeth's head because he knew how to make love to a girl, a woman. There were disappointments in her life she could no more forget than she could speak of them to her husband. There had been times, not so long ago, when she had wanted to feel such passion, and she had seen the disapproving look on his face. She had believed that there was something evil and wrong in her. And the times when she had wanted to be taken and even hurt, and Philip had not helped her. Bernard must be different. He was not religious. Maybe he was pagan. She knew that these were bad thoughts a woman her age shouldn't have. But sometimes she had them. She'd sit and think, or she'd be walking on the street and see young boys and remember when she was a girl. She'd think of Bernard and Elizabeth that way, and it happened that even thoughts of herself and a young man would come to her. Oh, sometimes she regretted she was old.

They sat looking past each other, neither capable of telling the other his real thoughts.

"But, Philip, she still thinks of us."

"I wonder how they're really making out. I can't believe they are doing as well as she writes. And she ran off without even a word beforehand. Didn't she lie to us once?"

"But she's our child. Now she's going to give us a grandchild," Mrs. Whelan reasoned, but her joy was tempered by a kind of envy.

"If he ever does her any harm," Mr. Whelan said, straining his muscles and slowly clenching and unclenching his fist as his face was turning purple, "if he does—I'll hold him accountable. I'll . . ."

"Philip, it was a blow, wasn't it? You have never said all you feel, have you?"

His shoulders slumped, and he looked at her pleadingly.

"No. We lived for her and worked for her. She was our dream girl. It wasn't just who she married—it was the way she did it. Forgiveness is hard, very hard."

Mrs. Whelan's lips tightened. She said nothing.

"I'm not a hard man. You know I'm not, Ruth," Mr. Whelan

said in a quiet, gentle voice. "In all my business life I've never broken my word. I've never betrayed anyone. I've never broken my word to you."

Guilt threatened him. He remembered three conventions when he'd drunk with some of his fellow morticians and they'd all gone out, and he'd gone with girls. But was that betrayal? These strayings were past, and they were not important. He had suffered a great private guilt because of them. No, they hadn't been any real betrayal.

"We can't blame their little baby," he said.

Her face lit up with a smile.

"Philip, you are going to go, aren't you?"

He answered yes with a strained smile. Then he had to go to the funeral parlor. Mrs. Whelan wrote to Elizabeth immediately.

August 15, 1932

Dear Daughter:

Your father and I were so happy and overjoyed to receive your letter with the news, and we are going to visit you and see New York over Labor Day. Elizabeth, I trust that everything is for the best, but sometimes I think you are too young to have a child. But what is done is done, and your father and I would not say a word against you, because you are our daughter. We have forgiven you. We only hope you are taken care of. If Bernard is a good husband to you, then he is our son. We are not the kind that holds grudges, and our only thought and wish is for you, our only daughter, to be happy.

We are well and we never complain. Your father works hard, and sometimes he comes home very tired and worn out with the strain of his cases and the business, but he is well, and, thank the good Lord, he has kept his head above water in this depression when so many sink and go down. I pray for you every night and only hope that you are taken care of and that you will come through the ordeal that is in store for you. It is a heavy responsibility to be a mother, and it is dangerous for a girl. She goes down into the valley of the shadow. I did when

I bore you, but I have never been sorry or regretted it. I hope
you will never regret it.

We will come to see you over Labor Day.

Your loving mother
Mother

IV

Bernard and Elizabeth turned the corner onto Fifth Avenue.
It was twilight, and the street was almost deserted.

"Fifth Avenue's dull on Sundays," Bernard said.

"There's a girl who's going to have a baby, too," Elizabeth
said, nodding her head in the direction of a pregnant young
woman.

"Before you became pregnant I only noticed girls on the
street who weren't pregnant—now, I only notice them when
they are."

"I must look awfully big now."

"You've never looked more beautiful."

"But you do want me slim again?"

"Naturally—I don't want to raise a baseball team, or a whole
squad for the next war to save democracy."

The years ahead couldn't be smooth and peaceful. He
wanted to spare her from worrying about things she couldn't
understand. God, this sense of impending catastrophe had
been in the back of his mind for some time now. He didn't
really know how it had developed. Way back early in 1927,
before he'd come to New York, he'd awakened one day thinking that prosperity couldn't last. Back in 1926 or 1927 he'd
decided, on the basis of reading some European history, that
there had to be another war. But it seemed that this alone hadn't
given him a nervous sense of impending catastrophe.

"People in Chicago don't talk about war the way they do
here."

"We used to on campus sometimes."

"Does it make you afraid, Bernard?"

"Fear is a waste of emotional energy," he said curtly, because he knew how frightened he would be if he allowed himself to think about the dangers of another World War.

She slid her arm in his and said admiringly,

"You're so brave, Bernard."

"I wish I were."

"You are."

All his life he'd worried about his courage. He wondered if he were a physical coward. And would he be able to measure up to all that men would probably have to face during his lifetime? But walking toward Eighth Street at this hour, with the street so peaceful, after such a peaceful day of work, how could one think of any catastrophes to come?

"I did something foolish last week, Bernard. I was taking a walk."

"Was that foolish?"

"Don't tease me," she laughed.

"Why?"

"Because you don't like to be teased yourself."

"I don't mind it."

"You do so, Bernard."

"Well, what about your folly?"

"Oh, we passed the building—it's back on the other side of the street. There's the Brevoort, Bernard, and we haven't had our Sunday-morning breakfast there yet."

And she thought this was only one of the many things they had talked about doing in New York that they'd never done. She knew that she shouldn't blame Bernard, because he had worked so hard for her, and they couldn't afford it. Glad as she was becoming about having a baby—and, yes, she was glad— she was—still, it would have been better if they could have had a few years together alone.

"If you didn't have to work, we could see a movie."

"Honey, the sooner I finish this book, the sooner we'll get the rest of the advance due me."

"Bernard, I don't waste money . . . except for little sweets —and a pregnant woman does have cravings."

"Honey, I was neither complaining nor criticizing you—I was merely stating the facts."

"I'm not a hindrance to you—am I, Bernard?" she asked.

He took her to him and kissed her.

"Is that the answer to my question, Bernard?" she asked, wide-eyed.

"Yes," he said with feeling.

Her face broke out with joy. He took her arm, and they crossed Eighth Street, walking on toward Washington Square.

"You didn't tell me about that foolish thing you did last week."

"Oh, that—I went to a real-estate agent. And—"

"I hope you didn't buy a house."

"I acted as if I were very rich. I fooled him. And I had him showing me big apartments in a building back there on Fifth Avenue. We passed the building. . . . Oh, Bernard, wouldn't it be wonderful if we could live there."

They were passing the secluded row of houses in Washington Mews, and she pointed.

"Yes—but it would be expensive."

"I heard Arthur Hampton telling Mr. Barber he thought your book would have a good sale."

"I'll never make a great deal out of my books. If we can get a simple living out of them, I'll be satisfied."

"You never can tell, Bernard."

They crossed over into Washington Square and sat on a bench.

The Square was lively. In back of them many Italians were talking loudly and spiritedly. Boys were running about and shouting. Couples passed, arm in arm. Overhead the sky was full of stars.

"Bernard, we don't have to go and do exciting things to be happy, do we? We can be happy just being together."

"We've already gone through a lot of troubles, haven't we?"

She thought for a moment.

"It's four years next month. Our first time. I was so afraid.

And I was afraid, too, that if I didn't, you wouldn't love me."

"Was that the only reason you did it?" he asked.

"Bernard—I was only a girl then."

They sat. Bernard was calm and melancholy. Now that he had almost finished the revision of his book, he seemed to regard Eva differently. She had become bound up in his mind with the character he had based on her. His regrets about her had gone into his book. He had resolved them. The writing of his book seemed to have made her a closed chapter of the past. He felt more tender toward Elizabeth. With a baby, she would grow and mature. The child would form a bond between them. Sometimes he was ashamed of himself for not having wanted it. Wasn't parenthood a common human experience? He shouldn't want to avoid it. And yet the prospect of being a father did bring with it the melancholy realization that now the freedom of youth was over. He had had so little youth. He had sacrificed so much of it to ambition, to his desire to learn, to his determination to have a career as a writer. He was having that career. He couldn't complain, could he? Yet he had lost something. He had sacrificed most of his youth for a future. Going over his book, he had grown in confidence about his future. Yes, he could have one if . . . if he could only earn a living. And if there were to be any futures.

"Sometimes I have thoughts that would seem insane to most people," he said. "I have one now—you know, honey, the future of a writer may be better than that of a businessman. I'll bet they worry more than I do."

Elizabeth was silent. She was thinking that all her life she would be Mrs. Bernard Carr, and that she was going to be the mother of his child. Oh, that's what was so wonderful about marriage. Had her mother felt this way when her father had married her? Did Mother still feel this way? Elizabeth guessed that, yes, her mother did love her father. If anything happened to him, Mother would be just heartbroken. If anything happened to Bernard! But it wouldn't. He was strong and healthy.

She slid her hand along the few inches of bench separating

them and squeezed his hand. She had wanted to sit here tonight, because Bernard had sat in this little park years ago with that girl, Eva. But Bernard and Eva had never sat here, married, with Eva having his child inside of her. She was filled with a sense of quiet triumph.

Chapter Sixteen

I

Bᴇʀɴᴀʀᴅ read the telegram again.

FATHER STRICKEN SERIOUS. JAMES

"Bernard, you'd better go home," Elizabeth said.

"What'll you do? What if something happens to you while I'm gone . . . I wonder what happened to my father."

Why couldn't his brother have been more explicit? He wasn't going back. He owed nothing to his father. What difference did it make to him or to the world if his father should live or die? How did a poor worn-out drunkard count in the scales of the human race? Why should a son be responsible for his father? Or feel grief if there were no grief? These questions ran through his mind with cold, clear, automatic logic. He felt nothing, dull, dazed. Why should he be hurt by this news?

"I'll telephone . . . But I'm not going back. We can't afford it."

"Oh, Bernard, he is your father."

"I didn't ask him to be my father. What good can I do by dashing to Chicago on a wild-goose chase?"

"Oh, Bernard . . ." Elizabeth exclaimed, pained and bewildered.

"If I don't go back, people in Chicago will talk . . ."

"That's what I was thinking, Bernard," she interrupted, missing his irony.

"Why should I care what they say? What are they to me? What does Chicago mean to me?"

"But, Bernard, it must mean something. Even if you say it

298

doesn't. After all, Bernard . . . you lived there so many years
. . . that . . . those years in Chicago, they're in you."

"That's why I don't want to go back. I don't want that past
to remain with me. I want to drive it all out of my mind."

She glanced aside and stared at the wall in fright.

"Bernard, please go . . . if we need money, I'll ask . . .
I'll ask my father."

"I don't want your father to have to pay for the Carrs. It
isn't his lookout."

"Bernard, please don't look at it that way," she said, beginning to cry.

Why should she cry over his father? Wasn't it sentimental?

"I'll go out and telephone," he said, rising.

He and Elizabeth went to the drugstore at Eleventh and University. He got several dollars' worth of change, entered a telephone booth, and got a long-distance operator. He waited impatiently. Then there was the ringing. That ringing was in his
home in Chicago, miles away.

"Hello?"

It was Art.

The operator talked. He felt vague. His thoughts were
unclear.

"Is this Woodlawn 1891?"

He had forgotten the old number. They still had a phone,
despite the depression.

"Carr? Is this Carr? New York is calling."

"Yes."

The operator asked for his money. He dropped quarters and
dimes into the box and listened to the ring.

"Go ahead, New York . . ."

"Hello, Art. This is Bernard," he said, while Art said hello
at the same moment.

There was a brief but weighted and seemingly long pause.

"I got your telegram."

"Yes. Father had a stroke. The doctor's given up hope. The
priest was just here."

"When did it happen?" Bernard asked.

"At nine o'clock last night. He pitched over in the kitchen. I'm afraid it's the end, Bernie."

"Listen, I'll come. I'll wire you about it. I'll come as quickly as I can get there. How is Mother?"

"All right . . . It's not any fun, of course, but she's holding up all right."

"Can I speak to her?"

Bernard heard Art calling his mother.

"Hello, Bernard."

"Hello, Mother. I'm sorry."

"The Lord's will can't be gainsaid. Are you well and is your wife well, Son?"

"Yes, Mother. I'm coming home."

"We'll be here. Your father is in a bad condition. I was praying for his soul."

"I'll be home as fast as I can get there, Mother."

There was a moment of silence. Bernard felt tense. He didn't know what to say.

"I'll wire about arriving. I haven't made connections yet."

"Yes, Bernard."

"All right, Mother, and here is a kiss."

He blew a kiss through the phone.

"God bless you, Bernard."

"Good-by, Mother."

"Good-by, Bernard."

He hung up and stood in the phone booth, perspiring. He was weak, dazed, overcome with awe. He went out to Elizabeth, who was sitting in one of the booths.

"I'm going. It's a stroke. There's no hope."

"Oh!" she exclaimed. "But, Bernard, I'm glad you're going."

They got coffee.

As he lifted the cup of coffee to his lips, he thought that his father's life had been a long succession of seconds and minutes which were now limping to their end. The minutes of his own life were passing. He was growing away from his own youth.

Why did he now feel so drawn to the scenes of all that past bitterness and frustration?

"Bernard, don't feel too badly," Elizabeth said, sympathetically.

"No, I don't," he said, thinking he must show at all times that he was courageously rational. "My father always hated me. I pitied him. Now, any minute, he'll be non-existent, mere dead flesh . . ."

Elizabeth sat up straight, startled and shocked.

He was bitter. In his father's death, he could see the end of all man and the answer to all of the fables, the superstitions, the lies, the false dreams he had been told as a boy. To go back to see this death without fear would be a proof and justification of his own rationalism. He would go back to look at nothing, literally at nothing that had once been his father. He would go back like an intellectual ghoul.

Elizabeth reached across the table and took his hand. Touched, he dared not tell her that he felt no need of comfort.

"Bernard!"

He forced a smile on his face.

II

After telling the operator that he would accept the collect, person-to-person call, Mr. Whelan waited at his desk with a pounding heart.

"Hello, Daddy."

Her young, girlish voice, which he hadn't heard for so long, came over clearly.

"Hello, Elizabeth. What's the matter? Is something wrong?" he said, masking his joy and excitement.

"Not with me. I'm well. How are you, Daddy?"

"Why, I'm fine," he answered, surprised, as he nervously tapped his foot.

"I'm so happy to hear your voice, Father. Can you hear me clearly?"

"Yes, very clearly. And I'm so glad to hear you, too."

"How is Mother?"

"She's well. You should have tried to get me at home tonight when you could have spoken to both of us. Your mother will be sorry she didn't get to speak to you."

"But she'll see me soon . . . I think."

"Elizabeth, what's the matter?" he asked in an agitated voice.

"Bernard's father had a stroke. I want to come home with Bernard. I don't want to stay here alone in my condition."

"Why, of course, you must come. When will you get here? I'll meet you. Bernard can stay with us, too . . ."

"But, Daddy, I want to fly because the train takes so long."

"It's not safe."

"Oh, it's pretty safe, Daddy. I inquired. And I want to talk to you because, Father . . ."

"How much do you need?" he asked without reflecting. "I'll wire you your fare, fare for both of you. You take the first plane here—if the weather's good. How is the weather?"

"It's wonderful here, very clear, Daddy. They're holding a reservation for a plane this afternoon, and we'll see you to-night."

"Fine. How much do you need?"

"Daddy, could you . . . one hundred dollars? Bernard will be able to pay you back next year when his book comes out."

"I'll wire it immediately. You wire me here about your arrival, and I'll meet you. Are you sure you're all right?"

"Yes . . . only, I'm almost crying because I'm so happy. I'll see you tonight."

"Yes. I'll wire you the money immediately."

"Oh, Father, I'm so happy. Here, I'm blowing you a kiss . . . Did you hear my kiss?"

"Yes . . ."

He checked on her address and wrote it down.

There was a pause.

"Good-by, Daddy."

"Good-by, Elizabeth."

He heard the click of the receiver. He hung up, swung sidewise in his chair, and sat in a daze. Then, as he got up from his chair, he sneered. So, the cocky lad had had to come to him, and he did it through Elizabeth. They both had to come to him, the Babbitt. All these months he'd been waiting for his moment of revenge. And now he didn't want it.

III

Patrick J. Carr lay in extremis.

The bedroom smelled of death and urine. Two holy candles burned on the dresser. Art Carr gazed at his dying father and listened to the rattling expirations of breath with awe, fear, and fascination. His father had turned into a noisy lump of suffering flesh. The face was distorted and had aged. The sunken eyes stared at nothing with idiotic fixation. The hair had turned white. Art leaned a bit forward and continued to stare with absorption. He wanted the end to come. The sight of his father hurt him. He thought that he ought not to stand here gaping. He wished he could say something, that the old man could talk to him. He wished it hadn't happened at all. He wished it hadn't happened the way it had. The old man was a goner, but he was going hard and slow. Everybody would one day be a goner. And this was the way it happened. The death rattle, the smells, the helplessness of it all. Those eyes! He himself was young and strong. How could he ever change and become like his dying father? How could he ever die? Must everybody end like this? Yes, some day you and I, too, would roll by in a big, black Whelan hearse.

Art went to the parlor, where Jim and Marie sat quietly.

"We're waiting for Doctor Branhill to come back," Marie said.

"He can't do anything now," Art said.

"I still have hopes," Jim said.

"I never realized it before. Mother is a saint," Marie said.

Her brothers were silent.

"When's Bernard coming?" Marie asked.

"He gets here at ten o'clock, the wire said. He's flying," Art said.

"Gosh, I hope nothing happens to him," Marie said.

"I hope he gets here in time," Jim said.

"I didn't think he'd come," Art said.

"I'm glad he's coming. I don't know why, but I'm glad," Marie said.

Mrs. Carr joined them. She looked worn. They sat, quiet and thoughtful. Art got up and went back to the sick room to gaze at his dying father with awe and fear and fascination.

Chapter Seventeen

I

Philip whelan looked poised and sure of himself, but inwardly he was very uncertain. He didn't know how he felt. He was with his wife and Jim and Marie Carr at the terminal. The plane was coming in, and he was fearful of some mishap. How could he bear it if Elizabeth should die in a last-minute accident? All day, after talking to her on the phone, he had been blowing hot and cold, one minute feeling eager to see his daughter and the next, asking himself if he hadn't been a sucker. But as a father he knew he was now vindicated. Talking with Jim and Marie, he was polite and cordial. He observed Marie closely. She was a pretty girl, but she lacked Elizabeth's daintiness and manners. She was a girl of a different class. The Carrs were simple, good people.

Mrs. Whelan was talkative and friendly. She was highly excited at the prospect of meeting Bernard and of finding out what he was like. His brother and sister seemed common, but the girl was pretty.

Jim, who had been keeping check of the plane, said that it was coming in now. All four of them tightened up. They all had been cast out of their ordinary routine of life, and they were affected more than they knew or could have described, even to themselves. And the fact that they were at an airport rather than a railroad station added the sense of drama to their experience. Excitement and novelty had been introduced into their lives by Patrick J. Carr's death.

They all watched the runway. They heard the announcement that the plane was in and kept their eyes on the gate. Even the Whelans, who were here to meet their daughter, were thinking

of Bernard more than of Elizabeth. Mr. Whelan became even
less sure of himself. A few passengers appeared. They still kept
their eyes on the gate. All four of them instantly relaxed when
they saw Elizabeth appear with Bernard tagging about a foot
behind her. The Whelans were shocked at the sight of Elizabeth,
pregnant, but she looked neat and happy. Bernard was confused
and shy.

Mr. Whelan stepped forward and embraced his daughter.
She spoke gayly, and as though nothing had ever happened between them. Then Mrs. Whelan embraced her. Bernard was glad
to see his sister and brother. They might ease the strain he feared
and expected in meeting the Whelans. He and Marie embraced.

"I'd forgotten how pretty you were," he told Marie.

"Bernie . . . Father passed away at six-thirty tonight,
peacefully," Jim said, almost as though he had learned the announcement by rote.

Bernard accepted the news calmly. The moment he'd seen the
four of them, he'd been certain that his father had died.

"Bernard, dear, I'm so sorry," Elizabeth told him sympathetically. "Father just told me the news."

"Bernard," Mrs. Whelan said almost with professional solemnity, "I'm sorry about your bereavement. But I'm glad to know
you wanted to come back."

Mr. Whelan firmly shook hands with Bernard.

"Thank you," Bernard said, still shy and confused.

"Welcome, Bernard. Sad as this meeting is, Philip and I are
happy to welcome you as our son-in-law," Mrs. Whelan said.

Jim and Marie greeted Elizabeth.

No one talked for several moments. Then Elizabeth chat-
tered about the airplane trip. Mr. Whelan assumed control of
the situation, asked Bernard about their baggage, and said he'd
go out and drive his car to the entrance and pick them up. Jim
went with Bernard for their grip and insisted on carrying it.
They all went out front. Mr. Whelan drove up in a large black
limousine. Elizabeth sat in front with her father. As others got
into the back, Jim insisted on taking one of the folding seats.

Driving away, Mr. Whelan was pleased with himself. The sight of Elizabeth pregnant shouldn't have surprised him as much as it had. But he had gotten over that immediately. She looked well and healthy. She was a beautiful girl, and she reminded him of Ruth when she'd been carrying Elizabeth. And Bernard was comporting himself like a well-mannered and serious young fellow. Perhaps many of his judgments about them both had been exaggerated. He was glad to have Elizabeth back with him, especially because in these last months he'd come to fear he'd never see his daughter again. She looked well, and not at all as if she'd had a hard time. He'd done right in sending them the money to come. He'd been there when they'd wanted him. The lad, too, had lost his father. And the Carrs were poor. Carr was trying to make something of himself. If Elizabeth could only persuade him to forget about atheism, well, perhaps he'd turn out all right. And Elizabeth would give him a grandchild. Philip Whelan was more content than he'd been at any time since Elizabeth's elopement.

"Gosh, it is still a surprise to me to be here with everybody," Elizabeth said.

"I think you'll find us, and Chicago, much the same, Elizabeth," Mrs. Whelan said.

Bernard couldn't believe that Whelan didn't still hate him. Now that he was here, he wished he hadn't come, or, at least, hadn't come on Whelan's money.

"You are going to stop and see your mother, Bernard?"

"Yes, I ought to."

"Bernard, we want you to know you are welcome at our house." There was a slight and sudden throb in Mrs. Whelan's voice as she went on. "I fixed up Elizabeth's old room for both of you."

"Yes, Bernard, you're welcome," Mr. Whelan said.

"Maybe, Father, you could give him a key. He might want to talk with his folks tonight," Elizabeth said.

"Yes, I brought an extra one along."

"I was thinking, I might stay home tonight and come over in the morning."

"Just as you think. Your mother will want to see you in this hour, I know," Mrs. Whelan said.

"I have to go back to my establishment. Bernard, we're going to take good care of your father's remains. I talked with your brother, Jim, about it, but if you have any questions, why, we can take them up," Mr. Whelan said.

"Oh, I'm sure you know how to manage it, Mr. Whelan," Bernard said.

Bernard was indifferent as to how his father, or anyone else, should be buried. Discussion of the question would only bore him. Yet he sensed both a willingness to be friendly and a professional pride in Mr. Whelan's words. But this only confirmed all his feelings of difference, of separation, from his father-in-law. He looked out the window, seeing vacant lots, dark storefronts, wooden buildings, lampposts. The street looked dingy. This was Sixty-third Street, but not his Sixty-third Street. Elizabeth was talking away, about New York, about the airplane trip, about herself. Then she said:

"Oh, I'm so glad I came with Bernard."

"It gives us a chance to know you, Elizabeth," Marie said.

"Yes, Elizabeth, after all, I'm going to be an uncle now. I'll be Uncle Jim," Jim Carr said.

Mr. Whelan cut down to Marquette Boulevard and moved on, driving silently. Bernard knew he ought to say something. He was silent, with his eyes on the passing scenes of houses, apartment buildings, sidewalks. He didn't know what to say.

II

At the sight of his mother's sad, tired, lined face, Bernard was almost overcome with sorrow. His mother had aged, and her eyes seemed less forbidding.

"Hello, Mother," he said in a voice that betrayed agitation.

"Hello, Bernard."

She kissed him, and, turning, wiped away the tears. Then they went into the parlor.

"Hello, Bernie," Art said.

He and Art shook hands. The parlor looked shabbier than ever with its familiar furniture. He sat down in his father's chair and casually observed the frayed rug, the table in the corner, and the rocker with the faded pillow. All unchanged, the room spick and span, but so poor-looking. And his mother was staring at him in a strange way.

"Bernard, do you want coffee? You always used to drink so much coffee," Marie asked.

"I'll make it," Mrs. Carr said, starting to rise.

"Mother, you stay here and sit still for a while. Let me make it," Marie said.

"I'll help, Sis," Art said, leaving the parlor with Marie.

"Your father is gone. Poor man. He had a hard end," his mother said. "I prayed that you would get here before the end, Bernard. But my prayers weren't answered. We were all by his bedside. But then, God was sparing you. His end was an awful sight. The poor man suffered hard," his mother said.

"Yes, it hit me, it did," Jim said, looking guiltily down at the rug.

Bernard wished they would hurry with the coffee. Drinking coffee would give him something to do. How soon would he be able to get away from here, to get back to New York?

"You're looking well, Bernard," his mother said.

"I feel good."

"And so is Betty. Mother, you have to see her," Jim said.

Bernard wanted to know more about his father's death, but he couldn't bring himself to ask any questions. And, sitting in his father's chair, he felt a little ashamed. Jim, Marie, Art had borne the family burden. He had been contemptuous of them so often. He had sent his mother five dollars only twice since he had left. Before that, when he had gone to college, he hadn't been able to contribute much. He had really walked out on them, hadn't he? Why had he come back now in their hour of sorrow? But they seemed glad to see him.

Didn't they have things they wanted to do, aspirations, plans, hopes of their own? And in their own minds, were his needs, his desires to know, to think, and to write, more important than their own plans and needs? Maybe Jim, or Art, too, wanted to get married. Hadn't he left them trapped? But he was trapped. Everybody, almost everybody, was trapped.

Marie called them all out to the kitchen.

"Gee, now that you are here, I'm glad you're back," Marie said.

"I'm glad, too. And you look so pretty," Bernard told her. "Do I?"

Mrs. Carr quietly watched him. She couldn't tell if he had changed or not. He was so different from the other children. It wasn't only his learning, his education that made him different. There was something in him that didn't come out. Sometimes, God forgive them both, when he and his poor father would quarrel, it used to come out.

She gazed at her other children. They were all young and had their lives ahead of them. They were so far away from her. Watching Patrick die, she had remembered and regretted so much of her life, and she had felt so old, so useless. She couldn't explain how she felt. She couldn't talk. She didn't know how to let her children know that she was sorry to lose Patrick, sorry now to be so alone in life with her gray hairs and her tired heart.

While Mrs. Carr sat so silent and so sad, the children talked about trivialities. Bernard stared around the kitchen. So many of the objects in it had been in this kitchen since his boyhood. That old stove, which his mother kept clean. The sink. There was some rust on the pipes under the sink now. This table. There was new oilcloth on it. Objects, the objects of the circumstances of one's past life—how meaningless they could become! But why should he think of objects? His father had become an object. A corpse was an odorous object that had once been a human being. And his father-in-law was taking care of the odor.

"He suffered at the end, Bernie," Jim said. "The way he looked at us—he was trying to tell us something, trying to tell Mother something. I'll be sure of that till my dying day."

Bernard listened attentively, regretting he'd arrived too late. He'd really wanted to look his dying father in the face. If he could have faced his father on the poor fellow's deathbed, if he could have looked death face-to-face here in the house of his childhood, he would have learned something—he might have learned how much courage he had. He envied his brothers and his sister for this grisly experience. He had had so much more experience than they, had seen so much more, had learned so much more of life, yet he had missed this terribly vital experience, and they hadn't.

"It came so suddenly. We never know when we are going to feel the whip of the Will of God," Mrs. Carr said.

"Did he say much? What did he say?" asked Bernard with nervous intensity.

"He mumbled. You couldn't understand him. At times, he seemed like a little baby. I think he was afraid," Marie said.

Art began pacing about the kitchen.

"Arthur, sit yourself down and take it easy," Mrs. Carr said gently.

He paid no attention to her.

"It was in the kitchen?" Bernard asked.

Jim and Marie shook their heads.

"We carried him into his room," Jim said. "I didn't know what had happened to him. We called the priest right away, and then we got Doctor Branhill. Everybody has been swell. Father Kennedy came. He's a swell priest, swell. And Phil Whelan, he's been a prince to us."

"But he crumpled right here in the kitchen?" Bernard asked.

"Yes," Art said bitterly, as he sat down.

Bernard suspected Art was hostile to him. His suspicion was disturbing.

"He's dead," Art said, angrily spitting out his words.

"Arthur, pray. I'll pray with you," Mrs. Carr said gently.

"I just want to be let alone," Art said, rising and walking heavy-footed out of the kitchen.

They were all tensely silent. Bernard watched their drawn, tight faces. Was there something they hadn't told him? Had they all really loved their father? Mrs. Carr went quietly after Art.

"Bernard," Marie said with forced resolution, "Father was drunk. He had his fist clenched and his arm raised to punch Mother, and something came over him. He looked stupid, and then hurt, and he fell down. It was a stroke."

"Where did it happen? Where was he standing?" Bernard asked.

Marie and Jim both picked different spots. While they were arguing as to who had pointed out the exact spot, Bernard interrupted to ask:

"How did he fall?"

"He fell," Jim said.

"He crumpled up and fell sidewise. His head just missed hitting the table. That's why I know he was standing right on this spot where I'm standing now," Marie said.

"No, Sis," Jim began.

"Did he fall with a thud?"

"Yes, kind of," Jim answered.

"He foamed a little at the mouth . . . oh, let's not talk about it," Marie said, distressed. "Father was sometimes hard to take when he drank."

"Yes, it was my father's weakness," Jim said.

"Just before it happened," Marie said, "he was calling Mother names, saying that something was her fault, that she was a hypocrite and only cared about religion and not her family, and that she and nobody would ever know . . ."

"Ever know what . . . Marie?"

"I don't know. He just was wild, and his face got so red. I was afraid. He was like a madman. And Art got angry and jumped up and called him a sonofabitch . . ."

"I don't know how I'd feel if we hadn't got the priest. He did receive the last sacraments," Jim said.

"I just wish I hadn't been here when it happened. His face was swollen and ugly, as if it wasn't a face. I was just petrified, petrified with fear, and I thought, oh, he's going to kill Mother and what will we do . . ."

"I never thought I'd live to see such a thing," Jim said, his chin sunken dispiritedly on his chest.

Art sauntered casually back to the kitchen, and when he learned that they'd described to Bernard what had happened, he asked:

"Can you explain to me how I feel, Bernie?"

"Art, you haven't done anything you have to feel guilty about."

"I see your point, Bernie. But, after all, I just wish things were different."

"The world ought to be different," Bernard said.

"Well, as I see it, a person just has to go along, mind his own business, go along, and not have any hard feelings against anybody," Jim said.

"Now that he's gone . . ." Marie said, stopping, a very thoughtful expression crossing her face.

"I guess he couldn't help being a weak boozer," Bernard said softly.

"If you just come down to brass tacks, and admit it, all of us are weak, but we like to pretend we aren't. Hell, we aren't paragons, if I can use a dictionary word," Art said.

Bernard slowly shook his head in agreement. He was thinking of values, wondering what was really right and wrong, and telling himself that there was really no solving of the personal problems of human relationships. And yet, did people have to be so ugly to one another? What had made his father so ugly?

They all lapsed into moody silence.

III

Sitting at the kitchen table, with its new, red-checked oilcloth, and having a cup of tea with her mother, Elizabeth remembered how she and Bernard had stolen silverware from the
cafeteria on Sheridan Square, and how she had cooked in the
basement room on Fifteenth Street. She so much wanted a real
home and a well-appointed kitchen.

"Gosh, Mother, I'd forgotten what a fine, big kitchen you
have."

Her eyes took in familiar objects, the big refrigerator, the
large washing machine, the big iron skillet. The pantry door
was half-opened, and she knew that, as always, it would be
well-stocked with food.

"Don't you have a good kitchen?" Mrs. Whelan asked.

Elizabeth suspected that her mother might be trying to pump
her.

"Not like this. . . . You know, Mother, New York isn't
like Chicago, that is, unless you live quite a bit from the center
of things. The apartments are small. You won't find many
kitchens like this in New York, except in the most expensive
apartments."

Elizabeth and her mother were glad to see each other, but
they both shrank from speaking of what was on their minds.
Mrs. Whelan was somewhat surprised at her daughter's good
spirits and appearance of health. She had imagined that Elizabeth would return woebegone and penitent. And though she
was glad to discover her daughter looking so well and happy,
she hadn't become accustomed to her own surprise. And Bernard had not seemed at all like what she had imagined him. In
the car, he had been gentlemanly. Mrs. Whelan thought him
attractive. He didn't look anything like the devil-may-care,
romantic type she had imagined him. In fact, she had seen any
number of young men in Chicago who resembled Bernard. If
she hadn't known he was a writer, she never would have believed it. She had thought writers would be different. Philip had

misinformed her, and she was beginning to suspect that Philip was jealous of Bernard. A father looked on a daughter differently from a mother. She had always known that she was raising Elizabeth to marry her off well. That was the way most sensible mothers regarded their daughters.

If she had had a son! Elizabeth might be carrying a boy. When she had been carrying Elizabeth, she and Philip had expected a boy, and she still remembered his disappointment.

"You're happy with Bernard?" Mrs. Whelan asked.

"Yes, Mother . . . Mother, honestly, don't you think he's nice . . . and kind of cute?" Elizabeth shyly said.

"He seemed like quite a nice young man. I had imagined he'd be different . . . Bohemian."

"Oh, no, Mother, Bernard isn't Bohemian. He works as hard as Father. He's very ambitious. At the University, he worked very hard and won a Phi Beta Kappa key. He's kind of modest and doesn't wear it. But don't you think he ought to, Mother?"

Mrs. Whelan didn't know what a Phi Beta Kappa key was. Elizabeth explained it to her, and then Mrs. Whelan agreed that Bernard ought to wear his. She was impressed.

"In New York, Mother, Bernard is very well thought of. He is. Some day he's going to be rich and famous. When people meet him, oh, they just know this. Mother, don't you think Bernard is . . . oh, kind of different?"

"I thought your father was, too, when I was a girl."

"Well, Father is. Mother, he's really a dear."

"He was hurt," Mrs. Whelan said. "But I think he's very pleased that you're here. I think he's forgiven you."

"I know, Mother, and sometimes I felt badly. But I knew that in time you and Daddy would understand and forgive me. I love Bernard."

"I understand."

Elizabeth was conscious of a sense of equality with her mother that she had never before felt. She wanted to get her mother to go on talking about her father, but she didn't try. She didn't know why she knew it, but she knew that if she did, she would risk getting her mother angry and possibly set her against her. She was sure that Mother wasn't against Bernard, and perhaps would really win her father over to liking him. And she had a plan she hadn't even had time to think out.

"Mother," she said with seeming spontaneity, "it's so good to be here."

"And you are happy, Elizabeth?"

"Yes, Mother, I am. I am really happy. Of course . . ."

Mrs. Whelan leaned forward, alert, eager, her eyes keen now.

"Of course, being in my condition . . . you don't know. You feel things you never knew you'd feel. Oh, Mother, I so wanted to see just you, because you could tell me things."

"What is it, Elizabeth?"

"What was it like, the pains?"

"I can't remember. I just remember that your poor father carried on more than we women do, Elizabeth, when it happens."

Their eyes met, and they smiled knowingly. Then Elizabeth suddenly burst into tears.

"Elizabeth!" Mrs. Whelan exclaimed in alarm.

She went to her mother.

"I'm just so happy, Mother. I want to cry."

Mrs. Whelan drew Elizabeth's head to her breast and stroked her hair.

"You're still my little girl."

"Mother, I'm sorry if I hurt you. I didn't want to. Forgive me."

"You know we do."

"I love Bernard, too, but . . . but you get afraid sometimes, knowing you are going to have a baby . . . and you don't know. . . . Mother, just let me cry."

"Yes, yes," Mrs. Whelan said soothingly. "You just go ahead and have a good cry."

Mrs. Whelan began to cry, too. Tears streamed down her face as she held Elizabeth closely against her.

"Elizabeth, my own little girl," Mrs. Whelan said.

"Mother, let me cry," Elizabeth sobbed.

After they had calmed down, Mrs. Whelan and Elizabeth chatted gaily over more tea, feeling very close to each other.

Mr. Whelan came in, looking worn. He sat down and said he was tired. His wife asked him if he wanted tea. He didn't. His emotions choked up on him. He was shy. He couldn't speak, so he continued to look away from Elizabeth. Then he looked down at the table and said, speaking slowly:

"Elizabeth, I'm very glad you're here."

"Daddy, it's . . . it's hard to explain. I loved Bernard, and everything is going to come out all right. I am so happy."

"I hope so. It's been lonely here without you . . . but, then, I always looked forward to the day you'd get married. I wanted you to get married some day. A girl should be. Maybe it was flighty, the way you did it."

"I . . . Father, something came over me, that's all."

"I think I understand," he said quietly.

"I'm glad Bernard's brothers and sister called you, Father. He was going to wire them to."

"It's really an accommodation. They're poor, simple people, and they have little money. I'm giving them more than they're paying for. I'm burying him at a loss, but I want to. After all is said and done, Bernard is your husband. That makes him my son-in-law. And what would the public think if I didn't handle this case? People might have talked. They could have said that my own son-in-law wouldn't give me his father's funeral. That would have been embarrassing. But they called me."

"I'm glad, Father."

"Of course, if Bernard goes around spouting those wild ideas he used to have—I hope you'll talk to him, Elizabeth."

"Bernard's changed. He's changing, Father. He's good to me, and he works hard, very hard."

"He ought to. He has to take care of you. A man who won't work hard for his freely chosen wife and for his family is no good on earth. He ought to work hard."

"Elizabeth, I want you to know Bernard is now as welcome

here as you are. This is your home." Mrs. Whelan turned to her husband. "Isn't it . . . Father?"

Mr. Whelan hesitated a moment before he answered.

"Yes," he said, looking tenderly at Elizabeth.

IV

"I don't know why. I just don't want to sleep, Bernard," Marie said, sitting alone with Bernard in the parlor.

"Neither do I," he said musingly.

"I didn't think you'd come."

"Why?" Bernard asked.

"Oh, I don't know. I just didn't think you'd come, that you'd care about us."

"I wish I could do something. Hell, there isn't much I can do. We had to borrow the money to get here from Whelan."

"I don't like him."

"Nobody likes an undertaker."

"Bernard, I feel as if I'm in a rut. . . . I don't know. I don't know what it is. I don't want to live the way Father and Mother did."

"I won't."

"You don't have to now."

"I don't have any money. I'm not secure. It's been sheer grubbing for me since I went to New York. It's always been that for me."

"Remember when we were little?" she asked.

He waited for her to go on.

"I just thought, oh, I thought life was somehow going to be wonderful. Now, do you know, I'm twenty-one."

"So is Elizabeth."

"I don't understand," Marie said in an abstracted moody manner.

"What?"

"Oh . . . life."

Bernard tried to think of something to say to his sister. The silence between them seemed like a weight that kept growing heavier.

"I don't know what it is. I was thinking there must be something wrong with me . . . I don't feel sorry . . . or sorry enough. Bernard, do you feel very sorry that Father died?"

He hesitated for a moment.

"No, I don't. I'm sorry, but not in the way a son should feel sorry. I'm sorry because there's so much waste of life, so much futility. The fact is that his life just meant nothing."

"I don't hold anything against him, now that he's dead. But I was thinking—now, take Elizabeth—I saw her and her father. He loves her. I just feel that I want to cry because of the way I feel, but I won't. I won't cry! I feel Father never loved us or cared about us or wanted us."

"It doesn't seem as though he did."

"I had the funny thought that when he was going to hit Mother just before . . . just before he had his stroke, that he was doing it because she had us, and that it was us, us more than Mother. That's what I'd sometimes feel when I was little. I'd feel so badly, and I'd have no one to tell it to. Oh, Bernard, am I making sense, or is this all . . . childish and . . . and naive?"

"I understand," Bernard said, moved, a sudden feeling of protective love for his sister welling up in him.

During all these years she had been growing up, and he hadn't paid much attention to her. When she'd begun to develop, he'd sometimes looked at her with regretful longing, but he'd never known her or taken a real interest in her. Until this moment she had been virtually a stranger to him. They were all strangers to him, just as he was to them. And his father, too, had been a stranger. In effect, a stranger had died. The living, he reasoned, had the bitter triumph of outliving the dead.

"You never liked him, did you?" she asked.

"He never liked me," Bernard quickly replied.

"But you didn't like him, either, did you, Bernard?"

He didn't want to answer her question.

"I guess I didn't," he admitted.

"Do you think he hears us talk?"

"No."

She stared at him. He guessed she was afraid.

"Last night, I asked myself—is this all there is? Is it possible that there isn't anything left of us and for us after we die? I asked myself this question, and I was afraid."

"This is the only life we'll ever know," Bernard said bitterly.

Marie nodded her head in agreement and then said with feeling:

"I want something different."

"What do you want?" Bernard said.

They were both tense and looked off because of the sense of strain they were afraid to show. The room seemed charged with their emotions.

"Something I haven't got."

"It's something none of us will ever get."

They were talking slowly, with pauses now between each statement.

"What won't we ever get, Bernard?"

"Much out of life."

They sat.

"The dawn's coming up," Bernard said, noticing the gray through the kitchen window.

"Gosh, we've been up all night."

They went and stood at the parlor window. Bernard put his arm around his sister and she rested her head on his shoulder. The gray dawn was seeping over Maryland Avenue. Across the street, the gray stone house where the Daughertys had lived was taking shape. They had lost their home in the depression. Frank Daugherty had gone to school with him. What was he doing? He could ask Marie. But he didn't.

The street was quiet. In this dawn, Maryland Avenue was not the dull, familiar street he'd often cursed and hated. The three-story gray brick building. Cold stones, dead stones in the gray dawn. A car passed. Two men carrying their lunches under their arms. The sky was growing bright above the houses and buildings. His eyes swept along across the street, the gray brick apartment, the Daugherty house, the brick Kennedy house, with neat shrubbery, a dark, deep green in the dawn, the red-brick three-story house where Olson used to be janitor, the Carey house, clean and painted with a new white coat! That railing in front of the red-brick apartment. How many times had he jumped back and forth over it? And in these houses, sleeping people, people waking up to another day! Life! And himself and Marie looking out of the window.

"I never knew you before. You're nice, nicer than I thought you were, even if you are my brother," Marie said softly.

He squeezed her, wishing he could do something more for her, something to make her life better and richer.

"And I never saw the dawn this way, either," she said. "It's different. It's like . . . like I never saw it before."

All dawns were full of promise. The dawn was like childhood, the infancy and the childhood of a day full of so many seconds of rich possibilities, and then these were squandered, and his father, his father was dead and cold, a dead, cold commentary on the squandered dawns in a human life. Nietzsche had used the phrase, *the dawn man*. Now, he understood. The man of promise, the promise of life. But then, what was that promise?

They turned from the window.

"We better get some sleep," Marie said, her voice becoming matter-of-fact.

"Yes," he said, trying to stifle some strange embarrassment in himself.

Watching her, he was flooded with warm and protective feelings for her. He wanted to think. Life now seemed very simple. You could describe it as a period of heartbreaking sadness.

They stood a moment and then she started walking out of the room.

"Good night, Marie," he said, kissing her forehead.

Chapter Eighteen

I

EATING lunch with Elizabeth and her mother, Bernard couldn't feel at ease. He knew he would always be an interloper in the lives of the Whelan family. And, in addition, he was under obligation to them. He could only impress or please them by denying and masking what his real thoughts and feelings were. Pretending to listen to the conversation, he allowed his mind to wander, and he smiled in an effort to simulate interest. His eyes fell on the electric sewing machine in the corner. Elizabeth wanted a sewing machine. Once, his mother had borrowed a secondhand machine. How much had this machine cost? It was one of many symbols he could find in this smug home. The heavy polished furniture, the sterling silverware, the thick rugs, the linen, the ornate dishes—all these were symbols, too. And they were the fruits of death, when death was a business. Elizabeth actually wanted him to be a success so he could buy things like these for her. She had fitted right back into her home as though she had never left it. She liked all this. He couldn't.

"Philip was hoping you'd get here before he left, but he had to go," Mrs. Whelan said to Bernard.

"I stayed up late last night, talking."

"Of course, of course, I understand," she said with a note of sympathy that dismayed him.

"You look tired, Bernard, you poor boy," Elizabeth said.

"I feel all right."

"Bernard, now you must watch your health and keep well. Elizabeth, you must see to it that he does."

"Oh, Mother, Bernard's very healthy," Elizabeth said in a tone of familiarity and possessiveness. "Of course, he does drink too much coffee, and sometimes he works too hard and doesn't get enough sleep."

"Your father used to smoke too much, but I convinced him he shouldn't. But he is looking fine now, isn't he, Elizabeth?"

"Yes. Bernard, didn't you think so?"

"Yes, I do."

"Do you want something?" Elizabeth asked as Bernard rose.

"I was going to get some more coffee."

"See. I said he drank too much coffee. But since these are such special circumstances, maybe we ought to let him have an extra cup, Mother."

Elizabeth blew Bernard a kiss as Mrs. Whelan got him another cup of coffee.

"I missed you last night," Elizabeth said flirtatiously.

Bernard grinned. He didn't want to talk now.

"While you are with us, Bernard, I want you to know that this is just like home . . . it is home. Your second home," Mrs. Whelan said, coming back with his coffee. "Bygones are bygones, and now you are my son, and if you will let him, my husband will be like a father to you."

"I'm very grateful," Bernard said.

Elizabeth glowed. She was very pretty with this shining smile of happiness on her face.

"Well," Mrs. Whelan said, "I've got some things to do, now that I have guests. Food to order, and other things."

Bernard finished his coffee and sat a minute, feeling awkward.

"Bernard, you better run along now," Elizabeth said.

"Yes, I think I will."

He was self-conscious about kissing Elizabeth good-by in front of her mother. He stood by the table. She went up to him, kissed him, and said:

"Call me up, Bernard."

"I will. And take it easy now."

He started toward the hall that led into the dining room, but turned back and looked at his mother-in-law and said:

"Good-by."

"Good-by, Bernard. You'll be here for supper, won't you?"

"Yes, I will."

Bernard was glad to leave. But he was going to the undertaking parlor. Now he'd have to face Whelan, and he would look at the corpse of his father. He would take his time walking the few blocks from the Whelan home to the parlor.

He'd been away only nine months. But it was strange to be alone on the streets of the South Side of Chicago. He was oppressed. He looked at the houses. Most of them were squat, spread-out, two-story homes with well-tended lawns. Families like the Whelans lived in them. If you knew these people, you couldn't dislike them any more than you could the Whelans. The Whelans truly loved their daughter, and if he could take care of her, and give her a house like one of these, they would love him, or, at least, respect him. Why couldn't he accept their values? It wasn't merely because he wanted to write. He wanted to write because he was in revolt against what these homes symbolized.

He turned westward on Seventy-first Street. The Illinois Central tracks cut down the center of the street. Warning bells rang. The gates went down along the street. A three-car electric train passed, bound for the South Shore Station. There were stores on either side of the street, and quite a few women were out shopping. The pedestrians looked content, well-fed, and well-dressed. He stared at the people, hoping to meet someone he knew. Just ahead of him, an ordinary looking young girl was walking between two fat, middle-aged women. He overheard their conversation. One after another, they mentioned items of clothing they owned. The girl spoke of a new jacket she had. The woman on the outside said she had a new spring coat. The woman on the inside said she had a new dress. The girl said she had a new hat. Bernard's eyes popped, and he kept closely behind them, walked more slowly, listening. Then the conversation bored him, and he slackened his pace to avoid overhearing any more.

Elsie Cavanagh lived nearby. He could meet her, couldn't he? He hoped he would. Although he had no way of knowing, somehow he was convinced she'd read his book. He wanted her to read it, to like it, and to know that he'd adored her in his boyhood. But didn't he want to meet her in order to hurt her, to repay her for all the miserable envy he'd suffered because of her? Elsie Cavanagh, betrothed of Martin O'Hara, defendant in a case of criminal embezzlement. But he went soft, nostalgically remembering his boyhood dreams of her.

He bought a morning's *Chicago Clarion* at the corner of Jeffery and waxed into a mood of gay enthusiasm when he saw that the O'Hara trial was on the front page. Marty O'Hara's picture was in the paper, too. O'Hara had gotten fat. Bernard stood in front of the Walgreen drugstore, eagerly reading the story. A smile spread over his face as he learned that Marty O'Hara had been on the witness stand and hadn't been able to answer questions clearly and convincingly. He had signed and cashed checks for himself and his father about an hour before the banks had shut down. After reading this news account, Bernard folded up his paper, grinned, and thought that here was another illustration of the values of this world. O'Hara was considered a better person than he here on the Chicago South Side. If Marty hadn't been caught, who would have cared?

He crossed Jeffery and walked on down to the Whelan sign. He slowed down and even thought of turning around and not going there. If he could only walk off now, with nothing but the clothes on his back, and disappear.

Bernard entered Whelan's undertaking parlor with contradictory feelings. He felt vaguely like a condemned man, and then he changed, his feeling one of quiet triumph. At first he noticed nothing, although it was all familiar. He looked toward the small reception room on the left, with its plants, its heavy furniture, and its tone of impersonalized respectability. He'd once sat alone in there dreaming of the day he'd write. Now, he was a writer. He went into the long and rather narrow chapel. Camp chairs had been set up, and the casket was in front with flowers around it. The odor of the flowers was heavy and oversweet. The rug was a deep, purplish, ugly red. He walked slowly up the aisle between the chairs and stood in front of the casket.

There were neither words nor images in his mind. It was as though there were a hollow in his brain where the image of his father's corpse had been dropped and lost. He felt empty, empty rather than cold. He stared at the corpse.

The remains of Patrick J. Carr were laid out in a black suit, with a white shirt and a black tie. His face was an eerie, strange gray-and-white color in the light and with the powder on it. The hair was white, so different from the black and iron gray it had been nine months ago, when he had left Chicago. Black rosary beads were entwined in the folded, grayish old hands. This, Bernard reflected, was a crowning touch of, no, not of hypocrisy, but of mere meaningless sentiment. And the waxy, expressionless imitation of a youthful face! All suffering, all character had been taken out of this face. It was not even a calm, dead face. Just a dead face. Dead and cold. Powdered and dead and cold and prettified.

Bernard turned from the casket. He turned back to stare at it again, feeling he ought to have some thoughts, some feelings, some impressions which would well forth in a stream of descriptive words. All anger, all dissipation, all hatred had been shaken out of this face. By what? By death? Decay? Or by the undertaker's art?

He walked away and met Whelan just outside of the chapel. "Oh, hello, Bernard," Mr. Whelan said stiffly.

"How do you do, Mr. Whelan," he said formally.

They faced each other.

"You . . . you did very nicely with my father. It's dignified, and I like it, and I want you to know I'm very grateful."

"It's my business to do a good job," Mr. Whelan said.

There was an uncomfortable pause. Bernard was apprehensive.

"How does my establishment look after all these years?"

"The same. It's the same."

"That was some time ago. You were younger then. How old are you now, Bernard?"

"Twenty-six."

"I hope you have no hard feelings. This establishment is my business, my life work. I could see you wouldn't fit in here. You, you wanted to write. I have nothing against writing. It's not in my line. I don't claim I understand much about it. My daughter tells me you are respected in New York, and, well, you and she, you're younger . . . you're a different generation from my wife and me. I guess life changes, and new generations see things differently. But since you've tried to be a responsible lad, and my daughter loves you, here's my hand, Bernard."

Bernard took his hand. Whelan's grip was firm, and his direct, scrutinizing glance was discomforting. Bernard smiled to cover his lack of ease and said:

"Thank you, Mr. Whelan. It's very decent of you, and I'm grateful. I'm grateful for your . . . your kindness to us, and to my family. I try to do everything I can, Mr. Whelan. I work hard. When I was here, well, it wasn't right for me. . . ."

"Yes. I know. Now we understand each other."

"Thank you, Mr. Whelan."

"Don't mention it, Bernard."

Mr. Whelan smiled in a friendly way.

"I have some business to attend to. Smith and some of the boys are out there. Do you want to go back and see them?"

"I think I will."

"All right, Bernard."

Mr. Whelan turned and went up to his office.

Bernard stood for a moment, smoking and looking out the door of the establishment.

—Am I a hypocrite? he asked himself.

He was touched and a little humiliated. Whelan had acted decently. But, still, he was a Babbitt. How would he react to *Un-shapely Things*? And what would Whelan say if he knew how precarious their position was? He ought to go back to New York on Monday at the latest. He'd be stifled here.

He turned and walked out to the back rooms.

"Well, hello," Smith said to Bernard with constraint.

It was much the same. Smith was sitting at the table with two other lads.

"How are you?" Bernard asked.

They shook hands. Smith introduced Bernard to the other two as the boss's son-in-law. Both of them greeted Bernard respectfully.

"I'm sorry about your father, Carr," Smith said. "I hope you like the job we've done on him."

"I do. It's very good."

There was a pause.

"Are you back for good?" Smith asked.

"No, just for a few days," Bernard answered.

"Just a hit-and-run trip, huh? How's New York?" Smith asked.

"I like it."

"Is the mortician's business any different there than here, Mr. Carr?" Finley asked.

"I don't know. I don't know about it."

"I guess not. Everything is much the same all over these days," Smith said.

"What happened to my friend Clarke?"

"He just picked up and left us about two months ago. I don't know why he went. You and he sure argued, didn't you?"

"Yes," Bernard smiled, his confidence growing.

He realized that now, in this room, he was somebody, the boss's son-in-law. If he'd stayed here and let Whelan take him into the business, he'd be a success, a respectable person in the community. Lads like these would even envy him. Thanks to his marriage, he could win more respect in this part of Chicago than he could by all his efforts to be an honest creative writer. He saw instantly and with utter clarity why he had had to leave. And yet these lads seemed decent and happy. Whelan was decent, too. What was it then? What did his values mean when thrown against their values?

"Are you still writing books, Carr?"

"Yes, I am," Bernard answered.

"That's not a hard job, is it?" asked Finley.

"It's not a job, but it's hard enough. You've got to be your own boss and manage your own time."

"I wouldn't like that—that is, if it was working. My own time, when I got nothing to do but pleasure, that's jake. But telling myself I got to work, never, not for my money," Cooper commented.

"Well, Carr, I'm going to have my own place as soon as I can. The depression threw me back near the goal line. My old man was going to get me going, but he took a licking. As soon as things clear up, I'll have my own mortician's business," Smith said.

"I'm glad to hear that."

"Hello, fellows, what are you doing? Gassing about when my son-in-law was here?"

"More or less, Mr. Whelan," Smith said.

"Do you fellows know this is my son-in-law?"

Cooper and Finley nodded.

"I once fired him, but I guess he didn't want to stay fired," Whelan joked.

They smiled politely. Bernard's face was expressionless.

"And now he's going to make me a grandfather."

"Why, congratulations, Mr. Whelan," Smith said, and then, as an afterthought, he turned to Bernard. "Congratulations, Bernard."

The other two also congratulated Mr. Whelan and Bernard.

The pride in Mr. Whelan's voice was unmistakable. Bernard wondered if this were the real reason for the reconciliation. Whelan must have deeply wanted a son. Now he was sure he understood his father-in-law better. Whelan's name, his desire for continuity, for his name living on—all this must be very strong in the man. He, however, did not feel the need for a son to keep his name alive. He felt pity for Whelan as much as he did superiority. And his dead father in front. The hated son of a dead man was carrying on the name of Carr.

"Yes," Mr. Whelan said, giving Bernard a pat on the shoulders, "he's giving me a grandchild—a grandson, I hope."

II

Mrs. Carr and her four children waited in the chapel for friends and relatives to come and pay their last respects to Patrick J. Carr. Outside, it was bright and sunny. The chapel was dim and smelled of flowers.

"You know," Jim said, "I can't get over what Phil did to my father. It's nice to think that he looks so lifelike and young, and, well, it's nice to think he is fixed up the way he is and will have a dignified funeral."

"It doesn't do him much good," Art commented.

Mrs. Carr wore a black dress with a high collar. Her hands were folded in her lap. Her hair was nicely and simply combed, and she had no powder on her face.

"Poor man, he didn't have an easy life," she said.

Bernard was slouched in a chair, thinking that all the awe and terror of death were covered up by the repair work done on his father's corpse.

He glanced around the gloomy chapel. Behind the corpse there was a window of picture-postcard blue-and-red stained glass. The walls were a dull lavender. And the carpet! And the casket set as if on a stage! Here, in this chapel, Mr. Whelan found the basis for his pride, his sense of his own dignity. This was a man's life work. He asked himself whether he should laugh or be angry.

He went to the small smoking room off the chapel and lit a cigarette. It was brighter, and the chairs were comfortable. He fell into one. Soon he was joined by Art and Marie.

"Well, here we are," Marie sighed.

"What's it all about?" Art asked. "Hell, he's dead."

"I don't care what's done for me when I'm dead," Bernard said.

Art turned and looked at Bernard and said:

"You provided for that by your marriage."

"You know, I did, at that," Bernard remarked, smiling.

"Mother looks nicer than I can ever remember seeing her look," Marie said.

"You know, I never thought of this before. But she must have really cared more for him than I imagined," Art said.

"She cries when she's alone," Marie said.

"I wonder what they were like when they were young," Art asked.

"She seems to have always been the same to me, except that her hair was brown instead of gray," Bernard said.

"I wonder what the old man was like when he was young. I guess he was like us." Art stopped, looked a moment at Bernard, and then said, "I guess something like me."

"I can't picture Mother in my mind as a young girl, a girl who . . . well, who wanted dates and fun," Marie said.

"Father looked like a dude in their wedding picture," Art said. "He was rigged out like a high stepper. Mother looks kind of happy in it, too."

"They never talked much about their youth, except for the old man's recriminations," Bernard mused aloud. "They never sat down and talked about when they might have been happy. I wonder if they were ever happy together. I wonder what life meant to the old man."

"He complained more and more at the end. I guess you either get the right end of the stick or you don't. He didn't," Art said.

They squashed their cigarettes and went back to sit with their mother.

III

Mr. Whelan carved the roast beef. The table was piled with food. Mrs. Whelan had brought out her special set of gold-rimmed china, her sterling flat silver, and her silver cream pitcher and sugar bowl. The linen was fresh and clean. Bernard could sense that this was important to Mrs. Whelan, and he complimented her.

"How long can you young people stay with us?" Mrs. Whelan asked.

Elizabeth glanced toward Bernard.

"I think we'll have to get back as quickly as we can," Bernard said, thinking of the cost of the trip back.

"Yes, you know Bernard can't be away from New York too long," Elizabeth said.

"It's such a shame to make the trip for a short stay," Mrs. Whelan remarked.

"All writers don't live in New York, do they?" Mr. Whelan asked.

"No, but it's best for me to live there."

"After you've written a book, and the publisher is going to publish it, do you have anything more to do?"

"No, except to correct the proofs."

"But, Father, it is a question of contacts. Because writing is a business. There are all sorts of things, contacts, knowing people, hearing about what's happening—oh, there are a million and one little things . . . aren't there, Bernard?"

"Yes, but I don't care so much about those matters. I don't believe in trying to convince people to like my writing. I want it to stand on its own feet."

"If you think you're good, I don't see why you shouldn't say so. I give good service, and I know it, and I say I do. No man can dare tell me to my face that I don't. It seems to me that if writing is a business, and a man's livelihood . . . and his family's . . ." Mr. Whelan's tone changed and he pronounced *family's* with hesitation . . . "his *family's* livelihood depends on it, he can't be a modest, shrinking violet."

"It's different."

"You know more about it than I do. I never had time to read anything much except the newspapers and a magazine now and then. I don't know anything about the publishing business, but if it's a business, I'd think it would have to be run like one."

"The publishers do run it like a business," Elizabeth said.

"How are you paid, Bernard?" Mr. Whelan asked.

"By royalties. I get a royalty of ten per cent on the retail price of every book sold, up to five thousand copies, and then I get thirty-seven and a half cents, fifteen per cent, on any additional copies."

"Did your book sell many copies?"

"No, it didn't. It didn't make up the advance."

Elizabeth seemed nervous.

"Advance? What's that?"

"You usually get an advance of money on future royalties when you sign a contract with a publisher."

"I see. Is it much?"

"I got an advance of two hundred and fifty dollars on my book, and I got three hundred and fifty dollars on the book that is coming out next year."

"That isn't much to make out of a book. Is that what the publishers think you're worth?"

"When you are known more, you get more," Elizabeth interrupted. "It's the same, isn't it, Daddy, with any young person in business?"

"And your first book didn't make two hundred and fifty dollars?" Mr. Whelan asked.

"No, it didn't. But I expect my new book to do better."

"Ferris and Winter couldn't spend money advertising the book. But Bernard's publishers for his next book, Tolan and Rand, they're much better, and they have great hopes in Bernard."

After some moments of silence, Mr. Whelan looked at Bernard and asked:

"How did you happen to change publishers?

"Tolan and Rand, that's Bernard's new publishers, are better for him. . . . They have more prestige," Elizabeth said.

"My old publishers wanted me to write a book that would

titillate shop girls. I told them I wasn't that kind of writer. Now, I've heard they might go bankrupt. My new publishers are better, in my opinion."

Mr. Whelan seemed a little bewildered. He went on eating and then served second portions to himself, his wife, and Bernard. He spoke of how much he liked the dinner. Mrs. Whelan said Fanny, the maid, was a fine cook, but that today, because of the occasion, she had helped with the cooking. During a lull in the conversation Elizabeth mentioned that Bernard had a good chance of getting a Loewenthal Fellowship.

"What's that?" Mr. Whelan asked.

"It's a foundation, the Loewenthal Foundation that gives the fellowships. They make awards every year to writers, artists, and scholars to permit them to carry on their work."

"They're very rich," Elizabeth said.

"How much do they give?"

"Between two thousand and twenty-five hundred dollars," Bernard answered.

"What do you do to get it?"

"You apply. If you're a writer, you describe the book you plan to write. If you're a scientist, you describe the problem you want to work on."

"And they give the money?"

"Yes, Daddy," Elizabeth said.

Mr. Whelan was thoughtful for a minute. Then he asked: "Isn't it charity?"

"It's supposed to be a recognition of merit and promise," Bernard said.

"If you get one of these scholarships, can you write anything you want?"

"It's assumed that you'll write what you've outlined in your project. They're very liberal, and they don't interfere with you, I'm told."

"It sounds like coddling to me. I'd want to pay my own way," Mr. Whelan said.

Silently, Bernard resented Elizabeth. Because of her, his hands were tied. And he was sure that Mr. Whelan had meant more than the literal meaning of his words in this last remark. But he spoke calmly:

"When you look at writing from the standpoint of business, the young writer faces difficulties. Now, you take this young fellow, Marty O'Hara, who's being tried now for criminal embezzlement. I went to school with him. His father had banks, and he could go right in and work. Or if you become an employee with some business—that business pays your salary. But in writing, it's different. You have to finance yourself as best you can before you produce anything. Nobody is interested in the cost of your living while you write, and after that the publisher issues the book, and besides what you are to get, there is his investment. I suppose that from the business standpoint a writer is going in business for himself. But, he has to do everything first, and he only gets the returns, other than advances, later on."

"But you don't know what you are going to get in return, and so, under the circumstances, is it a good business?" Mr. Whelan asked.

Bernard knew that his answer to this question was . . . *No!*

"When authors are recognized and successful, some of them make a lot of money," Elizabeth said.

"How do writers start then?"

"It depends on who they are. Some get jobs and try to work at their own writing at night and when they can. Some have money, incomes."

"Wouldn't it be better for you to take a job and write in your free time?"

"I did for a while. I worked in a hamburger stand in New York for twenty-two dollars a week."

The news surprised Elizabeth's parents. Elizabeth looked critically at Bernard.

"What happened to you then?"

"I sold a story to a magazine, *The American Mercury*, for a hundred dollars, and I quit and wrote my book. Then I got my advance of three hundred and fifty dollars. It's best not to have to take a job, if you can avoid it. Since Elizabeth and I went to New York, I've made about nine hundred dollars writing. That's about an average of a hundred dollars a month. That's more than an ambitious young fellow like Smith makes at the start in your business, isn't it, Mr. Whelan?"

Bernard didn't look at Elizabeth. He knew that his remarks would make her angry, but he was determined to answer the questions truthfully and not to pretend before the Whelans.

Mr. Whelan cleaned his plate. Elizabeth told them that Bernard might make a lot of money on his new book. Mrs. Whelan rang a little bell, and Fanny, the maid, came in. She removed the plates and served coffee and the apple pie. Elizabeth expressed enthusiasm for the pie.

"I was thinking about what you told me . . . Bernard," Mr. Whelan said. "Now, there's a drivers' union. Smith does well. But a young fellow starting in my business naturally couldn't do as well as you say you've done when he starts."

"That's what I was getting at. I meant someone learning the business, or learning to become an embalmer and going to school. Or take a young lawyer. I know a number of chaps who studied law at the University. They go into a law office and earn much less than what I've made so far. And I'm riding against the depression."

Mr. Whelan looked seriously and sternly at Bernard.

"All that's all right if you don't have responsibilities. But when you do have responsibilities, it's something different, isn't it?"

"Mr. Whelan, I have a lot of confidence in myself," Bernard answered in a tense voice.

"Yes, I see you have," Mr. Whelan said ambiguously.

They ate in silence for a while.

"How is your mother, Bernard?" Mrs. Whelan asked.

"She's well."

"She's a fine woman. In my business, you can't help but see

character. After all, what I see in my normal course of business
—there's a book to be written. Writers can't begin to tell about
life the way I have to see it."

Bernard looked toward his father-in-law with an expression
of interest, of absorption.

"I'll bet you must see many sad things, Daddy," Elizabeth
said.

"Elizabeth, your father is a strong man. He has borne hard
strain," Mrs. Whelan said.

"A real man stands up to life," Mr. Whelan said, speaking
in a solemn voice, and then, half-turning toward Bernard, "Yes,
I've seen many a poor devil. When I get a call, I never know
what I'm going to run into. About nine months ago . . . I had
a case. A man's son was a gangster. He was shot by another
gangster. And this poor father, his name was Engle, didn't
know it. The poor man thought his son was as honest as the day
is long, as honest as he was himself. It was pitiful, it was. My
heart went out to him. And nobody had the heart to enlighten
him, to tell him the truth—that his son was a hoodlum and a
gangster. Well, a story like that, that's nothing to be surprised
at in my profession."

"It's very sad," Bernard said.

"You two are still young yet. There are things you'll have to
learn—how older people feel about their children. Some of the
saddest cases I run into are cases of old parents whose children
have passed away, sometimes by getting into trouble. Girls. I
had a case like that, a girl dying from an illegal operation. I can
say these things to you now, Elizabeth, because you're a married
woman now and you're going to be a mother."

Elizabeth blushed, and Bernard nervously played with his
fork.

"Any man who has stood up to life knows what goes on.
That's something he doesn't need a book to tell him. That's why,
if I read, I'd read something different. And I think most people
feel that way. They have to stand up to life, and they know
that. They want something else when they want to read. That's

what I think you ought to know if you want to be a writer and support your family as a writer."

"Yes," Mrs. Whelan said. "People are often so sad. When they read, they don't want to read sad things. It's the same when a person goes to the movies. They want to forget."

"That's what I think. If writing is a business, well, it would seem to me that it's got to be the same as it is in any other business. You have to give something if you expect to receive payment and become a success. And I don't think people want to pay for sadness, for books full of misery. Now, it may be art, but I don't think people care. They don't want it. That's what I think."

"There're so many good things to think about, too," Mrs. Whelan said.

"But you have to write about what you feel and know. Otherwise, it isn't yours, it isn't your writing," Bernard said.

"Well, you don't have to feel gloomy all of the time. I don't, even though people in my profession are supposed to."

"Bernard doesn't, either, do you Bernard?" Elizabeth asked.
"No."

They had finished eating. Mr. Whelan pushed back his chair, and dropped his napkin on the table.

"But, Bernard, I have to admit this, I see you've tried hard. I'll be honest with you. I didn't think you were the kind who'd take a job in a hamburger stand after having a college degree. Now, that impresses me. Maybe I don't like your ideas, and I didn't like your book. But I like the character you've shown."

Bernard said nothing. He was a trifle pale.

"The thing that concerned me was that I was afraid you were one of these young fellows who thought the world owed him a living. I'm glad to know I was wrong." He looked at his watch. "Well, folks, it's about time we were on our way."

IV

There were about eight or ten persons in the chapel when Bernard entered it with Elizabeth and her mother. He looked about quickly to see if he knew anyone. They walked up front. Mrs. Whelan and Elizabeth knelt before the coffin. Bernard went over to his mother, who was sitting alone. Her eyes were fixed on the casket. He asked her how she was feeling. Elizabeth and Mrs. Whelan came over to her. Bernard introduced them, and Elizabeth smiled and kissed Mrs. Carr affectionately. They expressed their sympathies and condolences, and then took chairs on either side of her. Hard work had left many marks on Mrs. Carr's face and hands. Mrs. Whelan's face was beginning to wrinkle, but it wasn't marked by the signs of work or passion, as was his mother's. And Mrs. Whelan had made up, using too much powder. Bernard, observing both of them, doubted if his mother had ever used cosmetics in her life. In his boyhood he had been ashamed of his mother, and he'd have been prouder to have a mother like Mrs. Whelan. Now he was ashamed of that feeling, but he wasn't responsible for the false values and snobberies of his boyhood, was he?

Bernard couldn't tell whether his mother was being timid or cold. She seemed shy. She listened to Mrs. Whelan talk, now and then saying a word. Mrs. Whelan said she hoped Mr. Carr had had a happy end, and added that he looked handsome. He must have been a fine-looking man. And she was certain that Mrs. Carr's children were a great consolation to her—it must be a real consolation to a woman to have three grown sons. And she complimented Mrs. Carr on her children, adding that, after all, she could talk as family.

"Yes," she repeated, "We're really of the same family now."

Mrs. Carr looked tenderly at Elizabeth and said softly:

"You're a sweet girl. You must take care of yourself."

Bernard was surprised by his mother's gentleness. He was sure she liked Elizabeth. Mrs. Whelan immediately countered by praising Bernard.

"Maybe she'll do good for my son," Mrs. Carr said. And Bernard imagined his mother meant that Elizabeth might bring him back to the church.

Mrs. Carr gazed at her husband's casket, and asked herself

if she might not have been a better wife. There he was, dead. Cold and helpless. And he had been stricken when he was going to beat her. His death was so like a punishment of God. But had God been punishing only poor Patrick? Wasn't it punishment for her that her husband should have been coming at her, to beat or even murder her, almost when he was at death's door? And this girl who was now her daughter-in-law looked young and good, and she seemed like such a happy girl.

Mrs. Whelan was observing Mrs. Carr closely. Bernard's mother was the type of poor woman you had to feel sorry for. She seemed to be taking her husband's death hard—she must have loved him. You could tell that here was a woman who had sacrificed for her husband and her family. Poor thing, she had perhaps been happy sacrificing. She herself had so often been unhappy, thinking that she had to sacrifice, and yet she wanted to sacrifice. She envied Mrs. Carr. She guessed that Mrs. Carr had had the kind of busy, hard life in which there was no time for nervousness. She wasn't a nervous woman. She sat so still and held her hands together without moving them. And she kept looking at the remains of her husband, poor man, Lord have mercy on his soul.

Mrs. Whelan shivered with inward fear. How would she act, how would she bear it, if Philip were to be called? But, no, she knew she would go first. Some day she'd be laid out like that man.

Mrs. Carr's silence and the quiet of the chapel oppressed her. She plunged into conversation, talking of Elizabeth's pregnancy.

Bernard excused himself. As he turned to go to the rear, he glanced at the motionless corpse of his father. Death meant absolute rigidity. He forced thoughts of death out of his mind and went to the back of the chapel.

v

Jim and a big, powerful-looking, light-haired lad approached Bernard.

"Bernie, this is an old friend of yours."

"Don't you remember me, Bernie, Steve Zymoski?" the tall lad said, showing a number of gold jackets in the front of his mouth as he smiled.

"Why, hello, Steve, how are you?"

They sat down in the last row of chairs. Jim went to sit with a group of cousins.

"Bernie, I'm sorry about your . . . misfortune."

"Thanks. . . . What are you doing now, Steve?"

"Workin'. I work in de steel mills."

Bernard recalled Steve in grammar school, a skinny kid, a dumb Polak. Steve grinned gently and stupidly. Bernard noticed his huge hands. They bore the marks of hard work, just as his father's hands had.

"What are you doing, Bernie?"

"I live in New York, but I came back because of my father."

"Gee, I didn't know that. I ain't seen you since grammar school. Dat was a long time ago, wasn't it, Bernie?"

"Yes, it's a long time ago."

"I ain't seen you in a long time. But you say you live in New York? What d'youse do?"

"I write."

Steve said nothing for a moment.

"Write? What do you mean, you work on a newspaper?"

"No, I write books."

"Who'da thought it?" Steve asked, bewildered and respectful.

"Do you like your work, Steve?"

"Most of de men, dey don't work," Steve grinned. "I pour de steel in de moulds. It's hot, red hot, like red-hot water, and de odder fellow and me, we pour it from de bucket in de mould. I wear big glasses and gloves. It's hot. But dey keep me. I pour so fast."

"I'm glad to hear it."

Bernard tried to think of something to say. He couldn't.

"I seen about your fadder in de newspaper, and so I remember and I come here. I remember—remember Bernie?—we had a fight."

"Yes. Neither of us won. Sister stopped it and made us stay after school. That was in sixth grade."

"When I saw about your fadder, I said, I would come and pay my respects, and tell you, all dese years, I tought of dat fight, and I want to say I am sorry. I didn't mean to have dat fight."

"Hell, Steve, we were just kids."

"Yes. It was my fault. I was a kid, too, you know, and I tink, tink you don't like me because I'm Polish."

It was true. As a boy, he'd been like all the other kids and had looked down on Poles.

"Yes, I tought a lot of dat fight," Steve said. "I tought, sometime I'll tell Bernie I'm sorry. I didn't want to fight. I didn't know better. I'm an ignorant kid."

"Steve, but it was my fault," Bernie said.

He'd really picked that fight in order to show off.

"No, I tink. I tink for one week about it, and den I fight wid you. I'm sorry."

Bernard was inarticulate; he was touched.

"My fadder, he's dead. He died in twenty-nine. He was in de shop, and a piece of steel hit him," Steve tapped his head, "hit him on de head."

"How do the other workers feel at the steel mills?"

Steve didn't understand Bernard's question.

"What do they think of Russia?" Bernard asked.

"I dunno."

"Are any of them Communists?"

"Communists? But, they're bad. My fadder, Bernie, he loved America. He always say dis to me when I was a kid. He work hard. I work hard. He said to me America is a good country—'Steve, it's your country.'"

Bernard didn't know how to go on with his questioning, and he and Steve talked of boyhood days. Bernard realized how he'd never known Steve, and how prejudiced he'd been. To him, Steve had merely been dumb and stupid. But there was something so kind and gentle in this huge, slow-thinking lad, who kept twisting his cap, and smiling shyly, and talking of trivial, forgotten little incidents of childhood. He wished he'd been different as a boy, more friendly with Steve. But that was all lost now. He was pretending now as he and Steve reminisced. He didn't want to pretend. He wished the common bonds of their childhood were deeper.

Their conversation came to a halt.

"Bernie . . . are you Communist?" Steve asked, suddenly and suspiciously.

"Not exactly, but I think they want to help you."

Bernard tried to think of some way in which to explain Communism convincingly to Steve. He wanted to tell him that it wanted to make a better world for the workers. But Steve fixed suspicious eyes on Bernard. He was thinking of his dead father's words about America, and of how he wanted to work and have a family like his father and become part of the life of this country in which he had been born. He had always liked Bernard, but Bernard was educated and American, and Steve didn't understand why Bernard should talk to him of Communism and the workers. He kept looking at Bernard. The difference between them suddenly seemed even wider than it had been in childhood.

"Bernie . . . Communists are bad."

"They don't understand you workers, but they mean well. And with unemployment . . ."

"Dey make it worse."

"How?"

But Steve didn't want to talk. And soon he got up to leave, looking shyly into Bernard's eyes as they shook hands.

VI

Mrs. Carr was tired from having seen so many people. She was grateful, but she was also aloof. Expressions of sympathy, gossip, chatter, talk of the past all went in one ear and out the other. With Patrick's death something had come over her. He had passed away yesterday, just a little more than twenty-four hours ago. This seemed a very long time to her. Since then, she had been very sad in some moments, and very happy in others. She condemned herself severely. Last night she had knelt before the bed in which he had died, and she had broken into tears in the midst of her prayers. She hadn't been able to say her Act of Contrition as she usually did; she hadn't been able to talk to God in sorrow and with a heart filled with penance. She had had evil thoughts. While saying her prayers, she had suddenly wished she were a young girl once again.

Today, she had seen so clearly and with sympathy that Marie's heart was full of a girl's dreams. And then she had seen the pretty child Bernard had married. Her daughter-in-law had seemed so happy, carrying her son's child. Had she missed something in life? She watched Elizabeth sitting sedately near her and then glanced across the chapel at Marie, who was laughing as she talked with another girl. Weren't you flouting the Will of God when you wished yourself young again?

She gazed at the casket.

These good people couldn't know what was in her. Until yesterday, she herself hadn't known what was in her. Now, she knew. She knew how weak we all are, how easy it is to sin.

She turned to Lizzie Delehanty, a first cousin seated beside her, and said in a restrained voice:

"When we were first married, Patrick used to talk of getting a house of our own, and of the things he'd do. He sometimes used to talk of building the house himself with the help of the others he would hire. But we never managed to do it," Mrs. Carr said, realizing she hadn't thought of this old dream of Patrick's now for years.

The stout Mrs. Delehanty told Mrs. Carr she understood.

Yes, she had gone on, year after year, and she had hardly ever thought of the past. Now it came pushing up, and she kept recalling scenes and thoughts she had forgotten.

She gazed at the casket and said silently:
—Forgive me, Patrick.

VII

Bernard looked at his second cousin, Mickey McDermott, as though he weren't there. His father had boozed with Old Man McDermott when they were both young. Mickey was his own age, tall and lean, with hawklike eyes and a tight mouth. He wore a conservative but expensive blue suit, a dark tie, and a clean white shirt.

Mickey recognized Bernard but quickly turned. He hadn't seen Bernard for years. When they were boys, he'd never liked Bernard. He considered him harum-scarum and improvident. Twenty years from now he'd be much farther up the ladder than his cousin. He'd studied law at night school and was proud of his education. Bernard Carr wasn't the only educated person in the family.

He walked up front, looked at the corpse, and became momentarily afraid. He knelt and said a few prayers. His thoughts wandered. The Democrats were going to win this fall, and he was on the way up. These were the wrong thoughts to have, kneeling before a dead man. He was sorry to let his mind wander this way. He rose, blessed himself, and, with a condescending smile, he walked over to Mrs. Carr.

She wasn't crying. His own mother would be crushed with grief under similar circumstances. His father had always said that the great mistake of Paddy Carr's life was marrying that cold-blooded woman. He planned to marry for love, but you could love and marry advantageously.

"I'm very sorry about your husband," he told Mrs. Carr in a practiced voice.

She thanked him, stared at him for a moment, and then said:

"Oh, you're Mickey McDermott. How are you, and thank you for coming. My husband always spoke well of your father."

"Dad and Mother are coming later."

"How are you, Mickey?" Jim said, coming up and offering his hand.

Mickey greeted Jim with false cordiality and sat down next to Mrs. Carr.

"We were all shocked by the news," he said. "My father had been saying how he wanted you all to come over to see us."

"We understand, Mickey," Jim told him.

Mickey resented Jim's tone of familiarity. The Carrs didn't know their place, but he talked politely about his family with Mrs. Carr. Jim was getting anxious. Should he ask Mickey to be a pallbearer or not? The handling of the funeral arrangements was in his hands, and the question of what pallbearers to get was worrying him. His father would have liked it if he could have known that Mickey would be one of his pallbearers. Even in these hard times Mickey was getting on in politics and as a lawyer. He was going places, all right.

Jim called Elizabeth over, and introduced her to Mickey as Elizabeth Whelan Carr. She told Mickey that Bernard had often spoken of him, and was proud that he was getting along so well. Mickey was too surprised to answer.

"Bernard's here, isn't he?" Mickey finally said. in order to cover up his surprise.

He wondered how Bernard could have gotten a wife like this. He knew of her father, and they'd often talked of the marriage at home. She was a sweet girl. She seemed simple, and he was impressed by her manner. He wouldn't be ashamed at all of having a girl like her as a wife.

"I don't know Bernard well, of course," Mickey said to Elizabeth.

"But Bernard speaks proudly of you as his cousin. He's very happy to know of your success."

Jim Carr listened with pride and admiration. His sister-in-law was sure one wonderful girl, and she sure knew how to dish it right back to the McDermotts.

"Mickey," Jim said, "we'd all be mighty thankful to you if you could be one of my father's pallbearers."

Mickey paused. This was an imposition. He'd always considered the Carrs as climbers, and this proved it. They wanted to be able to say that Mickey McDermott, the young lawyer, was one of Patrick Carr's pallbearers. They wanted to associate their name with his. He wasn't born yesterday, was he?

"I'm terribly sorry, Jim," he answered with his manner of false friendliness, "but I have to be in court tomorrow."

Jim's face dropped. At this moment, Bernard sauntered up.

"Hello, Mickey," he said condescendingly. "You look prosperous."

Again, Mickey was taken aback.

"Oh, I'm doing all right. I'm building up a good practice, and I'm going into politics. We're going to make a sweep this fall, city, county, state, and nation."

"Yes, Mick, it looks sweet for our side, real sweet," Jim Carr said.

Bernard wasn't interested. Contempt was written clearly on his face. Mickey looked at him with suspicion. He felt like telling Bernard that he knew all about him; yes, he knew that Bernard was an immoral atheist and a no-good renegade from the Church. He thought that if he ever became District Attorney, and had a chance, he would certainly enjoy prosecuting his cousin for something or other, maybe for writing dirty books or for being a Red. Some day it might happen, too.

Bernard excused himself and sauntered off.

—Yes, he told himself, Mickey McDermott has all the makings of a politician and the soul of a prosecutor.

VIII

Bernard's old friend, Corcoran, went through the ritual of expressing his condolences. They sat together in the rear. Corcoran was jolly and beginning to get fat. Bernard compared himself physically with Corcoran. He himself was lean and trim, and probably in better condition than Corcoran. This pleased him. But his teeth. His tongue found a cavity and played with it. He kept putting off going to a dentist. He was just afraid. Did he want to be toothless one day? The question was depressing. Corcoran told him he looked fine, and he said the same to Corcoran. He asked Corcoran how he was doing, and Corcoran said he was doing well, selling real estate, but that a lot of the boys they both used to know were out of work.

"This depression is no joke any more, Bernie," Corcoran said seriously.

They were quiet. Bernard still liked Corcoran. But what did they have in common?

"I'm mighty glad to see you. I've thought often of you, Bernie, and I would have written, but, well . . ." Corcoran smiled genially. "I'm not a writer myself. Bernie, I never would have imagined you becoming a writer; no, I guess I never would have."

"There was a time when I wouldn't have myself," Bernard answered.

Corcoran talked about old times and gave him news of the lads they used to know. Frankie Vincent had been saving his money to get married, but he'd lost his savings in the O'Hara bank crash. Another lad, Danny Lindell, had gone to California to get rich, and he'd come back broke and divorced. Bernard listened with interest and thought of how destinies unfolded in such an unpredictable manner. Corcoran had exhausted the gossip he had to tell. They just sat without saying anything.

Bernard saw Peter Mannheim and signaled to him. Corcoran excused himself to go and talk with Mickey McDermott. Peter was a quiet chap whom Bernard had known on campus. He told Bernard that he'd passed his bar exams, but that it was hard to get going these days.

"Hell, Bernie, I don't want to be a shyster or an ambulance chaser. But I'll make out. . . . Bernie, who are you going to vote for? I think we need a change, and I'm going to vote for Roosevelt."

"Peter, I think I'm becoming a Communist."

Bernard had made this remark spontaneously. He wanted Peter to think he was an extreme rebel. He glanced about the parlor, enjoying the idea that by saying he was a Communist he could shock all of these people and drive them to hate and condemn him.

"In college you were different, more outspoken than the rest of us," Peter said.

"Our whole system is going to pot," Bernard remarked with a wave of the hand.

"Yes, it seems so. But is Communism the answer? I've been reading a series of articles on Russia in *The Clarion*. They must be worse off than we are. Why, according to this *Clarion* reporter, they have people working there as slaves in camps, and they haven't enough to eat."

"*The Clarion* is a reactionary paper," Bernard said. "For years it's printed Riga rumors. It would like Russia to fail. All it wants is rugged individualism . . . the rugged individualism of breadlines and Hoovervilles."

"I'd like you to read these articles. I know what *The Clarion* is."

"The world's greatest newspaper," Bernard cut in ironically.

"But these articles sound true."

"There's a press campaign on against Russia. Hoover won't recognize the Soviet Union. This is all old stuff. When we were kids, look at all the false rumors they printed about Lenin and Trotsky. Now the reactionary papers say there's a famine. I know people who've been there. They say there's no famine. Peter, I often think the real future is there, not here."

Bernard wondered why he was speaking this way. It was so different from the way he talked with Communists in New York. And he hadn't read these articles, nor actually had he read much serious factual writing on the Soviet Union. He was really fairly ignorant about this question. He did know he had his own serious doubts about Russia and he was a little ashamed of himself for having talked in this way in order to make an impression.

"Bernie, I'm not a reactionary. I don't know much about politics. I just want everyone to get along and be free. I'm just a young lawyer trying to get along and be free myself. But I don't like Communism. I know what Beard wrote and we read in college about the Constitution. It's true, I guess, but I don't think there's anything in the world as great as the American Constitution. I want to save it. It has worked for over a century. It saves us from much violence. Violence is no good."

"There's violence everywhere. Look at the war to end all wars," Bernard said bitterly. "There's going to be another war. What about the violence of Hoover, and McArthur's troops against the Bonus Marchers? I read of violence every day in the papers. The police beat up Communists. They break up demonstrations. They beat up Negroes. People haven't got enough to eat. And look at the farmers' strike. And at these people here. They don't even know what's going on in America, let alone in the world."

"I know it. But they aren't bad people. They just aren't educated as you and I are."

"They're prejudiced, prejudiced in favor of ignorance," Bernard said sharply.

"I don't know the answer. But I don't like Communism," Peter said.

"I'm beginning to think it doesn't matter what we like. It might be what we have to accept, what's inevitable. Sooner or later this capitalist system will run down completely."

"Bernie, I respect you and always have, ever since we first met on campus. But, Bernie, here you are, more educated than most people. And if you say you don't care who's president, why should others care? People who haven't your education, your understanding, your brains?"

"Peter, I'm a rebel," Bernard said in a voice that was low, intense, and defiant.

"Maybe that's why you are a writer. But, Bernie, I wouldn't go with the Communists," Peter said.

Bernard looked off, gazed around the parlor, stared at the

coffin, and then smirked weakly as he turned back to talk to Peter.

IX

Jim was still worried about getting the right pallbearers. And all this had to happen just when Gerry was away on a vacation. If he only had her here to give him support. But maybe it was good she was away, because he felt, well, kind of funny about the idea of introducing her to his mother

He didn't know who would be right and who wouldn't. He wouldn't think of troubling his mother with this question, but Art and Bernie might have given him some help. Bernie said he didn't care, and Art had told him it didn't matter either. But he'd bet they'd criticize him if he got the wrong ones. And he was wondering about his old friend, Biscuits. Would they approve? He and Biscuits Boyle sat in the smoking room puffing on cigarettes.

"Well, my father is gone," Jim said.

Biscuits didn't answer for a few moments. Then he said:

"Yes, Patrick Carr went into the Beyond, Jim."

"But how are things with you, Biscuits?"

"Didn't you hear, Jim? My father closed up his bakery last week."

"Well, your father is getting along in years. It's always best for a man to retire when he's advanced in years."

"No, he had to close up because he was losing money."

"I'm sure sorry to hear that, Biscuits. That's a tragedy. And your father was such a fine man," Jim said with concern.

"It's this depression. My father was hit hard. He isn't the same man any more. He walks around the house like . . . you know, like he was lost and he didn't know what to do with himself. It hurts me. A father is the best friend anybody will ever have, except for his mother. That's why I felt so bad, Jim, when I heard about your father dying. I looked at my father, the way he sits and thinks about his bakery, and it hurt."

"Yes, I know, Biscuits."

"My dad put all the money he had into his bakery. I don't know what he'll do. He's too old to have to go to work for somebody else, and I just don't know what he'll do."

Jim decided that he'd ask Biscuits and let them disapprove if they wanted to. He'd given them a chance to make suggestions. They had no kick coming.

"Biscuits, the family would all be mighty grateful to you if you could be one of my father's pallbearers."

"Jim, it's an honor for me to say yes."

Jim felt good. He had one pallbearer lined up. Good old Biscuits.

x

"If you ask me, Paddy Carr died of a broken heart," exclaimed a man; he had graying hair, a red nose, blotched cheeks, and work-worn hands.

A thin, dignified old man wearing a very high stiff collar agreed with a profound nod and clucking sounds.

They passed Bernard without noticing him and stood talking at the other end of the smoking room.

"It was that son," exclaimed the one with a high collar.

"I always told him—the razor strap. Spare it, and you go to an early grave, a brokenhearted father."

"I'll not die a brokenhearted father. I taught my sons respect. They're twenty-six and twenty-three now, but they still bring home their pay, because they know who's master of the house."

"That woman of his is too religious. He wasn't happy. You know what I mean?"

"Who could have thought it would turn out so? She was a pretty girl—pretty and shy. I remember her when Paddy was courting her. Shy, a shy one, and she changed. Well, I have a different kind of woman. She prays and goes to church, but I'm master of the house."

"The way I look at it from my experience is that, after a man marries, his life isn't his own."

"Let's have a snifter to the memory of Paddy."

"If I knew Paddy, he'd like it."

The two of them sneaked into the lavatory off the smoking room with the air of mischievous boys.

XI

Tom Lyons came into the smoking room. He was about Bernard's height, and dark and nervous.

"I'm glad to see somebody who's civilized," Bernard said.

"Come on, Bernie, I've known you too long for you to pull sophisticated New York gags on me."

Bernard started to explain himself and his remark, but Tom cut in on him:

"I joined the Socialist Party."

"Yes, I knew that."

"Well, what's your comment?"

"That's like an atheist getting religion and joining the Unitarians instead of the Catholic Church."

"Bernie, do you seriously run with the Commies?"

"I know a lot of them. The Socialists are milk and water. What the hell are they ever going to do?"

Tom and Bernard were launched on politics before they had said anything personal or casual to each other. Bernard thought that Tom's going only halfway to the Socialists instead of whole hog to the Communists indicated the difference between them. He remembered how they used to argue about whether one should stay in Chicago or go on to New York, and that Tom had nearly always defended the idea of staying in Chicago. This was in line with his being a Socialist—Socialism was like Chicago; it was a halfway stage of radicalism.

"Bernie, you're intelligent enough and you've lived here in America long enough, to know that outside of New York the line and ideas of the Communists don't go for this country," Tom Lyons argued.

"They're only trying to exploit misery for their own ends. Even with our depression we are less miserable than most of the people in the world, including the muzhiks.

"What peaceful evolution can there be? We're living in a time of political and economic devolution. Biologically, that's what cancer is—devolution. Not only America but the whole capitalist world has a political and economic cancer. You can't treat cancer the way you do warts."

"You're talking like a writer. Bernie, I know you know lots more about many things than I do, but not about politics."

"I studied political science at college."

Tom Lyons laughed at this remark.

"Bernie, you're too smart to talk that way, and you ought to know that the Commies don't think American. They have no future in this country, and they're no goddamn good, anyway."

"Maybe Americanism has no future in America. America itself may not have a future."

The two old men came out of the lavatory, glanced furtively at Bernard and Tom, and left the smoking room.

"Those poor old fellows were cronies of my old man," Bernie commented.

"How do you feel about your old man's death?"

"I'm not a sentimentalist," Bernard said with a shrug. "My old man died an Irish death. He was drunk when he died."

"That ought to be the happiest death a man can have."

"My father was never happy."

"Is that why you're such a dour Irishman?"

Bernard told Tom Lyons about his father's death.

"Christ, how awful. How does it make you feel?"

"Cold. It didn't surprise me. Somehow or other I always felt the poor old fellow would come to some terrible end."

"Bernie, I think I know you better than you know yourself. . . . You always look for the worst."

Bernard disliked this remark. He didn't correct it because he feared there might be some truth in it.

"Snap out of it, Bernie. You ought to move back here and

live closer to reality. I've learned a lot. I've changed. I think
I'm more mature intellectually."

"But how are you going to change things?"

"Politics is the instrument of change. If you use politics
and pressure in this country, you can bring about change."

"When I do anything, I go the whole hog," Bernard interrupted. "And this country is just politically backward."

"When you talk that way, you're kidding yourself, but not
me."

Bernard knew that he just hadn't made up his mind firmly
about all these questions.

"You'll learn—if New York doesn't get you," Tom said.

"Writing, not politics, is my life. And as a writer, how could
I live in Chicago?" Bernard asked.

"If you want my advice, stick to writing, let politics alone,
and don't touch the Commies, not even with a ten-foot pole."

"Don't worry, I'll go on writing," Bernard said.

"I went to see that Russian movie, *The Old and the New.*
And . . ."

"Did you like it?"

"It didn't mean anything to me. A Commy made a speech
before they showed the picture. He bragged about how they're
producing pictures like this in Russia to educate the people.
They're teaching them to use tractors. It was a joke. Nearly
every American grows up a mechanic. We don't need movies
to tell the farmers they ought to use tractors. I got into an
argument with this Commy, and he sprang the line on me
about political backwardness. I asked him what the hell's so
politically forward about Europe. We have a depression, a
goddamned awful one. But, hell, that's only the normal state
for Europe. And what the hell do the Commies do—they talk
about social fascism. What the hell has social fascism got to
do with anything social?"

"Social fascist merely means political sonofabitch in Commy
jargon," Bernard cracked.

They laughed.

"You're not really a Commy, Bernard. It's a pose."

"I just finished another book," Bernard said, wanting to change the subject.

Bernard told him about it, and they talked more about themselves, falling back into a mood of their old days together. The rivalry which had been bound up in their political talk disappeared. Bernard then mentioned Elizabeth's pregnancy. Tom was surprised and sympathetic. They talked about personal matters, and Tom went to see Elizabeth in the chapel. Bernard got sidetracked by his brother, Jim, who wanted to discuss the problem of the pallbearers. Then, when Tom Lyons was leaving, Bernard walked outside with him. They stood in front of the funeral parlor, planning to meet again before Bernard returned to New York.

XII

"Are you tired, honey?" Bernard asked Elizabeth.

"Not particularly. People have been really nice to me here, and, Bernard . . . I like your family. I like your mother very much . . . and I think she likes me. . . . And I don't think people are as much against you as you imagined. Your sister Marie is very proud of you."

Bernard didn't want to talk about this. All night here at the wake, at odd moments, thoughts had popped in and out of his mind. When you really knew a person, it was hard to condemn him. A writer, at least, crippled his understanding if he condemned indiscriminately.

His eyes turned toward the casket, as they had repeatedly all evening. No, he didn't condemn his father or any of these people.

"I've hardly spoken with you all night. Everybody's been looking at you. They're interested in you, and most of them would really like you, Bernard, if you let them. . . . And, Bernard, I have some really good news." Her face became suffused with joy. "Mother likes you."

He didn't answer.

"Aren't you glad?" she asked, disappointed.

"Of course, I'm glad."

He was. . . . But he was remembering how, when he was growing up here in Chicago, his emotions and fears had been entrapped. He was afraid of becoming re-entangled. Why should he care?

"Come and talk to Mother for a few minutes, Bernard."

He went reluctantly and sat down beside Mrs. Whelan. She told him how much she liked his family, and that his mother was a very fine woman.

Bernard thanked her. She said it was a nice wake, and he mumbled agreement with her.

Mrs. Whelan alternated between being bored and excited. Most of them here were poorer than she. They were common people. But even though they were not of her class, she'd not acted above them, and she believed they'd liked her. They'd all complimented her on her daughter, and Philip should have heard some of these compliments, because they showed that she had brought up Elizabeth well. And now she thought she could understand Bernard better, and she could see why he'd wanted to marry a girl like Elizabeth. Bernard was an ambitious boy. She didn't think there was an ounce or spark of ambition in his brothers. And Bernard was good looking and healthy and had good manners. If Elizabeth could only bring him back to the Church, perhaps it would be a good match.

Bernard tried to think of something to say to his mother-in-law. He imagined that she was silently critical of his family, perhaps disdainful. She knew it was a poor family. She seemed insincere and stupid to him. But her stupidity was different from the ignorance of his own family. She talked about his father, saying that he must have been a good man and a good father, and he wondered what she'd say and think if she knew the real story. He listened politely. Then he excused himself, saying he had to see his brother Jim about the pallbearers.

"You must go right ahead, Bernard. Elizabeth and I will sit here," she said, as though she were doing him a favor.

He left, looking for Jim, and found him still in a fog about finding the right pallbearers.

XIII

Bernard saw Pinky Cullen near the rear of the chapel and walked over to him.

"Hello, Pinky," Bernard said cordially.

"What did you write about me for?"

"But I didn't write about you, Pinky."

"You did, too. Because you wanted to make money, you wrote about me."

"But Pinky—" Bernard said genuinely surprised.

"Don't call me Pinky. Why did you write about me?"

"How do you know I wrote about you? Did you read it?"

"No, but I know, I heard. I know what you did to me."

"Don't talk so loud."

"Don't you tell me what to do. You're yellow, Carr, yellow," Pinky sneered.

"Listen, Pinky, I smell the booze on your breath. Now, just quietly get the hell out of here."

"You're yellow," Pinky sneered.

Bernard faced him, pale and tense.

"Yellow! You did me an awful trick, writing about me." Pinky fixed his eye on Bernard, and Bernard met his stare. "Yellow. You're yellow. And you did that to me thinking I wouldn't get you, didn't you?"

Mr. Whelan, Art, and several of Art's friends all suddenly surrounded them. Pinky's hand went to his pocket, and as he was drawing out a knife and opening it, Art and Mr. Whelan both grabbed him.

"Let me get him, the yellow sonofabitch," Pinky shouted.

Others hurried toward the scene.

Art twisted Pinky's hand until the knife dropped onto the carpet. Mr. Whelan released his hold on Pinky, bent down, picked up the knife, closed it, and stuck it in his pocket.

"What's the idea?" Art asked Pinky.

"You better get out of here, fellow," a friend of Art's said, scowling at Pinky.

"I'll get you yet, Carr," Pinky said.

"This is enough from you," Mr. Whelan said, stepping in front of Pinky and looking down at him sternly. "I'm going to have you arrested and booked."

Pinky relaxed, and, looking up at Mr. Whelan like a guilty boy, he said:

"I have nothing against you."

"This is my establishment. You've come here, to a scene of mourning and sorrow, and you wanted to stab someone— my son-in-law."

"Bernie, let's take him out and give him the clouts," Art said in a low voice.

"Let him go. I won't have anything to do with him," Bernard said; he was very pale.

"I only meant to scare him for what he did to me," Pinky said meekly.

"Bernard, do you want me to have him arrested?" Mr. Whelan asked.

"Let him go," Bernard said.

"If we let you go, will you behave yourself?"

"Yes," Pinky said, awed, looking at Mr. Whelan.

"Smith," Mr. Whelan said, noticing Smith near him. "Will you go with a couple of these boys and walk him to a streetcar?"

"Yes, Mr. Whelan."

"I'll see that he gets on a car quietly," Bernard said, and Pinky scowled at Bernard.

Smith, Art, and two of Art's friends led Pinky out of the parlor, while Mr. Whelan took Bernard aside by the arm, saying:

"You better not go. Let well enough alone. It doesn't pay to monkey with hoodlums."

"I'm very sorry this happened, Mr. Whelan—"

"Forget it," Mr. Whelan cut in.

Bernard was distressed. Now, when it was all over, he was frightened. Elizabeth asked him if he was all right. He said he was. He went up to the front and looked at his father's corpse. His emotions began to quiet down.

He took in the scene with a glance, and thought that it could have been somebody else's father who was dead, instead of his own, and it could be other friends and relatives mourning and paying their last respects at a wake, and this scene would be pretty much the same as it was. One would even hear many of the same words and sentences uttered. Other corpses, all corpses, were laid out grand, and looked fine and at peace with the world. And other people said they were sorry for someone's bereavement and misfortune. But did other sons look so coldly at the cold corpse of their father? Tonight, he'd seen Corcoran, Steve Zymoski, and Pinky. He was now separated from them in mind and spirit. He was separated from the whole generation of boys he'd known and grown up with here in Chicago. Was he the only lad who had worshiped and adored an Elsie Cavanagh almost as though she were as pure as Mary, and who had then revolted? And was he the only one who had trembled in church with the guilt of sin and the fear of Hell, and had boldly declared that there is no sin and there is no God? Was he the only one who was different? Among all the lads he had known in grammar school and high school, among all the lads like them in Chicago and in other places, weren't there any others who would deny and fight? They must have much in common, must they not? Common memories, and common fears. A common religion. But if he had been betrayed, hadn't those other lads also been betrayed? And if he had raged against this betrayal, must they not also have felt some anger? What had put out the fires of love and life and resentment in all these people?

Yes, was he the only one?

Wasn't there something in common between himself and

those whom he knew in the past? Suddenly he knew that he wanted to find something in common. He thought of Elsie Cavanagh. She hadn't come to the wake. And he had wanted her to, wanted, perhaps, to find, through her, some common link in this lost, dead, rejected past of his.

Chapter Nineteen

I

B ERNARD came out of the Illinois Central Station at Sixtieth
Street and walked westward. Since Pinky had attacked
him last night, he had been in a mood of anxiety and depression that he couldn't shake off. Now he most desperately wanted
to get back to New York as quickly as possible. Pinky had told
Smith and Art that he was coming back tonight. He knew
Pinky wouldn't come back. But his reason was powerless in the
face of his fear. He was afraid of being assaulted. And how
stupid it would be, he thought, to be stabbed to death by some
poor drunken cluck. He shuddered.

Seeing the buildings and the towers of the University in the
sunlight, he sagged with relief. His anxiety vanished into a
pleasing melancholy. He was safe now. He had a free afternoon
ahead. He could relax and do nothing, or perhaps meet old
friends and acquaintances and chat.

He crossed the Midway, remembering how he'd done this so
often, bound for classes or for Harper Library. Sometimes his
hunger for knowledge had been almost like a physical sensation. And at other times he'd been depressed and fatigued. And
he'd thought that his own fight for an education and a place
in the world was hopeless. He used to ask himself the same questions which now came to his mind: Could the spirit of truth
and free inquiry ever penetrate and conquer the South Side of
Chicago? Could it ever mean anything in the lives of the Patrick
Carrs and the Pinky Cullens? Could their deep and prejudiced
resentment of truth ever be dissipated? Could art and ideas and
truth win in this world? Only last night he had tried to talk to
Art and Jim about reading and learning, but they'd put him off.

It seemed a useless effort, yet he didn't want to believe it was useless to try.

Bernard walked on, noticing the students, wanting to talk to them, and looking with eyes of desire at the girls, and he decided to go to the bookstore.

"Hello, Carr. Are you back with us? What brings you here?"

Mr. O. A. Timkins, tall, lean, and sandy-haired, faced Bernard on the walk in front of the bookstore. He spoke genially.

"Oh, hello, Mr. Timkins. My father died, and I had to come back to Chicago. I was just taking a walk around to see old sights."

Mr. Timkins expressed his sympathy.

"The old sights are much the same," Mr. Timkins said. "Some of our students are becoming romantically interested in Communism. They make the campus noisier than it used to be. In your day, a few years ago, it was good just to have one student like you around. Now, maybe there is a change, but it isn't for the better."

Bernard wanted to challenge Mr. Timkins, but didn't. He had been a good teacher, and had helped open up his mind to philosophy, to Dewey and Santayana and Bertrand Russell. He had gained a lot from Timkins's course. He wanted to like Timkins, but he didn't respect him.

"Are you writing another book?"

"Yes, I've just finished a second novel. It's coming out early next year."

"Congratulations. You know, Carr, I'm especially proud of you as a former student of mine because you became an artist, a writer, and you have a mind."

"Thank you, Mr. Timkins. I think that writers, as well as everyone else, should try to think." As Bernard talked, he became aware that Mr. Timkins was listening to him with attention, and he was pleased.

"I think you're right, Carr. I've been teaching for over ten years now. It isn't easy to get students to think. Of course, by the time many of them come to us, their minds have already been turned against thinking. It isn't easy." Mr. Timkins sighed. "But you have to keep trying. The liberal spirit isn't thriving these days."

Bernard felt he was now on a plane of equality with a former teacher. And this was gratifying. There was a world in which he was respected. He wasn't alone in the expression of his values. And wouldn't the world of ideas outlive that of prejudice? He shouldn't feel hopeless or afraid.

"Well, good luck, Carr. I'll watch your career from afar with interest and admiration. I know it's going to be a distinguished one."

"Thank you, Mr. Timkins. I hope I can justify your hopes."

They shook hands. Mr. Timkins ambled on. Bernard stood in his tracks, thoughtful. And then he suddenly called out:

"Oh, Mr. Timkins."

"Yes," Mr. Timkins answered, turning around.

Bernard went to him and spoke hesitantly:

"I'm thinking of applying for a Loewenthal Fellowship in creative writing . . . and I'd be terribly grateful if I could use your name as a reference."

"I'd be glad to. By all means. Have them send the material to me, and I'll be happy to give you a fine sendoff."

"Thank you very much. It will be of great help to me if I can get it."

"Don't mention it, Carr. You deserve it."

"I'm very grateful, Mr. Timkins."

"Well, so long and good luck again, Carr."

Bernard turned and cheerfully entered the bookstore. He picked up a copy of *Ethics and Society*, which Timkins had edited, and glanced through its pages. An article on Whitehead attracted his attention. He regretted that he no longer could follow the writing of the academic world. He might go up to Harper's now and go through some of the journals.

II

"You look a little drawn and tired. Are you sure that you're all right?" Mrs. Whelan asked Elizabeth.

"Oh, Mother, I'm really all right. I didn't sleep too well. I have to get up so much and go to the bathroom. It's getting uncomfortable. I can't turn in bed and be comfortable," Elizabeth told her mother.

They sat in the parlor.

"The last months were hard for me. I hope you don't have it as hard as I did then."

This frightened Elizabeth a little, and it brought to her mind the dreams she'd been having. She couldn't remember them much, except that she had dreamed something had happened to Bernard.

"Mother, did you have strange dreams?"

"It's so long ago, I don't remember." Mrs. Whelan became curious. "What did you dream about?"

"I don't remember, exactly, except that something happened to Bernard, and Father saved us . . . saved him. . . . Mother . . . do you believe there's anything in dreams?"

"I know there is. Whenever I dream that somebody is sick, sure enough, the next day or two, I find out that somebody I know really is sick."

Mrs. Whelan talked on about her dreams, recalling that many of them had been warnings of good fortune, bad luck, illness, and death. And as Mrs. Whelan continued to talk she hoped that Elizabeth would think that she was truly psychic. Elizabeth became very excited, and thought that perhaps she got her own powers from her mother.

"Men can't understand dreams. You'll almost never find a man who's . . . psychic," Mrs. Whelan said.

As her mother talked, Elizabeth tried to remember what Bernard said Freud said about dreams. She couldn't understand it all, but Bernard had told her dreams were subconscious wishes. But it would be a mistake to tell this to her mother.

Mother might guess what her dream meant. She was becoming more excited. She'd succeed in making Mother an ally in her plans.

"Your father laughs at me when I tell him about my dreams or that maybe I have been given psychic powers."

Elizabeth agreed sympathetically and laughed with her mother about men.

"Two nights before you and Bernard came I had a dream that your father was going away for a long time." She laughed self-consciously. "He was going away in a leaky rowboat." She laughed self-consciously for a second time. "The rowboat looked like a coffin."

Mrs. Whelan went on to say that after this dream she had just known it meant Elizabeth was coming. Elizabeth's manner didn't change, but her mother's dream seemed to her to be sad. She laughed nervously.

"Father would look funny going away that way, wouldn't he, Mother?"

"Elizabeth, you do look drawn. You aren't eating properly, and you'll have to have more cheese and milk. If you don't eat the proper foods, you can lose your teeth. An unborn baby can take all the health and strength a woman has if she doesn't eat right and get her rest. You go and lie down now."

"I eat enough," Elizabeth said, not wanting to admit that, except when she had cravings for sweets, she didn't eat too much because she didn't want to get too big.

"Your father is really excited about becoming a grandfather. He hopes so much that it'll be a boy."

"Mother, I want a boy, too. . . . And, I wasn't going to tell you this because I wanted it to be a surprise, but I'll tell. . . . We're going to name our baby Philip Whelan Carr."

"Oh, you are! You don't know how happy that will make your father."

Mrs. Whelan's old gnawing disappointments ate at her. It was an unhappiness no one could ever understand.

Elizabeth said she thought a little walk in the sun would be good for her. She powdered her face, combed her hair, and went out.

It was good to walk again on all these streets. She didn't feel the same way about people looking at her here and noticing how big she was as she did in New York. Here, you felt it was important to have a baby, and almost everybody congratulated you and told you how good you looked, and the mothers of other girls envied you and wished their daughters were going to have a baby. And all the fine big homes in this neighborhood! Some day, when Bernard was rich, she hoped they'd be able to buy a home and live here. She could be the envy of the South Shore, and she knew, too, that once Bernard was writing best-sellers, people would look on him in a different light and be proud if he came back and lived here.

They could have a lovely home here, with a yard for their boy. And she'd hire a French governess, and they'd take trips to Europe and go to New York every fall, and they'd be so happy.

She waddled on, crossed Sixty-seventh Street, and found a spot on the grass in Jackson Park, where she sat looking at the golf course.

Her face became serious. Maybe her dreams had been silly and impossible. But they had been nice, and maybe they would come true. Her dreams generally did.

The sun was warm. She watched golfers in the distance, fascinated. She sat, happy, and hardly anything seemed to be passing through her mind. Sitting here in the sun, with her feelings so quiet, she couldn't even imagine that anything that wasn't good could ever happen to her. Only good things had happened to her all her life.

Elizabeth lay back and looked up at the clouds. They had such fantastic shapes. She imagined that the clouds were floating in the sky just as her baby was floating in her womb. She grimaced with a pain. It was kicking. Now her baby was quiet, as quiet as the cloud above. A look of inexpressible joy came over

her face. It was alive in her, her baby, Bernard's baby, alive inside of her.

III

Bernard sat in his father's chair, anguished by his state of
inner restlessness. These words written in his father's ordinary
handwriting really spoke from beyond the grave. So many men
were doomed to die without leaving a word behind. His father
had feebly tried to avoid this fate in this pitiful document.

He read:

*An unhappy man here speaks, understood by none. I have
been unhappy for thirty long years of marriage. And I have an
ungrateful son, flesh of my own flesh, who is a writer. Well,
if a son can be a writer, the father can write. What is in the
son can only come out of the father. I am a writer myself, and
I am writing here, speaking my piece for all and sundry to read
after I am in my grave. Who will ever look at me in my grave?
Who will ever remember me, unless they remember me as the
father of an ungrateful son who has the liberty to lie and mis-
represent me? But those who read will know, they will know,
and they will know that I am a man whose cup of bitterness is
flowing over the brim.*

*How many times have I not cursed the day that I married
and not cursed the day that my ungrateful son was born. A
man must be master in his own house and I was never the master in my own bed. She didn't want me the first night and she
never wanted me and one would think that being a man and a
wife was the sin against the Holy Ghost, and here I am man
born of woman and never loved by woman, and a father, an
old father with his cup of bitterness too great for man or beast
to swallow. Did she know the bitterness that was in me, her
telling me a hundred times a day and in a hundred ways that it
was a sin, a sin that I did with her, that my children were the
fruits of sin? Time and again, I have sat in this house and
watched her, thinking that she could never know all that is in
me, and all that I wanted and I once young, and she was the first*

and only woman of my life, and I swear by God and man to the truth of this.

Bernard stopped reading. He had both known and not known all this. But to think that the pitiful man who had written these words was the same man who had so often filled him with terror! Yes, it was the same man on whom he had spent, wasted, so many precious and powerful emotions of anger and hate and fear. His father came back to him in memory, with his extravagant gestures, his elaborate but unimaginative and banal sarcasm and insults, and his drunken angers. When he'd been only seven, the old man had come home drunk and had beaten him for no reason at all. How he'd cried and sobbed and trembled. He remembered, too, how his father had then become so quiet, so peaceful. He'd thought—*he beats me up and he doesn't say anything.* His father hadn't wanted him because his mother hadn't wanted his father. He hadn't really described his father in his book. But then, he had not meant to.

He resumed his reading in a thoughtful state.

In my son's lying and ungrateful book, he makes me out a businessman, not a hard working man, as I have been all my years. Let him go around the city of Chicago and look at the houses and garages and buildings, and let him know that some hand like these good strong hands of mine laid every one of those bricks in fair weather and foul, in season and out of season, and who appreciates it? And the smart son is ashamed of the father who had worked as a bricklayer and writes a lying book about the father, saying that the father is a drunkard and a woman chaser and goes to whorehouses, when the curse of my life has been woman, the woman I married who accused me silent, accused me with her looks and her praying and her going to Mass and everything she did all of these long years. And for consolation, I have a little glass now and again and talk with friends, and I am no good, a drunkard, a bad father, and, well and good, the world condemns a bad father, but what about a bad wife who is bad because she is so good and what about a bad set of children? And my daughter, Marie

Bernard put the sheets of paper in his coat pocket and looked about the shabby parlor. What was there to think about this strange and pathetic document?

His brothers and sister came into the parlor, sat down, and waited for him to speak. Marie had found the document in an old cigar box and they'd all read it. They were hurt and didn't want to talk about it. They wanted Bernard to explain something to them, but they didn't really know what it was they wanted explained.

"I wouldn't let Mother see it or tell her about it," Bernard finally said in a low voice.

They all agreed.

"He wasn't happy. That's why he drank so much," Bernard told them gently.

"The way I figure . . . he wasn't himself when he wrote it," Jim said.

No one answered. Bernard was hurt because his parents hadn't been different from what they were, and that their life together had been so meager. But how could you ask anything of the past? What use was there in being hurt?

His difference from his brothers and his sister stood in his way now. He had a future, and an escape. Life couldn't make him wretched the way it had made his father, and the way it might make Jim and Art and Marie wretched.

"We don't want to live like that," he said.

"Nobody's any good anyway," Art burst out.

Mrs. Carr called them to dinner. They trooped out like guilty children. She'd fried hamburgers and last night's potatoes. They ate quietly. In their mother's presence, they were embarrassed not only for themselves but for her. Unobserved every one of them kept trying to watch her. She didn't know what had come over them. The young couldn't take death like the old, she decided. Jim made a few casual remarks. The others said little.

They finished quickly, got ready, and left for the undertaking parlor, walking down to Sixty-seventh Street to take the streetcar.

Bernard sat silently beside his mother on the streetcar. Marie, Jim, and Art were ahead of them. She sat erect, a woman in mourning, her hands folded in her lap, her face cold and expressionless. When some passengers stared at her, she seemed to be unaware of them. Bernard looked out the window at the bare walls of Greenland Cemetery. If the corpses beyond those walls could speak, might they not talk as bitterly as his father had? He didn't want to die in bitterness.

Would Pinky come back tonight? No. Still, Bernard was afraid. Then he thought that poor Pinky had tried to stab him with the same sense of desperation as his father had when he had written a last testament.

They changed cars at Stony Island Avenue and got off at Seventy-first Street.

"The weather is so fine. I hope your father has a good day for his burial tomorrow," Mrs. Carr said, as they walked toward Cornell Avenue.

"Yes, I'll feel creepy if it is rainy. The rain makes me feel sad lots of times," Marie said.

"Well, I hope we don't have more excitement. If Pinky does come around, I'm going to slug him," Art said, walking a little behind the others with Bernard.

"Mother, wouldn't it be nice if we could live out in this neighborhood?" Marie remarked.

"I'll live wherever my children want to," she said.

"We might look for an apartment out here. We'd find the rent no higher than ours, and the change would be good for us."

"I'd just as soon move," Art called up to his mother and sister.

"Oh, Mother, we want to fix up a new place. We could get some things on installment and make everything bright for you, and the change would do us all good. Gosh, we lived in this place so long," Marie went on.

"But maybe we shouldn't be thinking of these things until we have taken care of your poor father," Mrs. Carr said.

They came to the undertaking parlor and went in.

Bernard went into the chapel first and walked up front to look at his father. The rigid, ashen face, powdered and manipulated as it was, told him nothing. He felt the clammy hands and the legs under the trousers. This was the mere decaying nothingness of his father. And did it matter in the least if his father's life had been miserable and without dignity? Nothing mattered now concerning his father, nothing except the consequences of his father's life, the consequences in him and in his mother and his brothers and sister. The continuity from that nothingness that had once been Patrick Carr was in the very habits, thoughts, feelings, and resentments of the living. And why should these go on? Why? What would happen when his own child would be looking at his corpse? What would he want the child to feel and to think? There was no retribution. The living paid the retribution, the tribute for the dead. His was living tribute exacted as the payment for the sins of his father, and the tribute he paid was what? His character! He must finish remoulding his character so that it would be everything that was different from the character of this man who had been his father. That was his real, inner struggle.

He turned away from the coffin, went outside, and stood smoking a cigarette and gazing at the sky.

IV

Philip Whelan sat in the parlor with his wife and daughter, relaxed and fresh. He had come home to supper fatigued. On and off during the day he had had troubling thoughts that he might not be quite the man he used to be. But, after eating, he felt fine again. This was a very good moment in his life, sitting here, puffing on his cigar, and letting his thoughts drift in a fog of happiness. Elizabeth had told him that if she had a boy, it would be named after him.

"Have you and Bernard talked over your plans yet?" Mrs. Whelan asked.

"We haven't had time, really."

"You couldn't locate yourselves here instead of New York? Couldn't Bernard get a job, say, on a newspaper, writing here in Chicago?" Mr. Whelan asked.

"I don't think so. He has to be in New York. Father, you know, it's a matter of whom you know, too. I guess it's like most everything else. It's . . . it's literary politics."

"But how will you be taken care of in New York, all alone?" Mrs. Whelan asked.

"I have lots of friends."

If you could be here in Chicago, it would better. Your mother could watch over you. And we could have Doctor Sparks look at you, and we'd feel more sure about everything."

Elizabeth was thoughtful.

"You could stay here, and Bernard could go back to New York for his business and then come back here, but I don't counsel letting a young husband off by himself, no matter how much you think he loves you. I wouldn't have let your father go off on his own, and your father, Elizabeth, is true as true, true blue."

"Oh, Bernard hardly thinks of anything but his work. He's so absent-minded. Why, once he went out to the store to get oranges for me, and guess what? . . . He came back with eggs. When I scolded him, the poor boy looked so surprised and hurt. He just asked me, 'Didn't you want eggs?' I don't even know if he'd be able to take care of himself alone when he gets to working hard."

"Does Bernard really want to name the child . . . after me?" Mr. Whelan asked.

"Oh, yes. We talked about it before he left today."

"Elizabeth, tell me the truth . . . Bernard isn't a Communist, a Red, is he?"

"Oh, no, Father."

"That's good. Now, tell me, Elizabeth, do you and Bernard need money?"

"Bernard's proud, Father."

"Did you have a hard time in New York?"

"Yes, hard, but not too hard. We both just had to be careful. I didn't want to write and make you worry and neither did Bernard. We were worried when . . . when I told Bernard about . . . about me."

"And how are you going to take care of the baby?"

"Bernard is going to try and get an advance on another novel. And if he gets that Fellowship and his book comes out early next year—the publishers decided to postpone publication from this fall to next year—they think it might be a good seller then. I really think it's going to be a bestseller . . . I do."

"And in the meantime?"

"Father, Bernard doesn't know I wanted to talk to you about it, but if you could . . . could give us a loan," Elizabeth said.

"I'd rather give you the money, if I knew that it wouldn't be wasted," he said.

"Is Bernard careful, and are you careful, Elizabeth?" Mrs. Whelan asked.

"We are. We've had to be. After all, we did start . . . being married with nothing, and I think we did well, considering the times."

Nothing was said for several moments.

"I'll tell you, Elizabeth. I didn't approve of your marriage. And I was angry. But you are my daughter. Your child will be our flesh and blood. It's all we'll have, you and it. Since Bernard seems to have settled down, and both of you are really trying to make a home, I'm going to make you a present. I want you and your child to have care."

"Father . . . oh, Father, I don't know what to say. I don't know how to thank you."

Mr. Whelan rose and walked quietly out of the room.

Elizabeth looked off uneasily, fearful. Her mother stared at her.

"Your father loved you so much," she said.

"Yes," Elizabeth said guiltily.

Mr. Whelan returned with a check and handed it to Elizabeth. She looked at it.

"Oh, Father," she exclaimed.

She rose and went to him with outstretched arms. He held her. She cried. He kissed her forehead, held her.

"Your father is good to you and forgives you," Mrs. Whelan said. And then she added, "And I forgive you."

Elizabeth kissed her mother. Mrs. Whelan looked at the check.

"A thousand dollars, that's a lot of money in these times. You manage it, now, because you have a sensible head."

"You were always so good to me," Elizabeth said, crying.

"When your own child grows up, Elizabeth, you'll understand a lot more. I tried to be a good father, and I want to be a good grandfather, too."

"You're the best father . . . Father. I only want Bernard to be as good a father as you are . . . and for me . . . for me to be as good a mother as Mother has been to me."

Mr. Whelan kissed her again, and said that he had to leave. Elizabeth said she was too tired to go to the wake, and asked him to have Bernard telephone. He promised to do this and left home, feeling proud of himself. His ruddy face beamed, as he slowly and confidently walked to his undertaking parlor. Now, the hard work he had done this year, keeping his head above water in the depression, was justified. He had hopes of the business going on. And he could afford this gift, because he would easily net eight thousand dollars this year. Once again, he was a happy man.

v

"It's all over except for tomorrow," Marie said moodily, as the Carr family sat alone in the chapel.

There were sighs and words of agreement.

They wanted to stay here longer, and were grateful to Mr. Whelan for having allowed them to remain for a little while after the regular closing hours. Every one of them looked forward to the funeral in the morning, and at the same time wished that it could be postponed. The corpse seemed to hold them in their chairs. Death had come into their lives, but in the morning, when the coffin would be lowered into its grave, life would go on for them. They were all glad to be alive, but they were guilty about their desire for life in the presence of the dead. They wanted to stay longer in that presence. The experience of death had not touched them as they had imagined it would. Now, after having come here for the wake, after having sat and talked with many people, they were familiar with death. They wanted to be hurt by it more than they had been. They wanted it to mean more to them than it had. They wanted the many words of sympathy and condolences which they had heard to touch them more than these words had touched them.

Now and then, one or the other would glance at the corpse, as if to make sure it was dead and could not accuse them of living. Yet the rigid image of Patrick Carr in his casket accused them of being alive.

"I'm all set on the pallbearers. Gee, Pat Looney is a swell fellow," Jim declared proudly.

"He was a good friend of your father's," Mrs. Carr said.

"Lots of people liked Pa. After all, Pa had a good turnout. He would have liked his wake, having all of his friends here to pay their last respects to him," Jim went on.

Art got up and paced back and forth. Jim lapsed into silence. They didn't appreciate what he had done in handling the funeral arrangements, except for his mother. He was more of a Carr than they were. His father hadn't meant what he'd written, and he hadn't really meant to hit and hurt his mother that night. . . . Why, it was only three days ago, and it seemed as if it had happened so long ago. Poor Pa, it seemed that he'd been dead for a long, long time.

Art sat down again.

Mrs. Carr turned toward the coffin and exclaimed:

"It must have been coming on him for some time before it

happened. If we'd only known what was coming, we would have been different to him."

"You did all you could, Mother," Jim said with empty reassurance.

"Who knows what another is like, and what might be in another's heart?" Mrs. Carr asked, her eyes still fixed on the coffin. "Who knows what the dead might think of the living?"

Her words subdued them all. Bernard looked with pity toward his mother, but he, too, succumbed to the feeling of depression his mother's words had roused.

The Carr children looked at one another. Their mother's remarks had reminded them of their father's document. Bernard watched her, thinking that she didn't have to read what his father had written. He was sure that she knew what his father had felt.

"I was thinking—we ought to have a lot of Masses said for Pa out of his insurance money," Jim suggested.

Bernard frowned.

"We will, Jim," Mrs. Carr said.

"But, Mother, you ought to use that money for yourself," Marie said.

"There's nothing I need that's in this world," Mrs. Carr said, her eyes still fixed on the coffin.

"Yes, I think so. I think that with times as they are and nobody certain, the money ought to be for Mother and the house. If things get worse, where are we? With banks failing all over the lot and things as they are, I think God will understand that we can't spend too much on Masses for Pa, not that I begrudge him any," Art commented.

"Whatever we give to God will come back to us," Mrs. Carr said with intensity.

"We'll have to be leaving now," Jim said.

No one moved. Then Mrs. Carr went up and stood alone, gazing at the corpse. If she only could have gone first. And in the other world, he would know what was in her heart. Would he have pity on her? She stood staring at the corpse.

They fell into an embarrassed silence. Bernard wandered up front and stood off from his mother, looking at the corpse. It seemed changed. The grayish hands seemed thin. The wrists were thin. The face, too. The odor of the flowers was disturbing. Too sweet. The face seemed to change again. It was less thin. The closed, thick lips. Gray skin over the closed eyes. The bulbous nose. Nothing was on the face. Ashen and cold and dead, expressionless, meaningless, an idiotic face, a face that had ceased to be a face. He had the strange illusion that it had moved, that some flicker of expression had crossed the grayish face. He was in terror for a moment. There was no motion. It had been merely his own fear. His father couldn't come back. The dead were nothing. And was this nothingness the cause for fear? What was there to fear here? What was there to fear in death?

The others joined their mother and knelt before the casket. Then they all slowly left the chapel.

They walked toward Stony Island Avenue. Bernard pondered about the way that death just hurt people. No matter who it was who died, no matter what one thought of the character of the person who died, that death could leave a scar, it could have left the real Confirmation mark on the soul, and always, always, people tried to cover up, to salve, to vaseline that hurt, to forget it. But you really couldn't do with the living souls of people what his father-in-law could with their dead bodies. You couldn't prettify souls.

VI

The organ music and the singing were dirgelike, and the slow High Mass was very tedious to Bernard. It was dim and shadowy in this small but charming Romanesque church lit up with candles, and Bernard was moved by the fact that he was actually in the church of his childhood. As a boy of seven he had knelt before this same altar rail and received his first Holy Communion. And now, his father's casket was in front of the rail. What real continuity was there between that boy

and himself? All that was familiar in his boyhood seemed so
unreal—the Mass, the chanted Latin, the black vestments of
the priest. There was wonder in them, and in this ceremony.
But didn't the wonder of religion take the place of the wonder
of life? There was his mother near him, praying fervently.
This Mass must explain something to her, give her something.
Didn't it explain death in Latin words she couldn't understand? But how could women like her bear life without this?
How could people with lives like hers, or like his father's, bear
life if death was the end? To the church, the end, the purpose,
of life was death. But death hurt people, hurt them deeply.
This hurt must be soothed for them. His father's meaningless life acquired meaning and dignity from the man wearing
black vestments. This softened the hurt of death, didn't it?
And the Mass told his mother, and most of the others here, that
they belonged somewhere in life. He didn't belong. He was a
stranger in the surroundings of his boyhood. Yet so many of
his boyhood memories were linked with this church. Here, in
this same church, he had cowered before God and had confessed
sins of his puberty. Here, he had knelt and dreamed of Elsie
Cavanagh and looked at her across the aisles during Sunday
Masses. Here he had knelt and asked God and Mary for help
and grace. Here he had prayed in defense of his purity. Here
he had feared life. And all these memories and pleas and
fears and aspirations and dreams were dead within him; they
were as rigid in the depths of his own consciousness as his
father was rigid in a casket. He had made a coffin within himself and in it had laid away his past. The return to St. Catherine's had opened that coffin. Now he could see the interred bones
of his boyhood.

They sat for the sermon. The priest's weak voice echoed
through the church. The man who was dead here had been a
good man, a father, and he had left a good family behind him.
Bernard half listened to and watched Jim and his mother. She
leaned slightly forward. Her body was taut, her face absorbed.
Jim's lips were closed tightly, and his face was washed with

solemnity. Art stirred, sighed, and noiselessly tapped his feet.
Marie's face was blank. Elizabeth was at the outside of the
pew with her mother. She listened with the same expression
she wore when people in New York talked of proletarian
literature.

The priest spoke of the many virtues of Patrick Carr. To
Bernard, this was grotesque, and he was inwardly angry. Why
was this necessary? He looked about. He knew the answer to
his question. All this was necessary for the living. And the
flickering flames of the candles. The crucifix hanging in shadows over the altar. The priest droning, speaking of the immortality of the soul. Bernard was glad when the sermon was
over.

As the Mass continued, he thought of Elsie Cavanagh and
of his story, *Someday.* Then the coffin was carried out and
loaded into the hearse, and they started on the long drive to
Calvary Cemetery. In the limousine Jim said:

"That was a fine sermon. Father Gilligin is an educated
man."

"I thought it was just right," Elizabeth said.

Bernard frowned and looked out of the window. Cottage
Grove. Then, through Washington Park. The lagoon. A man
in a rowboat.

"When a man dies, he's in the hands of God," Mrs. Carr
said with intensity.

The remark was disturbing, but Bernard didn't know why.
This entire experience in Chicago was a strange interim in his
life. It was something he had never expected to happen to himself. Yet here he was rolling through Washington Park. Then
Grand Boulevard. The statue of George Washington on horse-
back. The talk was casual. Everyone was constrained.

The ride seemed long. And then Calvary Cemetery was
bleak with cluttered stones in the August sunlight. The casket
was unloaded. There were prayers, and they knelt at the
opened grave. The casket was slid into the hole. Patrick Carr
was laid to rest. They turned away. Mrs. Carr watched alone,

and, for the first time since her husband had died, she shed
tears in public. Jim and Art each took her arm. Bernard wanted
to go to her. He couldn't. He walked gravely behind her. Elizabeth took his arm.

"I feel so blue."

"Don't be upset," he said tenderly.

He looked about at gravestones and vaults of all sizes and
kinds. Tomorrow he would return to New York.

Chapter Twenty

I

BERNARD and Joseph Leonard were strolling up and down Fifth Avenue, talking. It was a pleasant night, and quite a few people were out. Bernard was glad to be back in New York and alone for a few days. Elizabeth and her parents were coming on at the end of the week. On the day coach last night, he'd hardly slept, but he had arrived in New York eager, enthusiastic, and restlessly alive. New York now was utterly wonderful. He'd loafed and wandered about all day, thinking, dreaming, looking. He'd dropped in at *Mass Action*, and Sophie had told him that Lloyd Street was leaving as editor. Jake was running the magazine temporarily, and had talked mysteriously about Street. Barber had been busy but cordial, and would have lunch with him next week. All day he'd hoped to meet some lovely girl. Tonight, he'd made this date to take a walk and chat with Joe. But Joe hadn't been too interested in his account of the Chicago trip. Sensing this, Bernard remarked:

"It's a different world from this. It's a world practically without books; without respect for all that you and I value."

Bernard observed a passing girl out of the corner of his eye.

"Bernie, why should you care what undertakers, bricklayers, clerks, stenographers, accountants, and Communists think about you?"

"I don't," Bernard insisted.

"Then you give a damned good imitation of concern."

They stopped at Eighth Street, turned around, and strolled back north.

"Your background is no more awful than mine. It's just different. I come from the gilded ghetto."

"It's my laboratory of life. And I keep asking myself—how did I get from there to . . . to here . . . from Sixty-third Street and from Maryland Avenue to lower Fifth Avenue?"

"The important thing is that you did get here."

"Maybe. But I was thinking of something else. Sometimes, in restaurants, I've looked at people through the windows and they've seemed only half real. They'd pass, voiceless human beings, voiceless strangers. I'd get a queer feeling. And at times it seems to me that people in literary New York are sitting in an esthetic restaurant and looking through a window at voiceless strangers."

"Suppose those outside all stormed into the restaurant, where would you and I be?"

"If they only would, we'd have a bigger restaurant. But they aren't interested. Joe, it's about a thousand miles from here to Chicago, but the psychological distance is greater. It only costs thirty-two dollars and seventy cents to get a coach ticket from there to here. The psychological cost of that journey is far greater."

Another girl. She had such plump arms.

"Bernie, you said you're worried because your father-in-law gave you some money. The artist has a right to take any help he can get from society."

"Even some of my Communist friends don't see anything wrong in my getting help from my father-in-law."

He wanted approval, support, someone to assure him that he was justified in accepting all the help he could get. He wanted someone to tell him he hadn't compromised.

They walked over to Childs on Union Square and had coffee and English muffins.

Bernard knew he was really afraid of himself. If he became a success, what would happen to him? Now, with a thousand dollars in the bank, with the economic shackles off until the baby came and his book was published, he was beginning to fear the new temptations he might have to face. He had always been poor and harried. This had spurred him on. Could he spur himself on if he were economically secure? No one could give him reassurance about this question. It was irrelevant to seek it from others. Yet he was indulging in this irrelevancy.

"Carr, I know that one day the name of Joseph Leonard will be part of the history of the literature of the world. Nothing else means that to me," Joe said, snapping his fingers in contempt.

They finished their coffee, paid, and left the restaurant. Joe walked Bernard home. Standing in front of the house, Bernard said:

"William James once said something to the effect that all the differences in people is in the small area of consciousness—what they think and say."

"That's true," Joe said.

They parted. Bernard let himself in and climbed the stairs to the top floor. The room was orderly but dusty.

He fiddled about restlessly for a few moments, and then sat down and wrote a letter to Elizabeth.

August 29, 1932

Elizabeth Honey:

It was exciting to get back to New York, but I wished you were here with me. Now, it's late, and I am in our room writing this letter before going to bed. I saw Joe Leonard tonight, and we walked a bit and talked about literature. All day, I half-enjoyed my loneliness. I wandered about. At twilight, I saw the skyline from Central Park. The colors melted around the buildings and over the trees. It was like being in fairyland, and I wished you were here. There was a smell of autumn in the air.

I am going to start rustling books to review tomorrow, and

*am thinking about future writings. And I'll also get to work
on my Fellowship application, not to mention getting references.*

*But, Honey, I think of you, and I want you to be all right.
I want you to be well, but I know you will be taken care of.
Write to me.*

*Give my regards to your mother and father, and all my love
to you, Elizabeth honey, and to the newcomer who waits his
time. Kisses without beginning and without end. Write me.*
                                                Bernard

He addressed and sealed the envelope, and then sat down
and smoked.

He'd never stated his desire for immortality as baldly as Joe
Leonard had tonight, but he really had the same feelings. How
often, for instance, did he not think of each move of his, every
thought he had, every experience as of possible value to posterity? And then the times when he would think with sadness
and fear about death. His final thoughts might die with him,
unrecorded. Balzac had once said that the writer had to be an
egotist. Where did the line stop? The line between wanting to
impose your own feelings and ideas on the world and just down-
right megalomania? Was it a matter of compelling by conviction? But, then, couldn't someone who was crazy compel by
conviction?

His thoughts wandered. What was Elizabeth doing in Chicago? He'd come back after talking with Joe, determined to
write something, for his own morale and self-confidence if for
no other reason. But he couldn't write tonight. It was lonely
here in this room. He had these few days of freedom, but he
didn't know what to do with them. Would he use them for
fun and experiences, for adventures? For work? Or would he
just piddle them away? He seemed to be utterly dislocated. All
this restlessness, nervousness, confusion, seemed to him to be
related to sex. These last months, he had been thinking that
monogamy was the best state. Was it? Was man born to be

faithful and monogamous? What girls did he know? And if
he were to go with one, and Elizabeth found out, wouldn't she
be crushed? But why did this have to be? Why couldn't
people be rational? Why couldn't everyone own his or her own
body?

He got up and paced idly about the room. He noticed the
dust in the corners and a thin layer on the table and the furniture. He looked at the bright curtains Elizabeth had made, at
their clothes hanging in the opened closet, at the books on
shelves in the corner, at a few of Elizabeth's bottles and jars on
the dresser, and at a pair of old red slippers on the floor in
front of the bureau. All these objects looked pathetic, weighted
with meaning. They were the symbols of a common life, and
they seemed to speak to him with all the pathos of everything
that was deficient in their common life, the symbols of so much
that had been wished for and never realized.

There was no escaping the moments of restlessness and guilt
and desire he was now experiencing. And was there any use
in the exercise of self-control? Whelan would consider him a
sonofabitch. He was an artist. At least, he had the ambition to
be an artist. And as an artist, didn't he need change, endless
change and variety and excitement? Endless intoxication with
life? Was he growing emotionally rusty? Was he living by routine, killing all those responses to the world that he must keep
fresh and alive?

The gloom of his thoughts grew thicker and thicker, like
a penetrating fog that creeps over a city to paralyze all its
movement and business and normal living. He went to bed,
and tossed restlessly.

II

Dear Bernard:
   I miss you, especially at night. It gets lonesome, and if I wake
up because sometimes I feel dreadfully uncomfortable, I look
and there is nobody beside me, not my Bernard beside me, and

then I miss you, and I am counting the days until I see you again.

Mother and Father are wonderful to me, and, Bernard, they have grown to like you. They didn't know you before we came here. Father is busy again. He was called out in the middle of the night on another case. And then he came home and had to be out early. Bernard, he's really been very fair to me.

Tomorrow I'm going to go and sit in Jackson Park in the sun again and think of you, and of all the good things we're going to have, and of little Philip. Because I just know our baby will be a boy. And I'm going to take a parasol and perhaps I'll read a book. But I will sit and think of lots of things. I'll think about the times when you and I walked in the park, and I'll find a spot to help me remember our walks, and I'll think of when I'll be back in New York. Father got airplane tickets for himself and Mother and me. Gosh, I never imagined I'd become a regular airplane traveler. Father and Mother are looking forward to it, only Mother says she is afraid she will get sick in the plane, but I don't think she will . . .

Bernard, you see about a room for them in a comfortable hotel from Saturday until Tuesday morning. And you must be careful when I am not there about what you eat, and just don't eat hamburgers and gobble down your food, and get your rest, because I know how you like to stay up late and talk. I don't mind it, but I will worry if you aren't getting your rest and eating properly and if your laundry isn't attended to, because you are careless about things like this. There, now, get mad at me for saying it. You can't do anything to me, even if you do get mad, because I'm far away.

I have not seen your mother, but I am going to visit her before I come back. I think it will make her feel good, and I really want her to like me, because I like her. I like your whole family. And I'm going to go downtown with Mother and get another dress and some things. Mother and Father want to get a lot of things for our baby, too, and I told them they could get them in New York, but they are going to get them here

*and have them shipped. Please, do take care of yourself. I'll
be home soon, and you think of me. Be a good boy, and be sure
not to forget about the hotel.*

    Love and oodles of kisses from

                              Your wife

                                     Elizabeth

III

Bernard finished working over his review. He had been a
little uneasy about accepting this book from Brady because
it was about biology. But now that the review was written, he
was glad he'd done it. He had summarized and stated the contents clearly, and the only critical remarks he had made were
in his last paragraph, when he agreed with the author about
vitalism. This was a philosophic and interpretative question,
and not one of a strictly scientific order, and he was not being
pretentious in expressing his own opinion. Reading this book
had been a stimulating experience. Old ambitions and curiosi-
ties had been awakened, and he had been shocked at how intellectually narrowed his life had become. Since coming to
New York he'd read at least thirty-five books for review, and
not five of them had been worth reading. He'd heard many
discussions and arguments about politics and literature, but
these always boiled down to the same few questions. He had
even come to have some vanity about living in an advanced
milieu. Now he wasn't so sure of how advanced it was. It was
cramped, and limited. One could be absorbed in it so easily and
end up mistaking an endless series of loudly spoken big words
for concepts and meaning. How different was the spirit of this
English scientist who wrote so well, reasoned so carefully, stated
his case so fairly, and voiced such a tolerant and curious spirit.
These were the qualities of mind he really admired, but he had
almost lost his sense of them here in New York. He must find
time to read books like this, to sink himself more in the best
ideas of this age, and to take less seriously so much of the bub-

bling literary journalism and living-room and cafeteria talk
of New York.

He heated coffee in the kitchen, brought a cup back to the
room, and sat down to drink it and smoke. It was very quiet.
Here in this attic room, New York was far away. Its roar was
muffled.

He wanted to plan. During her last months, Elizabeth
wouldn't be going out much. It would be easier to read more
and work more. He could set time aside to study. He needn't
feel hurried and harassed now. He'd read more philosophy,
more science, more poetry. He must live more of a life of the
mind. He must hold tightly to a love of ideas for their own
sake. Perhaps now, with some of the money he made on reviews, he would buy a few books and start building a permanent library.

He recalled his college philosophy courses under Dr. Em-
meron Dwight and Mr. Timkins. He'd been on the verge of
tears when he heard of Dwight's death last year. The best
minds of men weren't immune to all the ills that flesh was heir
to. How he'd used to sit in Dwight's classes lost to the outside
world, listening to the old man talk in a casual and fluent
manner, thinking everything out on his feet before the audience, getting chalk dust on his hands and clothes, throwing out
ideas, suggestions, turning the thought of philosophers into
something living and exciting! And Timkins, too, had helped
him. Now those hours seemed so precious.

But he could have hours like this all by himself. He'd had
them when he was reading the book by the English biologist.
And why was the desire for these hours a sign of weakness?
Why was all this clamor and clatter of the world so important?
Why must politics be the dominating dictatorial interest of
life? The political news bored him. The political speeches of
the candidates were worse than the news stories. Hoover said
Roosevelt was wrong. Roosevelt said Hoover was. The Communists said they were the only party and that they were the
voice of the workers, opposing the three capitalist parties, in-

cluding the social-fascist Socialists. Why should he be drawn
into this campaign of howling?

The stark misery of people! Newspapers full of an indigest-
ible diet of political promises, predictions of businessmen that
the worst was over, and the suffering people. Despairing mothers killing their starving children. Suicides, riots, cries for food.
The life of ideas and of writing couldn't alleviate this condition. God, from the rockbound coast of Maine to the sunny
shores of California, this land must be one of suffering! Empty
bellies, fears, violent thoughts.

This was the last day by himself. He wished he had a few
more days alone. There had been none of the adventure and
excitement he'd hoped for. Elizabeth couldn't accuse him.
Instead of coasting on Whelan's help, he'd seen Brady and gotten
the book, and also permission to use the old man's name on the
Loewenthal application. But as time went on there would be
many reasons for friction with his father-in-law. It just wasn't
in him to be the kind of son-in-law Whelan would want. Still,
Whelan wouldn't live forever. What if their plane crashed
tomorrow and three died? Or if Whelan should be killed? Or
both of Elizabeth's parents? He and Elizabeth would inherit the
business, and they would be fixed for life. He didn't want
Whelan to die. If it happened, it would be no fault of his. If
they were all killed and he were free! He wouldn't get married
again. But how few girls and women he had had in his life.
He was so limited in experiences. What little enjoyed freedom
he'd had! And now to be free might mean something different.
He'd proven himself, and he had more knowledge, more confidence, and, yes, a little more experience than in 1927. He
could make friends, and perhaps women would find him attractive. Now was the time for him to be free. And he wasn't.
But if something happened!

He imagined himself living alone in a small room, in which
he could do as he pleased, coming and going unobserved.

Halting his daydream, he felt frustrated and guilty. He sat
down and tried to outline a statement of his project for a

Loewenthal Fellowship, but his ideas for a novel were too vague. He went to lunch at a dimly lit, clean restaurant around the corner on Eleventh and University Place, and sat alone, in a booth. He heard a familiar voice in the booth behind him. It was that of David Bergman. Then he heard other voices. He thought of joining Bergman and the other fellows, but he didn't. They were talking about German politics, and he listened with interest while he went on eating. David read out the totals and percentages of the vote in the recent German Reichstag elections and then compared these with the statistics of the earlier elections. Bernard heard him pound the table and say:

"Comrades, it's clear. The Nazis are stopped. From now on the curve is going to be ours, a rising curve that will end in Soviet power."

They all talked spiritedly and enthusiastically, cutting in on one another. Then David Bergman spoke pedantically. After making some further expository remarks about the strength of the Communists in Hamburg and Berlin he argued that, whereas the Communists were a unified force standing as the vanguard, the Nazis were a block made up of irreconcilable discontents, and, in the last analysis, dependent on the cowardice and class-collaborationist policies of the Social-Democratic leaders.

"All we need is Germany," he declared. He made noises clearing his throat. "Comrades, that's all—Germany."

Bernard sat up, wide-eyed. He wanted to laugh. But they were talking very seriously. Their conversation was no joke.

"France? What's France? Usury imperialism, luxury goods. You can't be master of Europe selling champagne and collecting interests on Balkan loans. It's Germany, and, outside the Soviet Union, comrades, that's where we're strongest."

There was an emphatic smash on the table, and then David declared with finality:

"In Germany, comrades, we're irresistible."

"If we can smash the Social Democrats in time."

"They don't worry me, comrades. Not in the least. We know how to lick Kerenskys," David said.

"Kerensky," one of them sneered. "You know, he and Dan and Chernov and Miliukov and Trotsky all ought to be arrested for loitering in history."

They laughed.

"Not Trotsky, comrades," David said, "Trotsky is counter-revolutionary. But subjectively he's a revolutionist. He's a dialectically unresolved man."

They talked about Trotsky, and David mentioned having heard some of the top Party leaders discussing Trotsky, and one of them had said:

"Trotsky, what a revolutionist! What a tragedy he is!"

David then said that this same Party leader had told a joke. When Trotsky was Commissar of War, he would sit on a fine white horse watching the May Day parades, and everyone would exclaim: What a man! Then Veroshilov became Commissar of War, and he sat on a fine big white horse, watching demonstrations, and everyone would exclaim: What a horse!

Bernard heard some of them laughing. One of the group challenged David and wanted to know what Party leader he was quoting.

"Since we're all *kosher* here, I'll tell you . . . Eldridge."

"And the C.I. rep, Bush, was there. Bush laughed at the jokes."

"Who's Bush?"

"You don't know who Bush is?"

"He's the C. I. rep.," one of them said, and they laughed.

"Yes, directives come through Bush. He's a real revolutionist, too. He's the man who convinced Lloyd Street to go underground."

They began talking about Street in hushed terms.

Bernard finished his meal and left without speaking to Bergman.

Chapter Twenty-one

I

Riding from the Newark Airport to Manhattan, Philip Whelan was less sure of himself than he'd been in Chicago. He had kept looking out at streets and buildings and telling himself that Chicago was homier than New York. He was impressed by the hotel. Elizabeth explained that the manager, Mr. Daniel, liked Bernard's writing and had been glad to do a small favor like this for her and Bernard. He asked how Bernard and Elizabeth had come to meet Mr. Daniel.

"He wants to write himself," Elizabeth said.

Zip Daniel had personally met the Whelans. He had been gracious and had seemed to be a decent sort of person and probably a good businessman. The East River Hotel was small, only six stories, but elegant, and Mr. Whelan assumed immediately that the man who managed it must know his business. He had instantly observed that the hotel was efficiently run. There were elderly and sedate people in the lobby, and he had decided the hotel was proper and respectable. But he was puzzled to think that a man running a hotel like this should want to be a writer.

"This," he asked, pointing around the room, "doesn't put you and Bernard under obligation, does it?"

"Oh, no, not at all, Father. Mr. Daniel was glad to make this accommodation."

"If we wanted, we could get a suite here for ourselves at reduced rates," Bernard added.

"Well, a man always learns," Mr. Whelan remarked.

He glanced about the elegant room. He had met all kinds of people in his life, but never before a successful businessman who wanted to be a writer. However, New York was different from Chicago. He knew that, even though he had seen very little of the Big Town.

Mrs. Whelan excitedly told Bernard about the airplane trip. She was still amazed to think that she had really flown all the way to New York. And she hadn't been afraid, either, not for one minute. Mr. Whelan only half-listened. He'd enjoyed the trip and had even been a little proud of himself for having taken it. Thoughts that he'd had in the plane came back to him. To think that he had flown over so many hundreds of miles of America, looking down at fields and houses and cities and mountains and lakes and rivers. What a wonderful country this was and how so many wonderful things could be done here. There was so much to look forward to. It made a man wish he were younger. All the changes that had come about in his own lifetime had only scratched the surface of what would be done and accomplished in the future. When you thought of all this, you felt out of life. You were afraid you were being passed by.

He quietly noticed Bernard and Elizabeth. He'd met many young fellows in his life, but never one quite like his son-in-law. Bernard bewildered him a little, At times, he appeared to be a very serious, decent, and ambitious lad. And again, there was something about him, the look in his eyes, the way he pressed his lips together, the way he jutted out his chin, the way you felt he was speaking of only some of the things on his mind! Whelan didn't know what all this meant. Might it be that Bernard was one of those chaps who wasn't going to let the world pass him by?

Whelan and his wife went into the bedroom to wash up before they all went out to dinner.

Elizabeth loked at Bernard and said:

"They are dear, aren't they, Bernard? But they aren't young any more. . . . Oh, Bernard, I get sad whenever I think of you and me growing old."

They sat waiting for the Whelans to come out of their bedroom.

II

"Philip, I think the children will get on well. Did you notice how happy Elizabeth was to see him?" Mrs. Whelan said as she stood before the mirror, powdering her face.

"Yes . . . and I say, if he turns out decently, I'll never regret what I've done for them as long as I live."

"Philip, I watched the young people very closely when they were in Chicago. Bernard will do whatever Elizabeth wishes. I never saw a young wife manage her husband better than she does. I have no worries about them now."

"Do you really think so?"

"I'm positive."

When the Whelans were ready, they all went out for dinner. Elizabeth selected a restaurant on lower Sixth Avenue. As they rode in a cab, she chatted away gaily and pointed out streets and buildings. At first, Mr. Whelan and Bernard were silent, but they gradually warmed up as Elizabeth continued to talk. Bernard also pointed out some of the streets and places of interest. Mr. Whelan asked questions about business in New York, and Bernard explained how New York was different from Chicago.

He pointed out that there was much more basic industry in Chicago than New York, and illustrated this by a reference to the steel mills. In addition, Chicago was a transportation center. In New York, he said, you would find the most powerful banks, and it was primarily a center for the sale of services and ideas. It was also an ocean port and relatively close to Europe. He said he had often thought about the differences. Mr. Whelan became interested. He and Bernard hadn't talked like this when Bernard had been in Chicago, and he was favorably surprised by his son-in-law's remarks. Elizabeth and her mother chatted away.

"In Chicago," Bernard went on, "the whole city has grown as a result of transportation. Real-estate values are related to transportation."

"I'd never thought of that," Mr. Whelan said.

Besides being pleased to be able to talk interestingly and yet honestly with his father-in-law, Bernard was also clarifying what he already knew. And regarded in the light of American problems, Chicago was more interesting and significant than it had seemed when evaluated from the standpoint of his own desires and emotions.

The taxicab stopped. Mr. Whelan paid. The restaurant was large and old-fashioned, with wood-panelled walls, on which were hung paintings of plump nymphs and of sailing vessels and clipper ships. The place was less than half filled, but the diners were well-dressed and were conversing in low voices, with an air of politeness and good manners. The array of silver, the shining platters, the spotless linen, and the efficient waiters added to the sense of ease and grace they all felt as they were ushered to a table in the rear.

Mr. Whelan complimented Elizabeth on having selected this restaurant. They all ate with relish, and said little during the meal. Mr. Whelan ate his steak with especial gusto. When they finished, they sat back contented. Mrs. Whelan commented on the food, and then Mr. Whelan said his steak had been as good as any he could ever remember having had in Chicago. Bernard smoked and drank a second cup of coffee while Mr. Whelan puffed on a cigar and gazed about.

"This is an old restaurant," he said. "Why, Elizabeth, it's the kind your mother and I could have gone to when I was courting her and wanted to make a particularly good impression." He turned to smile with knowing affection at his wife. "I once did court her, you know." He beamed. "And I had to beat off competition. Elizabeth, your mother was no wallflower in her day."

"That's the way he won me, Bernard, when I was a girl," Mrs. Whelan said.

She looked lovingly at her husband. She wished there were music here, oldtime songs and waltzes she'd heard when she was a girl, music which had helped her dream and had promised her so much in life. It would be sad to hear oldtime music, because it was sad to remember when you were young, but tonight it would be the kind of sadness you enjoyed. Oh, to have something of her girlhood back.

She was far away from home, in New York, and she had come here thinking that this would be like a second honeymoon. She was far away and yet she was as secure as if she were home. She was with her family, and she was as happy as she was sad. Her son-in-law was now part of her family, and he was a presentable young man. Yes, she liked him.

Elizabeth casually took one of Bernard's cigarettes and lit it.

"Why, Elizabeth, do you smoke in public?" asked her mother.

"Mother, it's even fashionable to smoke now. I only smoke now and then, after dinner. One after dinner won't be bad for me, and it . . . it tastes nice."

Mrs. Whelan looked anxiously toward her husband. Bernard was nervous. But Mr. Whelan surprised them with a relaxed smile.

"Of course, now that you're married . . ." Mrs. Whelan exclaimed.

Girls could be more free now. If she had dared to smoke when she was Elizabeth's age! If she dared now! She wanted to, but Philip wouldn't be so tolerant of her as he was of his daughter.

Without articulating his thoughts or expressing what he felt to himself, Mr. Whelan knew that something had just happened within him. A change in his feeling toward his daughter had come about. She was still young, even though her face was full. But she wasn't his little girl, and now she had lost that little girl's face he'd always had fixed in his mind as that of his daughter. He was relieved. A burden was lifted from him. Some unknown strain in his mind had snapped painlessly. After all, he thought, he had no right to tell Elizabeth not to smoke, and he could see by the way she held her cigarette and puffed at it that she wasn't smoking like a chippy. She seemed less close to him. He hadn't ever known the little girl who had been his daughter. But he knew this pregnant married woman even less than he had the girl. The anxious responsibility he had felt for her since her birth was now ended. He looked across the table at Bernard and suddenly felt closer to him. Bernard, like himself, was a husband. He remembered what Ruth had said in the hotel room about Elizabeth having her way with Bernard. He was glad. He wanted to chuckle. Now there were things this lad was going to know and to learn. Still, these were good. At least, they were right. He turned again toward his daughter. She was a flower off the same stem as her mother. He saw in her eyes the same confidence he'd so often seen in Ruth's eyes. He vaguely remembered Ruth when she was pregnant. Elizabeth resembled her. Yes, Elizabeth was a woman, with the strange confident power of a woman in her eyes. And she was not ruined. Things had worked out well, and she would be able to keep Bernard in line. They were sincere young people, building a home. How right he'd been to help them! And how glad he was for being here.

"You know, I was thinking," he said in a gentle voice, "it has taken me a little while to get used to what happened, and I never gave you . . . well . . . gave you my blessing. You two have it."

"Father," Elizabeth said, her face growing ecstatic.

"Thank you, Mr. Whelan, and I'm . . . I'm very grateful," Bernard said politely. He was startled; then he was moved. He suddenly liked his father-in-law. At least, he wanted to.

"And you two know you have my blessing. I'm so happy we are all here. We do have a family, don't we, Philip?"

Mr. Whelan sat back, nodding agreement with his wife. Perhaps his grandson would really be a chip off the old block.

—Young Master Philip Whelan . . . Carr, he said to himself.

He paid the bill, and they left.

They decided to take a walk and then go to see where Elizabeth and Bernard lived. Elizabeth chatted about their attic room. Bernard knew she was preparing them for it, but he wasn't concerned with their reaction. They were both better than Elizabeth had led him to believe, or than he had believed himself. He was even pleased that they were going to name the baby after Whelan if it were a boy. And he hoped it would be a boy.

"It's so comforting a feeling to have a family," Elizabeth said with emotion as they strolled toward Fifth Avenue.

"It's worth all the worry and trouble it brings," her father told her.

—Is it? Bernard asked himself.

His doubt troubled him, especially because he knew he had been genuinely moved. There was still that small area of consciousness in people where they differed from one another. And for the concepts and feelings in that small area, for the expression of those concepts and feelings—how far should one go?

Elizabeth told her parents about lower Fifth Avenue and how much she liked it. They strolled on.

III

Philip Whelan had awakened in the strange hotel bed, depressed. Never before in his life had he experienced anything quite like his evening with Elizabeth and Bernard the night before. He had felt so much more than he had revealed; he had been so much happier than he had seemed. Now, in a state of early-morning weariness, he distrusted his own emotions. Had he been a sucker? Had he allowed himself to become the victim of his own feelings?

He and Ruth were going to eat in their room. He had ordered a large breakfast, more than he really wanted, and he ate everything, his grapefruit, oatmeal, bacon and eggs, and muffins, because eating distracted him from his own feelings. He looked across the table at his wife. Her face was slightly wrinkled, her complexion bad, and her skin, once so soft, was a little coarse. Ruth resembled the girl he had married, and yet she didn't. He had looked across tables at this face so often, at breakfast, luncheon, dinner, that he was too used to it to observe how the signs of age were insidiously leaving their marks. This morning it was a shock to look at her. He tried to remember her when she had been his bride, but couldn't visualize her clearly. Her features were mixed up with images of Elizabeth.

"Somehow I woke up feeling like a girl this morning, Philip," she went on.

"This trip has led me to thinking—America is a wonderful country. All of the inventions, all of the comforts. And cities like Chicago and New York. My God, the buildings they have here! If Roosevelt can only be elected and pull us out now."

"But there are so few trees in New York. This is no place for young people to raise a child."

"Yes, you're right."

Ruth was nervous. She pressed her legs together under the table and tapped her feet on the floor. Mr. Whelan became uneasy because of her nervousness.

"Philip," she said tenderly.

He was frightened by her look. She went to him, took his hand, drew him to his feet, and said:

"I feel like a girl."

She embraced him passionately. In a submissive mood, he allowed her to kiss him and cling to him.

IV

Walking around, he was alternately dull and interested. It had been years since Ruth had acted as she had in the room this morning. And, thinking of their age, he was filled with shame. There was something frightening in women. And Elizabeth was a woman also. He had disturbing images of her with Bernard in bed. And at such moments might she not think of him and Ruth, and think of the time she was conceived? She wouldn't possibly imagine that he and Ruth acted as they had in bed this morning. He was glad he wasn't seeing Elizabeth.

Ruth walked along Broadway at his side. They were alone and tied together in some conspiracy of shame. They knew about each other what no one else knew. He had thought that those first feelings were now under control, that marriage, a settled life, a business, and maturity had helped to escape from them. But this morning, at the age of fifty-three, with Ruth, herself fifty and with streaks of gray in her hair! She had become suddenly like a young bride, and he had tried to be a young lover. He was more ashamed of her than of himself. He was afraid of her.

His feet were beginning to be sore.

"Goodness, Broadway is not what I had imagined it to be. So many advertising signs and moving-picture shows and all of these stores."

"They look like sucker stores," he commented.

"And so much noise. I swear to goodness, New York is the noisiest city I ever heard tell of," she went on.

"Elizabeth said it's usually more crowded, but that many people go away for this weekend. It seems to me that, except for the Loop in Chicago and State and Madison at the rush hour, you could never see so many people on the streets as we've seen this morning."

"They all walk so fast and they're in such a hurry. It almost tires a person just to look at them. On Fifth Avenue, I counted it, four people bumped into us," she said.

Ruth had said nothing about it since they had left the hotel. He was sure it was on her mind, but she didn't seem to be ashamed. Women must know no shame. He remembered, but not too clearly, how gradually, and especially after Elizabeth had come, that he had had decreasing desires for her. For years he had always just wanted to finish and had so often done it because he had imagined that if he didn't she might think that he wasn't a man. He suspected that she was critical of him. She might think how all of these years, he might have . . . might have given her so much more pleasure.

He unobtrusively stared at two young girls. Why need one feel the disgust afterward?

They paused to look at the *Times* Building.

"So this is Broadway and Times Square."

"Philip, there's one of those tour busses. Maybe we ought to take it and see more of New York," she said, pointing at a blue bus by the curb.

"Let's take it."

They took a rubberneck bus and enjoyed the sights of New York, and then they walked more, had dinner alone, saw a movie, and returned to their hotel, tired and quietly happy.

"My feet are almost killing me," Mrs. Whelan said, sitting by the bed and taking off her shoes. "My ankles are a little swollen."

"You rest now . . . Mother."

She gave him a tender glance. For a moment he did not see her clearly. She seemed like the same beautiful young bride he had once known and taken in his arms.

"We carried on like youngsters," she said half-guiltily.

"We're human, Ruth," he said apologetically.

"A person never knows what's in them—how much love there is in them."

He nodded agreement, because he didn't know what to say.

"Philip, are you sorry?" she asked.

"What?" he asked in return, feigning not to have understood her.

"Are you sorry that we carried on like youngsters?"

"The youngsters wouldn't imagine that there is still a lot of juice in the old folks," he said, smiling, surprised that he was able to carry off this remark without revealing his shame and dissatisfaction.

"I feel ten years younger . . . except for my feet."

She fussed with the pillows before lying down. Her movements and gestures reminded him of Elizabeth.

"Philip," she said with gentle authority, "you come here and put your head on my lap and rest the way you used to."

He shyly and awkwardly obeyed her. She patted and caressed his face and hair, and he lay with his eyes closed, removed from the world. He remembered how they had gone on a picnic and, sitting alone with her under a tree, he'd put his head in her lap for the first time in his life. That was about twenty-five years ago. Now, at his age, you felt desires without any romance, without that feeling of the sun and the world and the sky and of the moon and the songs of your youth. Suddenly he thought of corpses.

"Don't be so nervous, Philip. Just rest, rest like you used to."

"I'm not restless."

"You're still my boy, my lover," she said very affectionately.

v

Elizabeth had dragooned him into coming to Mass here at St. Patrick's. He was trying to restrain his resentment. But it wasn't so trying kneeling here in St. Patrick's. He was paying little attention to the Mass. Automatically he knelt, stood, and sat at the proper time. He bowed his head and stroked his breast as the Sanctus bell rang.

Coming here was important and pleasing to the Whelans; when they went back home they could say that they'd gone to Mass at St. Patrick's. When they had all met a little while ago in front of the church, the Whelans had been strangely quiet, and a little wistful and apologetic. What did it mean?

He looked toward the altar, brightly lit with candles. The priest was before the tabernacle. This ritual was a mystery, sacred, inexplicable, strangely and utterly anachronistic. He needed none of this in his own life. Was he the only atheist at this Mass? How could all this ever be ended? All these men and women kneeling in homage to a non-existent God, believing in the symbolism of this primitive dance drama! They outnumbered him. They were the multitude.

He was aware of Elizabeth's slight movements beside him. At his left, Mr. Whelan knelt, controlled and motionless, his face calm, solemn, and without emotion. The crust of Bernard's doubt and contempt seemed to break. He sensed a different mood growing within him. He dare not give himself to this mood. He couldn't open his senses to the appeal of the

Latin, to the poetry of this spectacle, even though he admitted
to himself that here was a kind of legendary human poetry
which had been perpetuated through the centuries. He was
filled with a yearning for inner peace. The altar bell tolled
again. He knew what really hid behind this mystery. Death.
His father's funeral Mass came back to mind. It had been a
shield between human fears and emotions and the naked and
brutal facts of that death. His father's life had acquired a meaning by the Mass. A corpse, a soul, was delivered up to a God
Who made the entire world significant, Who endowed each
and every thought and wish and desire of human beings with
meaning. And here he was, struggling to give a meaning to
everything he did and felt and thought after having rejected
these traditional sources of meaning. The Mass was part of the
common world of art. For art alone gave a necessary inner
meaning to human life.

He looked around the huge church, at its stained glass windows and enormous pillars. The dome of air filled the building
as though the very air itself possessed form and shape. He wondered about the people attending. The bald-headed man in
front of him, the girls and women near him. And the Whelans?
Did they know what this meant to them?

The remainder of the Mass seemed to pass quickly. They
left the church.

The sunshine on Fifth Avenue struck Bernard almost like a
blow. He became aware of light and gay voices, and of laughter
near him. He had often heard little sounds of joy, passing
laughter from people as they emerged from church. In fact,
he had been hearing this all his life without knowing it. Now,
for the first time, he understood it. In some manner these people,
consciously or otherwise, must have had moods, feelings, fears
like his. They must have felt the strain of death in church. Now
they were relaxed. They were happily returning to the world
of the living. He observed how relaxed several men were as they
walked. He noticed the measured, slow walk of Mr. Whelan as
he led them through the crowd on the sidewalk.

A man in a derby passed, swinging a cane.

"A lot of important people go to Mass here on Sunday, don't they?" Mr. Whelan remarked.

"Why, yes, Father, I think Al Smith goes to Mass here," Elizabeth said.

"Oh, I liked it—going to Mass in a church like St. Patrick's Cathedral. I always wanted to do that," Mrs. Whelan said.

"It's bigger than the Holy Name Cathedral in Chicago," Mr. Whelan said.

"Yes, it is. I guess it must be one of the biggest churches in America," Elizabeth said.

Men and women who, a moment ago, had been part of a group with eyes fixed on the altar, were now reduced to the status of being the unknown moving atoms, the moving human scenery on the streets of New York. The brilliant warm sun, the clear blue sky, the lines of buildings on either side of the street, the Public Library, visible ahead, the dresses in the windows, the books in a bookstore window, maps in a travel agency, shining silver and elegant dishes, the well-dressed men and women, a shiny and elegant gray roadster moving slowly north near the curb, a tall, handsome policeman strolling past— all this was like some connected spectacle. The streets here were as full of life as the church had been of death, of the impending final sadness of all men. He envied these people. They could now forget death because they had appeased it. They had eased in church what he had exposed in his own nature. What they had closed in their hearts, he had opened up in his.

"Now, let's find some jolly restaurant and have a fine good Sunday-morning breakfast," Mr. Whelan proposed.

"Oh, Father, let's. We'll go to the Brevoort on Eighth Street," Elizabeth said.

VI

"My work is as hard as any man's," Philip Whelan said, his voice slightly thick.

"Yes, Philip. I know. I look forward so much to the day when you will be able to take it easier," Mrs. Whelan said sympathetically.

"How many people appreciate it? How many people think the undertaker isn't human, that he's just somebody wearing black clothes, like a cartoon of pessimism and thinking only of robbing and cheating the bereaved?"

She nodded her head in agreement.

They sat in the hotel room. He leaned forward and gazed at the rug.

"Philip, now, please don't drink any more," she begged.

"I'm not drunk," he said.

His surly voice frightened her, but she said nothing.

He was trying to think. He knew that he wasn't drunk. He didn't get drunk often, at the most only a couple of times a year. A man in his business had to do something. Nobody knew what it was like unless they were in it themselves. Stinking corpses, ruined homes, men and women going crazy with grief. Entering houses of death at all hours of the day and night and taking away the bodies of loved ones in boxes! Meeting suspicion as if you were a murderer! And you always were forced to be tactful and hold in anything you thought. Smiling and showing tact with people who would cheat you out of your money. And seeing corpses, corpses, one after another, seeing them embalmed, laid out, taking them out of their homes smelling, seeing them made over, made to look younger and presentable so their families and friends could look at them. Yes, he had some right to relax, to forget. But how could he ever forget? He rarely thought like this of his work, and yet these thoughts were always there in the back of his mind.

He stared at the fresh pink coverlet on the bed. In that bed on Saturday he had let his wife make a fool out of him, and at his age. He had known since then that this was coming on.

"I took a walk and found out where I could get a good drink. I had a few drinks. A man has a right to a few drinks when he does what I do."

"I know, Philip. I understand. Only, please, Philip, please don't drink too much."

"I'm not."

He pulled a bottle out of his hip pocket and took a drink.

"I just don't want anybody to see you . . . drinking," she said with a look of displeasure.

"I'm as good a man as any man. I'm as good a man as my son-in-law."

"You're better. And if others had to do what you do, they, too, would want to forget sometimes."

"Just feel good," he said, starting to walk around the room. "I'm not getting drunk, I'm just feeling good. After the summer I had, I've earned two or three drinks. What pleasures do I allow myself? What do I do all of the time? I keep my eye on the ball, my business. There isn't a funeral director more honest and conscientious than Philip Whelan in the whole city of Chicago . . . in the whole damned country."

"Yes, Philip. But please, please, for my sake, don't go on drinking."

He went to the bathroom. Ignoring her as she called in to him not to drink, he closed the door and took a big swig of whisky. He remained in the bathroom a few minutes and then pushed the lever to make his wife think he'd had to go in. He stood indecisive, with his shoulders swaying slightly. He came out of the bathroom smirking.

"Philip, let me order you a cup of black coffee."

Not answering, he let his chin sag against his chest. He felt inexpressibly sorry for himself. At fifty-three how much had he lived? How much had he gotten out of life? The best years of his life gone, gone in work, work and the faithfulness and responsibility that a good husband and a good father ought to show. And now, what had he to look forward to? And who knew what it had all cost him? Who knew?

He turned and pointed to the telephone. "See that phone? It's not going to ring. I'm not going to have to answer it and hear that Mr. Connelly, or Mrs. Carr, or Johnny O-Damned

Fool or somebody else is calling that somebody is dead and that I'm to come with the box and get them. It's not going to bring me another case."

She looked at him with fear but said nothing. He went to the bathroom again and returned with a glass partly filled with water. He poured in some whisky and slapped the bottle down on the dresser. He sat, holding the glass in his hand.

"Now, don't worry. I'm not going to get drunk."

Coming home, he had been feeling so good, so high. Now he was so low. It was as if there were a pressure within him which was slowly mounting and mounting and would burst out in words he wanted to utter but was afraid to.

"You act as though you don't care for me. You act as if I made no sacrifices, did nothing. Here I am with you in a strange city, and you sit drinking. I know how hard it is. I know that you sometimes need to forget. And have I ever thrown it up to you?"

She sobbed. He looked at her pathetically. He stared at his glass. He gulped down the remainder of its contents and frowned.

Bernard and Elizabeth came in. Bernard immediately sensed that something was up. Mrs. Whelan had been crying. Now she was sitting quietly on the bed. Elizabeth sat in the chair, saying nothing. Bernard was afraid there was going to be an unpleasant bust-up and that Whelan would get nasty. Whelan's hatred of him might come out. He didn't know what to do.

"Come on, Bernard, you aren't a plaster saint. Have a drink with your father-in-law," Whelan said.

Bernard knew he was younger than Whelan and in better physical condition. He had no real need for being afraid. Yet he was.

"Here, I'll get another glass for you," Whelan said, staggering to the dresser.

Elizabeth signaled, nodding for him to take the drink.

"Thank you," Bernard said.

Mr. Whelan raised his glass.

"Drink," he said.

Bernard lifted his glass, smiled with constraint, and took a drink as his father-in-law did.

"Do you like it? Is it good?" Mr. Whelan asked.

"Yes. Yes, it is."

"It cost seven dollars,"

They waited for what Mr. Whelan would say or do next.

"Every so often I take a few of these. . . . Do you know why?" Mr. Whelan began.

"There's nothing wrong in it," Bernard said.

"To relax," Mr. Whelan continued. "To relax. All year I manage other people's grief. I have no time for troubles of my own, no right to them. I'm a public servant, servicing the grief-stricken."

He laughed bitterly and finished his drink. Bernard took another small sip.

Mr. Whelan fixed himself another drink. Elizabeth and Mrs. Whelan looked at each other, troubled, and Bernard and Elizabeth exchanged glances. Bernard was as triumphant as he was fearful. For now he saw Mr. Whelan, really saw him, and for the first time. Underneath his formal front he was an unhappy, pathetic man.

"Have another," Mr. Whelan asked, holding the bottle of whisky in his hand.

"I still have this," Bernard said politely as he held up his glass.

"What are you doing? Holding back to make an impression on me?"

"No, I just don't drink much."

"You know, I can tell if anybody is trying to impress me. I've seen too much not to be able to read character."

He stared directly at Bernard. Bernard knew he mustn't flinch. He faced his father-in-law with determination. Elizabeth and Mrs. Whelan looked on, tense and alarmed.

"Oh, Father . . ." Elizabeth said.

He dismissed her remark with a wave of his left hand.

"Go ahead, drink," Mr. Whelan commanded.

"I am, I'm drinking," Bernard said tensely.

"Are you afraid to drink me, glass for glass?" asked Mr. Whelan.

"I don't want to," Bernard answered.

Their eyes continued to meet. Then Mr. Whelan smiled meaninglessly. He drank. Bernard took a sip.

"We don't really understand each other, Bernard," Mr. Whelan said. "We're not the same type. But I'll hold nothing against you if you take care of her."

He pointed to Elizabeth.

"I try to," Bernard said.

"That's all, that's all. That's enough understanding for the two of us."

"I—"

"Just a minute," Mr. Whelan said, interrupting Bernard. "Do you place value on your word?"

"Yes."

"Raise your glass and give me your word of honor you'll take care of my daughter and be a decent husband."

They raised their glasses and drank, but Bernard was boiling within.

"Is that your word of honor?"

"Yes. It is."

"Will you shake hands on it?"

They both stood up and met in the center of the room. They shook hands. Mr. Whelan was teetering slightly. His hand was large and perspiring, and as he held onto Bernard's, he continued to teeter. Then he relaxed and, turning, dropped back onto his chair. Bernard sat down, limp. Mr. Whelan let his head hang forward.

"Nothing, nothing," Mr. Whelan mumbled. "Nothing to go on for, nothing. Doing my duty."

"Father, let me order you some black coffee," Elizabeth said.

"I don't want black coffee . . . I want a grandson."

His head fell.

"Nineteen thirty-two. In nineteen-fifty I want to train my

grandson. You hear me. Philip Whelan . . . Carr. Nineteen-fifty, nineteen thirty-two. Fifty-three. He looked up, rolling his bleary blood-shot eyes. "How old will I be in nineteen-fifty? How old? Eighteen years. Eighteen plus fifty-three is, eighteen plus . . ."

"Seventy-one," Bernard said.

"I'll be old, an old man. Fifty years service, fifty years distinguished service."

He got up and swayed from side to side. His wife leaned forward, taut. Elizabeth stood up. Bernard went near him. He swayed again and dropped back into the chair. He fell onto the floor, and passed out. Elizabeth caught herself as she was going to scream. Mrs. Whelan sobbed. Bernard was momentarily paralyzed with indecision.

"Oh God. My God, why must this happen to me?" Mrs. Whelan wailed.

"Mother, Daddy is just drunk, and he deserves a little, a little relaxation."

Bernard looked down at Mr. Whelan sprawled out on the floor in an ungainly fashion. He bent down and tried to lift him. Mr. Whelan was limp. He put Whelan's arm around his shoulder and slowly got him to his feet. He half dragged him to the bed and let him fall. He took off Whelan's tie, opened his shirt, removed his shoes, and then lifted the feet up onto the bed. Elizabeth put a pillow under her father's head. Mr. Whelan groaned. Bernard thought of his father-in-law handling corpses. Mr. Whelan was like someone dead.

"Elizabeth, get a cold cloth and wipe his face. It might bring him to, and then we'll get him coffee," Bernard said.

Elizabeth got a cloth and, sitting down beside her father, she spoke softly to him and with caressing gestures wiped his face. He mumbled, groaned, and kept stirring.

"Bernard, you are a dear, understanding boy," Mrs. Whelan said.

Bernard was suddenly sure that in a crisis he could be stronger than his father-in-law. After this scene he need have no worries

or fears in relation to him. He looked over at the bed. His sense
of pity was stirred. Elizabeth, pregnant, sitting there wiping
her father's face, talking to him gently, her voice so sweet, her
words endearing, talking to him as though he were a child.

Mrs. Whelan wiped her eyes and spoke calmly:

"You young people just go now. I'll manage Philip."

"Can't we do anything?" Bernard asked.

"Please, let me here alone with him. I've taken care of him
before like this."

As they left, saying good-by, she had started to take off his
shirt.

VII

Philip Whelan and his wife sat together in the club car. He
looked rested. Mrs. Whelan turned to look at him with affectionate eyes.

"It'll be good to get back home. After being away a few
days, there is no place like home," she said.

He nodded. He had been glad to leave New York. After a
meal on the train and a night's sleep, he had awakened this
morning feeling as fresh as a daisy. But he'd had the worst hangover in his life. Ruth hadn't reproached him, but he wasn't sure
as to what she might be thinking. He hoped that the minute he
got back into the harness, he would get a case. When he had a
case, he gave all his attention to it, attended to everything himself. It kept him busy, though many of the things were so familiar he could do them in his sleep. He always knew exactly what
to do, what kind of funeral to sell. Even down to having smelling salts ready on his desk when needed, he was Johnny-on-the-
spot in his work. He wanted to get back in harness, where he
belonged.

"When we get off at Englewood, I'll have Smith take you
home and then I'll go right out to the place."

"But you'll be home for supper? I was just thinking . . .
when I get home I'll go shopping, and then I'm going to cook
supper myself."

"We could eat out."

They lapsed into silence.

Opposite him several passengers began to look out the windows. Mr. Whelan listened to catch what was going on.

"We ought to see the golden dome of Notre Dame," a young lad about twenty-four said.

Then Mr. Whelan began to watch, and he found himself becoming eager. He, too, wanted to see the golden dome of Notre Dame.

"We're almost in South Bend now," exclaimed an elderly man.

"Goodness, what is it they're looking for? I don't understand," Mrs. Whelan asked.

"They're watching out to see the golden dome of Notre Dame," he said.

"The University?" she asked.

"Yes. There is a golden dome on one of the campus buildings."

"That must be nice," she said.

She leaned forward, also eager to see. The train moved on toward South Bend. Thirteen passengers strained at the window. The train pulled into the South Bend station, stopped, started, moved on, and gathered speed, but no one of the thirteen passengers caught a glimpse of the golden dome.

"It would have been nice to have seen it," Mr. Whelan said.

Chapter Twenty-two

I

Eᴌɪᴢᴀʙᴇᴛʜ was sitting on the couch in their first-floor furnished apartment on West Ninth Street. They had two large rooms, a smaller room where they would keep the baby, a bathroom, and a small alcove which had been made into a kitchen.

"I never believed we'd be paying sixty dollars a month rent. But since we didn't have to sign a year's lease, we don't have to worry."

"Oh, Bernard, we aren't going to be poor, really poor again."

"I hope not."

He was sitting prettier than perhaps any writer his age in America. They actually had a little over a thousand dollars in the bank, and he was free now to say what he pleased, and to write. The depression had become less real and imminent in their lives.

"Some day, of course, I want to pick out our own furniture and have a place to fix up just the way we want to. But this is all right, isn't it, Bernard?"

"Yes, it is," he commented, looking around at their new home and thinking that, so long as he worked, his physical surroundings didn't matter.

The furniture was old but sturdy. There was a studio couch in a corner. Across from it was a table at which he could write, and there was a row of bookshelves along one wall. In the corner was a folding table they used for their meals. It had delicate legs. There were also some straight-backed chairs, two upholstered chairs, and several lamps. It was really comfortable here, much better than he'd ever expected to have.

"I'm going to get busy now and draft my Loewenthal project," he said.

"Bernard, I was more worried than you know . . . thinking, thinking that because of me it was so hard on you. . . . Oh, but that doesn't matter, and now I'm glad we're having our baby."

"So am I," Bernard said rather casually. He was touched by the quality of joy in her voice and by the happiness that shone on her face.

She was happier than he. But, then, he took pride in thinking that his destiny precluded happiness for himself. And he knew he had been the instrument of her happiness. Eventually, might his writing not serve as the instrument of the happiness of others, even of those who were yet unborn? Had his own mother ever been like this when she was pregnant? He was beginning to understand more clearly now that there was something of his mother's nature, something of her temperament, in himself. For they were both living for things not of this time and place, not of this world.

"Bernard, you'll wheel the baby carriage, won't you? Lots of men do. You will, won't you?"

He nodded.

"And won't it be wonderful, watching him grow, teaching him to walk . . . and, Bernard, when he is old enough to go to school, we still won't be too old."

"We'll try to bring him up better than we were."

"I don't know a thing, and I'll be so afraid I won't be able to do what's right. But, Bernard, we won't let it be just a burden. It's going to be fun, isn't it?"

"I hope so."

He nodded again, and then, rising, said:

"Well, I'll get to work now."

He went over to his new work table.

Elizabeth decided she had become used to the idea of having a baby, and she was very, very glad. At times, she didn't feel too strong, and she had trouble sleeping because of her bladder and because she couldn't sleep on her side and would wake up, stiff. But she was glad in spite of everything. Because this was what a woman was for, and he knew that she was now a woman.

She hummed softly. Until she'd started having a baby, she had never thought so much, or enjoyed thinking about herself and how she felt. Now she would just be lost to the world, and she'd sit this way, as if she were in a world all by herself and were so snug and cozy in it that there was nothing you could be afraid of. And she felt as good as she sometimes felt after It, when something happened to her, and she would lie beside Bernard, oh, feeling warm, feeling just tired, and moist and warm, when you weren't sleeping and you weren't not sleeping.

"Oh, I almost forgot. Today's my day to see Dr. Zimmerman," Elizabeth suddenly exclaimed.

"You'll have to hurry. Why don't you take a taxi, so you'll be more comfortable and not be jounced around?" Bernard said, turning from his work table.

"The subway is faster for me . . . but it is a long trip alone."

"Honey, I just have to keep working."

Her face dropped.

"You haven't met Dr. Zimmerman yet, Bernard."

"I will, but I have to stick at this."

She said nothing and slowly got ready to leave. When she kissed him good-by, he saw the disappointment in her eyes. He wanted to change his mind and go with her, but he couldn't. He must work every day now and hold to a sense of obligation about his writing. If he had a job, he couldn't get off to go to the doctor with her, could he? He had to boss himself. All that was at stake for him would be decided in these small decisions, these small renunciations, these moments when nothing seemed to be at stake.

She left. He sat at his desk, striving to work out the statement about his project.

He was sorry that he hadn't gone to the doctor with her. But weren't his reasons unselfish? He thought of her, alone, riding on a jolting subway train. She might be afraid.

He began to pace the room, trying to think clearly.

II

They were having dinner with Florence and Abe, their first dinner guests in their new home. Elizabeth had prepared creamed chicken and baked potatoes au gratin. Florence and Abe liked the food and appreciated the way she had arranged the table. Eating by candlelight put them in the right mood.

"I'm so happy for you kids," Florence said. "Now you can live like human beings. I'm so glad that some people can; so few are able to these days."

Florence wanted to mean what she said. But against her will, she was beginning to see Bernard and Elizabeth in a different light. They had everything that she and Abe had, but they didn't have to go out every day and earn it for themselves. Of course, Bernard wrote, but he didn't have to work eight hours every day. And he had a bourgeois publisher who'd given him an advance. His new book was merely a love story, and he'd written it this year, in 1932. Bernard was using his talents only for himself—not for the workers.

Of course, it was a joy to see a girl as sweet as Elizabeth just beaming with happiness. The way Elizabeth fussed over her guests and went to pains to make everything just so was touching and charming. But you couldn't do that if you worked all day in an office and then had to rush home on a crowded subway and cook. During the summer she'd often thought of Elizabeth and Bernard as brave and unselfish, daring to have a baby when they were so poor. But hadn't Elizabeth, hadn't both of them known that they could fall back on her parents? She no longer could admire them as much as she had, nor feel as close to Elizabeth as before. She had been naive and sentimental, even imagining they could become almost like sisters. They came from different worlds, and Elizabeth could never really escape from hers. Elizabeth was like that girl Mildred Feldman, except that

she wasn't Jewish. Both of them knew they could play with
poverty, because they had fathers who would always take care
of them. Florence thought of her own poor father, an immigrant running a little candy store. She didn't want to be envious
and consoled herself with the conviction that what she was
thinking was true.

Bernard, Elizabeth, and Florence talked about unimportant
matters. Abe was silent. Then he remarked that a De Leonite
friend of his had asked him to sign a petition to get the De
Leonite's candidate on the ballot in the presidential election.

"I accused him of being an autograph hunter," Abe said,
pleased with his own wit.

They laughed. Bernard thought it was funny. Then he asked:
"Don't you want them on the ballot?"

"Why should they be on the ballot? They'll only take votes
away from the Party," Florence said testily.

"Haven't they a right to compete with the Party? And didn't
Lenin say De Leon was the only Marxist who had made a contribution to Marxism?"

Abe said the De Leonites were screwball sectarians.

"I heard a story today about a girl who was expelled from the
Party on charges of white chauvinism," Bernard said. "She
went to a dance with the chap she loves and intends to marry.
They wanted to dance together. They were in love. She was
ordered to dance with Negroes. She isn't prejudiced, but she
wanted to dance with this chap, and she didn't like being told
whom to dance with. Now she's going to be denounced in *The
Fist* as a white chauvinist, and her picture will be printed along
with the denunciation."

Florence was shocked, but she didn't want to admit it to
Bernard.

"Who told you the story?" Florence asked. "Maybe it isn't
true."

"Florence, we talked about things like that ourselves," Elizabeth said.

"A Party member told me . . . Sam Leventhal."

"Of course, it isn't right. But have we the right to criticize if we don't do something ourselves? And when the Party grows, things like that won't happen. You don't find anything like that happening in the Soviet Union."

"I don't think they should have done that to the girl," Elizabeth said.

"Of course, they shouldn't. But look at the big things, the Party's fight against war and unemployment and starvation."

Florence's word sounded hollow. She was relieved when Elizabeth shifted the conversation to cooking. She and Elizabeth did most of the talking during the rest of the meal.

When they finished eating, Elizabeth and Florence did the dishes, while Bernard and Abe sat in the living room, saying little to each other because they had nothing to say. The girls joined them. The evening fell flat. Florence and Abe seemed to become a unit of silence. Believing it was very late, Bernard looked at the clock and was surprised to see that it was only twenty minutes to nine. He wished they'd go.

"I wonder how long life can go on like this," Florence said moodily and unexpectedly.

"Like what?" Elizabeth asked.

"Unstable, that's the best word I can think of to define it. You can't plan, you can't look forward to the future. You have to hang on by the skin of your teeth. You feel wrong even having a job when you know so many are miserable and out of work."

Florence was thinking how she had looked forward to something better and different ever since she had been a little girl. And in high school and college this expectation about the future had grown even stronger in her. She had thought she would live a life of culture and travel and love. It wasn't turning out that way. Now, with the depression, she was blocked. All that she had was Abe, and their love. Because of their love they would cling together in this dangerous world. Oh, she wanted a baby, but they didn't dare have one in this unstable world.

Elizabeth and Bernard talked about the baby, and his work.

Abe and Florence started yawning and left politely at nine-thirty.

"Abe and Florence were quiet tonight. They left early. Did we say something? Do you think she didn't like the way you spoke about the Party?"

"She's becoming *kosher*."

"We want more out of life than they, don't we, Bernard? And I think we're going to get it, too."

"Yes."

Elizabeth got out her knitting and sat on the couch, with her legs close together before her.

"Bernard, have you finished writing out your Loewenthal application?"

"I'm still struggling with it," he answered, picking up a copy of Thucydides's *The Peloponnesian War*. "Case, Brady, Barber, Bill Barclay, Sherman Scott, and Professor Timkins have all agreed to be references for me."

"I know you'll get it, unless you're cheated out of it by literary politics. You certainly deserve it."

"Merit doesn't count a hell of a lot in the literary world," he said cynically, as he dropped onto the couch with his book.

He still wanted to believe that one could trust in merit. But he had so much evidence to refute this. Maybe he had been naive holding to his eager ideals of 1927, to feelings and thoughts and dreams of his college years. He let these thoughts fade from his mind and began reading.

Thucydides seemed like a contemporary. His emotions became involved with Athens. Knowing what the outcome of the war had been, he kept forgetting what he knew, and as he read on he began hoping for an Athenian victory. Then suddenly he put the book down and looked abstractedly up at the ceiling. This war had happened hundreds and hundreds of years ago. All those who had figured in it had been dead for centuries. And here he was, in New York City in the year 1932, reading of the Peloponnesian War, admiring Thucydides and learning from his work. What did this immortality, this ability to interest and move and teach men now mean to Thucydides? He knew that if he didn't hold to his faith in merit, he'd betray himself. He went on reading.

The Greeks had often appealed to immortality, to the good memory of men who would come after them. How little this appeal was to be found in contemporary American Politics. And wasn't the appeal to immortality really the appeal to truth? But could that appeal be heard clearly before you were dead and the unpleasantness of the truths you had told stopped rousing passions and hatred? It was sometimes so cold, so chilling, trying to live for this ideal. But was it better to live for what Florence and Abe lived for, whatever that might be?

As he read on, he remembered having read in Lucretius that men who want power and will do anything for it were trying to cheat death. Many of those Greeks and Spartans had so tried to cheat death. Long ago, in a world as broken up as this American world of 1932, Lucretius had observed men trying to cheat death. Wasn't this the answer to his question about merit? If he had merit, he needn't try to cheat death. If he didn't have it, what good would it do him to cheat? Some day he would be with those Athenians and Spartans, with Thucydides, Lucretius, and Patrick J. Carr.

Elizabeth looked at him tenderly. She hoped that Abe and Florence and others were as happy as she and Bernard.

III

Tonight, Sam Leventhal was free to wander, to dream, to think about poetry. He had no meetings to attend, no Party assignments to carry out. And he loved New York most on September nights like this. There was the quality of both summer and early fall in the air. On this kind of night, there was a poetic dialectics of the seasons. People were out strolling and walking and, perhaps, dreaming. They were drifting around instead of rushing nervously to work, as they did in the daytime. On the East Side, tired, hard-working men sat in front of the tenements. They thought and dreamed and talked about the little things of the day. Fourteenth Street was crowded. And he considered himself to be the comrade of all of these people, even though they didn't as yet know it. He was on their side in the mass struggle and wanted to be their poet. He wanted to write poems which would turn their unconscious dreams of Socialism into blazing, conscious fires.

> *Comrade Masses*
> *Comrade Humanity*
> *Sharing your sorrow and dreams. . . .*

Some day he would get the poem right, his projected prole-tarian song of New York. To begin with the word Comrade and to assert that he was the comrade of the masses and of humanity would be bold, practically speaking. He noticed a patient little old man who stood by the curb near Irving Place, meekly trying to sell *The Fist*. This man was a comrade. Sam thought of *The Internationale*.

> *Arise, ye wretched of the earth. . . .*

Here was one of the wretched of the earth who had begun to rise. An old man he had never seen before who was a comrade and a pioneer of the new world to come.

He moved on to a noisy political discussion in front of the Horn and Hardart Automat. A burly workingman in a khaki shirt waved his arms about and loudly proclaimed that in the Soviet Union the Communists had a Five Year Plan for the hap-piness of the workers. But over here, the bosses and the capital-ists could only plan their own greed, for war and misery, for the starvation of the workers. Several of the listeners interrupted, all speaking at once. A man who said he was a Socialist but not a Communist said that the workers didn't enjoy freedom in Russia. The burly worker scornfully shouted that the bosses wept crocodile tears because the workers in Russia didn't live in the slavery that was freedom for the bosses.

Five or six men shouted at the Socialist at once. Comrade Leather Jacket, with a book under his arm, pushed into the center of the group and boldly announced that whenever he heard anyone cry for freedom he knew that he was in the presence of an agent of the bourgeoisie. He called the Socialist "Noske." The Socialist said that he was a worker and belonged to a union.

"Noske called himself a Socialist and butchered the German workers." Then, with withering scorn, he added: "And you call yourself a Socialist."

Sam wished the Socialists would only see that the position of the Party was correct, even though it had its flaws. But thinking of the old man selling *The Fist*, of the crowds of poor working people on the East Side, and of his own poetic ambitions, he reluctantly admitted to himself that the Socialists were betrayers. But there was Leather Jacket saying what he was thinking, and Leather Jacket was crazy. He smiled.

—Leather Jacket is our lunatic.

Leather Jacket spat in the face of the Socialist.

"Shame! Shame!" someone cried out in disgust.

Sam felt ashamed. He wished Leather Jacket hadn't done this, hadn't given the Socialists ammunition like this to use against the Party.

Leather Jacket shouted at his critics that Lenin had spat upon social patriotic fakers. He opened his book and read a passage from Lenin.

"See, Lenin is my justification," he proudly yelled.

A spectator asked to see the book. Leather Jacket handed it to him. The spectator looked at the title page of the book and handed it back.

"A Stalinist version of Lenin," the spectator said with a sneer.

About twelve men talked and shouted at once, and Sam walked away with uneasy feelings.

He had doubts, not in the Party, nor in its program or world outlook, but in some of his comrades. And he wasn't sure he always could give to the Party all it demanded. The tasks awaiting a good Bolshevik were endless. Party work could eat up your days and nights. The fraction meeting the other night had lasted until two in the morning. And then the next day he'd had to work on *The Fist*, get out publicity on the Scottsboro case, and at night do house-to-house canvassing. And at odd moments he'd kept thinking he wanted to write poems. Tonight, when he was free, he couldn't write. He felt emotionally drained. Sometimes he worried because comrades he least respected, like Jake Jackson, were able to stand this grueling work the best. And then, the suspicion among some of the comrades, the way they listened to your conversation and read your writing in order to discover deviations. Many of them looked on him askance because he was a poet, an intellectual. Lenin, they told him, had said the intellectual couldn't be trusted. Was this correct or was it cynicism? Couldn't he be trusted? Couldn't Jake be? He knew how dangerous it was to doubt. And he knew that in this period politics was more important than poetry. All poetry was politics as well as poetry. He didn't want to doubt.

He remembered a remark Jake had made the other day at *The Fist* offices.

—We're in politics. But ours is a new kind of politics, as serious and as broad as life.

Because Communism was so new, it was hard, hard on the individual. He had to make himself harder. If he didn't, he would betray the masses, the masses he wanted to address in poems of comradeship. If he gave way to doubts, what life would he have? In the future, there could be neither life nor victory outside the Movement. You would choke, stifle, die in spiritual isolation if you became a renegade. He had to measure up to the demands of the Party. He would try to. Only this urge to write, these moody feelings he was having tonight seemed so out of place when he was with his comrades.

He stopped on the corner of University Place and Fourteenth Street and watched the people. Were these people happy or sad? Looking at them you couldn't know. They looked so peaceable, so unharried. To stand and watch them pass, you wouldn't think they lived in a country ruled by Business Fascism in the midst of hunger and depression and on the eve of War? And, yet, was this not so?

He tried to make concrete the prognostications of the Party, to imagine what would happen when Wall Street declared war on the Soviet Union and sent the Japanese marching into Siberia as the spearhead of American imperialism. He walked on, confused and shaken. There would be terror and Palmer Red Raids. Owning a copy of Lenin's works would mean jail. The offices of *The Fist* would be raided. And would the masses rise? Would the Party be ready?

These people walking by didn't seem to know that all this was possible. The Party hadn't reached them yet. And that was the big task. Considering these big problems and tasks, weren't his small worries picayune? Wasn't the cynicism of some comrades, the accidental injustices imposed on comrades, the mistakes made in designating the few good but mistaken Socialists as Social Fascists merely picayune?

Sam walked on and turned onto Fifth Avenue, at ease with himself. He had resolved his doubts. And perhaps it had been these doubts that had really interfered with his writing.

Now he was in another world. The faces of the people on Fifth Avenue seemed different from those on Fourteenth Street. Here you didn't see women marked by years of housework in tenements. You didn't see the tired, stupefied look on the faces of men who had worked all day in shops and at hard physical labor. You didn't see human beings made ugly by toil and worry and poverty. The women and girls in particular seemed so different from those on Fourteenth Street. The difference wasn't merely in their clothes, but in their figures and faces. He knew that his impressions weren't quite true. There were many beautiful daughters of the working class. But he stared strangely at several attractive girls. Then he remembered Mildred Feldman. Was this why he had been so moody today? The news of her death in Savannah, Georgia, had shocked and saddened him. She had been so wonderful. In a sense, her death had been heroic. He wanted to write a poem about her, but the lines just wouldn't come.

Coming to Ninth Street, and having fallen into a fit of

depression, Sam thought of Bernard and decided to drop in on him. Bernard was reading and Elizabeth was knitting. They greeted him cordially, and he felt good just seeing them. They looked happy, and he was delighted with their good fortune. Bernie now would be able to write without distraction.

He and Bernard talked about books and literature. Sam mentioned poets he liked, especially T. S. Eliot and Hart Crane. Bernard agreed with him about Eliot, and quoted some lines, and Sam, others. But Bernard said he found Crane obscure. Sam tried to explain Crane's obscurity by asserting that Crane had seen no way out, and that Crane was a symbol of the end of the gifted poet under capitalism.

"Did Capitalism make him commit suicide?"

"He was too sensitive, and he saw no way out. He's the exception that proves the rule. Sherman Scott wrote a fine article showing that Crane is a symbol of the defeat of the poet under capitalism."

"In the Soviet Union, the poets Mayakovsky and Essenin also committed suicide."

"Essenin did it because of love. And you talk with Jake. Jake can explain Mayakovsky's suicide to you."

"Nietzsche said that a suicide is an optimist—he wants to better his conditions."

Sam was silent with embarrassment. "I'm blue tonight . . . Bernie, did you hear about Mildred Feldman? She died."

Elizabeth and Bernard were visibly shocked.

"Maybe I'm right or wrong about Hart Crane, but Mildred's case is different. You know, she had chronic appendicitis. She would have pains and do nothing about it. She left a month ago, hitchhiking, and four days ago she was stricken in Savannah. She could have had the finest medical attention if she had only called on her family. She wouldn't give the right name."

"I don't understand it."

"She didn't want her family to help her. She hated them because of their wealth."

"But wasn't that foolish?" Elizabeth asked.

"Maybe it was. In a way, yes, it was. But there was something grand and poetic about it."

Bernard seemed lost in thought.

"She was a grand girl. She had a beautiful character. The news has put me in the dumps all day."

"She could have had her family notified," Bernard said, thinking of Elizabeth's relationship to her father and of how Mr. Whelan had come to accept him.

"Pride. She was too proud. She had made an agreement with her parents not to see Communists and Negroes, and not to be . . . well . . . unconventional until she graduated from college. She broke her word—"

"Did she have to tell them?" Elizabeth asked.

"She told them because she wanted to be honest."

"It wasn't necessary," Elizabeth commented.

"It's tragic, isn't it?"

"What else happened?"

"Her appendix burst. After she died, her real name and address were found. Sophie says her family is crushed. She was their only daughter."

None of them talked for a while.

"There's nothing to say," Bernard observed.

"It was a form of suicide, because she knew about her condition. Remember, Bernie, how she burst in at Sophie's party? Well, I walked her home to her room, and I remember her saying she didn't think she'd live long. I didn't give any credence to her remark."

"It's sad," Elizabeth said.

"Sometimes I wonder what's really happening in America," Bernard mused.

Sam waited for him to go on. He paused and puffed on his cigarette thoughtfully.

"Now, I broke away. In a sense, Mildred broke. Others have broken. You have."

"I grew up in the Movement. I was a Young Pioneer."

"Most of the boys you knew on the East Side are different from you—they are neither poets nor Communists."

"Yes, I guess that's true."

"There's Mel Morris. And a lot of others, too—all of us in our twenties, and we are in rebellion against all the values in American society. Are we harbingers of something, or are we exceptions, social sports and eccentrics?"

Sam became pious and said one must have no doubts and one should see that the Movement was the only home for all of them.

"I change my mind so often, I don't know what I think," Bernard said.

"Is that good for you as a writer, Bernard?" asked Sam.

"It seems to me one of the luxurious compensations in being a writer. You can change your mind. Writers can be politically wrong. Look at Dostoievsky."

"That was true in the past. It can't be any more. Bernie, if writers like you joined, the sectarians wouldn't be in a sound position on the cultural front."

"I guess I haven't the temperament. I couldn't stomach meetings. And I don't know that writers should join."

"If you only knew how I felt," Sam said with a peculiar eagerness in his voice.

"How do you feel?" Bernard asked.

Sam seemed embarrassed.

"You can't describe it. Everything has significance. I was walking on Fourteenth Street tonight. Every face, every word I heard meant something."

Bernard said that no matter what a writer's views, everything he observed had possible meaning. Sam described the discussion in front of the Automat, the old man selling *The Fist*, the crowds, and he quoted Jake's remarks about Communism being something new in politics. Bernard listened, speculating about Sam's courage and wondering if Sam feared death.

"And so, Bernie, when I walk as I did tonight, I know I'm not alone. I know that some day the human race will be my comrades," Sam said, his face glowing, his eyes bright.

"Basically, I'm with you, Sam . . . but as a writer I have to be alone. Writing can be cruel and lonely. It's just not subsumable to dogma."

"Bernie, we don't have dogma, we have a world outlook. Writers who don't come with us will be drowning men, swimming until they become exhausted. That's why Mildred is a symbol. She tried to go it alone. Look at how tragically she died."

"I'm not Mildred," Bernard said, not knowing why he made this remark. "And, Sam, the world I grew up in is dead with all its values. A historic embalmer just hasn't gotten around to shooting the fluid into it. It goes on sans blood, sans embalming fluid in its veins. The old is finished. It's going to blow up in war or be blown up in revolution. I know that. But until the detonation, I'm going to write. That's the way I feel."

"Sam is a nice boy, Bernard, but do you really think you need a boy like that to tell you about writing?" Elizabeth asked, after Sam left.

"No. I like Sam, but as a poet he's only a proletarian Eddie Guest."

"Bernard, let's talk about our plans."

"But there's not much to talk about. We just have to wait."

"Yes, there is. Now, should we just get a bassinet first?"

"I know nothing about those things."

"Mother and Father got us a batch of things. Mother gave me a list of other things to get."

"Do I have to know all this detail to be a father?"

"You'll have to know something—how to change a diaper without sticking a pin into the baby. Will you be able to do that?"

"Am I an idiot?"

She laughed.

"Bernard, when you talk, I know you're so smart. I can tell you're much smarter than boys like Samuel or Melvin Morris. But I'm not sure I'll trust you to put a diaper on our baby."

"Swell, I always was lazy."

"You're going to be a good father, I know you are."

He smiled. He wanted to be a decent father. He thought of his own father.

Elizabeth undressed, and he sat reading.

"Bernard, don't you want to listen and hear its little heart-beat?"

"Yes."

She lay down on the bed, naked, with her abdomen a swollen misshapen mound. He put his ear to her belly and listened. He thought he heard a faint beat. He was overcome with awe. He listened again.

"Do you hear it?"

"Yes."

"Isn't it wonderful?"

"Yes."

A feeling of joy flooded him. The little heart beating inside of her was a sign of life, of mystery. It was more awesome than death. It was life and mystery, and merely to think of it brought such a strange and unexpected feeling of joy and pride. And for the informed destiny within her, with its little beating heart, everything was new and inexperienced. He was glad to know that it was alive and that it would be his. He stroked and kissed her belly, looked at her misshapen body, stroked her belly again, bent down to try to hear the heartbeat again, looked at her with a shy smile on his face, and said:

"There are three of us now."

Chapter Twenty-three

I

WRITERS HAVE NO STAKE IN CAPITALISM

FIGHT AGAINST CAPITALISM UNDER THE LEADERSHIP OF THE COMMUNIST PARTY

THESE slogans, in large black letters, were on a wall near Bernard's seat in the large, crowded hall. Reading them, Bernard reflected that a writer should be for or against an idea, not because of his personal stake in it but because he thought it to be true or false, good or bad.

"Bernie, you don't know how glad I am you came," Sam Leventhal said to him.

"This meeting will go down in the cultural history of America," Mel said.

"The crowd is much larger than I expected," Bernard said, looking around at the pattern of heads in the large hall.

"And we've got names. We have the names of most of the important American intellectuals," Mel said.

Bernard was glad he'd come. Last week, when Sam had asked him to go, he hadn't given him a definite answer, but tonight Sam and Mel had stopped by, and he'd come on an impulse.

A nervous tension seemed to grip the audience. It was made up mainly of intellectuals and of Party people. All around him Bernard could see many contrasts, hear them in the variety of accents.

There were Mel and Sam and himself, each with a different

431

background. Sherman Scott was one of the speakers, and he
had been to Yale and had lived in Europe. Another speaker
was Louis Waller, the writer whose books were so mystical and
obscurantist. There were students from New York colleges,
and kids just out of the Young Pioneers of the C.P. He saw
Negroes here and there. A beautiful mulatto girl sat seven
rows ahead of them, and Mel couldn't keep his eyes off her.
Two rows behind, there were three Chinese. Realistic and modernistic painters, native-born grass-roots American intellectuals, advertising writers, poets from Princeton and from
Greenwich Village, long-haired Bohemians, Fourteenth-Street
characters, girls like Sophie, well-groomed girls and women,
the wives, friends, and sweethearts of editors and writers, talented and attractive poetesses, literary critics with college de-
grees, sons of East-Side immigrants and sweat-shop workers
who wanted to be poets or revolutionary leaders, stolid-looking
Party rank-and-filers with Slavic or Semitic features, several
Irishmen with broad brogues, teachers of philosophy, promising and talented college graduates who had forsaken the
chances of success for the revolutionary movement, the important leaders of the Party, whose names were spoken with
awe by the Comrades and who were supposed to study and
plot and plan and organize and direct the course to a Soviet
America from the legendary Ninth Floor, Comrade Leather
Jacket and others from the lunatic fringe, men and women who
had gone to jail for their Communist beliefs and affiliations,
and boys and girls who wanted to go to jail, girls who had
been educated at Vassar and girls who had come out of the
shops of garment and fur trades, Mark Singer, the beloved
American Gorky, Johnson the Negro vice-presidential candidate, Eldridge, the heralded Lenin from Iowa, men who had
led strikes, even big ones, and ex-wobblies, ex-Socialists, Trotskyites, and other Communist dissidents who sat amid hostile
glances and were threatened with violence—the old and the
new radical generation were present.

The big shots gathered on the platform and talked in small

groups. Individuals in the crowd moved about and talked. Stern and tough-looking ushers, with red bands on their sleeves, ranged themselves all around, ringing the audience as the police might have surrounded a Union Square demonstration. Red banners were draped about the balconies. Slogans were busy on the walls. A large picture of Lenin, with intent, piercing eyes, was hung over the center of the stage, and it was flanked by smaller pictures of Eldridge and Johnson, the two election candidates. Under these was the slogan:

VOTE COMMUNIST
FOR A SOVIET AMERICA

People continued to stream into the hall.

"There's over a thousand here," Mel said like a schoolboy.

II

Eldridge stood before the rostrum and said:

"Friends and comrades, only the Communist Party, U.S.A., could mobilize as distinguished a group of writers, intellectuals, and professionals as we have with us in this hall tonight. Friends and Comrades, no other political party in the American capitalist jungle could bring together this band of outstanding and honest writers, intellectuals, and professionals. We are proud of our accomplishment. Our party feels honored in the support of you writers, you intellectuals, you professionals."

There was loud applause.

"And you should feel honored to support our party, the only party that fights the hunger and horror of capitalism and points the way to a Soviet America. We are the only party that fights for your interest, for the creation of a great proletarian culture which will free your pens and your minds from a capitalist culture of despair and exploitation."

There was more applause.

Eldridge was an undistinguished man of medium height, with a round, benign face and a small mustache. He wore baggy clothes. He was both characterless and without pretensions, and he spoke in a nasal, twangy voice, his words rolling out in monotonous succession. But he received enthusiastic applause. He said that the meeting was a historic one because it publicly emphasized the desertion of the best of the intellectuals from the camp of capitalism. But what were the galaxy of thinking and literary people deserting? A system that bred misery, mass hunger and war; a system that was moribund and could only die. This election was a historic one, for it revealed the expansion of the Communist Party as the mass party which would win the future for the broad masses of town and country. And what parties were opposed to the Communist Party? Three capitalist parties. The Republican and Democratic Parties were the parties of Wall Street. The difference between Hoover and Roosevelt was less than that between Tweedledee and Tweedlededum. And the third capitalist party calls itself Socialist.

"I will give passing attention to the Socialist Party, so-called . . . not that they deserve it," he declared with a hateful sneer in his voice.

The audience clapped.

"The leader of the Socialist Party, so-called, is Norman Thomas."

The audience booed.

"Under a flag which he has stolen from us, Norman Thomas preaches the enslavement of the workers. This gentleman thinks that slavery is Socialism. He is a *Socialist*. Listen to what this Socialist gentleman has written about the Soviet Union. I quote: 'The Russian government rules by tyranny and terror, with secret police, espionage, and arbitrary exclusions.'"

Hisses came from various parts of the hall. Eldridge rapped his right index fingers emphatically on the rostrum.

"That is what you read in the yellow press. And if that is the language of Socialism, then Morgan and Mellon, Hoover and Mussolini and the godlike Emperor of Japan are Socialists. And that is what the Socialist candidate for President has to say in America, capitalist America, in 1932. In Detroit, Michigan, workers wanting jobs to earn a pittance so they may put crumbs of bread into the hungry mouths of their families have hoses spraying ice-cold water on their hungry bodies. In Washington, the Bonus Marchers are shot. In Kentucky, striking miners are the victims of Cossack terror, and Louis Waller, whom you will hear shortly from this platform, was clubbed when he went down there as a public-spirited citizen to investigate the conditions of terror under which the miners live. In the rich farmlands of the Middle West, where I was born, the farmers are being evicted, are being driven onto the road to shift for themselves, dispossessed by the greed of the banks. In the South of the United States, Negroes are lynched and the legitimate aspirations of the Negro nation for sovereignty go unheeded. The Scottsboro boys are framed. Millions, thirteen millions, according to conservative estimates, are unemployed. And what does capitalism do as a way out of this crisis? It plots a war against the Soviet Union. The Socialist candidate, in a fascist land, has the unmitigated gall to say that, and I quote: 'The Russian government rules by tyranny and terror.' "

Eldridge stood with his hands palm downward on the rostrum.

"Is this ignorance on the part of the Socialist candidate?

"No, it is not ignorance. If it only were ignorance, it could be corrected by the truth. It is shameless and unmitigated slander and vileness. It is outright imperialist propaganda conducted by the Socialist Party to justify an imperialist war against the Soviet Union."

Cheers.

"We have in this hall tonight the men and women who represent the literary and the intellectual conscience of America."

Wild cheers.

"You honest writers, you honest intellectuals have joined us in the struggle because you are not fooled and deceived by this lying propaganda put out by the lackeys of capitalism. You know what the issue is. Peace or War? Plenty or hunger?

"Capitalism, groaning under the weight of its contradictions, which we long ago predicted, can only promise the broad working masses of town and country a future of hunger at home and war abroad as the only way out for the fascist madmen. That is why they look with eyes of greed and hatred and envy and fear at the Union of Socialist Soviet Republics, the land where Socialism is being built."

The audience broke into violent cheering. When it calmed down, Eldridge continued in his flat, twangy voice:

"There are two worlds. These two worlds are represented in this campaign. The hateful world of capitalism is represented by the three capitalist parties. The world of the workers and of the future is represented by our Communist Party."

The applause thundered.

"And today, everywhere on the face of this earth, our Communist Parties live and grow. In Germany, our comrades have stopped Hitler and his Nazis. In Italy, the bankrupt regime of the Fascist Mussolini totters so that not even his Wall Street can prop it up much longer. Everywhere the world crisis is deepening. On May first of this year, the Communist International prognosticated: ' . . . the revolutionary wave is rising, and the class struggle is sharpening.' That perspective has been confirmed by the logic of events. The success of our campaign further confirms this perspective. And that is why you are here on our side tonight. You are men of culture. True culture needs health. We are the force of health in this campaign . . . in this country . . . in this world. As such, and in the name of the revolutionary workers, we salute you writers, intellectuals, and professionals who have come to our side in the great struggle."

The outburst of deafening applause knocked all thoughts out of Bernard's head. Mel and Sam beside him were yelling and clapping. He saw enraptured faces. He felt as alone here as he had at the wake back in Chicago or at Mass in St. Patrick's Cathedral. While Eldridge was speaking, he had been pulled in opposite directions. He wanted to feel solidarity here, as he had felt it in August 1927 in Union Square and at times last May Day in the parade. He wanted to think of himself as one with all these intellectuals in struggling for truth and justice. At moments his own emotions had welled up, and he had been deeply moved. But this emotion had been washed away without warning by a thought that had come to him. He had told himself that if you wanted to deal with these people you had better go out and become somebody and gain a reputation on your own, so you could meet them as equals. You would fare badly if you put yourself into their power.

Eldridge was the first Party leader he had seen in action, except at the May Day parade. He was repelled, almost against his will. While Eldridge had been speaking he had feared that his own way of seeing life might be crumbling in his mind. But the attack on the Socialists and the sneering quality in Eldridge's voice as he had made this attack had not seemed fair. He was afraid of intolerance, because he had seen so much of it on a personal level back in Chicago. And Eldridge seemed intolerant. He himself had never seen Russia and he hadn't really studied the available facts about it. The Russians seemed right, and he wanted them to succeed. They were remaking human nature. But were there two worlds, and was there freedom there, and were all the stories against Russia fake, and wasn't there surplus value in Russian economy, and didn't Eldridge take orders from the Russians, and what did the Russians know of America, and how could they give advice on how to act politically in America? Eldridge and other Party people saw more of America than he, yet the Chicago he knew and the New York he was coming to know were not quite like the America reflected in Eldridge's speech. He wanted to drown these questions, but they kept rising above the recurring rivers of his feeling like beings who refuse to go under and down in a torrential current.

Mel turned to him with a look that as much as asked him how could he fail to agree now.

"I have a pain," Bernard said flippantly.

"What's the matter?"

"Hoover just gave me castor oil," he said.

Mel was utterly bewildered. But Eldridge was going on with his speech, and Mel listened. Bernard didn't know why he had made this joke, and wished he hadn't, because he didn't want to offend Mel and he didn't want Mel to think he was really against the Movement. But he had read about Italian fascism, and it seemed different from conditions here. And, yet, wasn't there terror and police brutality here, too?

Was he afraid, and was he merely rationalizing? Eldridge wasn't convincing him.

And the meeting was going on. Paul Drummond was delivering a panegyric on the Soviet Union. Bernard remembered how Drummond had hinted at different attitudes at Sophie's party last spring. He knew that the Party had worked on Drummond to change his mind. Why was Drummond, a celebrated playwright, doing this?

III

Sherman Scott was applauded politely. He cleared his throat, took a sip of water, and began by saying that he was a petit-bourgeois intellectual, but that next month, at the polls, he would vote against his own class. This brought loud applause. As he launched into a complaining characterization of American culture, Bernard gathered the impression that Scott was really playing to the audience and to the Party leaders on the platform, and he wondered if this were necessary. Scott stressed the fact that America had produced a stock-market culture which swamped good artists and promising talents with false values.

"The overthrow of capitalism is not only a political and an economic and social necessity, it is also a cultural imperative. That is why I am here, and that is why many petit-bourgeois intellectuals have come over to your side . . . to the side of the workers.

"It's not merely the depression that has led me to change

my mind. Culturally, the boom was worse than the depression. The boom corrupted the literary men, the penmen of America. In the depression they have found their salvation. They are coming to you with outstretched hands. This couldn't have happened in the nineteen-twenties before the stock market crash on Black Friday in Wall Street. I know it couldn't. I saw what happened to my friends in the great American boom. They wrote the tripe that the present order of society demands of the writer. Corrupted, stultified, prostituted, they could make no use of their talents. Why was this condition of affairs possible? I didn't know then, and I couldn't find out why when I lived in Bohemian ivory towers in Paris and here in Greenwich Village. Now I know. The lesson has been brought home to me, and to many of my own generation, by the depression and by the ideas and program of the Communist Party.

"Let me pursue my line of thought further. Let me ask this question: Why, then, did my friends become prostitutes of the pen? The answer is to be found in the social order itself, in the fundamental nature of a ruling class which exploits the workers—and its writers. The writer has no stake in capitalism. Experience has proven this fact. The boom disinherited the writer from himself. The depression put him on the breadline and Art was stripped of its false glamour. Our own outstanding proletarian writer, Mark Singer, has rightly said that art is no more mysterious than a cheese sandwich. And today it is hard for writers to earn the price of a cheese sandwich with their pens. [Laughter.] In capitalist society the writer is an exile. But now we exiles have found our own roots in the roots of the future. The Communist Party is the party of the future. That is why writers like me will vote Communist —for Eldridge and Johnson."

Again the audience broke into booming applause.

Louis Waller, a mild-looking little man in a tweed suit, read from a prepared manuscript in a soft and insinuating voice. In a rhetorical style, he described how man had lost his organic roots in capitalist society, becoming a half-man who was concerned only with power.

"All of this is gravid with meaning. It relates to this campaign. For we must answer this question: What choice can a civilized, socially-conscious man make? The Democrats or the Republicans? . . . They are both diseased, putrefied, rotten to the roots. And their disease has its genesis in the malignant system which they defend and represent. These parties are full of the pus of the malignant disease we call . . . capitalism."

Louis Waller was cheered.

"Then we come to the Socialist Party. It condemns capitalism. Some of its spokesmen denounce it in vigorous enough language. The Socialist Party affirms the ideal of a Socialist economic system. And I do not doubt but that, subjectively, many of the *gentlemen* who speak for the Socialist Party really consider themselves to be honestly dedicated men—men of good will. But they cannot lead humanity out of the capitalist morass. For the flaw in this party is to be seen in the fact that its leaders *shrink* from adopting the necessary means which will permit the achievement of Socialism.

"But there is one party which will not shrink from facing up to its historic duties—the Communist Party. It has proved its seriousness in the Great Russian Revolution, and in its heroic defense and noble—yes, noble—implementation of the victorious Russian Revolution."

The applause was thunderous. Louis Waller beamed. He softened his voice and began to plead as he read on.

"History itself now tells the American intellectuals to take sides. The writers, the artists, the teachers, the philosophers, the technicians, the clerks all must now let themselves be numbered among the sheep or the goats. Yes, history has pointed a gun at them and it says to them, to us—'Choose! Decide now!' Either you stay as you are, the active or passive servants of a singularly dull and coarse and brutal fascism which marches under the banner of democracy in this country, or else you openly proclaim yourself to be its enemies, and to be the friends and comrades of the revolutionary workers. . . . And we on this platform, we in this hall, have made our fateful choice with open eyes, and with pride and confidence and a sacred sense of our duty. We have taken the side of our comrades, the revolutionary workers."

IV

The meeting ended with the crowd standing and singing *The Internationale*. The speeches had left Bernard so drugged that he didn't respond to *The Internationale* as he usually did.

The crowd poured slowly out of the hall. All around him he heard enthusiastic remarks about the meeting. Some Italians sang *Bandiera Rosa*. Then, from the other side of the hall, he heard youths chanting like college students:

Vote Communist!

Vote Communist!

Vote Communist!

A noisy crowd was gathered in front of the hall. Bernard saw two men tearing up papers and asked what had happened.

"It's probably the Trotskyites trying to horn into our meeting," Sam answered.

Bernard pressed through the crowd. Torn papers lay all over the street near the curb. A thin youth was arguing.

A man swung on the thin youth.

"Let him alone," Bernard shouted.

"Here's another one," a brutal-looking man yelled, moving toward Bernard.

Mel stepped in front of Bernard and said:

"He's a comrade. He's no Trotskyite."

Others glanced at Bernard with hostility and suspicion.

"What did he want to sock him for?" Bernard asked, as the thin youth was chased away by several Communists.

"He was breaking up the meeting."

"No he wasn't. He was merely selling his paper."

"A splinter paper. If you read it you'll get your mind full of counter-revolutionary slivers," Mel said.

Sam tried to get Bernard to move on.

"I don't like it," Bernard shouted.

"Who are you that you should like it?" a man said loudly and sarcastically. "He doesn't like it. He doesn't like the workers' revolution, maybe."

"Come on, Bernie. You'll just make things worse."

"I'm not running away," Bernard said.

"He's right. Communists are not hooligans," another man said.

Several arguments developed at once. The crowd milled about in excitement and confusion, and Bernard was edged away from the curb.

"What happened, comrade?" he heard a man ask.

"One of our comrades was beaten up by the Trotskyites," a man answered.

Mel and Sam came along each side of Bernard.

"It's all over. Let's go," Sam said.

They walked away from the milling crowd. Bernard was still shocked and angry.

"The Party doesn't order such action," Mel said.

"It's goddamned hooliganism," Bernard said.

"I'm against such tactics, but nothing would have happened if the Trotskyites hadn't come around when they knew we didn't want them," Sam said.

"It might have been a provocateur," Mel said.

"I wouldn't be surprised if it were," Sam said.

Bernard had calmed down now, and he didn't want to press the point further. He didn't want to argue or debate, but, damn it, this was hooliganism.

Sam was relieved when Bernard let the subject drop. The incident had pained him. He was apprehensive lest this drive Bernie away from the Movement. And he hoped they would soon be stopped. He hoped that some day Trotsky would make peace with the Party. Jake thought this might happen after the

German crisis matured. But he was most uneasy, too, because he actually had been glad when Bernie had spoken up.

Mel didn't know what to say. He also hoped that the incident wouldn't drive Bernie away from the Movement. It probably wouldn't. And he didn't want Bernie to press him with arguments and questions. For, after all, the progress of the Revolution sometimes demanded a few Social-Fascist broken noses. When Bernie came closer to the Movement, he'd understand this hard necessity.

"Let's have some java," Mel suggested, as they came to the corner of Fourteenth Street and Irving Place.

v

The cafeteria was full. Loud discussions were going on all around. Bernard sat near Mel and Sam at a long table. Mortimer from the Ninth Floor sat at the other end of the table. Bernard kept looking at him. Mortimer, an undersized fellow, seemed unctuous.

"Carr, these guys are like the Social Revolutionaries in Russia. They made bombs to kill the Czar, and the bombs exploded in their own hands," Jake explained, breaking out into laughter. "These fellows make theories that explode in their own heads. All of them are more Left than we are. Did you hear about Rudolph? Rudolph is a Trotskyite splinter. He won't recognize the capitalist elections, and so he's setting up homemade ballot boxes in some loft near here, and he's invited the American workers to boycott the elections and go to his headquarters and cast ballots there in a worker's election for president."

They laughed.

"But should he be busted in the nose?" Bernard asked.

"Of course not, unless as a shock to make him sane. How can we advocate such tactics? It would violate all our theories, and we're proud of our theories," Jake said.

Jake laughed charmingly and told more humorous stories to illustrate the lunacy of sectarian Leftists.

While the comrades at the table laughed at Jake's stories, he slyly glanced at Mortimer. Bernard wondered why. And he privately took note of the fact that Jake had switched the conversation from the subject of violence against the Trotskyites.

"Jake, after the Revolution, whom do you want to shoot first?" Bernard asked flippantly.

"What do I want to shoot anyone for?"

"We'd have to shoot a few people. After all, could we let literary critics and editors live, not to mention publishers and censors? How about you, Mel, whom do you want to line up against the wall? When we bury them we'll merely imagine that we're tossing eggshells into a garbage can."

"Bernie, I might have to intervene to keep you on the safe side of the wall unless a lot more of the comrades develop a sense of humor like Jake's."

"Maybe we ought to use a guillotine. After all, that's in our tradition. Whose head will we chop off first? What about the editor of the *Literary Survey*? He not only went to college, but he was a professor, to boot. He has no proletarian origins like mine—my father was a bricklayer—no, he isn't a proletarian writer. Then, too, he has no brains, so if we chop off his head we won't be destroying any brain power."

"He's not a bad fellow," Jake said.

"But he's bourgeois. Maybe we ought to put him on the list. How about you, Sam—are there any rival poets you want to shoot?"

Sam grinned, but in confusion.

"Just an Irish terrorist at heart," Jake said to Mel.

"I think the liberals ought to be shot first."

Everyone at the table listened to Bernard, some of them with hostility.

"It'll be a lot of fun shooting writers. Instead of firing squads, we might issue proletarian hunting certificates to the Marxist critics and let them shoot the writers. . . . That'll keep them from writing books."

"Carr, in our Movement the relationships between critic and

creator are comradely and mutually helpful," Jake said. "In the Soviet Union, the critic guides the artist. If he criticizes, he does it in a comradely way."

"We'll be comradely, too. We won't kill one another. It's merely these others . . ." Bernard made a dismissing gesture with his left hand. "You know, these . . ." He repeated his gestures. "These bourgeois writers. After all, you read *Mass Action*, so you know that they're no good to the human race. They won't be any loss. Hell, we can't be soft with them. We've got to be hard. After the Revolution we can't let the workers read their books. There won't be time for it. We'll have plans, and constructions, and the workers will have our books to read in editions of millions."

"What are you doing, Carr, pulling our leg?" Jake asked.

"I'm serious," Bernard went on with a dead pan. "I think we ought to have a plan. So I propose, comrades, that we now scientifically plan our post-Revolutionary shooting party."

Bernard was carried away by his own humor. It gave him a sense of total release.

"Let's form a committee to organize the post-Revolutionary Liquidation of Writers. Now, I'll serve as Chairman, but we ought to have an Honorary Chairman, someone mild and respectable like Louis Waller."

"He gave a better speech than I thought he would to-night," remarked a comrade whom Bernard didn't know.

"It was a damn good speech," Jake said.

"A remarkable speech," Mortimer said unctuously.

"He's Honorary Chairman. I'm the real Chairman, and, you know, I just can't wait for the day when my Committee can function with the necessary efficiency," Bernard went on. "I'll liquidate bourgeois writers with proletarian bullets instead of capitalist bullets. Because, you know, just as there is proletarian science and literature and bourgeois science and literature, so will there be proletarian bullets and. . . ."

They were all tense. They got up. Jake was embarrassed. Mortimer smirked superciliously. Sam grinned foolishly. Mel blanched. Two fellows, strangers to Bernard, glared at him fiercely. Bernard was carried away by his own talk. He didn't understand why they didn't laugh at his humor.

"I forgot . . . I ought to give myself another name as Chairman of the Post-Revolutionary Committee for the Liquidation of Deviating, Despairing Writers," Bernard said coldly and dryly.

They all walked ahead of him. Then Mel dropped back and said:

"Bernie, Mortimer doesn't appreciate your humor. But, of course, I understand it. But Mortimer . . ."

"Who the hell's he?" Bernard interrupted.

"He's a big shot."

Bernard looked at the pompous little man ahead.

"Let's shoot him, too."

"Bernie, he's a Party Leader . . . he's in charge of Agit-prop—"

"We'll take that over after we shoot him, Mel."

Mel laughed uneasily and artificially. Bernard walked out of the restaurant, pleased with himself but puzzled by the reactions of the comrades.

Chapter Twenty-four

I

THESE endless nights of waiting interfered with Bernard's calmness. He became the prey of fears. Elizabeth was knitting. Her face was big and round, filled out. Sometimes her eyes were so luminous they seemed polished by a happiness not of this world.

"You'll be glad when it's over, won't you, honey," he said.

"It's just that I'm so tired of waiting."

"I think I understand."

He went back to his book, a dull novel of farm life that Brady had given him to review.

"I just had a pain."

"Is it starting?"

"No, I'm sure it couldn't be. It was just a little pain. It was nothing."

"We want to be sure that we act promptly when the real pains come."

"Yes. One of these days I'll have to pack a little bag and have it ready."

"Let's do it now," he suggested.

"Oh, there's time."

"Is the pain gone?"

"Yes. It was nothing, Bernard. . . . Don't be so worried."

"I'm not. I'm merely concerned. I want to act quickly and intelligently when I have to. But we needn't worry about getting to the hospital on time; we're in a good neighborhood for taxis. And if I can't get one quickly enough, I'll call the police."

"It's sweet of you to think of these things, Bernard."

The fear that she might give birth in a taxicab was beginning to obsess him. If she did, he wouldn't know what to do. He

447

wouldn't know how to cut the umbilical cord. He might make a clumsy and tragic mess of everything.

"You're pale, Bernard."

"I'm all right."

"I don't want you to worry." She paused and smiled knowingly. "Bernard, you're going to have a hard birth, too."

"I'm rationally concerned, that's all!" he said with a seriousness bordering on pomposity; he was flustered.

Elizabeth giggled.

"I've never had a baby before," he said, looking at her with boyish appeal.

She laughed more loudly.

"I have to act responsibly."

"Come here and put your head in my lap."

He obeyed her. He sat at her feet with his head in her lap. She stroked his hair. He couldn't completely relax. This waiting! Waiting through suspended days! It was as though he were walking across a bridge of anxiety and he didn't know how long the bridge was. The end toward which he was walking was lost in mist and dense fog. And if he were in such a state now, how would he have been if they had had no money? He hadn't been properly grateful to Whelan.

"I'll have . . . two boys," she exclaimed softly, as she continued running her hands through his hair.

They were silent for a period.

"While I'm in the hospital, you won't have to run around like a chicken with its head cut off buying things," she said moodily.

"Yes."

"And aren't you glad you helped me sew the covering over the bassinet?"

She patted his cheeks. He held her hand. The house was very quiet. They heard the clock ticking. Then he got up and got a copy of Bertrand Russell's *Education and the Good Life* from the bookshelf.

"We'd better start reading this aloud so we're at least a little prepared."

"Yes, let's. You sit at my feet and read it to me."

He sat down and began reading aloud.

II

Elizabeth's moan woke Bernard. He jumped out of bed and turned on the light. Her face was contorted with pain. Then she gave him a wry smile, sighed, and said:

"It was just a pain . . . Baby Philip was kicking his poor mother, that's all. I'm sorry I woke you up, darling. I'm all right now."

"What was the pain like?"

She couldn't describe it.

"Was it like pains you've had before?"

"I think so."

Bernard wanted to think she had had only an ordinary pain. He turned the light out and carefully got back into bed.

"Do you have any more pains?"

"No, I'm all right. You go back to sleep. Please don't worry about me."

"Is there anything I can do, honey?"

"Just go to sleep."

Bernard lay beside her, unable to sleep. He didn't know why he believed that this pain was the beginning. It was merely a hunch. Or was he overanxious? In circumstances like this, you could make a fool of yourself with worry. He wished it were morning. Then he could go out and telephone Dr. Zimmerman. If he called up now, and it was nothing, a false alarm, he'd seem ridiculous, and Dr. Zimmerman would be sore.

"Are there any more pains, Elizabeth, honey?"

"Just little ones."

Why should he care if he made a fool of himself? He got out of bed, turned on the lights again, and with a look of determination started dressing.

"I'm not going to take any chances."

"Bernard, it's nothing," she said with gratitude in her eyes.

"Tell me what I ought to pack," he said.

"Bernard, you're a darling, but please don't bother. I know it's nothing."

Bernard sat down and waited, tense and expectant. He wasn't afraid, as he often had feared he would be. He was keen and alert. His mind seemed sharp and clear, but, because it was, he was frustrated. He really didn't know anything about the physiology of childbirth. It was meaningless to be so keen when one was so ignorant. A decision would have to be made, and he didn't know how long to wait before making it. He'd have to wake up the doctor; and he could take Elizabeth on a futile, melodramatically exciting trip. All this pother of his was meaningless. If she had any more pains, he'd time them and take her to the hospital.

"Bernard, you go back to bed and get your sleep. It's a month—"

She stopped talking, grimaced in pain, bit her lips, and turned pale for a moment.

"I'm going out and call Dr. Zimmerman."

"Wait, we have time."

"You'd better get up and dress. I have a hunch."

She obeyed him, dressing slowly. He helped her put her dress on.

They sat.

"Do you really think it's happening, Bernard?"

"I don't know." He smoked nervously.

"We ought to pack something."

Elizabeth fussed excitedly as she threw a nightgown and a few other items in a small handbag. Another pain came on as she was powdering her face.

"I'll go and phone."

"Oh, God . . . I'm wet. The water burst."

"We'll phone on the way."

She put on her coat, and they left. Bernard held her arm as they walked slowly toward Fifth Avenue. The night was chilly.

"We ought to be able to get a cab here."

"What'll we do if we can't?"

He hailed a cab at Ninth Street and Fifth Avenue. He instructed the driver to drive carefully and stop first at an all-night drugstore. They drove north. The night seemed strange outside. New York was strange. The darkness, the streetlights, the solid buildings were all part of a world of strangeness.

"Don't be afraid, honey," he said.

"I won't."

She shuddered as another pain came.

The cab stopped at Times Square. Bernard rushed into the drugstore and phoned Dr. Zimmerman, and told him they were on the way to the hospital. The doctor asked why he hadn't phoned sooner. Bernard said he hadn't had time.

"How do you know it's labor? Are you a doctor?'

"I timed the pains. And the water burst."

The doctor told him to go on up to the hospital. He returned to the cab.

"You made me wait a long time," Elizabeth complained.

"I couldn't help it, honey, I phoned as quickly as I could."

Then he realized that she must be in great pain and worried.

"You'll be there soon."

The cab moved on. Broadway was deserted. As they passed each street, he thought this meant one block less to go, one block closer to safety. He wanted to tell the driver to go faster, but he didn't dare.

Columbus Circle. The black bushes and trees of Central Park. Up Central Park West. In 1927 he had ridden this way in a cab to go to a whorehouse. Block after block. Street lights. Cabs passing. Soon it would be over. He'd be out of danger of having it happen in a cab. She'd be safe in the care of the hospital.

"Don't worry, honey. You'll be there soon."

"I'm not worried. I only want it over with."

She gripped his hands, dug her nails in his flesh, and fought with herself not to scream.

"Is it happening?" he asked.

"The pains . . ."

"Can you go faster, driver?"

"You didn't want me to go too fast."

"You better go faster."

He turned to Elizabeth.

"Are you all right?"

"Yes," she answered.

Block after block. Eighty-third Street. Soon they'd be there.

"You'll stay with me, Bernard?"

"Of course, I will."

They sped on. He held her hand. He wanted to say something to cheer her up and assure her. There was nothing to say. They were near the hospital and safe now.

They drove in the courtyard at the rear of the hospital. A doorman came out, helped Elizabeth, took the bag, and followed her inside. The hospital corridors were dim. The office was lit up. One nurse led Bernard to a desk, and another took Elizabeth upstairs. Bernard answered questions, paid a deposit, and was sent upstairs to a waiting room on the fourth floor.

The light was dim. He had nothing to read, and nothing to do. He looked down at One hundred and tenth Street and saw a man walk by. He saw a church across the street, tall and black in the night. He smoked a cigarette, moved about the waiting room, and sat down. He got up and stood at the door, looking out at the dark corridor. A pretty nurse went by. He looked after her. He turned, found a soft chair, and flopped into it.

He was becoming a father. But it might take hours. Elizabeth was in severe pain and was probably screaming. This could be a matter of life or death for her. He ought to have important feelings and impressions at such a moment as this. He was nervous, and he seemed to have no feeling, and it didn't matter what he thought or felt—he was helpless, a helpless supernumerary.

Dr. Zimmerman unexpectedly appeared. He was tall, plump, and gray, and wore a white coat.

"Mr. Carr."

Bernard jumped up.

"It's good you got your wife in. It was a still birth," the doctor said casually, but he was watching Bernard with kindly, sympathetic eyes.

Bernard didn't understand for a moment.

"How is Elizabeth . . . my wife?"

"She's well. The baby came out before I could get to her—dead."

"She's all right?"

"You can see her in a minute."

"Does she know?"

"Yes. These accidents sometimes happen, no one knows why, but they happen. There is no one medical explanation for them."

Bernard faced the doctor. There was something he ought to say, and he didn't know what it was.

"There's no danger for my wife?"

"No, no. We'll have to keep her in bed for a week or so, but she's going to be all right. She's a little upset, but . . ."

A nurse came and informed Dr. Zimmerman that Mr. Carr could see Mrs. Carr. The doctor led him by the arm along the dim corridor. He went into the room. A stout nurse was by the bed. Elizabeth looked exhausted.

He went up to her, slowly, timidly.

"Are you all right?"

She didn't answer. He took her hand.

"My baby's dead."

She cried. The nurse told her to rest. Dr. Zimmerman patted her head. Bernard held her hand.

"You're not mad . . . disappointed in me, Bernard?"

"No, I love you, honey. I want you to rest."

"I'm tired, Bernard."

She sobbed, looked at him wanly, and then gazed off at the window. He stood by her bed in a hurt, embarrassed mood. The doctor said that Mrs. Carr had better rest now. Her eyes looked dull. They had given her sleeping pills. He kissed her, stared at her. She was relaxed and pallid and beautiful. He kissed her again and slowly walked out of the room.

Dr. Zimmerman spoke with him for a moment. They hadn't

had time to rush Elizabeth to the delivery room. The dead baby had come as the nurses were preparing her. There was no answer to the question about the cause. Bernard asked to see the baby, and he was led into a room. The baby lay on a hospital bed, a perfectly formed, cold little boy. He touched the soft, tender, clammy skin. It had hair and eyes and legs and fingers and feet and genitals. Years ago, he had had one like this in Whelan's morgue. And this was his son.

He gazed at it for some moments. He left the room, shook hands with Dr. Zimmerman, thanked him, went to the elevator, rode down, and left the hospital.

The night was windy. He walked slowly along One hundred and tenth Street to Broadway.

He was free, free of this responsibility. His career would be easier. He was hurt. He had a hurt, sick, hopeless feeling. He was awed. It was as though his dignity had been stripped away. He was powerless with the powerlessness of all men. The rude unconsciousness of death had taken their child, unconcerned with him or with Elizabeth.

The wind whipped against his face. A policeman came along, and he prepared himself to be questioned as a suspicious character. The policeman passed him. There were tall, dark buildings on either side of the street. A few automobiles shot by. He was alone with himself. He walked on with hurt, sick, hopeless feelings.

III

Bernard had cleaned the house himself and had put roses in vases in the living room. When he led Elizabeth in, she cried and didn't notice what he'd done. She was weak, but she looked radiant.

"I want my baby," she exclaimed in tears.

"Honey . . ." he began.

"I want my baby."

He stood over her awkwardly. He patted her head, but she shuddered. She gazed up at him with a peculiar, wild stare in her eyes.

"You're a stranger."

"Elizabeth, Elizabeth, don't you know me?"

"You're a stranger. You're not Bernard."

"Elizabeth, I love you and want to help you to forget."

She sobbed. He tried to comfort her.

"Please, oh, let me cry. I want to cry."

He sat by, feeling hurt and helpless as he watched her, saw her body quivering and shaking.

She quieted down, wiped her eyes, went to the bureau, powdered her face, sat down near him, and meekly said:

"Bernard, forgive me."

"I understand . . ."

"I was so sad. I'd dreamed so much of bringing our baby home. And in the hospital, the mothers were so happy and they had such cute little babies, and my baby's dead. It was all so gay. They were so gay. And I was so sad."

How could he explain to her that you had to accept and assimilate this fact? How could he explain that this was life, nature, evolution, that this waste and their defeated hopes were only part of life.

"Why did my baby die?"

"I don't know. There's no answer."

"It never lived."

Again she cried, inconsolably. Not knowing what to do, he made tea and blundered over to her with a cup. She didn't touch it.

"You were sweet to have flowers. It was dear of you, Bernard. They're gay. But I'll never be gay. My baby's dead."

Elizabeth sat with a wild vacant stare in her eyes. Every now and then she gave Bernard a meek smile. He sat with her, holding her hand and hearing the tick of the clock.

Chapter Twenty-five

I

BERNARD came out of the delicatessen store on Eighth Street and walked toward Fifth Avenue, carrying a small bag of groceries. He noticed that the people on the street looked calm and were passing by him just as they would on any other day. On Fifth Avenue a man had a dog on a leash. A uniformed doorman stood under an awning gazing about. A couple came out of the Brevoort, caught a cab, and got into it. The busses were running. There were automobiles on the street. Life looked normal. He wanted to stop people, to talk to them, ask them questions. He went on home and set the bag of groceries on the table.

Elizabeth was thin again. She looked girlish and pretty in a white apron.

"I didn't have any trouble. The delicatessen store man gave me credit."

"I should have remembered last night that we were out of coffee."

"Well, let's have some now."

"I'll make it," she said, taking the bag.

Bernard looked at the newspaper, with the headlines about the banks. Every bank in the nation closed. All sorts of questions came to his mind. What would Roosevelt do after he was inaugurated today? What would happen? The country was paralyzed, but Eighth Street, Ninth Street, Fifth Avenue were the same. He didn't know how to interpret the situation. This was really the crisis, and people in the street looked the same as ever. The delicatessen store man knew him slightly but had willingly given him credit. And he was going on planning.

Elizabeth set coffee and toast on the table, and they sat down.

"Is it exciting out?"

"No. It's just like any other day."

"What will happen to your book?"

"This might kill the sale." He laughed. "Here I get good reviews, good space in the two Sunday book sections, and the banks close."

"But they'll open again, won't they?"

"They'll have to."

"I got a letter from Father and Mother. They think it's all right for us to go to Europe on your Fellowship, only they wish we could see them before I go."

Bernard didn't answer. He didn't want to go to Chicago.

He held out his cup for more coffee. Elizabeth got it for him.

"Our baby dying really saddened Mother and Father. It was a terrible disappointment to them."

Tears came into her eyes.

"Elizabeth . . ."

"I won't cry. Only, Bernard, I wouldn't care, I wouldn't care if we couldn't go to Europe on your Fellowship if it only had lived. I wouldn't."

He slowly shook his head. He remembered seeing Mel Morris and telling him the news, and Mel had said that maybe it was for the better. He had been hurt by Mel's words. He was still hurt and angry inside. So was Elizabeth. Would this hurt go away with time? Their freedom, their good fortune had come with this bitter memory. At times he almost imagined he'd stolen their freedom from someone, from their stillborn baby. It was as though the baby's accusing eyes were focused on him from the grave.

"Let's talk about what we'll do in Paris," she said eagerly.

"We won't get there if Mr. Roosevelt doesn't open the banks."

"But they'll open, won't they?"

"Honey, I was just thinking how, when we first came here and lived from hand-to-mouth, I couldn't have walked into a delicatessen and gotten credit."

"But you told the truth."

"We have about a three-hundred-and-fifty-dollar stake in the capitalist system."

"We have the Loewenthal money."

"That's not until next month."

He held his cup out for more coffee. They talked about going to Europe, and Elizabeth grew eager and happy. Her eyes lit up, and she laughed in a childlike way.

"Bernard, I knew all along that good things would happen."

"We've been lucky."

They both became uneasily silent after this remark.

"It's merely part of the biological waste of life," Bernard said, angry at the very fact of death.

He finished his coffee and said he wanted to take a walk. Elizabeth didn't feel like going with him. He left the house and strolled over to Fifth Avenue and then wandered on toward Fourteenth Street.

Bernard was full of a suppressed anxiety; he felt an inner excitement which could find no outlet. And the street was so calm. The crisis gripping the country couldn't be real, with the well-dressed men and women on lower Fifth Avenue. It wasn't quite real to him, now that he had arrived. Yes, think of it, he had arrived. *Unshapely Things* was receiving fine reviews, and his winning a Loewenthal Fellowship was a sign of recognition. Everything had changed for him. And everything had gotten worse for America.

David Bergman almost bumped into him on Thirteenth and Fifth Avenue, and they said hello.

"Where's the Revolution?" Bernard asked, and his eyes wandered to the bank on the corner; his money was in there.

"The country's paralyzed, and where's the Party—what's it doing?"

"What do you think will happen?"

"Oh, they'll get the banks open. But what slogans have they got? Are they demanding—Seize the banks?"

"Who?"

"Roosevelt."

Bernard suggested coffee. Dave asked him if he had the cash. Bernard said yes he had some change. They went into a restaurant at Thirteenth and Fifth Avenue, got coffee and doughnuts, and sat at a table.

"Did you hear—I was expelled from the Party?"

"What was your deviation?" Bernard asked.

"The German events. I fought the German betrayal."

Bernard didn't understand him.

"The Party polled six million votes in October," Dave said, pounding the table, "Six million, and it didn't fire a shot when Hitler came to power. Not a shot." Dave grew heated. "It's the greatest crime against the working class in history."

"What could they have done?"

"Made the Revolution," Dave said, again pounding the table.

Bernard didn't know what to say. Just as the bank crisis had surprised him, so also had Hitler's ascension to power.

"If Stalin and the Russians had given the signal and mobilized the Red Army, do you know what would have happened, Carr?"

"What?"

"The World Revolution. We've been sold out. And then, the Byzantines on the Ninth Floor expel me and say I'm an enemy of the Revolution. I walked the streets of New York with tears in my eyes, with tears, when I read that this Nazi lunatic had come to power. For a month I didn't raise my voice. And then I handed in a document and called for a new turn. So, I'm a social fascist."

"You're the first real social fascist I ever met. You look human."

"This isn't something to joke about, Carr."

Bergman went on talking, drinking more coffee, and waxing more heated and emotional. Bernard listened but could neither agree nor disagree with him. Since he'd gone to that Communist Party election meeting with Mel and Sam last fall, he hadn't been able to decide about his political beliefs. He didn't know.

Bergman's passion and anger disquieted him. He had never talked or thought with such passion about anything except literature. And now his literary aspirations would be fulfilled. Had Bergman thrown into politics the same emotional force he had given to writing? And was this the voice of defeat and frustration? His sympathies went out to Bergman silently. He saw in David Bergman, talking volubly, denouncing, pounding the table, what he himself might have become but for success.

The thought surprised him. For, yes, it was true! He was becoming a success. In fact, if capitalism were as successful as he at this moment, his book might be a bestseller.

Bergman asserted that had the Communist Party of Germany fought Hitler correctly and had the Red Army marched, we wouldn't have the Party and the American working class sitting by powerless now, during the biggest crisis in American history. Bernard didn't follow him.

"We'd be growing now. Wall Street, Washington, Roosevelt would hear us and tremble," Bergman orated with a shaking voice. "But they, too, know the significance of the German defeat. So they won't worry. They'll be able to solve the crisis in their own way."

"Do you think they'll solve it?"

"Yes, but maybe with fascism."

Bernard still didn't follow Bergman. His analysis sounded unreal, but it was uttered with such intensity, and with the accompaniment of such emphatic gestures, that it seemed not only convincing but irrefutably correct.

They finished their coffee and walked to Thirteenth Street and University Place. Bernard watched Bergman cross the street and stand in a doorway, staring at the entrance to the offices of *The Fist* and the Party headquarters. He realized that Bergman was a man pushed out of his own world, a revolutionist without a revolution.

—In a hundred years, Bernard asked himself, will Bergman's revolution or my books be better remembered?

—Or will either?

Bernard walked on. He bought a copy of *The Fist* on Fourteenth Street. There were bold headlines:

FORGOTTEN MEN OF U. S.
FIGHT FOR THEIR DEMANDS
TODAY AS WALL STREET
PLACES ROOSEVELT IN
WHITE HOUSE

He read part of a denunciatory article which declared that Roosevelt, the new Wall Street President and enemy of labor, would call for war powers and become a dictator. He didn't finish the article. He glanced through the paper and noticed a picture of a man named Wallace, who was to be in the new cabinet, and he read the caption:

Henry A. Wallace, Secretary of Agriculture, in the new Wall Street Cabinet, who wants to make Roosevelt a dictator for the benefit of American kulaks and at the expense of the poor farmers and the workers of the city.

Bernard put the paper in his pocket and wondered what would happen. He crossed Fourteenth Street and saw a small, silent, nervous crowd milling in front of the Amalgamated building. There was fear in the faces of these men and women. They kept going up to the bank entrance and reading the sign which said that it was closed. A big policeman stood near the entrance, looking off with his arms folded. There were foreign faces in the small crowd. Now and then someone would make a remark, and Bernard heard questions asked in broken English. One woman, with a black shawl over her head, went up to the door three times and read the sign. Then, still not believing that the bank was closed, she asked the policeman if it were closed.

"That's what it says, lady."

She read the sign again and walked off. The crowd kept staring at the closed doors. Bernard watched them and looked off at

Union Square. He saw men walking about there, probably more of the homeless.

America, he thought, had today become one common fear, one common anxiety, one common paralysis. Talking with Bergman a few moments ago, he just had not known what to say. He wondered—did anyone in this country know what to say or think? Did these people in front of the bank, or the policeman standing guard over its possibly worthless money, or those homeless men across Broadway in Union Square? Or did his father-in-law, his brothers, his sister Marie, or Hampton or Barber or Louis Waller or Jake or Mel Morris or Sam Leventhal or Pinky Cullen back in Chicago? Did any of them know any more than Patrick Carr, who was in his grave? Yes, today America, this entire country, was like one lump of uncertainty. And soon he would be leaving it. For he somehow believed that the banks would be opened and he would get the Loewenthal Fellowship money. He would be going.

But would he find in Europe, in Paris, even in Russia, what he had never found in Chicago, in New York, in America? What was happening in Chicago now? Chicago! He had once been a boy there, a frightened and ordinary boy, and somehow that boy had grown into this Bernard Carr, an American writer, standing here and looking across at Union Square in the morning sunlight. How had it happened? How had he found his road and won the confidence he now felt? The seeds of this change were not here in New York. They had been planted back there, halfway across this American continent. His heritage was there, not here, and not in the cultured Europe he was about to see. And somehow out of that heritage he had developed this ambition to become part of the memory of mankind.

He turned and walked home, with Chicago still in his mind. He found Elizabeth on the bed, crying. She gazed up at him with a meek, tear-stained face.

"Why did my baby die?" she asked in a pleading, angry, insistent voice.

"I don't know," he answered tenderly.

"I . . . wanted him to live," she whimpered.

Bernard held her hand, patted it, and said nothing, because he knew there was nothing he could say to soothe her.

After her outburst, she was quiet.

"Forgive me, Bernard, for crying," she said sheepishly.

"There's nothing to forgive."

"Bernard, we are going to be happy, aren't we?"

"Yes. . . . Do you remember Jake quoting Saint-Just at Sophie's party—*Happiness is a new idea.*"

"Bernard, let's plan now what we're going to do in Paris. Let's talk about Paris," Elizabeth said, becoming suddenly and nervously gay.